THE LOST REALM

CROWN OF THREE

J. D. RINEHART

✦ BOOK TWO ✦

THE LOST REALM

ALADDIN

New York London Toronto Sydney New Delhi

This book is a work of fiction. Any references to historical events, real people, or real places are used fictitiously. Other names, characters, places, and events are products of the author's imagination, and any resemblance to actual events or places or persons, living or dead, is entirely coincidental.

ALADDIN

An imprint of Simon & Schuster Children's Publishing Division
1230 Avenue of the Americas, New York, New York 10020
First Aladdin paperback edition May 2017
Text copyright © 2016 by Working Partners Limited
Cover illustration copyright © 2016 by Iacopo Bruno
Also available in an Aladdin hardcover edition.
All rights reserved, including the right of reproduction in whole or in part in any form.
ALADDIN and related logo are registered trademarks of Simon & Schuster, Inc.
For information about special discounts for bulk purchases, please contact Simon & Schuster
Special Sales at 1-866-506-1949 or business@simonandschuster.com.
The Simon & Schuster Speakers Bureau can bring authors to your live event. For more
information or to book an event contact the Simon & Schuster Speakers Bureau at
1-866-248-3049 or visit our website at www.simonspeakers.com.
Book design by Laura Lyn DiSiena
The text of this book was set in OneLeigh Pro.
Manufactured in the United States of America 0417 OFF
2 4 6 8 10 9 7 5 3 1
The Library of Congress has cataloged the hardcover edition as follows:
Names: Rinehart, J. D., author.
Title: The lost realm / by J.D. Rinehart.
Description: First Aladdin hardcover edition. | New York : Aladdin, 2016.
Series: Crown of three ; 2 | Summary: "Triplets Tarlan, Elodie, and Gulph are no closer to
finding each other or gaining the throne. But as the threats to their existence grow, so do their
powers. Can the three survive, fulfill the prophecy, and bring peace to the land? Or will they
meet an untimely fate?" —Provided by publisher.
Identifiers: LCCN 2015045910 | ISBN 9781481424462 (hc) |
ISBN 9781481424486 (eBook)
Subjects: | CYAC: Fantasy. | Kings, queens, rulers, etc.—Fiction. |
Triplets—Fiction. | Brothers—Fiction. | Prophecies—Fiction. |
BISAC: JUVENILE FICTION / Fantasy & Magic. | JUVENILE FICTION /
Action & Adventure / General. | JUVENILE FICTION / Family / Siblings.
Classification: LCC PZ7.1.R57 Los 2016 | DDC [Fic]—dc23
LC record available at https://lccn.loc.gov/2015045910
ISBN 9781481424479 (pbk)

Special thanks to Graham Edwards

For M. K.

In Toronia, realm of three,

A tempest has long raged.

By power's potent siren call,

Weak men are enslaved.

Too much virtuous blood has spilt

In this accursed age.

When the stars increase by three

The kingdom shall be saved.

Beneath these fresh celestial lights,

Three new heirs will enter in.

They shall summon unknown power,

They shall kill the cursed king.

With three crowns they shall ascend,

And true peace, they will bring.

—Gryndor, first wizard of Toronia

PROLOGUE

Weighed down by the thick iron boots, Kalia's feet dragged on the cobbles. Heavy iron gauntlets enclosed her hands. Metal chains ran from these and into the hands of the two legionnaires who were escorting her along the corridor.

They have done this because they are afraid of me, she told herself.

One of the chains pulled tight, yanking painfully at her arm. Kalia almost fell, but recovered and stumbled on.

But I am not afraid of you, she thought.

She almost believed it.

The soldiers, dressed all in black, soft-soled and silent, had come for her in the middle of the night. They'd clamped the metal gloves and boots over her hands and feet before she'd been fully awake.

"What is the meaning of this?" she'd demanded as they'd hauled her from her bed.

Saying nothing, the legionnaires had shoved her through the door and into the hallway beyond.

"When the king hears of this . . ." she'd started to say. Then, seeing the savage amusement on their faces, she'd stopped.

Brutan will learn of this soon enough. Until then, I will do nothing to provoke them.

They dragged her through the secret ways of Castle Tor, avoiding the public passages and keeping to the narrow tunnels hidden deep within the massive stone walls. They held her arms tight, wrenching her shoulders with every turn. As she plunged deeper into darkness, Kalia's fear bloomed like a sick, black rose.

Soon the cobbles gave way to flint flagstones. Kalia's iron boots scraped along, creating sparks that flickered on the tunnel walls. After two more painful turns, the tunnel ended at a wide arch plugged by a stout wooden door. Etched into the timbers was an image of a crown with three points.

The crown of Toronia.

The crown of the king.

He sent them! Brutan sent them! And now he's waiting behind that door, waiting for his prize!

"I would have come," she said. "If you'd told me the king wanted to see me, I would have come willingly. Why would I not?"

She tossed back her disheveled red-gold hair, hoping she sounded defiant. Yet dread congealed in the pit of her stomach. . . . Why did Brutan have them snatch her from her bed? Why have her brought to him in chains?

The answer hit her like a blow to the stomach. Her heart faltered in her chest.

He has found my children. My triplets. And when he has shown them to me, he is going to kill them!

She bit her lip to stifle the scream.

"It's better if you don't talk," growled the first legionnaire from beneath his black hood. "Just do as you're told. It'll go better that way."

"When the king commands, even the king's mistress obeys," said the second legionnaire. His lip curled in a sneer.

Kalia flinched. Her status was common knowledge throughout Toronia; everyone knew that Castle Tor was home to the king, the queen . . . and Kalia. The three of them.

Three was a powerful number. And it held a special place in Kalia's heart.

My three! Oh, my children!

"Please, won't you tell me . . . ?" she began, but it was too late. While one legionnaire shoved open the giant door, the second hustled her into the chamber beyond.

She stumbled forward. There was no sound but the dull clang of her metal boots against the stone floor. She kept her head down, unwilling to look at what she knew must lie ahead.

After twenty paces, her guards brought her roughly to a halt. A cold hand gripped her chin and forced her head up. Summoning all her strength, she held it steady and stared straight into the eyes of King Brutan.

The king was seated on a simple wooden throne, slightly raised on a platform of oak. Beside him, on a matching chair, sat Queen Magritt. Despite the lateness of the hour, both wore the full ceremonial regalia of Toronia: red robes and gold chains.

"Kalia," said the king. "So good of you to come."

The words were sweet, but his voice rumbled like thunder. His cheeks—usually red—were pale. His whole face seemed hard and blunt, and Kalia had the sudden, dizzying sensation that topping those luxuriant robes was the head not of a man but of an animal.

"I would have come willingly," she said, "had you but asked."

"I didn't," Brutan grunted. Wordplay had never been his strong point; he was a man of action. Being around him was like courting an unruly bear, and that had always frightened Kalia. Yet sitting beside this brute was someone who frightened her even more.

"Welcome, dear," said Magritt. The venom in her voice was in complete contrast to the smile on her lips, and therein lay her power.

When you came right down to it, bears were simple creatures.

4

Magritt, however, was a snake.

From behind Kalia came the sound of footsteps, many of them. She heard the creak of leather and the clatter of arms. Soldiers, she guessed, forming ranks behind her.

She cast her gaze to the sides of the room, knowing there was no escape but seeking it anyway. This was the Undersalle, the chamber that lay directly beneath the great throne room of Castle Tor. Like the throne room, it was long and broad, dominated at one end by the royal platform. Unlike the throne room, it was dark, lit only by flickering torches set in black sconces on the walls. The ceiling pressed down.

Kalia wondered how many criminals had faced their fate in this court of judgment. How many had protested their innocence. How many had begged for their lives.

How many had been put to death.

I will not beg.

Silence had fallen once more. Kalia glanced around and saw exactly what she'd expected to see: an entire legion of Brutan's guard—one hundred men, armed and alert in their bronze armor, no doubt with orders to keep her here until the king's business with her was concluded.

In the Undersalle, that could mean only one kind of business.

"Traitor!" Brutan shouted, rising suddenly from the throne. "You lied to me! All along, you lied!"

"How so, my liege?" said Kalia. She hoped the formal address might soothe his anger.

It did not.

"First you said you were carrying one child. But there were three." Foam splashed from Brutan's mouth onto his bushy beard. "Three, as was foretold by the prophecy. The prophecy!"

"But the triplets were yours, my liege. Your blood."

"My blood is what they would have spilled!"

"They were stillborn. What possible threat could a dead child be to a king?"

"Do you deny the words of the prophecy? 'Beneath these fresh celestial lights, three new heirs will enter in. They shall summon unknown power. They shall kill the cursed king.' The three stars appeared in the sky that very night, Kalia. Who knows what other dark magic was afoot? Do you think me stupid?"

Maybe not. But if ever there was a cursed king, it was you, Brutan!

Aloud she said, as calmly as she could, "Three years have passed since the three stars appeared in the sky, my lord. Nothing bad has happened since. The prophecy has not come to pass. There is no danger."

"Oh, but there is danger, my dear," said Magritt from her throne. Her voice was as silky as her husband's was coarse. Still that maddening smile played upon her lips. "The danger is you."

Kalia snorted. "Danger? You had me brought here in shackles! What possible threat could I be to you?"

"You know very well why you wear the iron," Magritt replied.

"It is to stop your magic, you damned witch!" shouted Brutan, stepping off the platform and planting his meaty hands on his hips. His face was flushed, and his eyes gleamed, as did the sweat on his brow.

It was true. As long as Kalia's hands and feet were enclosed in the cold, unyielding metal, she couldn't use her powers. Even had they been free, she doubted her abilities would have aided her in this abominable place, in the presence of so many armed men. Like the earth and air that drove it, her magic was soft and subtle, made not for confrontation but for love.

Yet their fear of her talents gave her strength.

"I abandoned my magic years ago, as well you know," she said. She found Magritt's gaze and held it. "I put it aside for my king."

"Liar!" yelled Brutan. "You cast spells to hide the truth. You say the babies were dead? I say different. I say that when I came into your bedchamber that night, you tricked my eyes into thinking the children—the three children—were dead. You even fooled the wizard, faithful Melchior."

If only you knew, Kalia thought. It was Melchior who had fooled the king. She wondered what Brutan would do if he discovered the wizard's loyalty was not to him but to the very prophecy that predicted his downfall.

She glanced around again, this time looking at the door through which she'd been dragged. She willed Melchior to walk through it.

But Melchior did not come.

"The triplets are as dead now as they were on that day," she said, tasting the bitterness of the words. "Why would you say otherwise?"

Brutan wiped spittle from his beard with the back of his hand. Spinning on his heel—for a big man he was surprisingly agile—he snapped his fingers at one of the two legionnaires who'd brought Kalia to the Undersalle.

"Bring him out!" he roared.

Kalia's heart stopped. *Bring him? Bring who?*

Numb, she waited as the legionnaire retreated into the shadows behind the two thrones. Waited with dreadful anticipation for the man to emerge again carrying a three-year-old child.

Will it be Tarlan? Or Agulphus?

The legionnaire returned dragging not a child but a bedraggled tramp. Kalia's shoulders sagged with relief. The man's clothes were rags and his greasy hair was clotted with filth. His eyes rolled and his lips mumbled. When the legionnaire released him, he swayed, barely able to hold himself upright.

Kalia's relief turned rapidly to puzzlement as she wondered who this man might be.

King Brutan regarded the tramp with undisguised contempt, but Magritt rose smoothly from her throne. "Kalia," she said, "may

I introduce you to Sir Brax? He has quite a story to tell. Quite a story."

Kalia's hands tried to clench, but the restricting gauntlets prevented her from making a fist. *Sir Brax! You were Melchior's ally. Which of my children did he give you to look after?*

As she stared at the tramp, her horror mounted. It was impossible to imagine anyone less suited to caring for a child. She tightened the muscles in her face, resisting the urge to scream at him.

What have you done with my baby?

The legionnaire prodded Sir Brax with the hilt of his sword. After a brief pause—during which Kalia was convinced the wretched man would throw up—Sir Brax began to speak.

"We were each given a babe," he said, his words slurred with drink. "Mine was a boy. Castle, we rode away from the castle. Me and the babe."

Kalia leaned forward, desperate to decipher his muddled speech.

"Kept to the back trails . . ." Sir Brax mumbled. "Tavern in Isur . . ." His chin lolled to his chest and the legionnaire gave him another prod. He looked up, his eyes glazed. "Safekeeping, away from the king. . . . Secret . . . secret at all costs." Then: "His name— his name, it was . . ."

Kalia's blood ran cold.

"Go on," growled the legionnaire, giving him a shake.

Sir Brax squinted. "Name was . . . Allus, maybe? Aphullus?"

Agulphus! thought Kalia with a sudden surge that was part triumph, part terror. *That's his name! My Gulph. My poor little Gulph!*

Sir Brax's ramblings petered out and a flicker of hope sparked within Kalia.

If they don't know his name, they can't find him.

Brutan had turned away. He stood with his fists bunched, and his big bear's body trembled from head to foot. Magritt's smile never wavered.

"Poor Sir Brax," she said. "His mind is rotted with drink. Now, Kalia, to whom did you give the other children? And will you tell us, before the end?"

Before the end!

Magritt's words rang like cracked chimes through Kalia's thoughts. So they meant to kill her after all. Bringing her here, to the Undersalle, had not been about hearing her story, nor even allowing her to hear Sir Brax's.

They've already decided my fate, she thought. *Nothing I say could make any difference.*

She felt something wrench inside her. Now she'd never see her children again—never see them overthrow their father and take the crown, never see their destiny fulfilled. Hot tears rose to her eyes, but she forced them back.

They can kill me, Kalia thought, *but that doesn't mean they've won.*

She squared her shoulders. The weight of the iron gauntlets was almost unbearable, yet she lifted them all the same, spreading her arms wide.

"Look at me, Brutan," she said quietly.

For a moment he didn't move. Then, slowly, with infinite menace, he turned. His face was a dark knot of fury.

"Final words, Kalia?" he said. "If so, make them brief. I am sick of the sight of you."

"You tell me my children live," Kalia proclaimed, willing her voice to rise up from this dark and dreadful place, wishing her words up and out into the night, where all who roamed beneath the stars might hear them. "I tell you it is true. My babies lived then, and they live still, and their lives have but one purpose: to see the death of you!"

Brutan's lip curled. "I knew it was true! I will track them down. As for you—you will be silent!"

"I will not! What kind of monster are you that you see your own children as creatures to be hunted and killed? What kind of monster puts his one remaining child,—a boy of six—behind bars lest he prove traitor?"

"Silence, I said!"

"As Prince Nynus lies forgotten inside the Vault of Heaven, so your heart lies forgotten too! And as for your precious Toronia, was there any king who brought more suffering, more cruelty to his realm?"

Hauling the iron boots over the floor, she took two faltering steps toward him. Although her arms shook, suddenly the weight they bore seemed to feed her strength. Never mind that her magic was muted; she still had her voice.

"Do my children live? Yes! Will they see the prophecy fulfilled? Yes, and yes! They will end you, Brutan. I know it! You know it! All of Toronia knows it! The crown of three will once more find its proper place. And you? You will be gone from this world, as if you had never been here. None will mourn you, Brutan. And none will remember you!"

"SILENCE!"

Brutan drew his sword and advanced on Kalia, his voice crashing over her like a wave. She endured it, holding her ground as she awaited the killing blow. Reaching her, the king thrust the blade against her throat and bared his yellow teeth in her face.

"You will die, Kalia!"

For a long, agonizing moment she waited.

Then, hands shaking, Brutan lowered his sword and dropped it back into its sheath.

"A witch you are, and as a witch you will die," he growled. "Not for you the clean dispatch of the blade. For you, Kalia, the end will be slow." A scowl distorted his flushed and sweating face. "You will burn."

Behind him, still seated on her throne, Queen Magritt nodded once, her smooth face creased only by a tiny, satisfied smile.

◆ ◆ ◆

The same two legionnaires who'd dragged Kalia from her bed-chamber now marched her into the small yard that lay behind the Undersalle. It was set deep below the towering walls of Castle Tor. Kalia felt like she was at the bottom of a square, stone well.

In the center of the yard, a wooden stake rose from a pile of wood and straw.

I am going to die. The thought brought no fear, only a desperate ache.

The legionnaires lifted her onto the pyre. One of them pulled her arms behind her, wrapping them around the stake; the other tied her wrists together. The metal gauntlets felt as heavy as the world. Wood splintered beneath her iron-clad feet. The rest of the Legion filed into the yard, spreading out to line its walls. She was trapped inside a ring of bronze.

Brutan lit the pyre in silence, plunging a flaming torch deep into its wooden interior. He glared at Kalia as he did so. She returned his gaze with what she hoped was a look of defiance.

The king stepped away and the flames caught fast, rising into the night. Kalia waited for the pain, but it didn't come.

Why doesn't it hurt? she thought. But it didn't matter. Inside she was in agony.

She tilted her head back, stared up past the confining walls to the night sky, far above. Three stars shone there: one green, one red, one gold. The prophecy stars.

My children's stars, she thought as smoke closed over them, erasing them from view. *What will become of my three?*

She would never know.

Sudden movement caught her eye: someone on a stone ledge, high above. A yellow robe, white hair.

Melchior!

The wizard was looking down at her, a look of infinite sorrow on his wrinkled face. He teetered, his bare feet planted wide, and for a moment Kalia thought he would fall from the ledge. He steadied himself with his staff, gripping it with his gnarled hands. His fingers were moving over the runes she knew were carved into its surface; his lips were moving too. Kalia tried to make out what he was saying, but she couldn't see the words.

Then she realized they weren't words at all.

They were numbers.

Yes, Melchior! Work your magic! Take it away. Take it all away!

In a rush, the smoke enveloped her, lifted her, carried her away. The last thing she heard before the end was the voice of Brutan, roaring in triumph.

Then, darkness.

ACT ONE

Ten Years Later

CHAPTER 1

T o the postern gate!" shouted Captain Ossilius. "It's our only chance!"

He swung his sword, killing two undead warriors simultaneously. Gulph dodged past his friend, kicking out at the bodies, once, twice, tumbling them end over end down the steep stone stairs, where they scattered the oncoming enemy soldiers like bowling pins.

"That should buy us some time," he gasped. "What's a postern gate?"

"Our last chance."

Together, Gulph and Ossilius climbed the rest of the way up the stairs, ran along the battlement, and plunged down a steep ramp into a small, enclosed courtyard.

Here they halted, leaning against each other as they fought for breath. Gulph felt small against the burly, gray-haired captain, and wondered if he would always be as skinny as he was now.

Never mind growing up, he thought, massaging the aches from his crooked back, *I just wish I'd grow straight.*

"So where's this last chance of yours?" he said, stepping away from his companion, who was still struggling to breathe. Ossilius ran a hand through his gray hair and ushered Gulph over to a break in the wall.

"Look," he said, pointing through the shattered stonework toward a squat tower built into the city wall.

"I can see what looks like a door," said Gulph. "What are those things on either side of it? Statues?"

Ossilius nodded. "That's the postern gate."

Gulph stared skeptically at the stretch of ground lying between them and their destination. Swarms of undead warriors were fighting their way through ranks of terrified citizens, and thick smoke shrouded the scene, making it hard to see exactly what was happening. But Gulph could hear the screams clearly enough.

All the people of Idilliam wanted was to flee, but even as they tried to escape they were seized and made undead. This was the horror: the enemy didn't kill you.

The enemy made you like itself.

"Every time we lose a soldier," whispered Gulph, "they gain one. How can we ever win?"

For a brief moment the smoke surrounding a nearby tower cleared, and King Brutan himself strode into view. Flesh hung from his bones; his blood-streaked clothes flapped in tatters; his eyes burned red with fire.

Gulph closed his eyes, trying to remember how Brutan had looked when he'd been alive. But all he could bring to mind was the look of betrayal on the king's face when he, Gulph, had placed the poisoned crown on his head.

I didn't know it would kill you, Gulph thought. *I never imagined it would make you a monster.* He shook his head, correcting himself. *No—you already were a monster, weren't you?*

Brutan's left hand closed on the neck of a man; with his right he snatched up a peasant woman. He lifted them both off the ground and squeezed his skeleton fingers. They struggled briefly, then their eyes closed and their bodies went slack. Their skin turned white; their flesh sank in on itself.

When their eyes opened again, they were filled with flame.

Gulph watched, aghast. He'd seen this happen many times during their headlong run across the battlefield; still, it never failed to repulse him. What made it worse was the knowledge of who Brutan really was.

You're more than a monster. You're my father.

A fresh wave of city dwellers burst from a breach in the wall: ordinary people clutching bags and boxes and clumsy wraps of cloth.

Gulph gripped the rubble of the broken wall, silently urging them on, wondering what meager possessions they'd managed to collect, and where they thought they could flee to.

"They don't know about the bridge," said Ossilius.

Gulph held his breath as the first of the refugees reached the edge of the chasm. It encircled Idilliam as a moat surrounds a castle—except this moat was bottomless. One man led his children to the brink and stopped, staring dumbstruck at the ruins of the bridge that had once connected the city to the rest of Toronia. . . .

"They have nowhere to go," Gulph groaned. "There's no escape. They're trapped here. We're all trapped."

He lifted the golden crown he'd carried across the battlefield. His fingers were cramped from clutching it. Now that he had the crown, he couldn't imagine ever letting it go—yet part of him wanted to cast it into the chasm.

"Just this morning Nynus was wearing it," he said. He shuddered, remembering what Nynus had done to take the crown—and to try to keep it. He'd tricked Gulph into killing Brutan and come up with the insane scheme to destroy the bridge and isolate Idilliam. "Nynus was no better than his father," Gulph said. "*Our* father."

"Gulph—Nynus is dead."

"But the crown is still here! Was it the crown that made him do all those terrible things, Ossilius? What will happen to me if I put it on? If I try to rule? The prophecy says that I'm one of the three.

That it's my destiny to rule Toronia. But what if I turn out to be just as much a monster as Brutan or Nynus?"

He stared at Ossilius, his eyes wide, the crown held between both hands. Ossilius looked solemnly back.

"It is just a crown, Gulph. A piece of metal. What you do with it is your choice and yours alone."

Gulph stared at the gold band. What did it matter now, anyway? For a brief moment, just after Nynus had died, when Ossilius had picked up the crown and handed it to him, Gulph had believed everything might turn out all right. But the dead had taken over Idilliam and there was nothing left to rule.

"It's time to go," said Ossilius. Gently, he removed one of Gulph's hands from the crown and placed a sword in it. "Are you ready?"

"I don't think I was ready for any of this," Gulph replied. But he followed Ossilius as they crept through the hole in the wall, heads lowered, and began to cross the battlefield. In the shadow of the nearby tower, Brutan had closed his bony fingers around the throat of a boy of about thirteen—Gulph's age. The undead king hoisted the lad into the air and studied his face with blazing red eyes.

"Are you my son?" he bellowed. "Are you the one who killed me?"

"Leave him alone!" Gulph hissed, but when he started toward the horrific scene, Ossilius pulled him back.

"It is too late," Ossilius insisted.

The boy's whimpers were cut off as Brutan squeezed. A moment later, his life had ended and his new, undead existence had begun.

"Revenge!" Brutan roared as he marched on. "I will have revenge on my son and my treacherous people!"

"I have to do something!" said Gulph, shaking Ossilius's hand from his shoulder. "I don't care if it's hopeless. These are my people. I should be fighting with them!"

He started off through the smoke, but Ossilius caught him again. "I understand, Gulph. I do. But this is not the time for you to fight. This is the time for you to hide."

Gulph stopped struggling and stared at him, dumbfounded. "*Hide?* What kind of king hides when his people need him?"

"The kind of king who wants to stay alive."

"A cowardly one, more like."

Ossilius shook his head, exasperated. "You know already that you cannot win this battle, Gulph. But you can make plans for the future. You can gather allies and arms. If you lie low now, one day you will rise again."

Gulph looked into the face of the man who was old enough to be his father, perhaps even his grandfather. He couldn't imagine a more loyal companion. And yet . . .

"The Legion was my life," Ossilius pressed. "I know when

to fight, Gulph. And I know when to make a tactical retreat. Believe me when I tell you that time is now."

"But my friends are out here somewhere. Pip and Sidebottom John and the others. I won't leave them behind. I won't leave anyone behind!"

"Do you mean the troupe of performers you arrived with? Gulph, we cannot risk it."

Gulph looked out at the legion of undead. He knew his friend was right. What chance did the two of them have? If they tried to find his friends, they'd only die in the attempt.

"All right," Gulph said reluctantly. "Let's go. But we'll take whoever we can save with us."

They ran on, hugging the city wall as they tried to circle around the worst of the fighting. The billowing smoke was acrid; Gulph could barely see through the tears streaming from his eyes.

"Look out!" shouted Ossilius as a rotting warrior leaped out from behind a mound of bodies. Gulph folded his legs, tucked in his body, and rolled away from the warrior with an agility that would have drawn a round of applause from an audience.

Once a Tangletree Player, he thought giddily, *always a Tangletree Player.*

As he sprang upright, he realized he had dropped his own sword, but spied a short sword lodged beneath an enormous stone that had fallen from the wall. He grabbed the hilt, yanked it free, whirled, and slashed his attacker across the chest. There was no blood, just a spray of bone shards and dust. The undead warrior came on, grinning its skeletal leer through hanging strips of flesh.

Gulph bent his knees and threw himself into a clumsy backflip. He landed on top of the stone and drove the sword into the warrior's skull. At the same instant, Ossilius sliced the thing's legs off at the knees.

The warrior's dismembered remains collapsed, twitching and hissing with their strange semblance of life.

"Keep moving!" Ossilius cried. "The longer we stay out in the open, the more danger we're in."

Gradually, they forged a path toward their goal. *I haven't abandoned you, my friends,* Gulph thought as he ducked and wove through a shrieking knot of undead. *I'll come for you. If not today, then tomorrow. If not tomorrow, then the day after that. I'll come for you. I promise!*

"Help me."

The voice came from behind the stone. It sounded like a girl, surely no older than Gulph.

"Pip?" He peered into the shadows, his heart suddenly racing. "Pip, is that you?"

But the face that peered up at him was not that of his oldest friend. This girl was much younger. Her cheeks were streaked with blood and her blond hair was matted with filth. She was shaking all over.

"Come with us," said Gulph without hesitation. He stretched out a hand, but the girl just stared at it, too terrified to move.

"Gulph, hurry!" called Ossilius from ahead. "We cannot afford to stop."

"Wait, Ossilius!"

The captain appeared through a billow of smoke. His brow was furrowed, but as soon as he saw the little girl, his face softened. He plucked her gently from her hiding place and they hurried on.

"It's all right," said Gulph to the girl as they ran. "You're safe now."

He hoped it was true.

Ahead, the ruined mausoleum loomed out of the smoke. Built by Brutan as a towering monument to death, it was now a mountain of broken stone. As they clambered over the rubble, Gulph shuddered, remembering the unearthly power that had brought this mighty building crashing to the ground.

Limmoni's power.

Broken roof tiles crunched beneath his feet—perhaps the very tiles on which Limmoni had stood when she'd been executed. The order to take her life had been the final command of Nynus's short reign as king of Toronia. A bloody reign indeed.

Will mine be any different? Ossilius had said he thought so, but Gulph wondered if he'd ever be sure.

"There!" Ossilius cried. "The postern gate!"

Gulph blinked away stinging soot and saw the tower they'd glimpsed from a distance. Set into its base was a large stone door, flanked by the statues Gulph had noticed. On the left was a man with the head of a bull; on the right was a snake-headed woman.

"So you mean the door?" said Gulph. "Where does it go?"

By now they'd run clear of the fighting. Perhaps the smoke was keeping people—and unpeople—away.

"The postern gate is the back door to the city."

"You mean it just leads to more fighting? What good will that do us?"

"We will not be going through the door."

"But I thought . . ."

Ossilius was off again, dodging through the smoke with the little girl held tight against his chest. Gulph followed, reaching the tower just a few paces behind the grizzled captain.

No sooner had they stopped than a man emerged from behind the bull-headed statue. He wore the uniform of an Idilliam soldier and was brandishing a long sword. Gulph couldn't tell which part of his body was trembling more: his arms or his knees.

"Stay back!" the man cried.

"At your ease, soldier," said Ossilius. He lowered the girl to the ground and held out his hands. "Do you know me?"

The man squinted at Ossilius's grimy outfit, then his eyes

widened. "Captain Ossilius? Of the Legion?" Lowering his sword, he made a clumsy salute. "What are your orders, sir?"

Gulph spotted more movement behind the statue. "Come out," he said. "All of you. It's all right. We won't hurt you."

Two more figures appeared: a woman wearing a baker's apron and a man whose face Gulph recognized.

"You were with us in the Vault of Heaven," Gulph said, staring at the manacles still locked around the man's ankles.

"Never saw you," retorted the man. "I'd have remembered a little freak like you."

"Shut up, Slater," said the soldier. But his tone remained fearful.

"Shall I strike him, my king?" said Ossilius mildly.

Slater's eyes narrowed. The eyes of the others grew wide.

"No," said Gulph at once. "He's just afraid."

"'King'?" said Slater suspiciously. "What d'you mean, 'king'?"

Ossilius dropped slowly to one knee. "This is Agulphus, son of Brutan, born one of three. This is a child of the prophecy stars, who has slain his father and taken back the crown. See, he holds it now, in waiting for the time when the three shall be brought together to take the throne as one. If you would join his quest, kneel with me now and show your allegiance."

The soldier's jaw dropped open. The woman gasped. The little girl, crouched beside the kneeling Ossilius, stared up at Gulph with uncomprehending eyes. Slater snorted and looked away.

Gulph raised the crown he'd been carrying this whole time, but which the little crowd seemed only now to see. The crown was suddenly very heavy.

Is this what power feels like? I never knew it weighed so much.

Slowly, with infinite care, he placed the crown on his head.

"The prophecy!" cried the woman, sinking to her knees and clasping her hands in front of her apron.

"My lord," said the soldier, pressing his closed fist to his bronze breastplate. "My liege. I—Marcus of the King's Legion—am yours to command."

Slater looked back, seeming to see Gulph for the first time. His expression melted slowly from insolent to amazed.

"Can't be true," he said. "Can't be."

"It can," Ossilius replied. "It is."

"Suppose I might follow a king," Slater said after a moment's consideration. "If he had somewhere to lead me."

"As it happens," Gulph replied, "I do."

CHAPTER 2

The instant she awoke, Elodie knew something was wrong. She crawled over the blankets to the front of the tent. Throwing the flap aside, she scrambled out into the forest clearing.

An army encircled her tent. Hundreds of men and horses stood facing her under the purple predawn sky. In the gloom, their faces gave off a faint glow. They were translucent, like soldiers made of frosted glass.

An army of ghosts.

"What's wrong?" she said, suddenly wide awake.

One of the knights spurred his horse forward. He was old and haggard, yet his back was straight and his phantom eyes were bright.

"We wish to leave," Sir Jaken replied.

The words struck Elodie dumb.

She looked beyond the rank and file of the ghost soldiers to where the Trident camp was awakening. Through the glassy horses, she saw ordinary men and women going about their early morning duties: carrying water brought from the nearby stream; lighting fires; tending to livestock. They trudged with tired limbs and bowed heads.

You lost the Battle of the Bridge, Elodie reflected. *You lost your friends and comrades. Is it any wonder you look beaten?*

Yet they were still alive, these surviving rebels of Trident. And all thanks to this ghost army.

An army only I can see.

Filled with resolve, Elodie swept her red-gold hair back from her face.

"You can't leave," she said firmly. "You simply can't. We've come so far together. These people need you. I need you. You can't turn back now."

"It is not a question of turning back," Sir Jaken replied. "Rather of going forward."

Elodie shook her head in frustration. "There's so much to do. Gulph is still trapped in Idilliam. I have to . . . Tarlan and I have to find him. We're supposed to be together, the three of us. I thought that's what you wanted."

"Only fate can decide whether you and your brothers will be one. We have played our part. Now we seek peace."

Elodie scanned the faces of the watching ghosts. Red light was bleeding into the sky: a fiery dawn.

"Brutan is in Idilliam too," she said, determined to convince them. "He's the one responsible for your deaths. Have you forgotten the War of Blood? Don't you want revenge?"

"We are beyond revenge."

Elodie's dismay was turning into anguish. She'd placed her trust in these abandoned souls. Placed her heart.

"Please," she said, rubbing her eyes. She wouldn't cry, not in front of them. "Think about it. You made a new bridge to help us cross the chasm to Idilliam. We might need it again."

"Our bridge broke."

"And cast a whole legion of Brutan's undead monsters into the chasm! Don't you see what a difference you made? Without you, everything would have been lost!"

Elodie stopped, suddenly aware she'd been shouting. To anyone watching, it would look as if she were yelling into thin air.

A boy dressed in a squire's uniform stepped out from behind Sir Jaken's horse. She'd been hearing the voices of ghosts her whole life—though she'd only known it these past weeks—but Samial was the first spirit she'd actually seen and spoken to.

And become friends with.

"Samial," she implored, holding out her hands. "Surely you can make them understand? Together we're strong. If we part now . . ."

"We do understand," said Samial. He cast an anxious glance at Sir Jaken, who nodded for him to continue. "You brought us here, Elodie. You led us out of the Weeping Woods so we could take revenge against Brutan. You set us free."

"But we lost the battle," Elodie protested. "Brutan still holds Idilliam. He . . ."

"In freeing us," said Sir Jaken gently, "you brought us out of the shadow of death. You allowed us to fight our final battle. Now that battle is over. Vengeance has been served, and we are at peace."

The misty faces of the ghosts nodded in assent. Tears stung Elodie's eyes. "But you can't just leave."

Samial took her hand in his ghostly fingers. Cold as it was, his touch comforted her. "Elodie—this part of it is over."

She looked into her friend's eyes. "So that's it? You've just come to say good-bye?"

"No," said Sir Jaken. "There is something you must do for us."

"Me? What do you need from me?"

"We need you to set us free."

Elodie pulled her hand from Samial's and turned away. *But this was my destiny,* she thought, desolated. *I was born to lead a ghost army. I know it. I'm the only one who can do it. Without them I'm just . . .*

"There are other spirits in this world," said an old, cracked voice.

Elodie jumped. She hadn't heard Melchior's footsteps—but

then the wizard's feet, as always, were bare, and the carpet of moss on the floor of the clearing was soft.

Maybe he didn't walk here at all. Maybe he just ... appeared.

"You scared me," she murmured. A thought occurred to her. "Do you see them too, Melchior?"

The wizard stared out at the ranks of ghosts. His yellow robe glowed faintly in the dim light of dawn. His hands gripped his wooden staff so tightly that his bony knuckles turned white.

"No," he said at last. "That is beyond me. But I sense the weariness they carry. You feel it too, I think."

Elodie considered arguing. But Melchior was right; she *did* feel it: a slow, insistent beating, like the wings of a trapped bird eager to take flight.

She sighed. "What must I do?" As it often did when she was nervous, her hand stole to the green jewel she wore around her neck. It was as much a part of her now as the blood in her veins; like that blood, it joined her to her brothers.

"The ritual is simple but powerful," Melchior said. "You must take a talisman—a possession that means something to these lost souls—and bury it."

"Is that all?"

"That is all."

"Like a funeral?"

"Like a funeral."

"But what possession? Where can I . . . ?"

"That is why we led you here after the battle," said Samial.

Behind him, the phantom horses drew back, some to the left, some to the right. A corridor opened up in the body of the ghost army, at the end of which Elodie saw a huge oak tree.

"Let me show you," said Samial.

Elodie looked at Melchior, who planted his feet wide and placed both hands on his staff.

"I will be waiting," said the wizard.

As Samial led Elodie to the tree, she felt the ancient presence of the knights and their steeds pressing in around her. She walked as if in a dream, her head light.

The tree was age-worn and enormous. Its lower branches—themselves thicker than the trunks of many lesser trees—drooped almost to the ground. Guided by Samial, Elodie picked her way between them to the oak's tremendous base. Here she found a dark hollow edged with green fungus.

"Inside," said Samial.

As Elodie stretched her hand toward the hollow, the tree creaked. She glanced up, startled.

"Don't be afraid," said Samial.

Biting her lip, Elodie reached inside the hollow. Its interior was damp, but her fingers alighted almost immediately on something soft. She drew it out, held it up.

"It's a flag," she said in wonder.

"The Standard of Morlon," said Samial. "It carries the colors under which we fought, all those years ago."

"Morlon. He was Brutan's brother, wasn't he?"

Samial nodded. His ghostly fingers brushed across the rotten fabric of the flag, tracing stripes that might once have been purple, a crest that might once have been gold.

"Brutan stole the throne from Morlon and we fought to reclaim it. We failed. The flag was hidden here by the last of our standard-bearers, on the last day of our last battle."

As they left the tree, a second passage opened up in the ranks of the ghost army. Elodie followed it, awed that these dead knights were steering her through this final task.

Melchior was waiting for her at the other end of the corridor, stabbing at the soft ground with the end of his staff.

"Here it is," she said, raising the flag, "their talisman."

The wizard nodded and tossed her a short branch. "Help me dig, Elodie."

She began working at the ground with the branch, but soon found she made better progress with her hands. *Back in Castle Vicerin, I'd have made a servant do this for me.* She scooped out clods of earth, piling them beside the steadily growing hole. The Vicerins had raised Elodie as their daughter, but planned to use her to claim the throne for themselves. *They'd hardly recognize me now*, she thought, staring in wonder at her filthy hands.

Once they'd finished excavating, Elodie sat back on her knees. The hole looked like a grave.

"What do we do now?" she asked.

"I think you know," Melchior replied gently.

Elodie picked up the flag, folded it, and placed it at the bottom of the hole.

"Now cover it over," said Melchior.

"Shouldn't we say something?"

"Do you wish to?"

Elodie shook her head. She was too upset to think, let alone speak.

Melchior touched her shoulder. "If no words come, Elodie, do not fret. Everything has already been said. This is an act of deeds, not words."

Elodie's sadness swelled as she scooped up a handful of soil and scattered it on the flag. As she did so, a series of ripples surged through the ghost army.

"Another," said Melchior.

Elodie obeyed. With each handful of earth, the rippling

increased. Elodie closed her eyes, feeling the air move strangely around her as her hands continued their work.

"Ah, you are here, Princess Elodie. Melchior—good morning to you."

The voice jolted her from her reverie. She looked up to see Fessan's tall frame silhouetted against the red sky that was brightening rapidly to orange behind the trees.

"Another day begins," remarked Melchior, rising awkwardly to his feet.

"Our last here, I think," Fessan sighed. The low dawn light carved harsh lines into his face, making him look tired, and much older than the youthful commander Elodie remembered from their first meeting.

"I think we will break camp tomorrow," Fessan went on. "We lost many during the Battle of the Bridge. It is vital we recruit more soldiers. Besides, the men need a purpose. Trident must continue to . . ."

He broke off, seeming to see the hole in the ground for the first time.

"What are you doing?"

A little annoyed at Fessan's interruption, Elodie stood up. She brushed the earth from her hands. "I am honoring those who helped us, Fessan."

"Honoring? Honoring who?" The scar running down the side of Fessan's face twitched as he looked around the clearing, his gaze passing straight through the ghosts.

"My army. Our allies. The knights who saved Trident."

"The ghosts?" Fessan's eyes widened. "Are they with us now?"

"They're here. But they're leaving. Their work is done, and now it's time to set them free."

"Leaving? But, Princess, half the soldiers of Trident died at the bridge. Many who survived are injured. If not for your . . . your friends, we would have been defeated. You cannot let them go! We need them!"

Fessan's whole body was shaking. Elodie was taken aback. Had Fessan ever lost his temper with her before? She didn't think so. Yet his anger only served to make her angry herself.

"How dare you?" she snapped. "How dare you question the right of these . . . these *warriors* to find peace. They have done their duty. And I *will* lay them to rest."

"And I will not let you!" Fessan's white-knuckled hands clenched at his sides.

"But you will," said Melchior, stepping smoothly between them. He tapped the end of his staff on the half-covered flag. "This is a blood debt, Fessan. As a man of the sword, you must understand that."

Fessan's shoulders dropped. He appeared suddenly exhausted. "Trident looks to me. I have a duty."

"The spirits look to Elodie," Melchior replied. "And she has a duty too."

Emotions fluttered across Fessan's face. Then, abruptly, he said, "Very well. Do what you must. I only hope that Trident does not pay for this with more deaths."

Turning on his heel, he stalked away toward the camp. Elodie watched him until he was lost among the trees.

"He's done so much for me," she said. "Fought so hard to put me on the throne. He raised an army for me, Melchior. And he lost so many on the bridge. But . . . oh, why does he have to make this even more difficult?"

"Fessan is a great leader," said Melchior, "and so he carries a great burden. As do you, Elodie. You just carry them in different ways. He is a good man. That is why I chose him to lead Trident." He turned his attention back to the hole in the ground. "And now we must finish what we have started."

In silence they returned to their task. As Elodie covered the flag, she felt her anger at Fessan drain away. Everything drained away, leaving just her, and her hands, and the damp soil they touched.

"It is nearly done," said Melchior quietly.

Blinking, Elodie came out of her reverie. Only one tiny corner of the flag remained visible. Her hands were poised over it, holding the final scoop of soil. All around her the ghost army was watching, as still as a held breath.

She looked around sharply. She knew she had to release the army, but she couldn't bear to lose quite all of them—not yet. "Samial?"

"I am here." He appeared as if from nowhere, a tired smile on his thin, grubby face.

She closed her eyes, opened them again. "Samial, answer me truthfully. Do you wish me to set you free?"

"Not if you want me to stay," he answered at once.

Her eyes filled with tears. "I do, Samial. I do."

"Then take this." The ghost boy drew an arrowhead from his tunic. As he held it up, the sun sent a thread of light through the trees, painting yellow light down its edge. "It has always been my lucky charm. If you keep it, you will keep me, too."

Elodie's fingers trembled as she took the arrowhead and slipped it into her tunic pocket. She swallowed hard. Then with a shaky smile she looked around at Sir Jaken and the rows of shimmering knights.

"Good-bye," she told them. "And thank you." Then she placed the last of the dirt on the flag.

The ghosts of the knights and their horses glowed with a brilliant light and Elodie took a step back, dazzled, her hands shielding her eyes. The knights raised their arms in one last salute. Then they dissolved into the morning, fading like a forgotten dream.

Elodie stared at the empty trees for a moment. Beside her, Samial bowed his head.

"There," she said with a long, ragged sigh. "It's over. I just hope I did the right thing."

"What does your heart say?" asked Melchior. He stood some distance away, leaning against a tree.

"That I did my best. But was it enough?"

"So like your mother," he murmured.

His words cut through Elodie's grief. She snapped her head around to look at him. "My mother? You knew my mother?"

"Yes."

He said it in such a matter-of-fact way that at first Elodie thought she must have misheard him. But his small smile told her she hadn't. She strode toward him. "Tell me about her!"

The wizard cocked his head, seeming to consider this. He looked to Elodie like a heron poised on the bank of a river, waiting patiently for a fish to pass.

"Her name was Kalia," he said at last. "She was a witch-of-the-earth, and never did I see a mother more devoted to her children. She was prepared to give up everything for you. Even her life."

Everything inside Elodie had stopped: the beat of her heart, the pulse of her blood, the breath in her lungs.

"The Vicerins told me my mother was a peasant woman," she

said slowly. "But that was just another lie, wasn't it? She was a witch! No wonder they didn't tell me."

"And if they had told you?"

She felt a smile twitch her lips. "I might not have let Lord Vicerin treat me like a puppet. I'd have liked to see him try to get the crown without me." She glanced back to where Samial remained by the buried standard, kneeling on the ground beside it. A thought occurred to her. "So my mother had magic! Is that why I'm like this, Melchior? Could she see ghosts too?"

"It is possible."

"Where is she now?"

"I am sorry, Elodie. There is no easy way to tell you this. When Brutan discovered that you and your brothers were still alive, he had your mother burned at the stake."

Elodie felt cold all over. "Then she's . . ."

The old wizard nodded. "Yes. I am afraid your mother is probably dead."

She looked at him sharply. "Probably?"

"Indeed. As soon as I learned of the execution, I tried to intervene. But Brutan had barred all access to the Undersalle."

"The Under-what?"

"Never mind. I was forced to find another way. I made my way onto the battlements, but I was too late to damp the fires as I had planned. So I improvised."

"What happened?"

Melchior's blue eyes stared far into the distance, or perhaps back in time. His hands roamed over the etched surface of his staff. His toes curled in the soil.

"I attempted a spell no sane wizard would ever try to cast. Just before the moment of Kalia's death, I tried to withdraw her from the world."

"You . . . saved her?" Elodie felt numb and confused. Could she even dare to hope her mother was still alive?

Melchior's eyes regained their focus and locked on hers. "I do not know. The magic I used was ancient and . . . brutal. To withdraw a person is to take them beyond both life and death, into a realm that has little to do with either. The process is perilous. As for bringing them back . . ."

Elodie's excitement was mounting. "But you think you might have succeeded! You do, don't you?"

The wizard shook his head. "I cannot say. When I examined the pyre later, I found nothing but ashes." He sighed. "The older I get, the more I realize that wizardry is more about questions than answers."

"But your spell might have worked." Elodie wrestled with the idea, trying to squeeze it into her overloaded heart. "And I don't care about questions, Melchior—I'm just glad we have a wizard on our side!"

"Alas, currently you do not."

Elodie gaped at him. "What? What do you mean, you're not on our side?"

A smile appeared on the wizard's face. "That is not what I meant, Elodie. Never doubt my loyalty; I am with you to the end. I simply meant that I am no longer a wizard."

Elodie stared at him.

"The spell of withdrawing is forbidden. When I used it to save your mother—to *attempt* to save her—I broke all the laws by which magic turns. The instant the spell was cast, the stars took back my powers. Ever since that day, ten years ago, I have wandered the world in impotence. Oh, I have helped here and there; I helped Fessan to create Trident, for example. But now, I fear, you need more than just a frail, old man. It is time for me to recover what was lost."

"Get your powers back? Can you even do that?"

"I do not know. But I must try. I must go on a journey and, at journey's end, I must lower myself into the ocean of time and plead with the stars."

Now Elodie felt goose bumps rise all over her skin. It came to her that the man standing before her—this stooped old fellow in a scruffy yellow robe—was not a man at all.

"I tell you all this in confidence," said Melchior, placing one gnarled hand on her shoulder. "Trident must not know. Fessan must not know—he bears a heavy enough burden as it is. Until my powers are restored, it is our secret. Will you keep it?"

Elodie nodded dumbly. Since waking this morning, she felt as if her whole world had tilted, leaving her balanced precariously between past and future. She pressed her hand against her pocket, relishing the hardness of the arrowhead Samial had given to her. A lucky charm, he'd said.

Well, we could do with a little luck.

At long last, far behind the trees, the new sun rose.

CHAPTER 3

Hold tight!" Tarlan cried. "We're here!"

Bunching his fingers into Theeta's golden neck ruff, he bent forward as the giant thorrod plunged down toward the trees. The four women riding behind him gasped and clung to each other.

Tarlan glanced left and right, to where Nasheen and Kitheen flew in perfect formation, each with five more survivors on their backs. Plucking these wretched people from the smoke-shrouded Idilliam battlefield had been hazardous, and when they'd crossed back over the chasm surrounding the city, he'd been afraid his passengers would fall. Yet here they were, soaring over the Isurian forest, toward the Trident camp. The third rescue flight was over.

How many more will it take before I find my brother?

With a raucous cry, Theeta splayed her wings wide, slowing her descent as she swooped majestically into the forest clearing. She flew low over a row of tents; Tarlan saw lines of wounded soldiers lying outside them, their faces turned up in the pale light of the morning sun. His winged steed passed a makeshift forge, where blacksmiths toiled over broken weapons. He guided Theeta into an open space between an enormous fire pit and a corral of horses, where she touched down at last.

Their thorrod companions landed beside them, each bird silent despite its massive bulk. As soon as they were all down, Tarlan slipped to the ground and helped the survivors to dismount. Nurses arrived from the hospital tents carrying stretchers; gratefully, Tarlan handed the survivors over to their care.

"You did well, Theeta," he said, patting the bird's huge beak. He smiled at the other thorrods. "You all did."

"Fly again?" Theeta replied in her dry hiss of a voice.

Before Tarlan could reply, something heavy bowled into him, knocking his legs out from under him and spilling him to the ground. He rose laughing, throwing his arms around the two animals that had just felled him like a tree.

"Greythorn! Filos! Are you trying to kill me?"

The wolf and the tigron cub pressed against his legs, yipping and purring their pleasure.

"I am happy when the pack is together," said Greythorn.

"Me too," Tarlan replied.

"Your brother?" asked Filos. "Did you find your brother?"

Tarlan stroked the tigron's blue-and-white striped fur. "No, Filos. It's chaos over there. But I'll keep trying."

"Brother melted," said Theeta.

"Melted?" It took Tarlan a moment to work out what she was saying. "Oh, you mean he disappeared?"

"Brother melted," Theeta agreed.

Tarlan nodded, remembering that strange moment in the middle of the battle when he'd seen Gulph facing the undead monster their father had become . . . and suddenly turning invisible.

I talk to animals. Elodie sees ghosts. And Gulph . . . Is vanishing your only trick, my brother, or can you do more?

"He will be hard to find," grunted Greythorn.

"Yes," Tarlan agreed. "But I won't give up."

The last of the people he'd rescued—a young man with a broken arm and a deep gash on the side of his face—looked at Tarlan curiously as he hobbled past.

The only thing they can hear when my friends speak are growls and squawks, Tarlan thought, feeling a curious breed of pride. *We have a language all our own.*

He led his pack to the fire pit, where they sat eating strips of meat—cooked for himself, raw for the others. As they ate, Tarlan checked Theeta's injured foot.

"How does it feel?" he said, touching the bandaged stump

where Brutan had severed one of her talons during the Battle of the Bridge.

"Claw gone," Theeta mumbled through a beakful of meat.

"That's right." He patted her scaly leg. "You must tell me if you need to rest, Theeta. We've done three flights since the battle already."

"Brother there," Theeta replied, in a tone that told Tarlan they would be in the air again soon.

Once they'd eaten, Tarlan sat fidgeting. He knew they should rest at least a little longer before setting out for Idilliam again. But the Trident camp, with its constant human bustle, was just so *noisy*.

You're a human yourself, a voice whispered in his head. *These are your people.*

"No," he muttered. "I have my pack. I go my own way."

"And what way might that be?"

Tarlan turned to see Fessan standing a few paces behind him. The Trident commander's arms were folded, and his scarred face was stern.

"Back to Idilliam, if it's anything to do with you," said Tarlan, standing up. "Someone's got to help these people."

"You've done enough, my prince," Fessan replied. "I cannot authorize another flight."

"Authorize?" Tarlan snapped. He hated it when Fessan called him "prince." "You think I need your permission?"

"It is too dangerous."

"You think I don't know that? I'm the one who flew in there during the battle, remember? You didn't even get past the bridge!"

"Many of my men died on the bridge."

Tarlan supposed that Fessan was right. But was that any excuse for inaction?

"Everyone's just lying around licking their wounds!" he said. "At least I'm doing something! What other hope has my brother got?"

"Ah, so we come to it. It is not the citizens of Idilliam you care about. You just want to find your brother."

"Of course I want to find Gulph. So does Elodie. If I can help some others along the way, so much the better."

Tarlan realized he was advancing on Fessan, and that Greythorn and Filos were matching him stride for stride. The wolf and the tigron were both growling, and their hackles were raised. Tarlan could feel the curl of his own lip against his teeth.

Suddenly he saw that Fessan didn't look stern at all. He looked exhausted.

"Back," he murmured, dropping his hands to his companions' heads. Both animals looked up at him curiously. But they did stop growling. "Go back. It's all right. Just leave us a minute."

Reluctantly, Greythorn and Filos retreated, planting themselves among the waiting thorrods and looking on suspiciously.

"I suppose you've got a better plan?" Tarlan said to Fessan, speaking more quietly now.

Fessan regarded him through narrow eyes. "I do."

"Are you going to tell me what it is?"

"Are you going to listen?"

Tarlan couldn't suppress his smile. "I suppose I might."

Fessan bowed his head with a small smile of his own. "Very well, my prince. We will go back to Idilliam. You are right. Gulph must be found—the prophecy depends on it. We agree on that much, at least. But Brutan's forces are strong, and their numbers will only continue to grow as more of the undead join their ranks. To defeat them, we will need an army the like of which Toronia has never seen before. But that is not all."

"It isn't?"

Despite himself, Tarlan was fascinated. As soon as he started talking strategy, Fessan's eyes lit up with a kind of fire, and Tarlan began to understand what it truly was to be a soldier.

"No. Before we can cross the chasm, we must repair the bridge . . . or build a new one altogether. For that we will need engineers, and lots of them." Fessan looked south, staring through the trees as if he were seeing not the forest but what lay beyond. "Even *that* is not enough, though. Idilliam is only part of the picture. We will need a second army, to march on Ritherlee. The Vicerins have become too powerful."

At the mention of the name, Tarlan's skin crawled. The memories of his imprisonment by Lord Vicerin were too recent and bitter to forget. For a moment he could again hear the sound of Theeta's wings as she'd carried him away from his prison, and feel his anger at being forced to leave behind the mysterious green gemstone that matched those worn by Elodie and Gulph. Tarlan thought it through and shook his head. "Gulph can't wait that long. He needs us *now*. My brother needs *me*."

"And you will help him," said an old, dry voice.

Tarlan whirled to find himself staring straight into the face of Melchior. He'd thought his ears were as highly tuned as those of his pack; so how did the wizard always manage to sneak up on him?

"I'm glad you agree," he said.

"But you will not help him now," Melchior added.

Tarlan scowled. Everything the wizard said seemed wrapped in many meanings. Humans were hard enough to understand, but wizards . . .

"Gulph needs me," he said stolidly. "I have to go to him. For all I know, he might be dead."

"He is not."

"How do you know that?"

Melchior raised one bony finger to the sky. The other stars had now faded, but the three prophecy stars still winked against the rosy sky.

"They appeared the night you were born," said Melchior. "One each for the three. . . ."

"I know all that," Tarlan snapped. "I don't see what—"

"If we see them, we're safe."

It was Elodie, emerging from the gloom to stand beside the wizard. Of all the humans Tarlan had come to know, Elodie was the least strange.

"That's what you mean, isn't it, Melchior?" she said.

Melchior nodded. "Your sister speaks the truth. If Gulph were dead, his star would go out. And that would extinguish the prophecy itself. The prophecy—the fate of Toronia—rests not on one pair of shoulders but on three. It is all of you, or it is none of you."

Tarlan stared at the lights in the sky. What was he, that his fate was bound to these celestial fires? *And what right do they have to tell me what to do?* Not for the first time, part of him wished he could reach up, strike them from the sky, and be free.

"So, now that is settled," the wizard went on, "you must come with me, Tarlan. While Fessan and Elodie are busy rebuilding Trident, you and I have an important journey to make!"

Fessan, who had been turning away, wheeled around with a startled expression on his face.

"Melchior, have you lost your senses? As long as the triplets are separated, they are vulnerable. Elodie and Tarlan must stay together. And I need you here. Trident needs you."

Tarlan felt as surprised as Fessan looked—and pleased, too. *A journey!* Maybe he couldn't escape his destiny, but could this be his chance to get away from these crowded tents and fly free in clean air once more? How wonderful that would be.

Even if I do have to put up with a wizard for company.

He glanced at Elodie. What would she think of being parted so soon? They'd barely gotten to know each other. But to his surprise, his sister smiled at him.

"You should go," she said. "I can see you want to."

Fessan shook his head. "I cannot let you leave—neither of you."

"You cannot stop us," Melchior said gently. "Tarlan, will you come?"

Mirith—who'd raised Tarlan as if he'd been her own child—had always told him the best decisions were made quickly.

When your head and heart are at war, tell your head to lay down its sword. That's what she used to say.

"When are we leaving?" he asked.

The sky was darkening by the time Tarlan found himself loading a knapsack with pouches of dried food and skins of water. Melchior had insisted that he rest before they depart and he had to concede that the long sleep curled beside Theeta's wing had done him good. His limbs felt strong and his head clear. As he noosed the neck of the sack, Elodie came up carrying a small pile of spare clothes.

"I hope you'll remember to wash," she said, stuffing the clothes into the sack. "You know what you're like."

"You knew about Melchior's plan all along, didn't you?" said Tarlan. "Where is he taking me?"

Elodie glanced around furtively, then lowered her voice. "I don't know exactly. But I think you're going to help Melchior get his powers back."

"Powers?" At first Tarlan didn't understand. Then it dawned on him. "His *magic*? You mean he doesn't . . ."

He listened as Elodie told him a story that sounded like a tale to scare children, but which he knew was only too true. A tale of betrayal, and a witch burned at the stake, and a wizard so desperate to save her that he'd sacrificed his magic in the attempt.

"Our mother," he breathed when she'd finished. "I didn't think I could hate Brutan any more than I did. I will find him. And when I do, I will kill him!"

"He's dead already," Elodie said drily. "It doesn't seem to have made much difference."

Tarlan wasn't listening. "I will go with Melchior. We will get his powers back. Whatever he needs me to do, I will do it. I will do it for our mother, Elodie!"

He broke off. His sister's eyes were wide with some emotion he couldn't measure. Why were human feelings so complex?

"Be safe," she said.

"You could come," he said suddenly. "It's like Fessan said: We're safer together. Like a pack."

Elodie arched one eyebrow. "A pack of animals?"

"Exactly!"

Elodie shook her head, but she was grinning. "You'll be back soon," she said. "The prophecy will see to that. Besides, Fessan needs me to help rebuild Trident. You're not the only one with work to do."

She hugged him, then stepped away. The fire pit glowed behind her, surrounding her with an orange halo.

"So it's good-bye, then."

"Farewell, my brother. For now."

A hard, curved shape pressed into the small of Tarlan's back. He turned and touched his hand to the tip of Theeta's beak.

"Greythorn! Filos!" he called, leaping onto the thorrod's back. "Go to Kitheen! We're leaving!"

The black thorrod crouched silently, allowing the wolf and the tigron to leap on. As they nestled in his coarse feathers, Tarlan looked to his left.

"Nasheen?" he said with a grin. "How's your passenger?"

"Wizard heavy," the white thorrod replied. Thorrods were not known for their sense of humor, but Tarlan got the idea that the enormous bird had just made a joke.

"It is many years since I flew," Melchior said uncertainly. "And in those days I did not need wings."

On the ground, Elodie had been joined by Fessan. Even though the Trident commander sometimes made his hackles rise, Tarlan was glad his sister was under Fessan's protection. He couldn't imagine a more loyal ally.

"Will you not reconsider?" Fessan said.

"We've made up our minds," Tarlan replied. "We're going."

"Then go with speed and in safety. And return soon."

"We will!"

"We are in our right place," Melchior added. "As are you, Fessan. Your father, Ossilius, would be proud of you. You will make good choices. And one day you will lead Trident to victory."

Upon hearing his words, Fessan relaxed visibly. For a moment Tarlan thought he saw not a confident soldier but an uncertain boy, anxious for approval. Then Fessan's back straightened and his arm lifted in a salute.

"Fare you well!" he cried.

"Good luck!" Elodie added. "And come back whole!"

In a flurry of feathers, the three thorrods lifted into the night sky. Tarlan wound his fingers into Theeta's ruff, relishing the blast of cold air against his face as the giant bird accelerated over the trees and into the waiting darkness.

Into the world! he thought giddily. *Once more into the world!*

"Which way?" he shouted to Melchior as Nasheen and Kitheen rose up on either side of them.

"West," replied the wizard.

"Down sun," Theeta cawed, pumping her wings.

"While we fly," Melchior went on, "I will tell you more about *why* we fly."

"You haven't told me anything yet."

"No. But your sister has." Melchior was smiling.

"How did you know that she . . . ?"

"Allow a wizard to keep at least a few of his secrets, Tarlan. Did Elodie also tell you I cannot regain my powers without your help?"

Tarlan's chest swelled. He'd assumed Melchior simply wanted a companion on the journey—perhaps someone to help out in a fight.

"What do I have to do?"

"All in good time. Now, where is it? . . . Hah, there! Look up, Tarlan, to your left. Do you see that streak of light?"

Tarlan scanned the starry sky. Almost at once his eyes fell upon a faint white line drawn across the heavens. It was slightly blurred, and swollen at one end.

"It is a comet," explained Melchior. "It appeared three moons ago. Back then it was too faint for most mortals to see."

"But I suppose you saw it."

"My eyes are old, but they see far."

Something in the wizard's tone made Tarlan's flesh prickle.

"When I saw the comet," Melchior continued, "I knew my days of wandering were over at last. Beneath its growing light, I walked back into the world. Now the comet is bright enough for all to see. Over the coming nights, it will grow brighter still, until it outshines even the prophecy stars. Then it will swiftly fade."

"What happens then?"

"I have but one chance to regain my powers, Tarlan. One chance, on one night, when the comet blazes with the forgotten fire of the distant deep. If I fail, my magic will be gone forever."

"And the prophecy?"

The wizard didn't answer.

The thorrods flew on into the night, dark shapes in a darker world. Their flight, as always, was silent; the only sound that came to Tarlan's ears was the occasional grunt or growl from Filos and Greythorn, who were almost invisible on Kitheen's black back.

Tarlan's excitement slowly dwindled, leaving him feeling strangely dejected. His brother was lost, and here he was leaving his sister behind too. Ahead lay emptiness and the crushing threat of failure.

"Where are we going anyway?" he said at last.

The wizard's voice floated out of the blackness, unexpectedly jovial. "Why, Tarlan, we are headed west. Where else would we be going but to the sea!"

Tarlan gasped. "The sea? I've never even seen it!"

"I thought as much."

"Is it . . . is it as big as they say?"

"Bigger."

"And is it beautiful?"

"Tarlan, you have no idea."

The sea!

Tarlan grinned. He was free and clear, buoyed up by possibility and driven by adventure. The troubles he'd left behind would just have to take care of themselves for a while.

He was Tarlan, and he was flying.

CHAPTER 4

A t last they had reached the postern gate.

"So where's this place you're taking us?" Slater asked Gulph, shouting to be heard over the battle. He jerked his thumb at the huge door. "It had better not be through there. We only just got out of the city in one piece."

Gulph turned to Ossilius, as curious as the others. Now that they were here, he had no idea where they were going next.

"We must push the Tauritus aside," Ossilius explained. "Then all will be revealed."

Before Gulph could ask what a Tauritus was, Ossilius hurried over to the statue of the bull-headed man standing beside the gate. It was fully twice his height. Gulph joined him, the others following close behind.

"I have a special task for you, Gulph," said Ossilius. "Climb to the head. Reach inside the mouth. There is a lever."

"Will that open the door?"

"Not exactly."

Bemused, Gulph knotted the crown firmly to a loop of his belt, then scampered nimbly up the statue until he was perched on its shoulder. Stone eyes glared at him from beneath a granite brow. Ignoring their dead gaze, he grasped one of the bull-man's horns for balance and reached into its gaping mouth.

His hand fell at once upon a short, metal lever. He pulled it up. No movement. The rough stone inside the statue's mouth pinched his hand. Somewhere through the smoke came the guttural cries of the undead.

They're getting closer . . .

Impatiently, Gulph pushed the lever down instead. Still nothing.

"Ossilius!" he called down. "I can't . . ."

"Turn it!" shouted the captain. "You can do it!"

Gulph obeyed. The lever rotated with a satisfying click.

"Good!" Ossilius roared. "Now push, all of you! For your lives—push!"

Gulph looked down to see Ossilius pressing his hands against the statue's stone haunch. The captain strained so hard that the tendons in his neck stood out like ropes. Marcus, the soldier, set his weight beside him, the woman in the baker's apron and the little girl following suit. After a brief pantomime of reluctance, Slater joined them.

Slowly, the statue began to move, sliding sideways in a series of jerks that made Gulph's teeth rattle, then abruptly halted. Gripping the lever with both hands, Gulph looked down and saw that a narrow slot had been revealed in the pillar. It looked black and ominous. A secret doorway.

"Hurry!" cried Ossilius, urging the little group of survivors through the slot. It was so narrow they had to enter in single file. When they were all inside, he turned his face up to Gulph.

"In a moment, I will tell you to let go of the lever. When you do so, the statue will return of its own accord. Do not worry—you can move much faster than a block of stone. Are you ready?"

Gulph's mouth was dry. He imagined releasing the lever, then losing his grip and tumbling to the ground. He saw himself lunging for the doorway, saw the statue sliding back into place, bearing down on him as he lay helpless on the ground and slicing him in two. . . .

"I'm ready," he said.

"Now!"

Gulph released the lever. Immediately, he felt the statue juddering beneath him. It threw him off balance; he went with the fall, flipping forward until his hands were planted on the bull-man's chest, then somersaulting out into clear air. He landed hard, letting himself tumble into a roll, then sprang up onto his feet again.

He could almost hear the applause.

"Gulph! Behind you!"

Two undead warriors staggered out of the thinning smoke. Both looked badly burned, and at first glance Gulph thought they were hugging each other. Then he saw that the burns had melted their rotting flesh together.

Ossilius darted from the doorway and hacked off the head of the first warrior. With a second stroke he split its body in two. The second warrior stumbled, weighed down by the flailing remains, but somehow came on.

Gulph reached for his own sword, but he'd lost it during his fall from the statue. Snatching up a stone, he hurled it at the oncoming monster. It hit the thing square in the chest, smashing frail ribs and flying straight out the other side. The impact spun the warrior completely around, and for an instant, the path to the secret doorway was clear.

But the doorway was almost closed.

Gulph sprinted toward it. The statue rumbled over the ground, some unseen mechanism dragging it in a series of juddering lurches. Ossilius had already ducked back inside and was reaching for Gulph with outstretched arms.

"Hurry!" he shouted.

Two more warriors appeared out of the murk.

The statue continued to grind its way shut. Now the slot was no wider than a man. Gulph leaped. Ossilius jumped aside, seizing Gulph's outstretched hands and hauling him through just as the Tauritus slammed back into place behind him with a head-splitting thump. Gulph felt the statue's cold stone brush his heels as he sprawled on the dank earth inside. One breath later and his legs would have been crushed.

He lay, panting for breath, blinking into utter darkness. The silence was just as complete. No light. No sound. Nothing at all.

"Are we all here?" said the woman, speaking uncertainly in the blackness. "I can't see a thing."

Nearby, somebody started to whimper. Clambering to his feet, Gulph reached out blindly. Small hands found his: the little girl.

"It's all right," he said. "We're safe now. What's your name?"

"J-J-Jessamyn," she blubbered. "Where's my mama?"

"I don't know, Jessamyn. But you're safe. Just keep holding my hand. Nothing bad can happen as long as we're holding hands, can it?"

Something bumped Gulph's shoulder.

"Hey!" It was Slater, his deep voice unmistakable. "Give that back!"

"Give what back?" said Gulph.

"He means his sword," said Ossilius, a little to Gulph's right. "You were right when you said you'd seen this man in the Vault of Heaven, Gulph. I remember him too. He is not a man I would trust with a sword."

"Give it back!"

"Take it from me, if you would. But before you do, I would point out that I have been trained in the seventeen classes of combat. That includes combat in the full dark. Can you say the same?"

Slater hesitated, then grumbled something unintelligible.

"What did you say?"

"What good's two swords to a man?"

"I could show you. However, I do not mean to use this as a weapon."

Gulph listened to Ossilius's retreating footsteps. Then came an unpleasant screeching sound, followed by a metallic clang.

"I have used your sword to jam the mechanism that moves the statue," Ossilius said.

"So now we're trapped," sneered Slater.

"Now we are safe."

"When you two have stopped arguing," said the woman, "perhaps we could get some light in here?"

"You speak well, my lady," said Ossilius.

"Hetty. My name's Hetty."

"Well, Hetty, cast around with me. The chamber we are in is a storeroom. It is small, but it should be well stocked. We may find torches, perhaps even preserved food."

Gulph gently released Jessamyn and stumbled into the blackness until his outstretched hands struck a wall. Fingering his way along it, he discovered a row of little doors, which he began to open one by one. From all around him came shuffling and scraping sounds as his companions made their own explorations.

Behind each door was a small cupboard. The first was empty, as was the second. The third contained what felt like straw, the fourth something horribly soft and squelchy. With a shudder, Gulph withdrew his hand and tried the next. A pile of wooden sticks lay inside this one, slick and oily, along with a small metal box.

He pried it open. Inside the box was a set of hard, cold nuggets. He knew what they were at once.

"I've found something," he exclaimed.

Gulph plucked a handful of straw from the third cupboard and placed it blindly on the ground. He took two of the nuggets and struck one against the other over the straw. A spark flew, and the dry straw ignited. The light was painfully bright.

"Fireworks!" Jessamyn cried from the other side of the room.

Seizing one of the sticks, Gulph plunged it into the fire. A couple of breaths later, he was holding aloft a blazing torch.

"Well done, Gulph," said Ossilius, striding across the chamber to slap him on the back. Gulph grinned.

Ossilius handed the rest of the torches around. Soon everyone was holding a burning brand. The orange light flickered across their faces, casting wavering shadows on the storeroom. Gulph turned a slow circle, taking in the shelves and crates and piles of what looked like moldering uniforms. Closer examination of the squelchy object revealed it to be a dead rat.

Gulph's heart sank. "There are no other doors."

"So this was your great plan?" said Slater. "Bring us to a dead end?"

Wordlessly, Ossilius handed his torch to Gulph and crossed the chamber to the back wall. Embossed into the stone was a large, circular emblem: the sign of the King's Legion. He pressed the heel of his hand against the raised star in the middle, and pushed.

The star sank into the wall. With a pained grinding sound, the whole crest sank back too, then rolled sideways into a hidden cavity.

Gulph stared through the round hole thus revealed. Beyond it, a long tunnel plunged down and away into darkness.

"The Tunnels of the Legion," said Ossilius, with almost reverential awe. "A secret known only to the elite."

He looked back at his companions. Everyone—even Slater— looked amazed. Gulph felt the stirrings of something new in his heart.

Hope.

◆ ◆ ◆

They made their way down the steeply descending tunnel. Gulph scurried close behind Ossilius, his boots slipping on the damp stone floor. The clammy walls seemed intent on banging his elbows at every opportunity, and he lost count of the number of times he bashed his head on the rocks that protruded from the ceiling. It was like racing into the throat of some sleeping, underground beast.

Soon they reached a flight of rough stone stairs leading even farther down. Ossilius paused briefly, holding out the blazing torch he was carrying. Hetty and Marcus held up their torches too, but their combined light showed them almost nothing at all.

"What's down here?" Gulph whispered. The tunnel was empty and clearly long-abandoned; nevertheless it felt wrong to speak too loudly.

"A safe haven," Ossilius replied, leading them down. "Somewhere we can hide until Trident liberates the city. They will come, I know it. My son is at their head, and he will never give up. If anyone can find a way to cross the chasm, it's Fessan."

The certainty in the captain's voice was heartwarming. But Gulph found it hard to share his resolve.

Limmoni leaped over the chasm, he thought, *but she died. And the undead are so many now. . . .*

"Who made these tunnels?" he said, trying to shake off the melancholy that was creeping over him.

"We did," Ossilius replied. "That is to say, the men of the King's Legion. It took many years of sweat and labor."

"But why do it at all?"

"The tunnels were designed as a bolt hole. Do you know what that is?"

"Somewhere to run to?"

"Yes, but more than that. It was decided, long ago, that if ever the city of Idilliam was overrun, the king would be taken to a safe place. Somewhere the enemy could not reach, but from where he could still rule."

"A secret place," Gulph murmured.

"So secret, no king has ever known of its existence." He smiled at Gulph. "Until now."

Gulph shivered. Despite the crown hanging from his belt, he didn't feel like a king at all.

"It's hardly a royal palace," Ossilius went on. "But there's enough down here for us to survive. There are stores of preserved food—we should reach the first of these soon—and armories, meeting chambers, latrines . . ."

"It's like a city under a city."

Ossilius barked out a short laugh. "Hardly! Underground realms are the stuff of myth and legend, Gulph. This is a rabbit warren, nothing more."

They continued to descend, gradually using up the spare torches in Marcus's pack as they moved through the gloomy tunnels. Occasionally they passed a side passage. Each time they did so, Ossilius stopped, sniffed, and ordered them to continue forward.

"Are you sure you know where you're going?" said Slater at one of the larger junctions.

"Shut up and let him lead," snapped Marcus.

"So you can follow like a mule?"

"Are you calling me a mule?"

"Only because you stink like one."

"I know where I am going," Ossilius said mildly. He ran his hand over the wall, where faint cracks ran from floor to ceiling. "But we must be careful from here."

They plodded on.

Gulph grew steadily more tired. Behind him, Jessamyn was asleep on Hetty's back. Marcus and Slater continued to argue and he filtered out their voices, concentrating on putting one foot in front of the other.

Something groaned overhead. Ossilius lifted his hand sharply, and the straggling column stopped.

"What is it?" said Gulph.

"Something I feared," Ossilius answered, pointing to the wall.

Gulph saw more cracks, each one wide enough for him to plunge his fist into. "What's causing it?"

"The mausoleum," said Marcus. "Am I right, sir?"

Ossilius nodded. "I fear so."

"I don't understand," said Hetty.

"It happened when they executed the witch, or the wizard, or whatever she was," Marcus said.

"Limmoni," Gulph put in. "Her name was Limmoni."

"As you say." Ossilius gazed into the darkness ahead. "When she died, there was great magic. It tore down the mausoleum. It made the earth shake. Part of the city wall came down too. The magic must have gone deep underground. All the way down here."

Jessamyn, who'd woken up, began to whimper. Hetty pulled the little girl into a motherly embrace, but couldn't disguise her own fear. "We'll be trapped," she whispered. "Or worse."

"Crushed," said Slater with a curious kind of relish.

"We're safe enough," said Gulph quickly. He didn't like the look of defeat that had overtaken Ossilius's face. Someone had to keep them moving. "There's food ahead. Come on!"

The tunnel underwent a series of twists and turns. Beneath their feet, the ground grew steadily more uneven. Had it been made like this, or was it the result of the earthquake? Gulph couldn't tell.

Rounding a corner, he came face-to-face with an enormous pile of earth and rubble: a cave-in, blocking the tunnel almost completely.

"That's that, then," said Slater. "I knew we shouldn't have come down here."

But Gulph shook his head. "A few rocks won't stop us," he said brightly. "Hetty, can I borrow your apron, please?"

They all watched curiously as the baker slipped off the garment and Gulph wrapped the crown in it and slung it over his shoulder: a makeshift pouch was safer than leaving it on his belt.

"Easier with both hands free," he explained, waggling his fingers and flashing what he hoped was a reassuring grin.

Dropping to all fours, Gulph scuttled up the side of the rockfall, testing its solidity as he found the best route to the top. There was a small gap near the ceiling. Working quickly, he cleared it of stones, making a gap through which they would all be able to squeeze.

"One at a time," he called. "It's all right—trust me."

Marcus came first, shedding his pack and shoving it ahead of him as he climbed. He followed Gulph's route precisely. At the summit, Gulph helped him through and down the other side.

Next came Hetty. The baker was a big woman, and clearly found the climb hard, but Gulph thought he'd never seen anyone look more determined. Then Jessamyn made the ascent. Her tears forgotten, the little girl actually looked as if she was enjoying herself.

There was a brief pause as Ossilius and Slater eyed each other. There was some kind of challenge going on, Gulph guessed, with neither one wanting to turn his back on the other. At last Slater began to climb.

"Thank you, *Highness*," Slater said as he slithered through the gap, somehow making the royal address sound like an insult.

"Well done, my king," said Ossilius, who was following close behind. He took Gulph's hand and squeezed it. "Today you descend, Gulph. Tomorrow you will rise."

A lump formed in Gulph's throat.

"I . . ." he began, then gave a shout. "Look there!"

At the end of the tunnel was a stone archway. The light from Gulph's torch flickered over the carving in the wall above: the circular crest of the King's Legion.

"The central store!" cried Ossilius.

They ran toward it.

The archway led into a round chamber. Brass lamps hung from the low ceiling, which was perforated with a number of small, circular holes. Just as in the storeroom, the walls were lined with shelves and niches. On the far side was a neat stack of crates and barrels.

"Food!" Slater elbowed his way past Gulph. "At last!" He headed straight for the nearest crate and pried open the lid to reveal a mound of what looked like dried and salted meat. Scooping up a handful, he filled his mouth and chewed methodically. "Tastes like crud," he said. "But if it's all we've got . . ."

Gulph helped Hetty to open more of the storage containers, revealing pots of preserved fruit and kegs of what smelled like apple juice. Jessamyn found metal plates, which she arranged proudly on the floor, and Gulph and Hetty served out the food.

Meanwhile, Ossilius and Marcus had found straw and oil in one of the wall niches, and were using it to fuel the hanging lamps. This done, Marcus touched his torch to each lamp in turn. Soon the chamber was ablaze with light and heat. Gulph watched, fascinated, as the smoke from the lamps coiled its way into the holes in the ceiling, to be carried away by whatever artful ventilation system had been installed here, deep in the bowels of the earth.

"How far beneath the city are we, do you think?" he asked as the two soldiers joined the little circle. He handed Ossilius a plate, then tucked into his own food. The fruit was chewy and the juice was both weak and bitter. But his stomach received both with gratitude.

"We are as far down as Idilliam is high," Ossilius replied.

"That's a long way," said Marcus. "Here, Slater, pass us some of that meat."

"Get it yourself," Slater replied, hugging the crate to his chest. "If you dare."

"What's that supposed to mean?" Marcus stood, his hand hovering over his sword. Ossilius took his wrist, but the younger soldier shook him off.

Gulph and Ossilius exchanged a glance.

"It means the meat is mine," said Slater, getting to his feet.

Marcus took a step toward him. "We're all hungry, Slater.

There's no telling how long we'll be down here. We need to work together."

"Get back, soldier boy, or I'll work you *over*!"

"I'm sick of arguing with you. Now give it up."

"Enough of this bickering," ordered Ossilius, now on his feet too. "Share the food, Slater. Now."

But Slater took a step backward, glowering. Marcus reached for the crate and Slater shoved him away, then stumbled into one of the kegs.

Marcus drew his sword; the keen blade flashed in the lamplight.

"Wait!" shouted Gulph. He leaped in front of Marcus, his hands raised. The last thing they needed was for a fight to break out.

"Out of my way!" said Marcus. He seemed to check himself. "Er, sire."

"Put down your sword!" Gulph put all his heart into making his voice sound stern. What came out sounded more like a squeak. Nevertheless, Marcus obeyed.

"We have to stick together," Gulph went on. "Whatever happens, we have to—"

The ground began to shake. The plates rattled, spinning like gigantic coins and spilling food across the suddenly vibrating floor. Tiny stones broke loose from the walls and ceiling, dropping like hail all around them.

"What's happening?" wailed Jessamyn.

"Cave-in!" snapped Ossilius. "Everyone—against that wall!"

He herded the group toward the only wall that wasn't in motion. Gulph tottered as he ran, finding it hard to keep his balance on the floor's undulating surface.

Far down the tunnel through which they'd entered, something roared like a caged dragon. Just visible in the pinched distance, a cloud of dust billowed toward the chamber, carried on an icy wind.

"Out! Out! Out!" shouted Ossilius, urging them into one of the smaller passages leading from the food store. Marcus led the way, with Gulph and Hetty hustling Jessamyn between them. "Slater! Come on!"

To Gulph's amazement, Slater was crawling across the shaking floor toward the approaching dust cloud, chasing the crate of meat he'd dropped.

"Leave it!" yelled Gulph. "There's no time!"

Now the falling stones had become rocks. Not hail but an avalanche. Gulph clamped his hands to his ears as the dragon's roar multiplied a hundred times over, echoing through the disintegrating chamber. Dust exploded against his face, blinding him and choking his mouth with powder.

Flailing wildly, he blundered into the wall, then staggered back into somebody's arms. He clawed the dust from his eyes and saw Hetty staring back at him, mouthing words he couldn't hear. Jessamyn was clinging to her legs, her mouth drawn down in terror.

A shadowy figure rose up in the middle of the dust cloud. It was Slater, incredibly still carrying his crate of meat. He held the prize above his head in triumph and began to stumble toward where Gulph and the others were cowering in shock.

He was halfway across the chamber when the ceiling collapsed completely.

More dust. More rocks. Gulph cringed. The noise was beyond his power to comprehend, let alone hear. The entire world seemed to have tipped on its side. His teeth rattled in his skull. His head felt ready to burst.

Gradually the earthquake subsided. Silence fell; it was somehow worse than the uproar. Pebbles rattled down from the gigantic hole that had opened up where the ceiling had once been. The dust slowly settled.

The chamber was a ruin. The floor was canted steeply to one side and covered with fallen boulders. Slater's arm protruded from beneath one enormous rock.

Crushed! he thought in horror. *Even he didn't deserve to die like that.*

With an effort, he tore his eyes away from the gruesome sight. He tried to speak, but a fit of choking closed his throat. He coughed out a spray of white powder, then tried again. "Is everybody all right?"

Voices came to him through the lingering dust. Hetty and Jessamyn, Ossilius and Marcus. So they were all still alive.

Everyone except Slater.

One at a time they stepped out into the rubble. From far down the passage came a distant rumble, then all was quiet again.

"I think . . ." Ossilius began.

The floor lurched. A crack opened up in the wall against which they'd been sheltering. It raced down and across the floor, right between Gulph's feet.

The crack widened, becoming a gaping hole, then a chasm. For an instant, Gulph seemed to be hanging impossibly in the air. His companions were suspended beside him, each of them reaching frantically for something to hold on to.

But there was nothing.

Wind rushed past Gulph's face as he cartwheeled down into the blackness.

CHAPTER 5

"What are you doing?" said Samial uncertainly.

"What I should have done sooner," said Elodie, lifting the knife.

She adjusted the shield she'd propped in the corner of the tent, tilting it slightly so that her face was reflected in the polished inner surface.

Taking her hair in her other hand, she began methodically to cut it off.

Samial watched in silence as Elodie's long, red-gold locks fell to the ground.

"If you had told me a few weeks ago that I'd be doing this," said Elodie, "I'd have been horrified. But not now. Part of my hair was sliced off in the battle. I'm just evening it up."

"You are doing a lot more than that."

When she'd finished, Elodie put down the knife and appraised her reflection. Her hair was little more than a scruffy cap on her head. *Urchin hair*, she thought. "It's like there was another me all along, hidden underneath the first me. A secret me. And now I've set her free."

"You are still you," Samial replied.

But Elodie wondered.

"Come on," she said. "It's past noon. We're late already."

"Why do you like me to attend council? I am a ghost. Nobody else knows I am there."

"That's exactly why you're useful, Samial. You can hear the things I miss."

Samial grinned. "It is good to be useful again. Sir Jaken always used to say that a good servant was a better treasure than gold."

"You're not my servant, Samial. You're my friend."

Leaving the tent, they crossed the clearing to the flat patch of ground where Fessan's big tent had been pitched. He welcomed her into the circle of people gathered in the open space, then made his way around the others gathered there, clasping hands with some, clapping the shoulders of others. Elodie noted the respect in people's eyes as their commander moved among them.

He's more than a leader to them, she thought. *He keeps them going.*

She took her seat, Samial standing beside her. Although she was glad of his presence, she found herself suddenly missing Tarlan. Her brother had been gone only a day, yet his absence seemed to hang over her. She stroked the green jewel at her throat. Even though she knew Tarlan had lost his to Lord Vicerin, the touch of the cold stone seemed to bring him a little closer.

"We are Trident," said Fessan, taking up his place at the center of the circle, "and we have survived!"

The audience, which up to that moment had been a sea of distracted murmurs, fell silent.

"We are safe here, for now at least—our enemies do not know where we are. Yet we are vulnerable even so, for two reasons. We have wounded, very many of them. And our numbers are badly depleted. The problem of the wounded will be solved by time, as injuries heal and spirits mend. For once, time is a luxury we can afford.

"As for our numbers, on this we must take action at once. New recruits will not come to us; we must go to them. There is a town nearby—Deep Poynt . . ."

"We passed through the place last year," put in Ghast, one of Fessan's lieutenants. "The people there have no love for our cause."

"Nor are they against us. They are simply afraid to show allegiance to anyone. If we give them a reason to join us—show them a figurehead—I believe they will rally."

All eyes turned to Elodie. Their combined gaze struck her like a blast of wind, leaving her momentarily breathless.

"If it's support you want," interrupted a voice from the edge of the clearing, "you're looking at your first recruit."

A man in a brown cloak emerged from the trees. He tossed his thick gray hair out of his eyes and began swaggering toward them.

"Stown!" Elodie cried. She leaped up, drawing her sword.

Fessan was already holding his sword too, as were Ghast and the other lieutenants. When Stown was halfway across the clearing, Fessan called:

"Far enough, Stown! You have no business here."

"Now, that's where we disagree."

"You made it clear that you would only be content if you led Trident yourself. That's why I sent you away. Your exile is permanent. There is no way back for you."

"Exile." Stown rolled the word as if tasting it. "It's such a *royal* word. Something kings and queens command. What do you think, Elodie?"

Elodie felt her cheeks flushing. Seeing this man brought back her troubled early days with Trident: being jeered at on the road to Idilliam, the endless arguing, her friend Palenie's murder by an assassin who mistook her for Elodie . . .

And lurking in the background, always sneering, had been Stown.

"I think you should have stayed in exile," she said coldly.

"Seize him!" Fessan barked. Ghast and two others raced toward Stown, who immediately raised his hands in surrender.

"No need to do that," said Stown. "I'm a different man now, with very different friends. Soldier friends. All the soldiers you need, in fact. Want to meet them?"

He brought one hand down sharply. Behind him, men burst from the trees. Elodie recoiled in horror. There were hundreds of them, their faces masked by gleaming steel helms, their swords shining in the midday sun. Their armor shone too, flashing bright beneath their flowing cloaks. Their blue cloaks.

"Vicerins!" Elodie hissed.

Stown threw off his own cloak. Underneath, he wore blue too.

Samial grabbed her arm. "Elodie, you must hide!"

But Elodie shrugged him off. Her grip tightened on her sword. "I'm not going anywhere."

The circle of people broke apart. All around her, Trident was in motion as green-clad soldiers grabbed swords and bows from the racks where they'd stored them. Tired as they were, Fessan's men were still fearsome warriors. Yet Elodie knew that the Vicerin forces had the advantage of surprise.

In the confusion, Stown had broken free from the Trident men and drawn his own weapon. He parried with a Trident soldier, sending him to the ground, then bellowed, "You stole something from Lord Vicerin! Now he wants it back!"

Suddenly Elodie knew why they'd come.

Me! He means me!

"Get behind!" roared Fessan, dashing in front of Elodie as a pair of blue-cloaked Vicerins sprinted toward her. He stabbed his sword at the first, struck at the second.

"I can fight!" she snarled, drawing her own weapon. "Let me fight!"

"Take her to safety!" Fessan cried.

Before Elodie could protest, Ghast was hustling her inside a protective ring of Trident troops.

The clearing filled with the tumultuous sounds of battle: sword on shield, blade on flesh, grunts and shouts and the strangled cries of the dying. The Trident army fought as bravely as they had on the bridge, but Elodie could see that they were hopelessly outnumbered. Even as they cut down the Vicerin attackers, more of the enemy flooded out of the trees.

"I can fight!" Elodie cried again, but Ghast seized her arm and bore her away from the battle. Two members of the escort stayed behind to fight off an onrushing band of Vicerins, and as the swords of the men clashed, Elodie glimpsed a pair of rocks rising as if by magic from the ground. They floated briefly in the air, then smashed into the skulls of the enemy soldiers, who fell senseless.

Samial!

Before she could see more, Ghast was pulling her through the camp and past a hospital tent, where a row of wounded Trident men were struggling to lift themselves off their stretchers. A group of Vicerin soldiers was bearing down on them. Two nurses stood in their way, hands raised. When the attackers reached them, they cut the nurses down, then worked their way along the line of the injured, stabbing each man where he lay. Blood spread rapidly from one stretcher to the next, turning the white canvas to red. "Butchers!" she screamed. She pushed against Ghast's arm and felt it give way.

"Queen Elodie! No!" cried Ghast as she fought her way to freedom.

"I'm not a queen yet!" she shouted over her shoulder. "If I were, I'd be protecting my people!"

The metallic stench of blood filled her nostrils. All around, Trident soldiers lay dead or dying.

They'll all be killed, she thought. *Unless I give the Vicerins what they want* . . .

She raced to a nearby wagon and clambered up to the driving board. Standing tall, she took a deep breath and yelled, "I AM HERE!"

Around her the chaotic fighting continued unabated. But as she scanned the clearing, she saw two faces turn up toward her: Fessan and Stown.

"Elodie!" Fessan roared. "No!"

He ran toward her. Almost immediately a sea of blue cloaks swallowed him up. Elodie strained forward, her heart in her mouth. An instant later Fessan broke free, blood spraying from the tip of his sword. Behind him three Vicerin soldiers dropped to the ground.

"Stop him, you idiots!" yelled Stown. Yet more blue cloaks appeared, making a wall in front of Fessan, and this time he was swallowed entirely.

Stown strode toward the wagon, gathering even more Vicerin troops in his wake. Elodie watched in terror as they surrounded her.

"Stop fighting!" she yelled. "I'm here!"

Her cry was heeded. Across the battlefield the sounds of clashing steel died slowly away. The forces of Trident and Vicerin alike lowered their weapons and gazed at her.

Elodie had opened her mouth to speak again when the wall of blue cloaks parted and Fessan was thrust toward the wagon. His face was bloodied and his hands had been bound behind his back. He was shoved down the line of Vicerins, all of whom were jeering. When he reached the end, two of the enemy seized him, while a third held a knife to his throat.

Meanwhile, Stown had reached the wagon. He grinned up at Elodie, revealing a jagged row of decaying brown teeth.

"So, you've decided to surrender after all?" he said.

"Elodie!" shouted Fessan. "Don't do it!"

Beads of blood trailed from the knife and ran down his neck.

Stop struggling, she willed him. *Stop struggling, or they'll kill you!*

But she knew Fessan would never stop. There was only one way to save him, to make him give up the fight for her.

I'm so sorry, she thought. *Please forgive me.*

Then she squared her shoulders and summoned all her old haughtiness.

"I will do what suits me," she told Fessan. "I am glad someone has finally come to save me from you and the rest of these cutthroats!"

Fessan stopped struggling and blinked in surprise.

"Elodie!" he cried. "What are you doing?"

"What I had always planned to do." Elodie's heart broke a little as she heard the coldness in her own voice, still more when she saw Fessan flinch before her words.

"I don't believe it! I don't believe *you*!" She felt sick to her stomach. But for her plan to work, Fessan had to be convinced. An idea came to her.

"Why do you think I buried that standard? To leave Trident undefended."

When he heard this, Fessan's face finally crumpled. His chin sank to his chest.

"You called them 'cutthroats,'" said Stown slowly.

"Of course." Elodie turned to face him. "Do you think I like being here? Ever since they kidnapped me, I've been dreaming of rescue."

"Really? I always thought . . ."

"Oh, I've played along. What choice did I have? I thought they'd kill me otherwise. But I knew my father would send someone eventually. It's just a shame it had to be you."

Elodie held her breath. Insulting Stown might anger him beyond reason—or it might just convince him she was telling the truth.

"It's quite a turnabout," said Stown suspiciously. "But that doesn't matter now. We have you at last."

"Yes, at last! I can't bear to stay with Trident a moment longer. I presume you've been ordered to take me back to my father at Ritherlee?"

"Just as soon as we've finished off your Trident friends."

"They're not my friends." Elodie thought quickly, trying not to let her alarm show in her face. "Besides, they're finished already. They're not worth your time."

"We'll fight you to the last man!" shouted Fessan, struggling in vain to free himself. "Elodie—you can't do this!"

"Stay where you are, young lady," said Stown. "I wouldn't want you to get hurt while we finish our business here." He turned to his men and shouted, "Round up every last one of these Trident scum!"

Elodie watched with mounting horror as the Vicerin soldiers moved swiftly among the Trident ranks, disarming the green-clad soldiers and forcing them to their knees.

"What are you going to do with them?" she blurted.

Before Stown could respond, a man rode up on a huge black horse. He was almost skeletally thin, his skin as dark as mahogany. Adorning his Vicerin uniform was an array of gold brocade and a pair of gleaming medals. He glared down at Stown as his mount champed restlessly.

"Captain Gandrell," Stown muttered. "I wondered when you'd show up."

"I have been here all along," said Gandrell. His piercing green eyes flicked to Elodie. "Princess, are you in good health?"

Elodie knew she was gaping, but she couldn't help it. Captain Gandrell had been a familiar figure throughout the thirteen years she'd lived at Castle Vicerin. If he wasn't drilling soldiers in the battle yard, he was standing watch on one of the towers or consulting with Vicerin himself in the council chamber.

A face from my former life, she thought faintly. *The first I've seen since being taken from Ritherlee.*

With a deep breath, she gathered herself. "I am very well, Captain Gandrell," she said. "What kept you?"

The thin man's eyes remained unreadable. They always had been. Elodie remembered Gandrell as being tough on his troops but always entirely fair. *"There is no straighter arrow than Gandrell,"* Lord Vicerin had said once.

Will he be fair now?

"You will ride with me, if it pleases you," Gandrell said.

"She'll ride with me," said Stown, with the tone of a petulant child. "Lord Vicerin put me in charge of the mission, or had you forgotten?"

Captain Gandrell regarded him, stony-faced, then turned his attention back to Elodie. "I have orders—that is to say *Sergeant* Stown and I have orders—to take you straight to Lord Vicerin. This we will do, as soon as we have dispatched the rest of the Trident rabble."

"No!" cried Elodie.

Gandrell raised an eyebrow. "Which aspect of these orders does not please you, Princess?"

"I'll come with you. But there can't be any more killing."

Stown snorted.

"I have my orders," said Gandrell. "None are to be spared. This is Lord Vicerin's wish."

Elodie looked out across the clearing. The men and women who'd fought beside her—fought *for* her—knelt defeated, their faces exhausted and empty.

Fessan's head was still hanging, which meant she couldn't see his face at all.

"But they're no threat," she insisted, aware of the panic in her voice. "Look at them. They're tired and hungry and injured. They're—" Elodie searched for a phrase this military man might comprehend. "They're a spent force."

"Wounds heal," Gandrell replied. "Tired men may sleep, and awaken refreshed." He spurred his horse and drew his sword. "Enough talk! The time has come!"

"Stop!" From her tunic pocket Elodie snatched the arrowhead Samial had given her—and pressed it against her own throat.

Gandrell's eyes widened with shock. "Princess, what are you doing?"

"If you kill them," Elodie said, "I die too."

Fessan raised his head. His eyes were full of pain. Beside the wagon, Samial's ghostly face looked paler than ever. All around, both Trident and Vicerin soldiers were watching to see what would come.

"Why would you save this rabble?" Gandrell said. "Tell me, Princess. I am very curious."

"I'm sick of bloodshed," said Elodie truthfully, still holding the arrowhead steady. "I've seen enough for a thousand lifetimes. Now, what message would you take to my father? That you have destroyed Trident? Or killed his daughter?"

Captain Gandrell gazed at her for a long, appraising moment. At last he dipped his head.

"It will be as you ask, Princess. No harm will come to them.'"

Stown cursed and spat on the ground. Captain Gandrell ignored him.

"Lay down your weapons!" Gandrell yelled at the Trident ranks. Some did as he said, but others looked around in confusion or gripped their swords as if still unwilling to concede defeat.

"Looks like we'll have to kill them anyway," growled Stown.

"No you won't," Elodie snapped. "Fessan—tell them!"

Fessan's eyes locked briefly on Elodie's. His trembling chest heaved. Then he called out:

"Do it! The battle is over."

The Trident soldiers began to murmur. Then, slowly, those who still carried their swords gave them up. Elodie fought back tears as Gandrell sent his blue-cloaks to gather up the Trident weapons. Unarmed, the Trident troops were gathered in the center of the clearing, where the Vicerin soldiers forced them to sit with their hands on their heads.

Meanwhile, more of the Vicerin men tore down the tents. The Trident camp was soon a waste ground of scattered bedding and the few scant belongings the wandering army had managed to gather. Everything that would burn was stacked and set alight. Three of the wagons were filled with Trident's weapons, appropriated now for use by Lord Vicerin. The sun had barely begun its descent into the afternoon before all trace of the Trident camp—except for its miserable inhabitants—had been destroyed.

Elodie cast one last look back at her defeated Trident friends. Those who returned her gaze looked either dazed or hateful.

Let them hate me, she thought sadly. *At least they're still alive.*

"Time to leave, Princess," said Gandrell.

She tried not to flinch as he helped her onto the bench at the front of one of the wagons. "No," she said quickly when he made to sit beside her. "A lady does not ride with a soldier."

The only company she could bear for the journey to come was Samial's. Her friend perched beside her and she gripped his cold fingers.

"Have I done the right thing, Samial?" she whispered. It was too late now. The wagon lurched and the convoy began to depart. As it rolled through the trees, a sleek gray mare drew level with Elodie's wagon. She glanced up and saw that its rider was Stown. He leered down at her, and something in the malevolence of his grin made Elodie look back.

Marching behind him came a trio of Vicerin soldiers. Held between them, gagged and chained, was Fessan.

Elodie felt cold. "What are you doing with him?"

"We might have left the rest to rot," sneered Stown, "but not this one. We've got other plans for him."

"I don't understand."

"Oh, it's very simple, *Princess.* Your friend's coming with us. I can't wait to see what Lord Vicerin will make of him. Can you?"

CHAPTER 6

The wings of the three giant thorrods beat a steady, silent tattoo against the air, driving Tarlan and Melchior on toward the coast. Below them the dense Isurian forest was a tangled green carpet. Above hung a faint smear of light: the comet.

"You can see it in the day now!" Tarlan shouted across the expanse of air between the flying birds.

"It grows brighter as it comes closer," the wizard called back, "and will grow much brighter yet."

Mirith had told Tarlan about the stones that occasionally fell from the sky, blazing hot. He'd sometimes watched their white trails in the night but had never actually seen one come to ground.

Is that all the comet is? he wondered. *Just a big stone?*

But it was more than that, he knew. The comet was somehow

wrapped up with Melchior's powers. It was strange. Perhaps the comet wasn't glowing with light at all. Perhaps it was glowing with magic.

As evening cast a blue shroud over the trees, Tarlan guided the thorrods down toward a stand of ancient oak trees.

"Land by that stream," he said to them. "The water should be fresh and the trees will be good cover." He grinned across at Filos and Greythorn, nestled together on Kitheen's black back. "As for you two—I bet you can't wait to stretch your legs!"

Tarlan was right. The instant the thorrods touched down, the wolf and the tigron cub leaped from Kitheen's back and bounded off into the trees, ears pricked, nostrils flaring.

"Good hunting!" Tarlan laughed.

The three thorrods dug a shallow scrape near the tree line and flopped into it, clearly exhausted. Tarlan went to each of the huge birds in turn, stroking their beaks and smoothing their feathers.

"Greythorn and Filos will bring you fresh meat. Try to stay awake until they get back. Melchior, do you want to fetch the firewood, or shall I?"

But when he turned around, the wizard was hurrying away from the clearing, making his way over the stream. His grubby yellow robe was bunched up under his armpits, exposing scrawny white legs. For an instant Tarlan thought he was walking on water. Then he saw the stepping-stones lying just beneath the surface.

"Where are you going?" he called.

"I saw a village. There will be an inn."

After spending a whole day flying through the fresh, uncluttered air of Toronia, Tarlan felt cleansed. The last thing he wanted was to throw himself back into a crowd of noisy, smelly humans. He gazed around the little clearing.

"It's nice here," he said wistfully.

"Yes, but we are not just travelers, Tarlan."

"We're not?"

"No, we are here to learn."

"We are?" Tarlan's heart was sinking.

"Of course! How can we solve the many problems which undoubtedly lie ahead if we are not fully informed about them? Besides, you will one day be king, Tarlan. There is no better place for you than among your people!"

Grumbling under his breath, Tarlan picked his way across the stream and followed Melchior into the trees on the other side.

Do you know how annoying you are, old man?

Ten paces ahead, the wizard chuckled to himself. Tarlan's skin prickled as he considered the possibility that Melchior could read his thoughts.

The village was tiny and, like most human settlements, looked odd to Tarlan's eyes. Having grown up in a cave high on a cold Yalasti mountain, he'd never really understood people's compulsion to cut up natural materials and turn them into walls and roofs.

The buildings were simple wooden lodges. Rough streets meandered between them, little more than packed earth, with torches burning at intervals along them. At the end of a straggling row of small, identical dwellings rose a larger building with a wide porch. Its small windows flickered with light, and from inside came the sound of raucous singing.

"The Double Stag!" proclaimed Melchior, clapping his hands together.

"What?"

The wizard pointed at a swinging sign carrying a painting of a huge deer with two heads standing proudly in a forest glade. "It's the name of the tavern!"

"Oh," Tarlan replied, not wanting to betray that fact that, for all Mirith's attempts to teach him, he'd never been very good at reading.

Melchior strode up to the inn. Tarlan had an urge to turn tail and run back to the clearing. The idea of spending the night under the trees with his pack was almost too much to resist.

Then he remembered Mirith's dying words.

You told me to take my jewel to Melchior. Well, I've lost the jewel, but at least I've found the wizard. And I'm not letting him out of my sight!

Melchior opened the tavern door and Tarlan followed him inside. He'd expected something like the dining hall at Castle Vicerin:

a big, open chamber with diners seated politely at a long table. Instead, a low beamed ceiling brushed the top of Tarlan's head. A large fire threw up a flickering glow and clots of smoke; never had Tarlan breathed air so thick. The smell of soot was strong, but there were other smells too: beer and roasting meat, spice and sweat.

And the tavern was packed full of people.

Isurians. So these are the folk who live in the forest.

Their clothes were patched, their hair long and shaggy. Most of the men carried wood axes at their waists; the women wore simple dresses, less grand than those he'd seen around Castle Vicerin and much thinner than the bulky wraps worn by the women of icebound Yalasti. And there were so *many* of them. Their combined conversation was a constant, pounding roar.

A few heads turned as Tarlan and Melchior entered. Most carried on drinking and eating. In a far, dark corner a woman shrieked with laughter; in another, several men roared out a bawdy song.

Melchior pushed his way to a trestle table stacked with small kegs and plates of food. Tarlan stood frozen. He felt trapped, as if the noise were trying to crush him.

Can't stay! Got to run!

Melchior returned carrying a large platter of bread and meat in one hand, and two tankards in the other. With an effort Tarlan quelled his panic and followed the wizard to a vacant table, where they sat and began to eat.

The bread was wonderful: fresh and doughy. The meat had a tang like nothing he'd tasted before. For several long moments Tarlan forgot his discomfort, his attention wholly taken up by the food. As he devoured mouthful after mouthful, he became aware of Melchior watching him.

"So I'm hungry," he said defensively.

"Do you hear what they are saying?" said the wizard, picking birdlike at the bread.

Wiping his mouth with the back of his hand, Tarlan listened. It was hard to make out individual conversations among the hubbub, but certain phrases kept rising to the surface:

". . . marched on Idilliam . . ."

". . . heard the bridge has fallen . . ."

". . . children of the prophecy . . ."

Tarlan lifted the tankard, which was full of warm, foaming ale. He drank half at a gulp and slammed the tankard down with a satisfying thud. His belly felt tight and full. He hoped the thorrods and the rest of his pack had eaten as well.

"News travels fast," he said. He looked around, amazed all over again by the noise in the tavern. *Why do these humans talk so much?* Then the question came back to him: the one he hadn't dared to ask earlier. "How did you lose your powers, then?"

The wizard grinned. "Social niceties are not your strong point, are they, my boy?"

"What?"

"Never mind. It is a fair question. And it deserves a fair answer."

"So are you going to tell me or not?"

Melchior dabbed his mouth with the corner of his robe and sat back patting his stomach, even though he'd eaten barely a few scraps.

"You know how your mother died," he said.

Tarlan shifted uncomfortably on his stool. "Elodie told me. But what's that got to do with your powers?"

"Then you know that I tried to save your mother's life. But I had no way of knowing if my magic had worked. I suspected at the time—and have since come to believe—that it did not. Immediately after the execution, I was consumed by rage and guilt. I did something very foolish."

"What did you do?" Rage was something Tarlan could understand.

"I confronted King Brutan. In front of the entire court, I declared him a coward, a tyrant, and a murderer."

Tarlan's respect for the old man grew. "Really? What did he do?"

"Sent me to the dungeons, of course. Luckily for me, he put a fellow called Captain Ossilius in charge of my confinement. Ossilius is a good man, and he arranged my escape. Brutan put a price on my head and so off I went into exile."

Tarlan whistled. "Mirith wanted me to find you. But everyone told me you were dead."

"I spread some rumors to that effect. I am glad to know they took hold."

"So you just . . . waited?"

"What else could I do? My powers were gone. I was a marked man. But I did achieve two things. The first was to seek out Ossilius's son—Fessan. Like me, he had been banished from Idilliam."

"Did he call the king a coward too?"

"No. He used actions rather than words. He defended a carter whose wagon had overturned in the castle gate from being stoned by soldiers of the King's Legion."

"Stoned? Because of an accident?"

Melchior shrugged. "The broken wagon was holding up the royal procession. For defying the will of the king, Fessan was beaten to within an inch of his life and banished."

Tarlan fiddled with the edge of his cloak. He really knew nothing about the young Trident commander, he realized, and wished he could take back his harsh words at the camp.

"From the moment I found him," Melchior went on, "a young man in a ragged soldier's uniform with an equally ragged scar down the side of his face, I knew he possessed the same fighting spirit as his father. Together we set up Trident."

"What was the second thing?"

Melchior's wrinkled face seemed to contract. "Ah, that is something that weighs heavily on me. It concerns my apprentice."

"You have an apprentice?"

"I had one. Her name was Limmoni. She was . . . extraordinary. Had she lived, she might have been the greatest wizard ever to walk Toronian soil."

"She died? How?"

"I cannot say for certain. I sent her to Idilliam, to Castle Tor, in the guise of a serving girl. She was to be my eyes and ears. She performed her task extraordinarily well. But now, alas, I sense that she is gone."

"You . . . sense it?"

"Whatever the distance between them, no two wizards are ever completely apart." Melchior gave Tarlan a small smile. "I know you understand me, Tarlan. Is this not how you feel about your pack?"

Tarlan considered this. Would he know if Theeta died? Or Greythorn? Or Filos?

"Yes," he said quietly. "Yes, it is."

Casting off his melancholy, Melchior suddenly stood, picked up their empty tankards, and said, "Serious talk dries the tongue. Let me get us more to drink."

Tarlan watched the wizard force his way through the crowded tavern. He picked at what was left of the bread, tossing the crumbs moodily over the edge of the table. The fire crackled in the tavern's hearth, a high, popping sound that was just audible over the buzz of countless conversations. A strident voice rose above the noise, coming from a burly man seated at the next table.

". . . so I gets the chain round his neck and he goes wild, see?" the man was saying.

"That's bears for you," his skinny companion replied.

"Aw, I've kept bears for years. Once they're broken they're meek as babies. The trick is to keep 'em scared. That's the trick with all animals, Buster. Keep 'em scared."

Something snapped inside Tarlan. He stood, his legs wobbling a little. He didn't feel entirely in control of himself.

"Why would you want to keep a bear?" he said in a voice that wasn't quite his own.

The man stared up at him from his stool, his ruddy face a mask of annoyance. "What's it to you, lad?"

"Can a bear pull a cart?" said Tarlan. "Can it plow a field? A bear is a wild animal. A free animal. Why would you—"

"I'll tell you what a bear is good for," sneered the man. "A bear is good for dancing." He nudged his companion. "Ain't it, Buster?"

"Dancing?" The edges of Tarlan's vision were flickering red. "You keep a bear to make it *dance?*"

Before he knew what was happening, his fist was flying toward the man's face. Big as he was, the man moved fast, bringing up his own hand just in time to catch Tarlan's. Twisting free, Tarlan wrapped his fingers around the man's throat. His eyes bulged with pain and surprise.

"Tarlan!"

Melchior's voice penetrated the booming that had filled up Tarlan's ears. With a supreme effort of will, Tarlan released his hold. The man pushed himself away from his table, staggered upright. Tarlan stood, wavering, the red mist clearing from his vision. The tavern had fallen silent. Faces turned toward him, wide with undisguised suspicion.

The man Tarlan had attacked drew a long, shining knife from his belt.

Everyone in the surrounding crowd took a step back.

With a click Melchior placed something on the table in front of the man. Tarlan saw it was a large, silver coin.

"For your trouble," said the wizard.

"I'll give 'im trouble," growled the man, massaging his bruised throat and brandishing the knife at Tarlan. "Brat like that should be locked up. I've just the cage for 'im."

"He will be beaten," said Melchior smoothly. "Come, boy, and next time mind your manners."

"You're *paying* him?" Tarlan was incredulous.

Melchior raised his hand, though stopped short at striking him. "What did I say about manners?"

The faces watched them as they left. Tarlan suspected that fights were commonplace here. The arrival of strangers, perhaps, was not such a regular occurrence.

"Are you really planning to beat me?" said Tarlan as they escaped into the cold night air.

"Of course not. But I had to say something."

"I could have taken the knife from him."

"And what about the knives of his seven friends?"

This brought Tarlan up short. "What do you mean?"

"I mean the man in the green hat, the man with the limp, the woman with the broken tooth, the fat man with small eyes, the twin brothers, and the beautiful woman who carried the biggest dagger of all up the sleeve of her dress. They were all standing behind him. Did you not see them?"

Tarlan opened his mouth, closed it. He'd always prided himself on being observant.

Just how sharp are your eyes, old man?

"I'm not sorry for what I did," he snapped.

"I understand that. But we went in there to gather information, not to get you killed in a brawl."

Tarlan's anger was still boiling. He resisted the urge to turn it on the wizard.

"I'm not leaving without freeing that bear!" He waited for Melchior to contradict him. To his amazement, the wizard grinned.

"Neither am I."

They retraced their steps to the edge of the village. After checking they hadn't been followed, Tarlan pursed his lips and whistled three times. Moments later a pair of shadows coalesced in the darkness, resolving themselves rapidly into two furry shapes.

"Greythorn! Filos!" Tarlan whispered. "Stay quiet, now. You have a job to do."

The wolf and the tigron sat obediently before him, awaiting instructions. Tarlan held out his hands and allowed the animals to sniff them.

"Do you smell the man?" he said.

"Yes," said Greythorn. "A big man."

"Sweaty," said Filos.

Melchior watched with interest. Tarlan allowed himself a smile.

You might see things I cannot see, old man. But I hear things you cannot hear!

"Big and sweaty, yes," he said, "that's exactly what he was. Can you find his scent? I think he must live nearby. Can you take me to where he lives?"

Immediately, Greythorn and Filos dropped their snouts to the ground and began to sniff, trotting in ever-widening circles as they sought the trail. Greythorn found it first, uttering a low *yip* as he shot off along a little-used forest track. Filos quickly joined him. The two animals wove in and out of each other's path, sharing the task of tracing the scent back to its source.

"Who needs magic?" Tarlan said to Melchior. "Come on."

Long before they reached a ramshackle hut hidden in the trees, Tarlan could smell the bear himself: a damp, soiled stench that hung in the night air like smoke. The smell led them to a large wooden cage hidden behind the hut. Inside was the biggest bear Tarlan had ever seen.

The instant he saw them, the bear snarled and threw himself against the bars. One massive paw slashed out between the slats of wood, his sharp claws raking down Tarlan's arm. Tarlan drew back with a hiss and circled the cage, being sure to keep his distance.

"Be careful," said Melchior. "He is angry."

"Of course he's angry!" snapped Tarlan. "Look at him!"

The bear's black fur was torn and striped with blood. Old scars shone through the matted pelt. Tarlan wondered how many years the man had kept him here, how many beatings the wretched creature had endured.

"It's all right," he soothed, reaching out his hand. "You're safe now."

The bear bellowed and swiped again. Tarlan dodged, barely avoiding another injury.

Maybe this isn't going to be so easy.

"I want to set you free." Tarlan conjured up images of wide, open spaces in his mind, trying to project them toward the bear. For some reason, all he could think of was sandy deserts, even though he'd never seen one. "Please, won't you let me help you?"

"He-elp?" growled the bear, eyeing Tarlan with suspicion. His voice sounded like falling rocks. "You speak? You he-elp?"

"Yes. I speak. I help. What's your name?"

"Brock!" The sound came out in a fit of coughing. "Brock! Brock!"

"Brock? Is that your name?"

"Brock!" the bear agreed, glaring at Tarlan with eyes like tiny furnaces.

"All right, Brock. Are you going to let me help you?"

"He-elp?"

Melchior's hand came to rest on Tarlan's arm. Tarlan nearly jumped out of his skin. "I cannot understand what he is saying," said the wizard, "but I do know he is dangerous, Tarlan. Perhaps this was not such a good idea."

"Too late. Like it or not, the bear goes free." Tarlan picked up a stone and smashed it against the lock. The simple wooden mechanism exploded into splinters, and the door swung open.

Before he could blink, the bear was out. The enormous beast moved like an avalanche, huge and irresistible. He crashed into Tarlan, knocking all the wind from his lungs and throwing him to the ground. Fighting for breath, heart hammering with fear and excitement, Tarlan stared up into those blazing eyes.

"Kill you!" thundered the bear. His mouth yawned, revealing immense yellow teeth. Saliva dripped onto Tarlan's face. The bear's breath was unspeakably bad.

"Kill me if you want to," said Tarlan, barely controlling his terror. "I can't stop you. You're free to do whatever you want now, Brock. You're free."

The bear drew back his paw. In the faint starlight, each claw looked like a sword. His rancid breath hung around his gaping jaws in a steaming halo.

Abruptly, the bear closed his mouth, lowered his upraised paw, and stepped away from Tarlan.

"Free," said Brock, as if tasting the word for the first time. He looked at the trees, at the sky, then at Tarlan. "You freed Brock. Brock thanks you."

"You're welcome."

Tarlan rose and stroked the bear's ragged muzzle with one trembling hand.

"Remarkable!" said Melchior. "I have seen many things in my long days, Tarlan, but never anything quite like that."

"Oy! What d'you think you're doing?!"

Tarlan turned to see the burly man from the tavern loping up to the cottage. One of his fists was clenched around a whip. His face was crimson with fury.

Instantly loyal to their new companion, Greythorn and Filos stepped in front of Brock, lowered their heads, and raised their hackles. Their growls filled the night.

"No," said Tarlan, waving them back. "This is Brock's fight."

The bear squinted at him, his ferocity replaced with such a look of confusion that Tarlan's heart broke.

"It's all right, Brock," he said. "You're free to do this, too."

Understanding dawned on the bear's ravaged face. Drawing back his lips to reveal those enormous teeth, he reared up on his hind legs. Tarlan gasped. He was tall for his age, but the bear was fully twice his height.

The man never stood a chance. As Brock crashed back to the ground and charged, he drew back his whip, but the bear was quicker, closing his jaws around the man's wrist and clamping them shut. Tarlan heard a sickening *crunch*, then the man's severed hand dropped to the ground.

"Aieee!" the man shrieked. "Don't . . . don't . . ."

Grabbing the man with his huge paws, Brock picked up his torturer and hurled him into the cage, still screaming. The man landed upside down, blood squirting from the stump of his wrist. His eyes rolled up to show the whites and his howls of pain reduced to faint bleating sounds.

Brock advanced on him once more.

"No," said Tarlan, blocking the bear's path. Brock snarled at him with such ferocity that Tarlan thought for a moment he'd gone too far.

"Don't kill him."

The bear swayed on his hind legs, staring down at Tarlan with rage-filled eyes.

"Want to bite him! All the way through!"

"No. Let him live. He'll tell his friends what happened here. They might think twice about keeping animals locked up after that."

The bear's black brow contracted as he considered this.

"Brock wants to kill him," he said, but his growling voice had lost its angry edge.

"I know. I understand."

At last, with a low grunt, Brock dropped to all fours and turned his back on the man who'd kept him prisoner.

"Where will Brock go?" the bear said.

"That isn't for me to say," Tarlan answered. "It's for you to choose."

After a long moment the bear asked, "What is *your* name?"

"Tarlan."

Another pause. Then:

"Brock will come with Tarlan."

Tarlan grinned. "I was hoping you were going to say that."

CHAPTER 7

G ulph was surrounded by cold. It enveloped him, sucked him down, turned him over and over. He flung out his arms and legs, and the coldness resisted. He opened his mouth to yell, and the coldness rushed into him. The coldness was in his eyes, his nose, his ears. The coldness was everywhere, and he was lost inside it. . . .

Water! It's water!

Gulph clamped his mouth shut and kicked out.

Which way is up?

He didn't know. Perhaps he was swimming deeper within whatever pool he'd fallen into, swimming down to his death.

His lungs were burning. Soon he would have to breathe.

When I do, I'll drown.

Finally he broke the surface. Flinging back his head, he drew in a ragged breath. The cold water drained from his face, leaving him gasping in warm, humid air. He churned his legs, fighting to stay afloat.

"Tip your head back," said a nearby voice. "Waggle your arms."

It was Jessamyn, treading water beside him with a small child's easy grace. She looked fearful but determined.

"My mother says that legs want to float," she added. "You just have to let them."

Gulph did as Jessamyn said, tilting back his head and waving his arms slowly just below the surface. To his surprise, his legs bobbed up. With almost no effort at all, he was floating on his back, staring straight up.

What he saw took away what little breath he'd managed to gather.

High above him was an immense arch of deep purple. It seemed to glow faintly. Within it, a thousand tiny pricks of light twinkled like stars. It was vast and beautiful, a breathtaking twilight sky.

The sky? How can that be, when we're so far underground?

Then he saw it wasn't the sky. It was the ceiling of a cavern, a gigantic chamber made of craggy purple rock. Rock that shone with an inner light.

Not rock. Crystal!

"Gulph! My liege! Are you all right?"

Ossilius swam up to him. Blood ran freely from a gash on his forehead. Gulph realized his own face was stinging; when he looked at his hands, he saw they were covered in scratches from the rockfall.

Close behind Ossilius was Hetty, who was struggling to keep an unconscious Marcus afloat. The soldier's head bobbed and he mumbled incoherently.

"I'm fine," Gulph told Ossilius. "Help him."

They clustered around Marcus, taking it in turns to support the soldier. The water lapped around them, tiny ripples sparkling in the purple glow of the crystal ceiling. To Gulph's amazement, the water itself also seemed to be aglow.

It's silver!

"We have to get him to the shore," said Hetty, as Marcus's head dipped briefly under the water.

"There is no shore," Ossilius replied.

Gulph saw that he was right. No matter which way he looked, all he could see was an expanse of silvery liquid melting slowly into darkness.

What now? he thought, panic rising.

Jessamyn gave an excited squeal. "Look! A boat! Over there!"

A slender vessel was gliding toward them through the eerie twilight. Two figures steered it with long paddles: a man and a woman, both dressed in flowing silk robes. Their faces were as pale as milk.

"Climb aboard," said the man as the boat drew up alongside them. "Be quick now."

Together they heaved Marcus into the boat, then clambered in one at a time. The man helped them, pausing occasionally to cast a wary gaze out across the water. The woman worked her paddle in silence, deftly keeping the narrow boat stable as its cargo steadily increased.

Gulph was last aboard. He flopped down in the curving hull.

"Thank you," he panted.

"You were lucky we were out here." The man's voice was low and soft. He nodded to the woman, and together they began to paddle the boat onward through the silvery water. The paddles made no splash, and no sound.

"Where are we?" asked Hetty.

"Celestis," said the woman, speaking for the first time. Her voice was as smooth as the water.

"Celestis?" said Gulph. "What's Celestis?"

"This is Celestis." The woman waved her arm out across the silver lake. "This is the lost realm."

Gulph stared at her.

The lost realm. Does that mean we're lost too?

He glanced toward Ossilius and saw that the captain's mouth had dropped open. The rest of their companions simply looked confused. Above, stars twinkled in the dimly lit ceiling.

"Once there were three realms," said the man. "Then came the time of change. Now there is a fourth. Yet none above know that Celestis lingers."

Gulph's head was filling up with questions. All his life he'd believed there were only three realms in Toronia: Idilliam, Isur, and Ritherlee.

Three realms. Three siblings. The crown of three.

Yet here he was in a fourth realm he'd never known existed.

A dreadful fear stole over him. *The prophecy only mentions three realms. What if it's wrong? What if we're fighting for something that isn't true?*

"Please," he said, "tell us more! What was the time of change you mentioned? Does anyone here ever go up to Idilliam? How—"

"You will hear more," said the woman, "when you are accepted."

"If you are accepted," said the man.

"If," the woman agreed.

"Accepted?" said Gulph. "Who by?"

"The Lady Redina," said the woman. "None can enter Celestis without her permission."

"We need no permission," said Ossilius through gritted teeth. "We have endured much hardship to reach this place, and none of it by choice."

Moving in perfect unison, and without haste, their rescuers laid down their paddles and reached beneath their silk robes. Each drew out a long sword and held it aloft. The blades shimmered, and Gulph saw that they too were made of shining crystal.

"Permission must be granted," the man repeated. "It is the way of Celestis."

He thrust his other hand toward Ossilius, who tensed. Gulph held his breath. If Ossilius drew his own sword, they were all going back in the water.

Then he saw the man was presenting Ossilius with a small white cloth.

"For your face," he said. "There is blood."

Eyeing him cautiously, Ossilius took the cloth and wiped his face. The cloth came away bloody, but to Gulph's astonishment, the wound on his friend's forehead had vanished.

"Is that cloth magic?" he blurted.

The man shook his head. "Not the cloth. The water."

"It heals," said the woman.

Gulph realized his own face was no longer stinging. He stared at his hands. The scratches were gone, with no trace of scars remaining.

At the far end of the boat, Marcus sat up, rubbing his head.

"Where are we?" he said.

While the two Celestians rowed silently through the silver water, Gulph sat with Ossilius at the boat's prow.

"There is an island, see?" Ossilius pointed. "The lake surrounds it, like a moat."

Gulph gazed in wonder at the approaching landmass. *Except it isn't really land,* he corrected himself. *It's crystal. This whole place is made of crystal.*

And so it was. The shore toward which they were gliding was a tangle of diamond shards, a thousand shimmering facets jutting from the water like a shattered crown. Beyond these rose slopes of green emerald set with smooth sapphire paths, meandering between tall, glassy buildings: an entire city made of crystal. Spires and soaring arches caught the sunlight and threw it back in a dizzying series of reflections.

No, Gulph corrected himself. *Not sunlight.* "There's no day or night down here at all," he said to Ossilius. "No weather." He studied the people who were beginning to gather on the shore. "No wonder everyone looks so pale."

He tried to imagine a life without sunshine, without rain. No storms, no seasons, just a perpetual twilight. *What a strange way to live.*

"There!" said Ossilius. He sat up sharply. "Do you see that light?"

Gulph could just make out a thin bright strip on the opposite side of the lake, far from the island city. It was broken into sections by pillars of crystal.

Ossilius turned to Gulph. "Do you know where I think we are? At the bottom of the chasm."

"What?" Gulph stared at him. "But that's impossible! The chasm's bottomless. Everyone knows that. . . ."

Just like everyone knows there are only three realms.

Could it be true? He peered out at the strip of light, struggling to organize the geography in his head.

We were in the tunnels under the city. Then we fell through into this cavern—a gigantic hole in the ground beneath Idilliam. So those pillars are holding Idilliam up above our heads. And what surrounds the city? The chasm.

"You're right," Gulph said with a shiver.

"So we can see the light of day after all," said Ossilius. "Very dim and distant, but there."

"Perhaps we're not so lost," Gulph murmured.

Jessamyn crawled between them, her small hand creeping into Gulph's.

"It's pretty here," she said.

"Yes," said Gulph, "it is."

"Prettiness may hide many things," said Ossilius.

"That's true too."

"We must be on our guard."

The silver water snaked between high crystal banks, finally opening into a wide pool. The woman moored the boat beside a set of steps leading from the water up to the grounds of a large house: a dazzling confection of diamond walls and ruby turrets.

The man led them ashore. Gulph ascended the crystal staircase with caution, afraid its surface would be slippery. But the ground was solid, and his feet found good purchase. At the top of the stairs, he stretched, working out the knots in his muscles. It didn't take long: his years as an acrobat meant his back was used to popping itself back into shape . . . even if that shape was more twisted than most.

A tall woman awaited them at the top of the stairs. Like their rescuers, she wore silk robes. Her face was round and open, her eyes an intense and beautiful blue. Her skin too was the color of milk.

"You have done well," she said, addressing the man who'd brought them. Her voice was slow and strong.

"Thank you, my lady." He gave a small, stiff bow, then hurried back down the steps to rejoin his companion in the boat.

"I am Lady Redina," said the tall woman. "Celestis is my realm. Are you hungry?"

As if on cue, Gulph's stomach growled, very loud. Jessamyn giggled.

Lady Redina extended her hand in a flowing, languid gesture and stroked the little girl's hair. "So beautiful."

"Pardon me, lady," said Marcus, peering past her shoulder, "but is all that for us?"

With a smile Lady Redina stepped aside, and Gulph saw a long table standing beneath a gazebo in the grounds before the house. Servants stood behind crystal chairs, awaiting their arrival. The table was piled high with food.

Gulph swallowed. Except for their impromptu meal in the tunnels, he couldn't remember when he'd last eaten.

"How did you know we were coming?" he said as their hostess led them to their places.

"I have observers," Lady Redina answered smoothly. She indicated to each of them where they should sit, her arms moving as gracefully as a dancer's. "Occasionally people fall. When they fall, they are seen. When they are seen, I am told. And I make ready to receive the newcomers. As I now receive you. Join me, please."

Gulph hesitated, remembering what they'd been told in the boat.

"Does this mean we have your permission to stay?" he said.

Lady Redina inclined her head. "First we will talk. Decisions come later."

The food was a thousand times better than the meager morsels they'd found in the tunnels. There was a kind of grilled fish that melted on Gulph's tongue, and plates of steamed vegetables that crunched deliciously, spilling spicy flavors down his throat.

Gulph tore into it all with gusto. He saw with no surprise that his companions were doing the same, snatching up spoonfuls of this and handfuls of that and shoveling them into their mouths. Lady Redina contented herself with small nibbles of white flesh from a crab's claw.

"Is there any bread?" asked Hetty, eagerly scanning the table.

"I fear there is only what you see," Lady Redina replied. She daintily dabbed the corner of her mouth with a napkin.

"Oh," the baker mumbled. "Well, it's very fine."

Gulph noticed that they'd not been offered meat either. *No grass,* he thought suddenly. *Without proper sunlight there can be no fields. Which means no animals and no grain.*

His belly was full now, but he swallowed the final mouthful of purple carrots in his bowl, leaned back in his chair, and let out an enormous belch.

"Forgive me!" he said, clapping a hand to his mouth. "But I do think that was the best meal I ever had."

Around the table, everyone chuckled, including Lady Redina. Her laugh was like a low, tinkling bell.

"There is nothing to forgive," she said. "Your satisfaction is evident. I am flattered."

"Gulph is right to thank you," said Ossilius. "You have been very kind."

"Yes, you have," added Gulph. "Do you always eat as well as this? I mean, where did it all come from? Not the fish, I mean—obviously you catch those." He stopped, suddenly aware he was babbling.

Lady Redina put down her napkin. "It is natural for you to be curious. But I do not think those are the questions you wish to ask."

Gulph glanced at Ossilius, who responded with an almost imperceptible nod.

"Well," he gulped, "I suppose we'd like to know more about Celestis."

"What do you want to know?"

"How does it come to be here? Has it always been here? I thought—we all thought—there were only three realms in Toronia."

"Then you thought wrong. Celestis exists—as you can plainly see for yourselves. It has merely been forgotten. Yet to be forgotten is to be safe. I am sworn to keep it that way."

"You rule here," said Ossilius. It seemed to Gulph that he was trying to get things straight in his head.

"I rule, yes. But more than that, I protect. I am the protector of the lost realm."

"But how does a whole realm get lost?" Gulph said.

"Many years ago—some say three hundred, some say more—Celestis stood beneath the natural sun. But war came to Toronia, and the ground shook and opened its great mouth, and Celestis fell. Buried beneath the rocks of the world, our realm has endured in darkness ever since. But also in safety. Part of my pledge is to ensure that war never touches us again. When war comes, realms fall. We in Celestis know this only too well."

Gulph adjusted the bundle on his back, suddenly aware of the weight of the crown he carried there, tucked away out of sight.

"Do you think we bring war?" he asked hesitantly.

"I think nothing. I merely listen. Then I judge. So, tell me your stories."

Gulph wanted to trust this woman who'd shown them such hospitality. But how much should he tell her? He opened his mouth, still unsure of what he would say, but before he could begin, he felt a sharp warning kick from Ossilius.

To his relief, Marcus spoke up from the far end of the table. "Begging your pardon, my lady, but it's war we've escaped from."

Lady Redina lifted an immaculate eyebrow. "Go on. I would hear from you one at a time. Tell me your story, soldier."

"Well," Marcus said, shuffling awkwardly in his chair, "there was the Battle of the Bridge, to start with. The Idilliam Bridge? A rebel force tried to cross into Idilliam, but Brutan's army fought them back. Brutan is king of Toronia now—at least he was. He died, but some evil magic brought him back. He walks like the dead, but he isn't dead, if you take my meaning. . . ."

Lady Redina listened in silence as Marcus described the conflict between Brutan's undead army and the attacking forces of Trident. When he'd finished, Hetty told of her experiences trying to escape the besieged city of Idilliam. Throughout, Gulph squeezed his hands together under the table, afraid that one of his companions would reveal his true identity to Lady Redina.

Ossilius is right, he thought. *As a hostess, she couldn't be more welcoming. But as protector of Celestis . . . how would she react to one of the prophecy triplets turning up at her door?*

He was relieved that just as Marcus had been more interested in telling Lady Redina about tactics and swordplay, Hetty seemed fixated on the effects of the battle on her bakery.

"My chimney fell into the whole day's batch before it was even half-browned," she mourned. "But I suppose there's few left in Idilliam now who'll appreciate a good loaf of bread. . . ."

As she chattered on, a servant poured dark red wine into their goblets. Gulph took one sniff and felt his stomach turn over. The man who'd been his guardian until the age of four—Sir Brax—had been a drunkard, and it hadn't taken long for the young Gulph to develop a hatred of alcohol.

As he wondered what to do with the wine, Lady Redina began to question Ossilius. "So this Nynus was the son of Brutan?"

Taking advantage of the distraction, Gulph contorted his arm behind his back and, with a deft flick of his wrist, emptied his wine goblet into a nearby vase.

"Yes. Nynus ruled for a short time after the death of his father." The captain answered courteously and with a straight face, betraying no emotion as he spoke.

"Yet his father lives again?"

"I do not know if 'lives' is the right word. He stands. He fights. But he is no man. He is transformed."

"Transformed, yes." Lady Redina rolled the word around her mouth as if tasting it. "So Toronia has been overtaken by a plague. A plague of the undead."

"Yes."

"Could this plague infect Celestis, do you think? I believe you came here in innocence, but might these undead creatures not have followed you? Might you not have brought your war to Celestis after all?"

"Forgive me, but it is not 'our' war, my lady. War overwhelmed us. We are simply trying to survive it."

"You have not answered my question. Is Celestis vulnerable?"

"No," said the captain. "The way here is closed. I am certain of that."

Lady Redina turned to Gulph. Her face possessed a breed of beauty that seemed to show no age. Yet Gulph fancied there was something lurking beneath the blue of her piercing eyes.

Something underneath, he thought, suppressing a shiver.

"Now you," Lady Redina said. "Tell me who you are."

Gulph swallowed.

She must not know.

"I'm, er, sort of an acrobat," he said. "A traveling player. We were performing in Isur—the Tangletree Players, I mean—and we were caught up in the fighting and taken to Idilliam."

"And where are the rest of these players now?" asked Lady Redina.

Gulph stared into his lap. "Dead. I'm afraid they must be dead."

I hope they are at least, he thought miserably. *The alternative is just too horrible for words.*

He looked up again and realized that his companions were staring at him in surprise.

"An acrobat?" said Hetty. "But I thought—"

"So you see," said Ossilius loudly, "we all found each other in the heat of battle, escaped, and by a miracle found our way here to the sanctuary of Celestis. And I cannot imagine a more perfect place in which to hide from the war above. May I have more wine?"

Marcus and Hetty stared at Gulph in surprise, but they said nothing. Jessamyn was eating some lemon-yellow sweets and didn't seem to be following the conversation at all.

Gulph allowed himself to relax just a little. For now his secret was safe.

A servant refilled the goblets as Lady Redina's stern gaze strayed out to the lake.

"Perfect," she mused. "Do you think Celestis perfect?"

An awkward silence fell.

"Well, I suppose—" Gulph started to say.

"Appearances can be deceptive," Lady Redina interrupted. "Celestis may not be at war, but this realm is blighted nevertheless."

"What's 'blighted'?" said Jessamyn.

Lady Redina's face softened. Gulph thought she looked a little sad. "A blight is like a shadow, my dear. Or perhaps a disease."

"Disease?" said Marcus, eyeing the fish in his bowl with sudden distaste.

"Not in the way you imagine," replied Lady Redina. "Still, you might say that Celestis is as plagued as Idilliam."

"Plagued by what?" said Gulph.

"A monster."

Jessamyn gasped and huddled against Hetty. The baker stroked her hair and gave Lady Redina a reproachful look. "No need to frighten the little one, my lady."

"On the contrary. There is every need. Beneath the silver waters of the Celestial Lake lurks a creature of untold evil. Few have seen it ... except for those it has killed. It moves by night, emerging silently from the water to prey upon the unwary. All attempts to catch it have failed." She smiled again at Jessamyn. "They say that the bakaliss swallows its victims whole and that it takes them three days then to die, as they lie suffocating inside the monster's toothed belly."

The little girl shrieked and buried her head in Hetty's dress. Gulph wanted to comfort her too, but his thoughts were ringing from the word Lady Redina had just used.

"Did you say 'bakaliss'?"

"It is the name of the monster. You are familiar with such beasts?"

"Yes. Well, no. Sort of."

"Which is it?"

"It's just that ... I once heard a story about a bakaliss."

"Really?" Both of her eyebrows rose. "Tell it to me."

"There's nothing much to it."

"Tell it!"

Flinching, Gulph blurted, "The bakaliss was an evil serpent that lived under a mountain. One day a king set out to kill it, but the serpent killed him instead."

His words echoed in the sudden silence. On the far side of the table, Marcus dropped his knife with a clatter.

"It is not much of a story," said Lady Redina icily.

"No," said Gulph. "I suppose it isn't."

He bit his lip, resisting the urge to say more. She *wanted* him to say more, he could feel it. Those piercing eyes burned into him, pulling at him. He put his empty goblet to his mouth and pretended to drink, all the time trying to beat back the thoughts that were fountaining in his head.

You want to hear the real story? Then I'll tell you. One day, an evil queen called Magritt and her crazy son, Nynus, made a boy called Gulph dress up as a bakaliss so he could put a poisoned crown on the head of King Brutan. And that boy was me, and the king was my father, and as soon as I put the crown on his head he turned black and died foaming at the mouth, and now I'm king, and I might not be wearing that stupid costume with its red fur and orange frills anymore but now you're telling me there's a real bakaliss, and it's here, and it kills people, and guess what? I'm a king, and I've journeyed under the mountain, and if I stay here the bakaliss is going to eat me alive, because that's what the story says!

CHAPTER 8

It took the Vicerin column two days to reach the bridge spanning the great Isurian River. As the wagon carried her across the broad wooden deck, Elodie remembered the last time she'd passed this way. Then she'd been a prisoner in a carriage driven by Fessan, who'd kidnapped her and whisked her away for what she'd been sure was ransom, or perhaps execution—but had turned out to be the first step on the road to her destiny.

Now it was Fessan who was the prisoner, stumbling along, his hands tied to the rail of the wagon rolling behind her. Never had she seen a man look more broken.

The clatter of hooves turned to soft thuds as they passed from the bridge to the packed-earth road beyond. The road arrowed due south, but Elodie knew it would soon swing west, steering her back to the place she'd started from: Castle Vicerin.

What did it mean, now, to be retracing her steps? Was this the end of the prophecy? Was she retreating like a snail into its shell, never to emerge again?

No! I'm not retreating. I'm attacking.

"I will find Tarlan's lost jewel," she whispered to Samial, who sat beside her at the front of the wagon, unseen by all but Elodie. "Then we will rescue Fessan and escape. Fessan will rebuild Trident. And I . . ."

Ahead stretched the vast patchwork farmland of Ritherlee, green rolling fields stitched together by dark hedgerows. The sky was flat blue, scratched with chalk-line clouds. A flock of starlings danced in the distance, ten thousand birds drawing impossible shapes in the sunshine.

My home.

The farther they rode into Ritherlee, the more Elodie saw that her homeland had changed while she'd been away. There were fewer laborers in the fields, and many of the farmsteads looked abandoned. Some had been burned to the ground.

"What has happened here?" said Samial.

"Lord Vicerin," she said tersely. "The man I once called Father."

They passed a burning village. The wind brought shouts and the thin clash of steel. A rider emerged from the smoke. Reaching the two men at the head of the column, he saluted.

"Captain Gandrell. It's good to see you again, sir. Did all go well in Isur?"

Before Gandrell could reply, Stown said, "Trident was exactly where I said it was. Tell Lord Vicerin that I led his men straight to them."

Captain Gandrell scowled. "Sergeant Stown has been of use. He is now looking forward to taking up ordinary duties in Lord Vicerin's guard. *Very* ordinary duties. Now, what news from Ritherlee?"

"The battle is almost won, sir," said the rider. "Another barony conquered for Lord Vicerin!"

Stown called over his shoulder to Elodie. "That's four in two days! At this rate you'll be on the throne before the season turns!"

"Still your tongue, Sergeant Stown!" Gandrell snapped. "Or I will explain what that means with the flat of my sword!"

Elodie was pleased to see Stown put in his place. All the same, his words made her uneasy. *It wouldn't be me on the throne. It would be Lord Vicerin himself. I'd be his puppet, just as he planned all along.*

Stown shot Gandrell a mutinous glance, and Elodie wondered how he had managed to rise so quickly through the ranks of the Vicerin army. It seemed only yesterday that he'd been slinking out of the Trident camp, banished and beaten.

"Scum always rises to the surface of the pond," whispered Samial in her ear.

Elodie stifled a giggle. "How did you know what I was thinking?"

"Because the same thought had come to me. That man will betray anyone who trusts him, sooner or later."

Elodie nodded. Stown was as treacherous as her former stepfather. *No wonder Vicerin likes him.*

From behind, she heard a sudden cry of pain. She knew who it was immediately.

"Get up!" a man shouted. Elodie heard the crack of a whip.

The cry had come from Fessan. His legs had finally given way, but the cart had not stopped. His hands bound by a short length of rope, he was being dragged full-length through the dust while the Vicerin soldiers jeered.

"They are such monsters!" cried Samial. "Why do they not stop?"

His face contorted with effort, Fessan staggered to his feet and tottered on, grunting in pain. Elodie bit her tongue and fought back tears. The former Trident commander could barely stand upright; his clothes were in tatters; his cheeks were covered in blood and filth.

Stop it! Why do you have to be so cruel?

She gripped the railing at the front of the wagon and began to get up, ready to leap down and run to Fessan's aid. Samial's ghostly hand tightened on her arm.

"You can't," he said.

Elodie tensed against him . . . then sat down again. "I know."

The Vicerins had to believe she was on their side. How could she help Fessan if she was locked up as well?

"What's going on?" said Stown, having ridden back to survey the scene. Gandrell was close behind him.

"Stop the cart," said Gandrell wearily. "Put him aboard."

"I don't think—" Stown began.

"That is correct," Gandrell interrupted. "You do not think."

Elodie watched in silence as the cart juddered to a halt and Fessan was thrown onto it. He landed bonelessly, like a rag doll.

"What are you going to do?" whispered Samial.

Elodie clenched her fists in her lap. "I'm going to save him," she hissed. "And then I'll bring them all down."

They reached the castle as the day was drawing to a close. Red stone towers filled the skyline, turned to blazing beacons by the setting sun. The column thundered over the drawbridge and up to the large east gatehouse; the iron portcullis slid smoothly upward to admit them.

Home, Elodie thought as the wagon carried her and Samial under the arch. *I used to love every stone of this place.*

As the portcullis slammed shut behind her, it felt as if she were entering a prison. An icy wind seemed to rush through her. In saving Trident, had she doomed herself?

Most of the soldiers headed straight for the barracks on the south side of the castle, leaving Stown and Gandrell to bring Elodie to the central keep. To her surprise—and relief—the cart carrying Fessan came too. That was good—at least she could keep her eye on him a little longer.

They were waiting for her on the lawn in front of the high stone tower: Lord Vicerin, Lady Vicerin, and their daughter, Sylva. As the wagon carried her and Samial toward them, Elodie was struck by a swimming sense of unreality. Everything looked so familiar: the red stone of the castle burning in the sunset; the ornate and ordered rows of flowers standing to attention in their beds; the proud peacocks strutting across the grass, just as if the castle belonged to them. Everything the same, and yet . . .

Everything's changed.

"Our lost daughter has returned!" cried Lord Vicerin, lifting his arms to help Elodie down. There was a smoothness about all his movements; it matched the gleaming blue velvet of his jackets, the slickness of his boots, the powdered perfection of his skin. Suppressing a shudder, she let his soft hands clutch hers and stepped to the ground.

Pasting a smile on her face, she looked up at him. "It's wonderful to see you again, Father."

He beamed, displaying large teeth like those of an animal. A horse, perhaps. Elodie could smell his sweet, sickly scent lingering around her.

Lady Vicerin reached to embrace her. Her face was artificially white, her lips painted red. The skirts of her dress were so full that she had to lean forward to hug Elodie, and the result was a brief squeeze and kisses blown into the air.

"Welcome, dear daughter," Lady Vicerin said.

"I'm so glad to be home," said Elodie, hoping her words sounded more convincing aloud than they did in her head.

Then Sylva was hugging her—a real hug that tugged at Elodie's heart. Sylva's cheeks were as rosy as her mother's were pale, and Elodie was surprised to see that her gray eyes were wet with tears. Sylva blinked quickly, as if not wanting anyone to see. "I'm glad you're all right," she said softly.

Lady Vicerin ran her fingers down the hem of Elodie's grubby Trident tunic. "We really must get you out of these dreadful clothes. All of your best dresses are waiting for you." She drew a fan from her sleeve and waved it in front of her face, wrinkling her nose with distaste. "I am sure you cannot wait to bathe and get into something clean. You can spend the whole of this evening choosing what to wear tomorrow, just the way you used to."

"I can't wait." *Did I really use to do that?*

"Such a feast we shall have," added Lord Vicerin. "There will be quails in jelly, your favorite."

"Yum."

Lord Vicerin strolled to the rest of the convoy. Stown and Gandrell, who had by now dismounted from their horses, saluted him.

"You have done very, very well," said Vicerin.

"Thank you, my lord," the two soldiers said simultaneously, then scowled at each other.

Vicerin peered over the side of the cart. "What, pray tell, is this?"

"The commander of Trident, my lord," said Gandrell, stepping in front of Stown.

"We're going to interrogate him," said Stown, shouldering his way past Gandrell to stand at Vicerin's shoulder.

Vicerin's long nose wrinkled in distaste. "So, my fine captive commander. What do you have to say for yourself?"

To Elodie's surprise, Fessan somehow managed to sit up. His face was blackened with bruises and covered in mud. When he opened his mouth to speak, she saw that two of his front teeth were missing.

"You'll learn nothing from me," Fessan croaked.

"Oh, I rather think I will. And when you have told me everything I wish to know, I shall think of a suitable punishment for you." Vicerin walked slowly around the cart, making a show of rubbing his chin. "Yes, this is a subject on which I shall have to think very hard. Very hard indeed."

He flicked a speck of dust from his immaculate velvet jacket and turned to Gandrell and Stown. "Would you not say that this situation merits the very deepest consideration, gentlemen?"

"Yes, my lord!" Again, the two men spoke together. Again, they shot each other a hateful glare.

Vicerin leaned close to Fessan, who returned his gaze with a calm authority, and Elodie's heart filled with pride. She wanted to run over and push Vicerin away, to put herself between them and protect the man who'd done so much for her. Instead, she forced herself to play her part, and stood and watched.

"You took something very precious to me," Vicerin hissed between his too-large teeth. "The price to be paid for such theft is high. Very high indeed. Would you not say so, Elodie?"

She flinched, not because of Vicerin's question, but because Fessan's steady gaze was now fixed upon her.

"No price could be too high," she said through numb lips. "This creature deserves everything he gets."

Without breaking his gaze, Fessan said, "Do what you will. I have already suffered the pain of betrayal. No torture can be worse than that."

Elodie looked away.

"By the time I have finished with you," said Lord Vicerin, "you may think differently. Now, which of you loyal fellows will take this wretched thing to the dungeon?"

Stown and Gandrell glowered at each other, neither man saying a word.

"Very well, since you have proven yourselves to be such a fine team, the duty is yours to share."

"Yes, my lord," said Captain Gandrell, saluting once more.

"As you wish," said Sergeant Stown, bowing low.

They escorted the wagon away. As it rolled past, Fessan's eyes caught Elodie's once more.

"I wish I'd never set eyes on you," he said. Then he did something strange with his mouth, pursing his lips but faltering as his tongue caught on his broken teeth. As the cart disappeared out of the courtyard, Elodie realized what he'd been trying to do.

He was trying to spit on me.

She told herself that was good. Lord Vicerin was clever—frighteningly so. The only way he would be convinced by her performance was if everybody else was convinced as well.

Including Fessan.

But, oh, it hurts!

"Now, I have many affairs of state to attend to, my dear," Lord Vicerin said, making off across the lawn. "I will see you at dinner."

"I'm looking forward to it, Father."

Dinner? I hope you choke on it!

Lady Vicerin whisked Elodie and Sylva up the endless staircases of the keep, all the while keeping up a constant stream of chatter about the latest goings-on in Castle Vicerin.

"We had to get rid of three of the cooks, you know," she prattled. "They were found throwing dice in the kitchens, and simply had to go. The food was ghastly for a while, but we eventually found suitable replacements."

They passed a window, giving Elodie a brief glimpse of the castle wall outside, and the green fields beyond. They seemed impossibly far away.

"Servants have been such a problem," Lady Vicerin went on, slowing her talk no more than she slowed her pace. "That dreadful maid Daphne disgraced herself with a stable boy, and as for the seamstresses, well, you should see the mess they made of Sylva's new reception dress. I mean to say, do these wretched people have any idea how hard it is to find good silk these days?"

Elodie let the talk wash over her. Since leaving the castle, she'd learned much about what she now considered to be the real world. Out there, life was hard. For some people, even finding enough food to eat was impossible.

You live in a bubble, she thought, staring at Lady Vicerin's rustling skirts as she turned onto yet another landing overlooked by gold-framed portraits of long-dead nobles. *Sooner or later the bubble will burst.*

Samial was still with her, climbing the stairs two paces behind. His eyes were wide as he took in the opulent surroundings.

"Anyway, I'm sure you'll settle back in soon enough," Lady Vicerin was saying, addressing Elodie directly now. "You have your sister to help you. And perhaps your brother will return too."

Elodie stopped, her whole body turning suddenly stiff. "Wh-what?" she quavered.

Why is she talking about Tarlan? He'd been briefly held prisoner here, she knew, but she couldn't believe that Lady Vicerin would even mention him, let alone that she would want him back inside her spotless castle in a hurry.

Lady Vicerin stared down her nose and fluttered her fan. "Cedric. Your brother. Surely you have not forgotten him?"

Of course!

Cedric was Sylva's older brother, and the three of them had grown up together: Cedric and Sylva and Elodie. They'd played and fought and done all the things ordinary siblings did. She hoped he'd return soon too.

"I am so proud of my Cedric," Lady Vicerin went on. She stopped beneath an ancient painting of a knight on a war horse. Old as the picture was, the resemblance to Cedric was unmistakable in the knight's high cheekbones and aloof gaze. "So proud that he fights for our house."

Elodie recalled the day Cedric had marched away to war, the single glance he'd thrown her from his place at the head of his regiment. The look of excitement on his face as he rode toward glory in some future, imagined battle.

Only that's not what war is like. I know that now.

"Yes," she agreed. "Cedric is brave."

"Such a shame about your hair." Lady Vicerin frowned at Elodie's shorn locks. "That red and gold was always so striking. Still, it will grow out again. Indeed, my dear, I do believe *you* have grown, even in the short time you have been away. We shall simply have to throw out your whole wardrobe and start again. Sylva, tell the head seamstress to meet me in Elodie's room in the morning. There is a lot of measuring to be done."

"I will, Mother." Sylva bobbed a curtsy to Lady Vicerin, but her gaze was fixed on Elodie.

You know something, Elodie thought as they climbed the final flight of stairs to her tower chambers. *No . . . you're trying to tell me something. But what?*

They reached the door to her old room. It looked solid and impenetrable.

Elodie's hand stole to the green jewel around her neck, then up to the collar of her tunic, which seemed suddenly tight and suffocating.

The room looked exactly the same as when she'd left it. In the center stood a huge four-poster bed. Beside the window was a large dressing table covered in jewelry and bottles of perfume. It was at once familiar and very strange.

"Rest, my dear," said Lady Vicerin, kissing her forehead. "You must be tired. Soon we will dine. Sylva, come."

Sylva gave Elodie another hug. But when she pulled away, the look she gave Elodie was so searching that she felt a jolt of worry.

Has she seen through me? After all, Sylva knew Elodie better than the other Vicerins. She had been Elodie's shepherd, always two steps behind her, always playing the part of the protective older sister. Elodie knew that the real reason Sylva had kept close to her side was to make sure she didn't try to run away from the Vicerins. She could still remember the panic on Sylva's face that day when Trident kidnapped her from among the market stalls, how she'd chased desperately after the carriage Elodie had been bundled inside. Had she simply been worried about the trouble she'd be in for losing her? Or had she been fearful for Elodie, too? Elodie wasn't sure.

And if she has seen through me, what will she do?

Two castle guards arrived at the top of the stairs and took up station outside the room.

"For your protection, my dear," Lady Vicerin said smoothly, perhaps seeing the expression of alarm that had crossed Elodie's face. "There are Trident sympathizers everywhere. You are too precious to lose twice."

As Lady Vicerin and Sylva left, the door closed with a solid clunk. Elodie turned to Samial.

"What she means is she doesn't trust me not to run away," she muttered, dropping her voice so the guards outside wouldn't hear.

Samial nodded. He was sitting on the windowsill, staring around at the room.

"It is very grand," he said.

"Yes, it is," Elodie agreed. "But really it might as well be a prison cell."

She sat beside him, and something caught in the window frame brushed her hand. It was a feather.

Elodie pulled it free. The feather was soft and downy, and very long—far too long for an ordinary bird.

"It looks like gold," said Samial in wonder.

"It's Theeta's," Elodie said.

Carefully, she tucked the feather into the same pocket that held the arrowhead Samial had given her. The two objects nestled together like old friends.

You were here, Tarlan. And you escaped. I'm going to escape too.

CHAPTER 9

The sea was a sudden, dazzling explosion of light. They came to it unexpectedly, after a difficult afternoon of flying through increasingly narrow canyons. Rock walls had turned to and fro, forcing the thorrods this way and that, their wings clipping the walls. Tarlan had been about to suggest they fly higher when the walls peeled back, spitting them out into a breathtaking vastness. The rich tang of salt, which Tarlan had been smelling all day, hit him like a punch to the face.

"The Warm Sea!" proclaimed Melchior. "Also known as the Western Ocean or, in the old tongue, Dup-an-Aegis."

"Big water," cawed Theeta. Her scratchy thorrod voice was filled with excitement.

Tarlan laughed. He felt giddy. "That's right, Theeta! I've never seen so much water in one place!"

As the thorrods carried them out over a black sandy beach, he drank in the view. The sea stretched to an impossible distance, both marking the horizon and surpassing it. The sea was everything to his left, and everything to his right. It was ahead and beyond, a huge rippling blanket of color and light and endless depth.

I can see into it, Tarlan thought in wonder, staring down through green shallows to the coarse contours of a winding coral reef. Lifting his gaze, he observed how the sea changed from green to gray, and how in the places between it contained all the shades of blue he could ever have imagined, and a thousand more besides. He saw whitecaps of foam hurl themselves against toothed rocks. Far out toward the horizon, he saw the ridged back of some immense monster break the surface for a single, breathless second before vanishing once more into the unknowable depths.

"It is beautiful, no?" said Melchior.

"I've never seen anything like it."

"Seethan saw," Theeta put in.

"What?" said Tarlan. "What did Seethan see?"

A lump came to his throat. It was still hard to talk about the old thorrod who'd given his life to save them from the elk-hunters. That terrible day in Yalasti seemed so long ago now, yet his grief was still fresh.

"Endless lake," Theeta responded. "Long ago."

Tarlan knew that was all she would say on the subject. Like all thorrods, Theeta used few words. It wasn't because her mind was simple. In fact, Tarlan was sure, the opposite was true. Thorrods merely struggled to squeeze their thoughts down into anything so crude as speech.

"A village," said Melchior, pointing south along the coast toward a cluster of low buildings. They appeared to have been constructed on stilts. Long-hulled boats swarmed in the waters around the village; a fishing fleet, Tarlan supposed.

"Is that where we're going?"

"No. Did I not tell you? We go west."

Melchior swung his arm straight out to sea.

Tarlan squinted. The afternoon was drawing into evening, and the sun lay low in the sky, directly ahead. Its golden light was beginning to turn the surface of the sea into a field of tiny fires.

"I don't see . . . Oh!"

Far offshore, an island had materialized out of the haze. It was black and rocky, jutting from the water like a giant's hat.

"The Isle of Stars," said Melchior.

Tarlan shivered. "It looks . . . bleak. Are we going there now?"

"No," said Melchior. "Night will fall soon, and the Isle of Stars is best approached by day. We will make camp and wait for the rest of your pack to arrive."

They landed in a small cove surrounded by cliffs. Tarlan and

Melchior climbed down from their thorrod steeds, after which Theeta and Nasheen made a rough nest among some rocks. While the birds settled themselves, Kitheen flew back along their trail.

"Your pack members are loyal to their leader," said Melchior as the black-feathered thorrod disappeared into the canyon. "To each other as well."

It was true. Without being asked, the thorrods had taken it in turns to fly at ground level, brushing their wings through the undergrowth in order to leave a trail of scent that Greythorn, Filos, and Brock could follow.

"It won't take the others long to catch up," Tarlan said. "I'll build a fire."

He gathered dry driftwood from beneath the cliffs, then started collecting rocks. The wind from the sea was strong, and he would have to build a low wall to protect the flames.

The best rocks were to be found near the waterline. As the sun began to sink below the horizon, Tarlan approached the sea with trepidation, unnerved by the bellow of the waves as they pummeled the black sand. A sudden rush of surf raced toward him, moving faster than he'd expected, and crashed around his knees. Laughing, he fought for balance, entranced by the sucking sensation of the waves as they withdrew, dragging away the sand from beneath his feet.

Returning to the camp, he began to lay the rocks in a circle. Some were black and glossy; others shone like large jewels.

"Are these precious?" he asked as he piled a gleaming green gem on top of a shining red one. He touched his hand to his throat, suddenly missing the beautiful green stone Mirith had given him . . . oh, it seemed so long ago. "They are sky rocks," Melchior answered. "And all such stones are precious."

"Precious? Why?"

The wizard's piercing gaze fell on Tarlan's fingers, still at his throat. "I do not yet know. I only know that your jewel is valuable, just like the jewels that belong to your brother and sister."

"I wish I hadn't lost it. Will I ever get it back, do you think?"

"I do not know that either, Tarlan. What is lost may not always be found."

Tarlan laid the last of the rocks on the circular wall. "Did Mirith get my jewel from here, then? I didn't think she'd ever left Yalasti."

"Mirith received your jewel from me."

Tarlan looked at the wizard with renewed interest. "All right. Where did you get it from?"

"From Gryndor." A wistful look softened Melchior's old eyes.

"Who's Gryndor?"

"The first of all wizards. He walked Toronia before . . . well, before it was Toronia. He walked this world when the seas were dry and the lands were dreams."

"I don't understand."

Melchior chuckled. "Let us just say that Gryndor was very, very old!"

"So where did *he* get the jewels from?"

"I cannot say. But I can tell you that when the sky rocks first fell, many ages past, they formed everything we see around us today. They made the realms, Tarlan, do you see?"

"Not really."

"Your homeland of Yalasti stands on sky rocks. So do Idilliam, Isur, and Ritherlee. And Celestis did too, of course."

Tarlan paused, his arms full of driftwood ready to be tossed within the circular wall.

"Celestis? What's that?"

"The fourth realm," the wizard replied. "City of Stars."

"I've never heard of it."

"It is forgotten. A lost realm. Where the city of Idilliam now stands, Celestis once stood. But now . . . now Celestis is gone."

Tarlan began stacking the timber. As he worked, his gaze strayed to the gleaming rock wall, then up at the high cliffs, then out to sea. Finally he found himself staring straight up into the darkening sky, where the three prophecy stars now framed the comet, which by now had grown very large and very bright. The world was big and strange, and full of endless wonder.

There's so much I don't know.

"What happened to this . . . Celeris?"

"Celestis." Melchior tossed a handful of driftwood onto the pile Tarlan was making. "Celestis was once ruled by a king. An evil king."

"There seem to be a lot of those around."

Ignoring him, the wizard went on. "The cruel acts of this king were so hurtful to his people that Gryndor allied himself with two of his fellow wizards. Together they plotted to bring the tyrant down."

"Three wizards against one king? Did they succeed? They must have done."

"They died," said Melchior tersely. "The king killed them before they could work their magic. As they died, their powers burst across the whole of Celestis. Their magic undermined the city, pulling the rock out from under it and burying it deep underground."

Tarlan thought about how the sea had tried to drag him under, and shuddered.

"How long ago did this happen?"

"A thousand years."

Tarlan frowned. "Then . . . people talk about the Thousand Year War . . ."

Melchior was nodding. "The death of Gryndor and the collapse of Celestis started the war that has raged in Toronia ever since. Ah, but those were terrible days."

"You talk about them as if you were there."

"Oh, I was just a young wizard at the time. I searched in the wreckage for survivors, but the Celestians were beyond all help. The entire city was gone, utterly crushed. It was made of crystal, you know, very beautiful to behold. Such a terrible loss. In time a new city rose: Idilliam, built upon the ruins of what had gone before."

Tarlan had been about to use the flint from his cloak pocket to ignite the fire. Now he stopped. "You're a thousand years old?" He could scarcely believe it.

"I am as old as my eyes and a little older than my teeth," Melchior replied with a mischievous grin. He stretched, his joints cracking like thawing ice. "And tomorrow I shall be reborn."

Before Tarlan could ask any more questions, Greythorn was bounding toward him over the black sand. Next came Filos, with Brock lumbering behind. Silent as an owl, Kitheen swooped through the twilight to join his thorrod companions in their nest of rocks.

"You found us!" Tarlan said as his pack gathered around him.

Filos looked around the beach, her blue-and-white stripes shining beneath the light of the prophecy stars.

"What do you think?" Tarlan asked.

The tigron sniffed the air. "I smell salt. And fish. I like fish."

"I prefer a hot haunch of deer," growled Greythorn.

Tarlan realized Brock was standing a little apart from the others and beckoned the bear over. "Come closer, Brock," he said. "You're part of the pack now."

"Brock likes the pack," the bear rumbled, squeezing between Filos and Greythorn. "Hard to run fast, though."

"You kept up well enough," Greythorn said.

"And you kept going when we got tired," added Filos. "I think you could run all day, Brock."

"Running reminds Brock he is free."

Tarlan ran a hand through the bear's shaggy coat. "As long as you're with me," he said, "free is what you'll stay."

The morning brought gray light and low, ominous clouds. The tide had climbed halfway up the beach toward the dead remains of the fire, and the waves were thick and angry. The wind was strong and laced with salt.

After a meager breakfast of dried meat, Tarlan and Melchior climbed silently onto their thorrod mounts. As Tarlan settled himself on Theeta's back, he felt Filos nudge his foot.

"I'm sorry," he said. "You have to stay here."

"Don't go," said Filos.

"A storm is coming," said Greythorn, sniffing toward the Isle of Stars, the top of which was shrouded in mist. "This is a bad day to fly."

"This won't take long," said Tarlan. He had no idea if that was true, but he was anxious not to delay further. "We'll be back."

I don't know if that's true either.

No sooner had they taken to the air than rain began to fall. Far out to sea, lightning scratched thin lines between the sky and the water. Distant thunder boomed, making the air tremble. Ahead loomed the Isle of Stars, a conical mountain peak with a flattened top.

"Once this was a volcano," Melchior called as the thorrods carried them in from the angry sea and over the black slopes of the island's foothills.

"What's a volcano?"

"A mountain that spits fire."

Tarlan decided he didn't want to know any more.

The foothills steepened swiftly to sheer mountain slopes. The thorrods climbed steadily, working their wings hard against the buffeting wind. The lightning was closer now, white sheets slicing through the clouds directly above Tarlan's head. The thunder was a constant drumbeat in his ears, in his chest.

This must be where the fire came out, he thought when they finally reached the island's peak, where a vast crater yawned like the mouth of some monstrous troll. The thorrods were big, but the crater swallowed them whole. Its walls were smooth and shiny, like black ice, capturing each burst of lightning and turning it into a thousand jagged reflections. Sucked down by the crater, the air swirled around them in a treacherous whirlwind.

At the bottom of the crater was a lake. Despite the spinning, howling wind, the water's surface was completely still. To Tarlan's astonishment, it was also the color of silver.

Rising from the center of the lake was a platform of smooth, black stone.

"Here!" shouted Melchior over the roar of the wind and the crash of the storm. "We are here!"

The three thorrods flew down toward the lake in a lurching descent that made Tarlan's stomach feel as if it had turned inside out. Just when he thought he would throw up, they dropped the last few wingspans and landed on the platform, which was just big enough to hold the three of them side by side.

As Tarlan and Melchior dismounted, the giant birds held their wings wide so as to shield their passengers from the worst of the rain. Tarlan went to each of the thorrods in turn, silently touching their razor-sharp beaks with his hand to demonstrate his thanks and trust.

"The Silverenne!" Melchior cried. The wind blew his hair and beard around his face in a white froth. He pointed at the lake. "Once it flowed through all of Toronia. But no more. The silver waters have long since retreated underground, except in this one special place."

"Why is it silver?" Tarlan had to cup his hands over his mouth to be heard.

"It holds the light of the stars! And by their light, and their magic, I shall be restored to everything I once was!"

Struggling to keep his balance in the gale, Tarlan studied the walls surrounding the eerily calm lake. Countless white stones were set into the rock. Some were the size of his hand; others were as big as the thorrods that had carried them here. Unlike the black rock that held them, these stones were dull and unreflective.

They look dead, Tarlan thought with a shiver.

"They are the constellations!" shouted Melchior. "Each has a number, and each number has a power. The sum of those powers totals the heart of a wizard. This is my task here today: to count the constellations back into myself."

Tarlan shook his head. He had no idea what the wizard was talking about. The thunder cracked, again and again; the noise was earsplitting, and with each boom Tarlan jumped.

"How will you do that?" he yelled, fighting to make himself heard over the din. Despite the best efforts of the thorrods to protect them with their wings, his clothes were drenched. As for the birds, they looked bedraggled and miserable.

"As each number is counted a new stone will light up!" Melchior shouted over yet another tremendous thunderclap. "When all the constellations are shining, my powers will be restored. Watch the stones while I am gone, Tarlan, and watch them well. Remember their pattern, and remember their number, for one day you may need them!"

"'Gone'?" Tarlan yelled back. "What do you mean, 'gone'?"

"As soon as I enter the water, I am vulnerable. You must keep watch. But you must also keep back! Until all the constellations are lit, until all the numbers are counted, nothing must disturb me, or all is lost. All! Do you understand, boy? Nothing must disturb me! Nothing!"

Tarlan gaped.

"Promise me you will not interfere! Promise me!"

"I promise!" Tarlan blurted.

Melchior dropped his staff. It fell to the ground, the clatter lost in the thunder. The wizard's face, so close to Tarlan's now that their noses were practically touching, fell abruptly backward.

"Melchior!"

The wizard's arms spread wide. His yellow cloak billowed like wings. He entered the water without a splash. Silver waves closed over his head.

The instant he hit the water, the air stilled and the sky fell silent. The lightning ceased, leaving only flat gray light. Tarlan's ears rang in the sudden silence.

Below the surface of the Silverenne, Melchior twitched once, then became utterly still, as if he'd been flash frozen by a Yalasti winter wind.

Tarlan dropped to his knees at the edge of the platform and thrust out his hands, intending to drag the wizard to safety. Behind him Theeta screeched a warning.

Tarlan drew his hands back as if burned.

Until all the constellations are lit, until all the numbers are counted, nothing must disturb me, or all is lost! All! Do you understand, boy?

Tarlan didn't understand. He didn't understand any of it. But he'd promised.

Below him, in the still waters of the Silverenne, the wizard floated as motionless as the dead.

"Hurry up, Melchior," he whispered. "Whatever you're doing down there, hurry!"

CHAPTER 10

The house overlooked the lake. Its floors were carpeted with a soft moss, and the rooms were filled with plump cushions embroidered with beautiful lacy motifs, but nothing could disguise the fact that it was made of crystal.

"This is such a peculiar place," said Gulph, running his hand down a wall made of milky opal. "Everything's so cold and hard."

"Including the Lady Redina," Ossilius observed.

"Do you think so?" said Gulph. "I don't know. She did let us stay, after all. And she's given us this house."

Ossilius snorted. "A grand gesture indeed."

Gulph threw himself down on one of the cushions. Upstairs he could hear the sounds of the others exploring and making themselves at home. Hetty had taken Jessamyn under her wing, promising her stories at bedtime; Marcus had just looked relieved to have found somewhere to lie down and recover.

But Gulph couldn't rest, and Ossilius's fitful pacing of the room told him that his friend felt the same.

"I don't really know what to think," Gulph said, gazing across the silver waters of the Celestial Lake. "I know we should be grateful, but . . ."

"But what, Gulph?"

"Maybe you're right. There's something wrong here. I don't know if it's got anything to do with Lady Redina, but . . . I just don't know."

Ossilius crossed to the window, stretching his arms above his head. "I feel an ache in my bones that goes all the way through to my soul. I am tired, Gulph. We are all tired. In the morning, when we have slept, our thoughts will run more freely."

"Do they have mornings down here, Ossilius? Do they have nights?" Gulph couldn't take his eyes off the lake. Tiny ripples twinkled dimly in the cavern's constant purple twilight. "Oh, we should never have gone into those tunnels. We should have stayed in Idilliam. We should have fought for our city."

"Had we stayed, we would be dead." Ossilius's tone was flat and final.

"Don't you mean 'undead'?"

"I suppose I do. Does that make it better?"

"Of course not. It makes it worse."

"We *will* fight, Gulph, when the time is right. Brutan *will* be defeated. You have my word on it. In the meantime, my job is to protect you. That is why we entered the tunnels: to keep you safe."

"Well, I don't feel very safe. And I don't feel very good about abandoning my friends. They could be dead or . . . worse. Don't you feel the same?"

"If you ask me if I want to be here, I must answer no. But coming to Celestis has at least given us shelter and put space between us and the enemy and given us time to think."

Gulph joined Ossilius at the window. He took a deep breath. "What do you know about bakalisses?"

Ossilius lowered his voice. "Is that what troubles you, my king? It is just a story."

"Pip used to say stories are like the roots of a big, old tree. Just because you can't touch them doesn't mean they're not real. Or important."

Ossilius put a hand on his shoulder. "It's the here and now that matters. Show me a bakaliss and I will face it down. Until then mythical monsters are not our concern."

Gulph spied movement on the path outside the house. A young man was trotting toward the nearby town square carrying a basket of what looked like fruit. He had his back to Gulph, but there was something familiar about his lopsided gait.

The man glanced back over his shoulder, and Gulph felt his face go slack with shock.

"John!" Gulph exclaimed. "Sidebottom John!"

"Who?" said Ossilius.

"He's my friend. One of the Tangletree Players. He's . . . I've got to go to him!"

Gulph raced from the house and onto the path. Reaching Sidebottom John, he grabbed the man's shoulder and spun him around.

"Steady, old lad," said John, his tone mild, his friendly face set with a bland smile. "Don't you go a-droppin' my fruits."

"John! I didn't think I'd ever see you again! How did you get here? Where are the others? Is Pip here? Is she all right?"

Gulph thought the questions would never stop pouring out of him. Then he noticed the blank expression on his friend's face.

"You be a chatty fellow," Sidebottom John said. "But I've got to be a-goin'. Bye-bye."

He turned to leave. Gulph pulled him back, more roughly than he'd intended. "John—it's me. It's Gulph." Sidebottom John stared at him with dull, uncomprehending eyes. "Don't you know me?"

"Be gentle with him," said Ossilius, having caught them up. "I have seen this shocked way before, in soldiers returning from war. Your friend's mind is wandering. It might even be lost altogether."

Lost?

"I wasn't trying to hurt him," said Gulph.

"I know that," Ossilius reassured him. "The sight of your friend has shocked you, too."

But Gulph didn't want to give up. "Don't you remember anything, John? The players? Performing at the castle? Remember how I used to turn somersaults over your head! Or what about that time when . . ."

He stopped. The vacant look in Sidebottom John's eyes was too much to bear. His friend was there and absent, both at the same time.

"I'll be a-goin' now," John said cheerfully. "There's fruitin' to be done."

"But . . ."

"Let him go," said Ossilius, gently gripping Gulph's arm.

Gulph watched, distraught, as Sidebottom John trotted down the path, turned a corner, and disappeared.

"It isn't right," said Gulph. "And you can't tell me it is. There's something about this place—"

A scream interrupted him. It echoed through the cavern, ringing like a bell off the surrounding walls of crystal.

"What was that?" said Gulph, unease pooling inside him.

"Someone in trouble."

They ran toward the lake. On reaching the shore, they found

themselves at the end of a long, narrow bridge of crystal extending out across the water like a pointing finger.

The scream came again.

"Come on," said Gulph.

They raced along the bridge. There were no handrails, and as they crossed, Gulph tried to ignore the fact that one wrong step would send him tumbling into the lake.

The bridge ended at the far cavern wall, where a wide opening yawned. Mist swirled through thin gray light. Cool air wafted Gulph's face and he knew at once where they were.

The bottom of the chasm!

They stepped cautiously outside. All around them, barely visible in the mist, were fields dotted with scrawny crops. Gulph could taste the damp air on his lips . . . only it didn't really taste of anything. There was hardly any wind here, no sense of weather, and the light—such as it was—seemed flat and lifeless.

Gulph looked up, straining to see through the haze. Somewhere up there was Idilliam, and Isur, and all the rest of Toronia. Another world, high above, forever out of reach to the people who lived down here in this hidden realm.

He turned, searching for Ossilius, when once more the scream rang out.

"Over here! By the three realms, over here!"

He found the captain beside a pile of bodies. He looked stricken with grief.

"Trident!" Ossilius said, pointing to the green uniforms, the image of a three-pronged spear stitched onto the tunics. "These are my son's warriors. They were here. Trident was here." He fell to his knees. "My son was here." His gray eyes grew wide. "I must find him. I must find Fessan!"

The nearest body was lying facedown. Ossilius rolled it over. Gulph gasped: one half of the Trident soldier's face was a raw, bloody wound.

"Not him!" muttered Ossilius, turning to the next body.

The wind gusted and the mist cleared a little. Gulph saw that this heap of corpses was just one of a long line of such piles stretching into the murky distance.

A figure emerged from the mist, and Gulph's heart rose into his mouth.

The dead are coming alive! Brutan's army is down here too!

But the figure was just a man clad in the silk robes of Celestis. He walked straight up to where Ossilius crouched among the bodies and laid his hands firmly on the captain's shoulders.

"We have worked hard to bring them to a peaceful place," the man said. "Let them rest."

"But you don't understand!" cried Ossilius. "My son! Fessan! Have you seen my son?"

The man waved his arm toward the rows and rows of bodies. Ossilius slumped to the ground in despair.

"People fall, from time to time," said the man. "But never so many. Others fell too, creatures we'd never seen before, men who were not living but . . ."

"Undead," finished Gulph with a shudder.

The man nodded. "We think there must have been a battle between these soldiers and those . . . undead. We are burying them. It is all we can do."

"They came to fight," whispered Ossilius. He began to weep. "They came to help Idilliam. And they lost."

It broke Gulph's heart to see his friend this way. He wondered if Ossilius's son—this young man called Fessan—really was down here.

"How many have you buried?" he said.

"Many hundreds," the man replied. "There are many hundreds more."

So that was that. If Fessan's body had fallen from the bridge, he might already have been laid to rest.

"Ossilius," Gulph said, dropping to one knee beside his friend. "I think . . ."

Something smashed onto the pile of bodies with a tremendous, sickening thud. Gulph cried out and jumped backward. Beside him, Ossilius staggered to his feet, reflexively reaching for his sword.

But Lady Redina had taken their weapons—one of the conditions under which they'd been allowed to stay in Celestis.

"Not another one," the Celestian man moaned.

The thing that had fallen was rising up from the scattered corpses. It was a corpse itself, Gulph saw with mounting horror—a dead man clad in red velvet robes. Red fire blazed inside its empty eye sockets. A huge white wig clung precariously to its naked skull, while pinned to its chest was the gold badge of the Idilliam treasury.

The undead treasurer lunged, and its skeletal fingers closed on the arms of the Celestian. The man shrieked and tried to pull back, but the thing's grip was unnaturally strong. It bared its teeth, and guttural sounds erupted from its torn throat.

"Here!" shouted Gulph, hurling a rock at it. "Over here!"

The undead creature released the Celestian, who scrambled rapidly backward. Even as it was lunging for him, Gulph took three rapid steps straight toward it—drawing a warning cry from Ossilius as he did so—and jumped high in the air. He flipped once, twice, and landed square on his feet on the other side.

The treasurer spun, unbalanced. Its wig flew off, revealing gleaming white bone. At the same instant, a second corpse staggered out of the mist. This one wore the remnants of a tattered green tunic and carried a notched sword. Its face was still mostly intact, but the rotting flesh had sagged, drawing its mouth down in an expression of infinite sadness.

A Trident soldier! thought Gulph. *How many more of them are down here?*

"Come to me, Gulph!" barked Ossilius. "Quickly!"

Circling back behind the treasurer, Gulph saw Ossilius prying a broken sword from beneath one of the corpses. But the undead Trident warrior had slipped between them. Gulph stumbled, momentarily disorientated by the cloying mist, the repetitive slap of dead feet on the damp ground, the hideous rasping sounds rising from deep inside the wrecked bodies of the oncoming dead . . .

A third figure appeared from the mist. To Gulph's astonished eyes it seemed to be *made* of the mist. Instead of limbs it seemed to move in silence on curves of swirling gray vapor; where its face should have been, there was a yawning hole.

The thing seemed to have no hands, yet it was carrying a sword.

Unaware of the strange creature's arrival, the two undead monstrosities continued to lumber toward Gulph, backing him against the pile of bodies. Ossilius was running forward, his broken blade raised, but he would not get to them in time.

The mist creature moved.

With a thin, hissing sound, its sword sliced through the neck of the Trident soldier. The walking corpse dropped like an unstrung marionette, its whole body jittering frantically. The instant it hit the ground, the rotten flesh smoothed over and it became just one more ordinary corpse.

The second blow cut the undead treasurer clean in half. Its bones jangled as it fell, losing in the space of a single breath all the hideous magic that had animated them. What landed at Gulph's feet was nothing more than a skeleton. The lifeless skull cracked in half, then all was still.

Gulph bent double, panting hard. His whole body was trembling.

"Look out!" shouted Ossilius.

Gulph glanced up to see the mist creature heading straight for him, its body a blur. Gulph cringed back, but just before he thought it would strike him down, the apparition came to a sudden silent halt, and he was amazed to see that it was just a person after all. A woman, in fact. Her slender body was completely shrouded in thin robes made from many layers of gray silk. A hood covered her head and obscured her face.

One thin hand was visible from beneath the robes. Its pale fingers gripped a sword made from pure white crystal. With a single liquid movement, both blade and hand vanished beneath folds of the sheer, gray fabric.

They stood in silence: the amazed Gulph, the equally surprised Ossilius, the trembling Celestian. And this ghostly woman of the mist.

"Th-thank you," Gulph stammered. "You saved my life. All our lives."

"That blade," said Ossilius. "No ordinary sword could have done that."

"Nor a blade of Celestis." Although her face was concealed, the woman's voice sang out clean and clear.

Why do you sound familiar? thought Gulph, although he was certain he'd never heard her voice before in his life.

"How did you . . . ?" Ossilius began.

Long fingers rose and drew back the hood. Gulph gasped. Half the woman's face was pale, like her hands. The other half had been burned a savage pink. The scars twisted along her cheek and jaw, and continued down her neck to where they disappeared beneath her robes.

"Witches have their ways," said the woman.

Her hood fell fully back, and a wave of red-gold hair tumbled over her face. She tossed it aside. Her eyes were fixed on Gulph. They were ordinary green, but like the eyes of the undead, they seemed somehow to burn.

"Kalia!" Ossilius cried.

A roaring sound filled Gulph's head. He felt dizzy; for an instant he was sure he was going to faint. The moment passed, and he stared in open wonder at his savior.

Kalia.

He'd heard the name before, of course he had. It had come from the lips of Queen Magritt as she'd stood beside the body of her husband, King Brutan.

Kalia seduced King Brutan. That was what Magritt had said, or something like it. *And she bore him three children—triplets indeed.*

The dizziness came and went in waves. Gulph staggered, convinced he would fall. Yet somehow he stood.

They said you were burned at the stake!

He stared at the dreadful burns scarring Kalia's face and neck.

Witches have their ways.

Gulph realized he'd been holding his breath. Slowly he exhaled. As he did so, all his strength fled and he sank to his knees.

With the last of the breath that was fleeing his mouth, he managed to say:

"You're my mother."

ACT TWO

CHAPTER 11

Gulph stared up into the face of his mother, his heart galloping. Tendrils of mist swirled wraithlike around her waist. Her whole body shimmered, and for an instant he was sure he was dreaming. Then the mist cleared, and she was entirely there.

"Mother. Mother, it's me. It's Gulph."

Kalia regarded him with a puzzled frown, showing no signs of recognition.

"Oh, I mean Agulphus. My name's Agulphus."

The frown remained.

She's beautiful, Gulph thought, seeing not the burn scars but what lay beneath.

"I'm one of the three—uh, your three . . . I mean, the triplets," he said. He was breathless and confused, and the words tangled in his mouth. "I'm . . . I'm your son."

"I have no children," said Kalia sharply.

Gulph shot a startled glance at Ossilius. Like Gulph, the former captain had dropped to his knees. He was gazing up at Kalia with reverence.

"Impossible," Ossilius said in a hoarse, breathless voice. "Were I not seeing this with my own eyes . . . Kalia, you died. Yet here you are."

"Died?" Kalia replied. "What nonsense is this?"

Gulph felt close to tears. "If it really is you, then it isn't nonsense at all. It's just . . ."

"A miracle," said Ossilius.

Kalia shook her head. Her frown deepened.

Rising to his feet, Ossilius spoke slowly to Kalia, as if to a small child. "It has been a long time. Thirteen years. Kalia, cast back your mind. Do you remember anything of the past?"

Kalia shook her head again, more vigorously. "You are wasting my time. I have no children. I do not know this boy. I do not know either of you."

She gathered her gray robes about her and turned away.

"No!" cried Gulph. "Please don't go."

"Castle Tor!" said Ossilius. "King Brutan—surely you must remember him. And Idilliam. Where you lived."

Kalia hesitated, her body tense beneath the layers of flowing silk. "My home is here. I have always lived in Celestis. Now please, I have had enough of your lies."

She sprang over the remains of their undead attackers and vanished into the mist.

Gulph leaped to his feet, shouting her name. He ran after her: ten steps, twenty. It was like chasing down a ghost. At last he skidded to a halt. She was nowhere to be seen. His mother had come to him—had saved his life—and now she was gone again.

He returned to where Ossilius was waiting. He felt like he had received a gift, only to have it snatched from his hands.

"I don't understand," he said. "I mean, I know she won't recognize me—I was just a baby. But . . ." He stretched an arm around, touching his crooked back. "Am I that much of a disappointment to her?"

"Never think that!" snapped Ossilius. "You do not disappoint, Gulph. You never could."

"I thought my father had her burned to death. Now I don't know what to think."

"But she *was* dead. Burned to ashes," said Ossilius. "Gulph, what I have never told you is that I saw it with my own eyes."

Gulph's mouth dropped open. "You were actually there at the . . . at the execution?"

"Not at the burning itself, thank the stars. I do not think I could have stood by and watched such cruelty. No, I was part of the detail sent to remove the stake and pyre from the execution yard. And to clear the remains."

"But if she died, how can she . . . ?"

"Magic, Gulph."

"Magic?"

"There is no other explanation. I do not pretend to understand it, but magic may explain why she is here. It may also explain the way of her mind. Consider this: she is not the only person we have met who has lost their memory."

"Sidebottom John!"

"Exactly. Which means the magic may be right here, in Celestis itself."

Gulph's thoughts were dark shadows. *If she died, and is here now, then she is one of the undead. Not like my father and his awful shambling soldiers, but she can't be truly alive. In which case . . . what is she?*

"Magic in Celestis," he said slowly, pulling back from this unnerving train of thought. "Magic that makes people forget. Will we forget things too, Ossilius?"

Ossilius sighed. "Think about what you have seen these past days, Gulph. Do you really believe you can forget such horrors? Can any of us?"

"I suppose not."

But how would we know?

"We should go back." Ossilius was staring at the pile of recovered Trident bodies. His mouth was drawn down in such sadness that Gulph put aside his own misery.

"You don't know that Fessan's here," Gulph said. "He's probably safe somewhere, planning the next attack."

"Perhaps," Ossilius replied.

The following day Gulph found himself seated once more at the table in Lady Redina's courtyard. He still felt dazed by his meeting with Kalia, and although he knew he should be hungry, the familiar selection of fresh fish and bowls of tiny steamed vegetables held little appeal. He was sitting close to the vase again, he saw with relief, so he could at least tip away his goblet of wine when he got the chance. He'd just have to try to eat the rest.

"And this young man is Gulph," Lady Redina was saying. With a start he realized she was introducing his party to the handful of Celestians also invited to the feast.

"Pleased to meet you," he mumbled, forgot the Celestians' names almost as soon as he'd heard them, then panicked as he considered what Ossilius had said about magic and memory.

Get a grip, Gulph! he scolded himself. *You're just distracted, that's all.*

As they picked up their forks, a sixth Celestian appeared around the corner of the house and crossed the courtyard to join them at the table. She was small, and very light on her feet. Her long, red-gold hair flowed like a pennant behind her.

It was Kalia.

His pulse racing, Gulph rose from his seat, his mouth filling up with formless words. Ossilius pulled him back down.

"Stay calm, Gulph," he whispered. "Let us see what unfolds."

"You are welcome, Kalia, if a trifle late," said Lady Redina. She spread her arms and addressed the whole assembly. "This is a feast of welcome for our new friends. I say 'friends' and not 'guests' because you are all part of Celestis now. It is your home for as long as the crystal endures."

There was something final about this that Gulph didn't like. But he heeded Ossilius's advice and bit his tongue. He glanced toward Marcus and Hetty. They were citizens of Idilliam—surely they'd heard the name Kalia before? Would they make the connection? But they showed no sign of recognition.

"It is pleasant to see you again," Kalia said to Gulph, helping herself to a plate of oysters.

Again, Gulph tried to speak, and failed.

"Oh. Do you know our new friends, Kalia?" Lady Redina's voice carried smoothly across the table.

"Not really. We happened to meet yesterday. They had wandered into the chasm. I helped them."

That's all true. Gulph held his breath, waiting for Kalia to reveal what he'd said about her being his mother.

But she said no more. His secret was safe, and that was a relief. Still, curiosity burned in him. Kalia clearly recalled meeting him, but had she forgotten what they'd talked about? Was she affected by whatever magic held sway here too? Or was she simply being discreet?

There were so many questions.

How can I ask any of them without giving myself away?

Then it came to him.

After emptying his wine goblet surreptitiously into the vase, Gulph cleared his throat and said, "Do you know someone called Sidebottom John?"

Lady Redina smiled warmly and spread her arms wide. "I know everyone in Celestis."

This idea was oddly unnerving. Gulph pressed on. "Well, I met him here yesterday. He was a jester in the Tangletree Players— we've known each other for years. But when I approached him, he didn't recognize me. Isn't that peculiar?"

"The poor man," said Lady Redina. "How very sad."

"Do you know what happened to him?"

"Your friend was discovered wandering by the silver lake. I believe he must have found his way down to Celestis from the world above, just as you and your friends did, Gulph."

We hardly "found our way." We fell.

"As for the state of his mind, I judge that he is suffering from the shock of war. You have told me about the recent terrible events in Toronia—the fighting, the atrocities. Is it any wonder his mind has closed up like a flower?" She shook her head. "The poor, poor man."

"I suppose you're right." Ossilius had suggested the same, after all.

"Perhaps . . . if your friend were to spend a little time with you, his memory might be stimulated."

Before Gulph could say anything, Lady Redina was snapping her fingers and telling a servant to seek out Sidebottom John and bring him to the feast.

Gulph didn't know what to say. He'd started out convinced that Lady Redina was hiding something, yet here she was clearly willing to help.

And if it works—if I can help him remember—perhaps I can help my mother, too.

"Thank you, Lady Redina," he said, toasting her with his empty goblet. "You're very kind."

With the meal over, the dinner guests left the table and began to mingle and chatter in the garden. Gulph strolled alone between rows of sculpted ruby roses and beneath overhanging crystal fronds that tinkled like chimes in the breeze. At any other time, he would have been curious to explore, but all he was really interested in was seeing his friend.

At last the servant returned. Trotting after him was a beaming Sidebottom John.

"I remember you," John cried immediately, seizing Gulph's hand.

Gulph grinned and felt his heart swell. "You do? You really do?"

"By the gollies, I do! We did meet on the path yesterday. I had my fruits!"

Gulph felt crushed. "Is that all you remember, John?"

"On the path." John nodded vigorously. "We was on the path. You, and me, and the fruits."

"Yes. Yes, we were. But what about before that? Do you remember Idilliam?"

"Iddle Ham?"

"We performed for the king. Then everything went . . . there was fighting and . . ."

Gulph's words dried up as Sidebottom John's face grew slack with incomprehension.

How can I get through to him?

"You like fruit, yes?" he said with sudden inspiration.

John's face lit up. "Fruits is my favorites."

"Stay there!"

Gulph grabbed three apples, as shrunken as the tiny vegetables, from a bowl on the table, then drew John to a secluded spot behind an outcrop of green crystal. Out of sight of the other guests, he bent his knees a little, then began to juggle the fruit.

"That's good!" John exclaimed, clapping his hands together like a delighted child. "That's is clever."

Gulph continued to juggle. The apples rose and fell in their endless round. It was a kind of practical magic—the kind of magic anyone could do.

No—not just anyone.

"You can do this too, John," he said. He stopped juggling and let the little apples drop, one after the other, into his left hand, then held them out. But Sidebottom John backed away, shaking his head.

"Oh no, John can't do the flippities. That's for the clever folk. Like you."

"But you *can* do it, John. You really can."

Something flashed momentarily across John's face: a fleeting expression of . . . what? Remembrance? Sadness? Fear? Gulph couldn't tell. It was there and gone too quickly.

"No," John said emphatically. "John doesn't do that."

"All right. How about this?"

Gulph dropped the apples, bent double, and went into a handstand. Still on his hands, he walked a complete circle around John. When he was back where he'd started, he jumped onto his feet again.

"That's clever too." John clapped halfheartedly, but his brow was creased.

"You can do it, John. You taught me how!"

"I doesn't remember that!" Tears sprang to John's eyes. He started backing away. "Why d'you tell me things I doesn't remember? I doesn't even know you. Go away! You makes my head hurt!"

Gulph pursued him. "Please, John, try!"

"Go away!"

"You have to remember!"

"You isn't my friend! Go away!"

Why won't you just remember! he thought, ashamed at the sudden wash of anger, but powerless to prevent it. By now he'd backed Sidebottom John against the green crystal outcrop.

"What did this to you, John? Was it some kind of magic?"

"Don't like magic!" John batted at Gulph with his hands, trying to push him away.

"Please, John, I just want to help you!"

"Don't need no help! Just want to go home!"

"Where is your home, John? Do you remember *that*?"

"Go away!"

Gulph's head felt hot and dry, as if a sandstorm were scouring the inside of his skull. *What's happening to me?* Then he recognized the sensation: it was the peculiar, arid feeling that came over him whenever he was about to turn invisible. What he'd come to think of as "*desert trance*," although what deserts had to do with invisibility he had no idea.

The feeling intensified. Heat thumped through him, filling him up. Just when he thought he was ready to burst, he felt himself spilling out of his body and into the humid, Celestian air. The sand was pouring out through his eyes, his nose, his mouth, and he was the sand, and the sand was him. John's face grew enormous before him, and then blurred, and then . . .

I am John. I am inside the cave of his head, looking out through the windows of his eyes. There is movement, dancing light. Sun through smoke. I am afraid, hiding, making myself small. A vertical line of stone: the pillar I am hiding behind. Into the shadows. Hide, John, hide! But my friends . . .

There is Willum, there is Dorry, and there, oh, there is Pip. The players. The Tangletree Players. My friends, in the sun, in the smoke.

In chains.

My friends are in chains, and the chains are in the hands of the undead, the rotting monsters, the bone-men, and they are herding my friends like cattle, and all I can do is hide and watch. I have escaped, but my friends are taken, my friends, oh, my friends are . . .

He was stumbling backward, panting hard, shocked to the core. The eerie sensation of *leaving his body* had come and gone in the blink of an eye. He'd been Gulph, then he'd been John, and now he was Gulph again. He palmed sweat from his forehead and sat down hard on the crystal ground.

"Is you all right?" said Sidebottom John. He looked puzzled but otherwise unaffected by their brief meeting of minds.

Gulph clambered to his feet. His heart was a horse bolting through his chest. He stared into John's eyes, the very eyes which, just a few breaths before, he'd been looking out of.

Not out of his eyes. Into his memory.

Was that true? Had that really just happened?

Are they really alive? Willum? Pip? All the others?

He'd never seen the undead taking prisoners before. They just transformed the living into more walking corpses. What cruel, new plan of Brutan's was this?

Gulph didn't care. If what John had shown him was true, there was only one thing that mattered now. He clapped Sidebottom John on the arm. "Thank you, John."

"What did John do?"

"More than you know."

Gulph marched back between the lines of ruby roses and made for Ossilius, who was standing near an elegant crystal sculpture of a swan, deep in conversation with Marcus.

"Ossilius!" Gulph hissed. "They're alive!"

"Who is alive?"

"The players. Pip. The others. My friends. They're alive, all of them!"

"Gulph, wait. How do you . . . ?"

"It doesn't matter. They're alive, and that's that. We have to go back. We have to go back to Idilliam and rescue them!"

"Whom do you wish to rescue?" The voice belonged to Lady Redina. Gulph hadn't heard her following him; she must have moved in complete silence.

He was about to repeat what he'd said to Ossilius, when he stopped himself. He'd already told her he thought Pip and the others were dead. How could he explain his sudden change of mind?

"Er, my friends," he stammered. "I was just saying that, er, that *if* they were alive, I would want to rescue them."

Marcus looked confused. He opened his mouth, about to speak. Gulph shook his head minutely from side to side, and to his relief Marcus's mouth closed.

"What makes you believe your friends might still be alive?" said Lady Redina.

"Oh, I don't," said Gulph. "Don't believe it, I mean. It's just . . . I just hope they might be. If John survived, maybe the others did too. That's all."

Yes. That's all. I don't have strange powers that let me see into people's thoughts. In fact, there's nothing unusual about me at all. I'm an acrobat, just an acrobat.

"I understand," said Lady Redina. "You are loyal to your friends. The fact that you wish to help them proves that. It also proves that you are brave."

She brushed the backs of her fingers down Gulph's cheek. Her hand was hot.

"Sadly, there is nothing you can do. Even if your friends were alive—and I doubt that they are—you cannot now leave Celestis. The lost realm must remain lost. It is the only way to keep it safe from the wars above."

"You mean we're prisoners here?"

She looked affronted. "Celestis is not a prison. It is a haven. I am not a jailer, merely the one who has granted you permission to stay. That permission cannot now be taken back. It is the way of Celestis."

Not a prison? I might as well be back inside the Vault of Heaven.

"What if I were to leave anyway?"

"Then you will be in exile. Those who leave Celestis may never return. All who try to enter the crystal realm a second time must die."

Her expression was stern. Her warning was clear. Yet her words brought Gulph grim hope.

So, people do leave. All I need now is to find the way out. And take it!

CHAPTER 12

E verything the same.

Everything different.

Elodie sat at the banqueting table in the grand council chamber of Castle Vicerin, just as she had hundreds of times before. The polished dark wood of the tabletop gleamed in the light of the hanging chandeliers. The silver plates and goblets gleamed too. On the chamber walls hung tapestries celebrating the many triumphs of the Vicerin family through the ages. Near the door to the kitchens, servants stood, awaiting their lord's command.

Everything just as she remembered.

Everything except me.

And yet, when she looked harder, Elodie saw that there *were* changes, small but unmistakable.

There are two footmen where once there would have been four. And the tapestry commemorating the Battle of Elder Gorge is frayed at the edge.

Glancing up, Elodie noted that only half the candles on the golden chandelier were lit.

The war is taking its toll.

"Have another cake, my dear," said Lord Vicerin, waving his hand across the table with a flourish. He sat at the head of the table as usual, with Elodie on his right. For now, they were the only diners.

"Thank you, Father."

She selected a tiny yellow cake from the plate. It was impossibly dainty, molded with flutes and flowers and iced with bright whorls of color. To Elodie, after weeks spent eating roast wild boar, dripping with fat and served on an upturned Trident shield, it hardly looked like food at all.

"Will anyone else be joining us?" She bit into the little cake. It was unbelievably sweet and sticky.

"I thought it would be pleasant to dine together." Lord Vicerin inserted a lurid green cake into his mouth, trapping it behind his large teeth and mulching it with his tongue. "Just the two of us."

His words echoed around the chamber. The vast expanse of the banqueting table stretched into the distance. Far away, in the corner of the hall, the servants stood impassively.

"Lovely," said Elodie, the last crumbs of the cake catching in her throat.

As she watched Lord Vicerin dab at his lips—they looked very red, as if he'd colored them with rouge—a sudden thought came to her.

Did you sit here, Tarlan? If so, what did you make of all this?

The idea of her brother in this ridiculous carnival of a castle— that wild boy from the frozen wastes of Yalasti, who spoke with animals and turned up his nose at the slightest hint of civilization— almost made her laugh out loud. She grabbed her own napkin and pressed it over her mouth.

"I cannot tell you how wonderful it is to have you back under our wing again," Lord Vicerin said, setting his plate aside. "The day you were snatched away by those dreadful ruffians . . . Oh, Elodie, it was the worst day of my life."

I bet it was, Elodie thought. *You'd lost your little puppet, and your key to the throne of Toronia.*

"I sent men after you at once, of course," Vicerin went on. "I scoured the whole of Ritherlee, offered rewards. I was so desperate to have you safe once more."

Under your control, more like.

Lord Vicerin beamed. Tiny blobs of icing had stuck to his teeth. "And now you have returned and our ordeal is over. Our family is whole once more." He paused, clearly expecting her to speak.

"I can hardly believe it myself," Elodie managed to say.

Clasping together his long, powdered hands, Lord Vicerin

leaned forward over the polished table. "And here you must stay. Your protection is now my priority, dear Elodie. That is why I must ask you some questions, just a few. Questions about those awful vagabonds who kidnapped you. And about what happened. You do understand, yes?"

"Of course, Father."

"Let us take this Fessan, for example. How much responsibility does he give to his lieutenants? Is he a dictator? Or is he one of those dreadful people who likes to talk out his problems until the sun goes down?"

"I don't really know what a dictator is, Father."

"Very well, then what of his tactics? I understand you were present at the Battle of the Bridge, although what a daughter of mine was doing in the middle of such a scene I cannot imagine."

I was using my sword to hack down undead warriors, if it's any business of yours. And I am not your daughter!

Elodie made herself nibble at another cake. "Yes. I was there."

"The knowledge makes my heart weep. Now, Trident attacked even though the bridge was broken in the middle. How did they plan to cross it? Do they have siege engines?"

"What's a siege engine?"

Lord Vicerin patted her hand. "Never mind. The attack was repelled, we know that. Trident's numbers must have been greatly reduced as a result."

"A lot of people died."

"Did Fessan plan to recruit new soldiers in Isur?"

"We passed through some villages. Most of the people threw rotten fruit."

At first Elodie had to work hard to keep her answers vague. But as the interrogation went on, she relaxed into the part she was playing.

It's only what you expect of me, isn't it? You think I'm a silly little girl who only understands dresses and pretty jewels. Maybe I used to be. But not anymore.

"You are a very brave girl," Lord Vicerin said, leaning back extravagantly in his chair. His tone—that of a parent speaking to a small child—reassured Elodie that she'd succeeded in her attempts to fool him. "Won't you take some more refreshment?"

He spooned pieces of fruit from a tortoiseshell bowl onto her plate. Each was carved into the shape of a rose.

"Oh, I nearly forgot." Lord Vicerin smiled expansively. "There is just one more question. Are those wretched Trident ruffians still spreading rumors that you are one of three? A prophecy triplet? And that your siblings are alive?"

His tone was light and breezy. Yet his eyes were as cold as steel.

"Yes," she said. She didn't like this turn of the conversation, and judged that any further lies would have to be dressed in the truth. "They all believe it."

Here it comes.

"And what about you, my dear? What do *you* believe?"

She chewed and swallowed a petal carved from a pear.

"I believe I *am* one of three," she said.

Lord Vicerin's eyes widened, then grew narrow.

"What do you mean, child?"

"I mean that I have a brother, and I have a sister: Cedric and Sylva Vicerin. *They* are my siblings. The only ones I know, or care about. I know I'm adopted, but that doesn't mean you're not my family, because you are. Castle Vicerin is my home. This is where I belong. With you." Onto her face she pasted the widest, most sincere smile she could muster. "I love you."

Vicerin beamed. "I am very pleased to hear those words, my dear. In fact"—he slipped his hand inside his velvet jacket—"let me show you how pleased I am."

When Lord Vicerin withdrew his hand, he was holding a knife. Its gold-plated hilt flashed in the candlelight. Elodie clapped her hand over her mouth. Her heart was thundering.

He's seen through me! He's going to kill me right here in the council chamber!

But instead of plunging the dagger into her breast, Lord Vicerin handed it to her, hilt first. It was then she saw that the weapon was still in its sheath. Its dazzling, jewel-encrusted sheath.

"It is startling in its beauty." Lord Vicerin gave her a sickly smile. "That is why you deserve it, Elodie."

Trembling, she took the ornate knife. "Thank you, Father. But . . . ?"

"But why? Simply this, my dear: if Trident attempts to snatch you again, I want you to be able to defend yourself."

Still shaking, Elodie tucked the dagger under the wide belt of her new satin dress. Warm relief flowed through her entire body. *If this doesn't prove he trusts me, what will?*

Behind her a servant coughed gently. Lord Vicerin dabbed his lips again.

"And now, my dear, I fear there are council matters I must attend to. You are excused."

As soon as Elodie had risen from her chair, another servant glided in and skillfully ushered her toward the door. She was glad their business was concluded. Suddenly she wanted nothing more than to be out of this hateful room.

On her way out she nearly bumped into a pair of castle guards flanking a middle-aged woman dressed in shining armor. The woman's brow was creased with worry lines. Following behind the woman came a line of men and women, all wearing formal yellow robes.

"Excuse me, Your Highness," said the first guard, giving Elodie a perfunctory bow. "Lord Vicerin doesn't want to be kept waiting."

Elodie stepped aside. As the parade of dignitaries swept past, the woman in the armor paused.

"You must be Princess Elodie," she said. She looked as if she hadn't slept for a week.

"Please," said the guard. "Lady Darrand, come this way."

Elodie said nothing. She had the peculiar feeling the woman was looking right through her. Then the moment passed.

"I hope we may meet again," said Lady Darrand, and with that she was gone, stepping wearily into the council chamber with her finely dressed entourage. The doors slammed shut, and the guards took up station outside with their hands resting lightly on the hilts of their sheathed swords.

"Best you run along, my lady," said one of them, an older man with gray hair and a kind face. "Your father will be in there for the rest of the day."

"Who's Lady Darrand?"

"A neighbor. And an enemy. It's a delegation. Lady Darrand wants to put an end to the war in Ritherlee."

Elodie nodded. "Will there be peace, do you think?"

The second guard, a younger man, nudged the first.

"Like I said, it's best you run along."

Elodie obeyed. But her curiosity had been aroused. How wonderful would it be to return to Trident with useful information about Lord Vicerin's military operations?

I'll be Trident's spy, right at the heart of the castle.

Another guard was waiting at the end of the corridor. He was dressed in the crisp black livery of a footman, but Elodie knew he was a soldier from the straightness of his back and the bulge of weapons beneath his tunic. Wherever she went in the castle, one of these guards in disguise went with her.

"*Your father wants you protected*," the men would answer when she asked why they were following her.

Lord Vicerin's gift of the knife made her believe that might be true. But she also believed something else.

He doesn't want me to escape.

"I'm going to take a moment before returning to my room," she called to the guard. "Don't worry. I'll be perfectly safe."

Before he could reply, she made a sharp right turn into a narrow, oak-paneled passage. Immediately the guard followed.

"Your father prefers you to stay in the open."

"This won't take long."

Dozens of paintings hung on the walls of the passage. Elodie kept count of the pictures as she walked past. When she reached the thirteenth, she stopped.

I think this is the right spot.

The painting was wide and showed a battle scene in which blue-clad soldiers swarmed through the shattered wall of a burning wooden fort. Instead of swords they carried crude clubs. The fort was an early incarnation of Castle Vicerin, she realized—a primitive wooden structure that once stood where now towered this mighty bastion of stone.

"Do you have any paper?"

"Beg pardon, my lady?"

"Paper. And a quill. I wish to take notes. You know how much I enjoy my painting classes."

"I, er, it's a long way to the schoolroom, my lady."

"You don't need to go to the schoolroom. They keep writing supplies in the store beside the council room door. How else do you think they keep records?"

"I, er . . ."

"Go and get me some."

"I'm not supposed to leave you alone, Your Highness."

"Oh, for goodness' sake. You know as well as I do this passage is a dead end."

"Yes, but . . ."

"But nothing! Nothing can come at me from that direction, and you'll be able to see the entrance from the main corridor. I'm really quite safe."

"I know, Your Highness, but . . ."

"Just go!"

The guard hurried away. Elodie allowed herself a smile. Playing the spoiled brat was even more fun than playing the spy.

As soon as he was out of sight, she pressed her ear to the wood-paneled wall the painting hung from. The first voice she heard was a woman's, raised in anger.

". . . you call yourself civilized when you steal from us?"

"Do you presume to call me a thief, Lady Darrand?" Lord Vicerin's purring voice was unmistakable.

"I do not call you a thief! I call you what you are! You are a child abductor, Lord Vicerin!"

Elodie pressed her lips together. Tarlan had told her how he'd rescued a group of children from the Vicerin dungeons. Had more been taken since then? She imagined Lord Vicerin striding up and down between the cells, his handkerchief pressed to his long nose, his powdered face wrinkled into a sneer. The thought made her feel sick.

"Can we not keep this meeting on a cordial footing, Lady Darrand?" said Lord Vicerin. "Can we not be at peace? If you will only sign this treaty, then we can do away with the throne altogether and rule Toronia as a council of nobles."

With you as its head, I suppose? Just you try to take the crown from me and my brothers!

Footsteps echoed down the passage. Elodie muttered a curse.

Back so soon? I've barely had time to hear anything. . . .

She pulled herself hurriedly away from the wall. When the guard rounded the corner, she was peering at the painting closely.

He held out the paper and quill. Elodie snatched them and scribbled enough notes to make her pretense at study convincing. There was nothing more she could do with the guard hovering beside her, so she marched back to the main corridor. The guard stumbled along in her wake.

"Begging your pardon, my lady, but what was it you learned from the painting?" Elodie adopted her most withering tone. "Vicerin history, of course. The most worthy subject of them all, wouldn't you agree?"

"Er, yes, my lady."

They threaded their way back through the labyrinthine castle corridors and a wide hall lined with suits of armor. When they reached her bedchamber in the tower, Elodie closed the door behind her, leaving the guard outside. Samial was waiting on the far side of the room.

"We've got a lot to talk about," she whispered.

"Yes." Samial didn't need to speak quietly, since Elodie was the only person who could hear him; nonetheless, he sounded agitated.

"What is it?" Elodie asked.

"I have found Fessan."

Elodie sat down heavily on the bed. She had to know more, yet dreaded to hear it.

"Where is he?" she hissed. "*How* is he?"

"He is in one of the deep dungeons. They call it the water cell."

"The water cell? What's that?"

"It is very small. They keep it flooded, almost to the ceiling. Fessan is chained to the wall. If he stands, he can just keep his chin above the water. The water is very cold."

Elodie felt as if she'd been punched. She tried to imagine it. She couldn't. "It's torture," she whispered.

"Every day they drain the water so he can eat. They check his wounds, but they do not treat them. The wounds are going bad, I think."

"Oh, poor Fessan. Poor, poor Fessan."

"Shall I let him out?"

Elodie stared at Samial agape. Invisible to ordinary eyes, like all ghosts Samial had a presence in the physical world. It had never occurred to her that her friend could simply set Fessan free. Yes, Samial could go back to the water cell, steal a key, and open the door. Fessan would run, and then . . .

Then they'd catch him.

She got up and walked unsteadily to the window. Down in the courtyard, a regiment of Vicerin soldiers stood in line. Captain Gandrell was pacing up and down before them, barking out orders.

If he's in as bad a way as Samial says, he won't get five paces before they catch him and lock him up again. If he can even walk at all.

"No." It was such a small word. Yet it broke Elodie's heart to say it. "We need a proper plan."

"Do you mean a battle plan?" There was a gleam in Samial's ghostly eyes.

"I suppose I do. But first we need information. Lord Vicerin is holding meetings with the other Ritherlee families. He's with Lady Darrand right now. I tried to eavesdrop on what they were saying, but they keep such a close eye on everything I do."

"There are no eyes on me, Elodie. Shall I listen for you?"

Despite everything, Elodie grinned. There was a way to gather intelligence after all.

"Yes, Samial. You can be *my* eyes. And my ears. What better spy than a ghost!"

CHAPTER 13

The sun was setting behind the castle's red towers. Elodie tagged along behind Lord and Lady Vicerin and Sylva as they strolled through one of the wide walled gardens near the south dining hall. The air was still and warm, and filled with the aroma of flowers. Beneath a tree filled with pink blossoms, a peacock fanned its glorious feathers and strutted around its mate. The hen pecked at the grass, apparently unimpressed.

"Tonight there will be stuffed trout and quail egg tarts," Lady Vicerin told her, smoothing the satin of her long, flowing dress. "You will enjoy it, I think."

Knowing how Fessan suffered in the dungeons below, Elodie doubted she'd enjoy one morsel.

Just as they left the garden to cross the outer courtyard, the castle gates swung open. A horn blasted and four horsemen galloped in.

As they rode straight up to them, Sylva and Lady Vicerin gasped and stepped back.

Lord Vicerin stood his ground, his face pinched with annoyance. "What is the meaning of this?"

The front rider was carrying a passenger: a hooded figure seated awkwardly on the saddle in front of him, its head lolling.

The rider said nothing, merely drew back the hood.

Now it was Elodie's turn to gasp. The face that was revealed belonged to a young man, just a few years older than her. His face was gray except for two hectic spots of red on his cheeks. He was achingly familiar.

"Cedric!" she cried.

By now the other riders had dismounted. Taking great care, they lifted Cedric down from the saddle. Though the boy's eyes were open, he seemed unaware of what was happening to him.

They brought Cedric's feet to the ground. As they held him upright, Cedric's cloak fell open, revealing his right arm. It was bandaged at the elbow.

Below the bandage there was nothing.

Elodie froze, unable to believe what she was seeing. *This can't be happening. It just can't!*

Cedric's forearm had been severed.

Lady Vicerin shrieked and fell to the ground in a dead faint.

"Fetch a healer!" snapped Sylva, stepping over her mother's

prone body and placing her arm gently around her brother's shoulders. "It's all right, Cedric. You're going to be all right."

Elodie wanted to join Sylva, but her feet felt as if they'd taken root. All she could do was stand and watch as Cedric was borne away.

Oh, Cedric. I'm so sorry.

Throughout it all Lord Vicerin stood in silence. When she glanced at him, Elodie saw that his quizzical look had been replaced by something else. It took her a moment to identify the expression. Then, at last, she had it.

Lord Vicerin looked disgusted.

The Room of Healing was situated at the top of a squat tower. The room was round, and although it had no windows, light flooded down from dozens of narrow apertures in the roof. It was quiet here, a place of sanctuary, a place of peace.

Elodie's mind was anything but peaceful. Seated with Lady Vicerin and Sylva beside Cedric's bed, she felt sick. Sick to see Cedric so horribly wounded, and sick that Lord Vicerin had not seen fit to visit, even when the healer had pronounced him close to death.

"I can't believe Father isn't here," Sylva whispered in Elodie's ear. Elodie jumped, startled to hear her own thoughts spoken aloud. "Cedric nearly died fighting in his forsaken war."

"Please, there is no need to whisper," said Lady Vicerin, regarding them both through tearstained eyes. "Oh, my boy. My poor, poor boy." She tightened her grip on Cedric's left hand.

His only hand, thought Elodie with a shudder.

"But why isn't he here?" said Sylva. Was that a note of defiance in her voice? Or just raw emotion?

"Your father is a busy man," said Lady Vicerin defensively. "He will come."

Elodie thought that unlikely. From the look on Sylva's face, it was clear she shared her doubts.

"How is he?" Elodie asked the healer, who had just finished adjusting the fresh bandage she'd wrapped around the stump of Cedric's arm.

"He will sleep," the woman replied gently. She was round and placid; her white apron was immaculate. "I have given him a sleeping draft. Given time, he will recover."

Bowing low, she left the room.

"It breaks my heart that my boy can no longer carry his sword," said Lady Vicerin. "All he ever wanted to do was to honor his father."

Who can't stand to look at him now.

With a flurry of petticoats Lady Vicerin rose to her feet. She bent and kissed Cedric's forehead. "Sleep well, my boy. Heal fast."

As Sylva and Elodie followed her into the corridor, a pair of guards fell into step behind them. Sylva waved them away.

"I will walk with my sister alone," she said.

"But we have orders . . ." the first guard began.

To Elodie's surprise, Lady Vicerin turned on him, her red-rimmed eyes flashing. "Do you refuse my daughter's request?" she snapped. "My son lies broken in that room and you will not let the girls grieve in peace? Get you gone!"

"Of course, my lady," said the second guard hurriedly. With some relief, Elodie watched him hustle his companion away.

Sylva kissed Lady Vicerin's cheek. "Thank you, Mother."

"Do not be late for dinner," said Lady Vicerin. She clutched her handkerchief between both hands. "You know how upset your father gets about such things."

She rustled away. Sylva turned to Elodie.

"I know you want to escape. I could see it in your eyes the minute you arrived. Don't deny it."

Elodie went cold.

So I was right. She did see through me!

"I don't know what you're—" she blustered.

"Elodie, we grew up together. I know you better than anyone. You can't fool me."

Elodie's dress felt tight around her chest.

"I . . . I was trying to fool everyone," she whispered.

To her amazement, a smile flashed briefly on Sylva's rosy face. "You *are* fooling everyone. Everyone except me . . ." Her voice trailed away. She looked suddenly sad. "This isn't the place you were meant to be, Elodie. You're lost here. But you're not alone."

Elodie hitched in a breath, let it out slowly.

"If your brother managed to escape, you can too."

Elodie thought she'd had her day's share of surprises. Now this. "You knew Tarlan was here? But you never said anything about it. I thought . . ."

"Oh, we're all supposed to keep quiet about him, especially around you. My father's very embarrassed about it, you know. Your brother freed a group of children from the dungeons, and as for those giant birds . . . what are they called?"

"Thorrods." Elodie grinned. The thought of Tarlan running rings around Lord Vicerin thrilled her deeply.

"They were spectacular!"

"You should try riding on one."

"Have you done that?" Sylva's eyes grew very wide.

"A couple of times. But Tarlan's the real expert. I can't wait to see him again."

"Nor can I!" Now Sylva's eyes were blazing.

"What do you mean?" said Elodie, growing serious once more. "Sylva, what are you going to do about me? Aren't you going to tell your parents the truth?"

"Oh, Elodie. Don't you understand? I want to escape too!"

◆ ◆ ◆

Another table. Another meal. Everything different. Everything the same.

They think this castle is the whole world, Elodie thought as the finely dressed ladies and gentlemen took their places along either side of the enormous table. At the head, powdered and proud, sat Lord Vicerin. *They think themselves so important. But it's really such a tiny place. And they are so small.*

Six servants placed an array of silver trays on the table. Each was filled with nests of pastry containing tiny hard-boiled eggs, no bigger than her thumbnail. The guests oohed their appreciation, while Elodie judged that this first dish in the nine-course meal to come would have fed half the men in the Trident camp.

But before the staff could begin serving, the big doors at the end of the dining hall crashed open. A grizzled man strode in, his gaunt face all but obscured by a long, ragged beard. His tattered furs swayed as he walked, his enormous boots thudding on the polished floor.

The guests shifted uneasily in their seats. Several of the women pressed their napkins to their mouths. Lord Vicerin's expression folded into a frown.

As the man made for the head of the table, a guard scurried in after him.

"Come back, you! Sorry, my lord. Begging your pardon. I told him to wait, but he just—"

"What is the meaning of this?" said Lord Vicerin, rising to his feet.

The visitor stopped just short of the table. He stood, feet planted wide, his big hands curled at his sides. Elodie got the impression that, beneath his furs, his body was as thin as his face. Yet he seemed to emanate strength.

"Oy, you! On your knees!" said the guard, drawing his sword. But Lord Vicerin lifted his hand and waved him back.

"I am not accustomed to seeing such a filthy specimen in my banqueting hall. I demand that you tell me who you are."

The man said nothing, simply glowered. Titters ran down the length of the table.

Warming to his performance, Lord Vicerin stepped away from his chair and began to circle the newcomer—though Elodie noticed he made sure to keep out of striking range.

"What are you, I wonder? A traveling bard, perhaps? Have you come to tell us a story? Or perhaps sing us a song? You'll need a tongue for that, of course. But, oh, it seems you have forgotten where your tongue is."

The titters turned to laughter. One of the diners, bolder than the rest, lobbed a piece of bread at the man. It bounced off his head and landed on the floor. Several people applauded.

Looking closer, Elodie saw that the man's eyes had a dazed look about them. And those big hands were trembling slightly.

Strong but thin, and unimaginably weary. What trials had he suffered?

And why are you here?

"I do have a story," said the man. His voice was cracked, as if he hadn't used it for a very long time. As he spoke, the laughter died away. "You may know it, Lord Vicerin. Or part of it, at least."

"I do not think—" Lord Vicerin began.

"Once I was an Eye. An Eye of Idilliam. You know of the Eyes, I think, my lord—rangers under the command of King Brutan. We traveled far and wide throughout the kingdom, seeking out those who caused unrest and . . . suppressing them."

"Look, my man, I really do not—"

"Those were difficult times." The man's voice grew deeper as he spoke, losing some of its hoarseness. His eyes brightened. "We were busy men. Very busy. Then a rumor came to Brutan. A rumor of a birth, of triplets born in the realm of Isur. Brutan's first thought was of the prophecy and so, even though no new stars appeared in the sky, he feared for his life."

Elodie sat forward, listening intently, for this was a story entwined closely with her own.

"This is all very interesting," said Lord Vicerin, "but neither I nor my guests wish to listen to your ramblings."

From the guests' fascinated expressions, Elodie could see that wasn't true. Despite this, Vicerin waved the guard forward.

"Wait," said a voice. "I would hear his story."

To Elodie's amazement, the speaker was Lady Vicerin. Had she ever challenged her husband in public before? Elodie couldn't remember a single time. Perhaps Cedric's misfortune had woken her up at last.

"My dear," said Lord Vicerin. "I do not believe it is appropriate to—"

"Let him speak," Lady Vicerin replied with a tight and haughty smile. "He is no bard, but his story is of interest."

Lord Vicerin's eyes flashed with rage. Nevertheless, he stopped the guard in his tracks. "Finish your sorry tale," he snapped. "Then I will show you what I do with uninvited guests."

If the man was intimidated, he didn't show it. "Brutan lived his whole life in fear of the prophecy. Whenever he heard rumors of a new birth, he sent out his Eyes to investigate. This time he changed his orders to match the depth of his terror. He commanded us to kill every newborn child we found."

A woman gasped. Lord Vicerin's frown deepened. Elodie suppressed a shudder.

"I am pleased to say I refused to carry out my orders." The man sighed heavily. "How could I commit such an atrocity? As for my colleagues . . . alas, they were not so squeamish. The first village they came to, they found me waiting for them." He paused. "They did not leave that village alive."

"Is that the end of your tale?" said Lady Vicerin. "I do not believe it is."

"There is a little more, my lady. Years later the prophecy finally came true. Triplets were born to King Brutan, and the three stars appeared in the sky. They hang there still, as you all must know. But before Brutan could kill the newborns, they were handed over to trusted guardians and carried to places of safety. The wizard Melchior did this."

The man paused again. He pressed his trembling hands to his face, then dropped them once more to his sides.

"I was one of those guardians."

Gasps rose from the listening guests. Elodie would have gasped too, only she couldn't breathe. Across the table, Sylva's normally red cheeks had turned deathly pale. Lord Vicerin had stiffened, his face an unreadable mask.

You looked after one of my brothers! Was it Tarlan or Gulph? By the stars, you were there on the night we were born. You were there!

"Captain Leom," said Lord Vicerin slowly. Faint pink glowed through the powder on his cheeks. "I thought you were dead! If only I had known it was you!"

The man—Captain Leom—regarded Lord Vicerin solemnly. "Thirteen years shut inside a cave changes a man."

"A cave?" said Lord Vicerin.

"I took the child to Yalasti. I myself had grown up there, and I planned to hide him in my home village. Yalasti is cold and remote, and would have been far enough from Brutan's grasp for us to be safe."

"What happened?"

"Just short of the village, I was attacked by Helkrags—vicious barbarians who track herds of elk. I took to my horse and fled. I thought I'd evaded them, only to find they'd surrounded me. There was no hope of escape. I wrapped the child in my cloak and hid him behind a snowdrift, near the track used by the villagers to forage in the woods. I hoped someone would hear his cries and find him."

"You abandoned a baby?" said Lady Vicerin.

Captain Leom glared at her, the new brightness in his eyes turning briefly to fire. "Given what the Helkrags would have done to him, it was the only choice I had."

Tarlan, Elodie thought. *This is Tarlan's story. He still has that cloak!*

One glance across the table informed her that Sylva had made the connection too. Lord Vicerin was shifting uneasily, his brow starting to glisten through the powder.

No wonder you're worried. What would happen if Leom found out you kept Tarlan prisoner here?

"The Helkrags captured me. They . . . they tortured me, forcing me to give up my ranger knowledge: knowledge of hidden paths, of the secret alliances between rival tribes. How to survive the Yalasti winter, which normally forces even men like themselves into hiding."

"How did you escape?" Lord Vicerin's eyes darted around the room. Elodie knew that, with so many people watching and listening, he had to keep up a semblance of politeness. She suspected that all he wanted to do was run Leom through with a sword. "After a long time, the Helkrags moved me from the cave to an ice fort. We hadn't been there long before they had some kind of squabble with a rival tribe who'd killed a thorrod. The squabble turned into a full-blown battle. In the chaos, I managed to steal a sword and fight my way to freedom. . . ."

Captain Leom's voice trailed off. He turned his head up to the ceiling and half raised one of his shaking hands.

"I saw a boy. I saw a boy rising up out of the burning fort. He was flying, riding on a thorrod, and flanked by two others. His hair was red-gold, just like the baby I'd left in the woods, all those years before. And I knew it was him. Don't ask me how. I just knew."

Captain Leom lowered his hand again. His audience listened in silence.

"I tracked the thorrods as best I could. But I lost the trail in the Icy Wastes. Still I forged on, and now here I am in Ritherlee. Lord Vicerin, you were ever an ally of the good-hearted, and no friend to King Brutan. That is why I come to you now, for succor and shelter. For a chance to regain my strength and pick up the boy's trail once more. He is the future king, you see, and he will need good men to stand beside him in the fight to come."

These last words came out in a kind of gasp. As he spoke them, Captain Leom staggered sideways, and his face drew down in a rictus of pain.

"Fetch him a chair," said Lady Vicerin. "Before he falls over. And something to drink."

Lord Vicerin snapped his fingers. A servant brought an ornate golden chair and deposited it immediately behind the hulking, fur-clad captain. Leom sat with a grunt, scattering dirt and smearing grime on the chair's fine velvet cushions.

Elodie wanted to cry out to him, to tell him that the boy really had been Tarlan, that the baby he'd saved was alive and well, and back with the wizard Melchior. But doing so would betray her true allegiance.

Maybe later I can speak to him alone. Not now.

A second servant handed Captain Leom a goblet, but the man's trembling fingers betrayed him before he could take a drop. The goblet fell to the floor, spilling the wine it had contained. Nobody moved to help him.

Elodie couldn't contain herself. Springing to her feet, she grabbed another goblet from the table and took it to Captain Leom. Holding it gently to his lips, she helped him drink. Half the wine soaked into his bushy beard, but the rest went into his mouth.

He nodded his thanks. Then his gaze fell on Elodie's hair. He stared, his eyes slowly widening.

"Can it be true?" he said at last. "Are you . . . ? Have I lost one of the three only to find another?"

Something cold wrapped itself around Elodie's fingers. It was Lord Vicerin's hand. It took all her willpower not to recoil.

"It is true," said Lord Vicerin smoothly. "We take great care to protect our princess. Is that not so, Elodie, my dear?"

"Yes, Father," Elodie replied through gritted teeth.

Her revulsion increased as Lord Vicerin brought his lips close to her ear. "Forgive me, my child," he whispered so only she could hear. His breath was unspeakably hot and damp. "It appears that at least one of your brothers is still alive. Your place as queen is assured, naturally, but we will endeavor to find the boy and keep him safe. Just as we keep you safe."

Elodie couldn't speak, so she just nodded and gave him what she hoped was a meek-looking smile.

"Your story is a remarkable one, Captain Leom," said Lord Vicerin, stepping away from Elodie and pitching his voice so that the whole room could hear. "And you are a remarkable man. I am glad you have come to seek sanctuary at Castle Vicerin, and I will do everything in my power to find this lost boy."

"Thank you, my lord," said Captain Leom, bowing his head.

"This boy," Lord Vicerin went on. "Yes, this lost boy. I worry about his fate. Certainly there have been no sightings of such a boy in Ritherlee, nor of these three thorrods—such birds certainly could not be missed, even by the most dull-eyed lookout!"

The other diners chuckled knowingly at this. Elodie guessed that at least half of them must have known he was lying. Lord Vicerin drank in the appreciation with a shrug and a wave. Elodie resisted the urge to kick him in the shins.

"As a mark of my respect for you, Captain Leom, I propose a rescue mission. It will leave for Yalasti immediately, first to defeat these barbaric Helkrags, and second to pick up the boy's trail. We have our princess. Soon we will also have our prince!"

This provoked cheers from the audience and a grateful smile from the weary Captain Leom. But Elodie could only wonder at the speed with which Lord Vicerin had switched from unguarded suspicion of this travel-worn guest to wholehearted support of his cause.

And puzzle over the fact that none of what he'd just said made any sense.

You've only just brought me back from the forests of Isur. You know that Tarlan must still be somewhere up there. So why send men to Yalasti? What are you really up to, Vicerin?

CHAPTER 14

W e're leaving," said Gulph. "Right now."

Ossilius regarded him, bleary-eyed. "What's the matter, Gulph? It's the middle of the night."

"There's no night in Celestis and you know it."

"The clock says it is time to sleep. Go back to bed, Gulph."

The clock stood on the other side of the dormitory they shared, a delicate construction of pipes and pulleys. Silver water dripped steadily into little waterwheels, which spun to power a slowly turning needle that marked off the hours.

According to the water clock, it was the middle of the night. But outside the window there was only the same drab twilight in which Celestis was perpetually smothered.

"I can't sleep. Ossilius, my friends are up there in Idilliam. Brutan's got them in his clutches, I know it. I've got to help them."

Ossilius propped himself up. He poured himself a goblet of wine from the jug on the nightstand and sipped it slowly, rubbing his eyes. "She says we must stay. The woman. What is her name again?"

"Lady Redina? I don't care what she says. If we can rescue the others and bring them down here, she'll have to let them stay. It would be too cruel to turn them away."

Ossilius frowned. "Remind me who these friends of yours are again, Gulph."

"Wake up, Ossilius! I'm talking about the Tangletree Players. Surely you haven't"—he stared at his friend, comprehension slowly dawning—"forgotten?"

The blank look on Ossilius's face told him everything he needed to know.

"You don't remember them, do you?" Gulph said dully.

"Remember who?" Ossilius drained his goblet and poured himself another. "Won't you take a drink, Gulph? It's really very mild."

"Never mind the wine . . ." Gulph began to say, then stopped. Understanding crashed down on him like an avalanche. "The wine!"

He knocked the goblet from Ossilius's hand. It flew across the dormitory, spraying red wine across the floor, and landed with a clatter in the far corner.

"Don't drink it! It's poison!"

Ossilius's eyes were dull. "What are you talking about? It tastes very fine."

"Never mind what it tastes like! I'm the only one who hasn't touched that stuff, and I'm the only one who hasn't started forgetting!" Gulph grabbed the jug and tipped the contents into the washstand, the liquid gurgling away. "Ossilius, you can't drink another drop. If you do, you'll never want to go home again."

Ossilius gave him a quizzical look. "But I am home."

"No." Gulph shook his head, denying not only Ossilius's words but the whole dreadful mess. "You've got to come with me. Let's go now. By the time we get to Idilliam, your memory will have come back."

I hope so, anyway.

"I'm tired," said Ossilius. "You must be too. Stop imagining things and go back to bed. Everything will seem clearer in the morning."

Gulph was about to protest, then thought better of it. "All right, Ossilius. Maybe that's for the best."

He crossed the dormitory to his bed. But he didn't get under the covers, just sat there, waiting. When Ossilius began to snore, Gulph picked up the bundle of clothes and food he'd gathered together earlier, and tiptoed out of the room.

First I'll find my friends, he thought. *Then I'll come back for you and Sidebottom John. My mother, too.*

Outside the house, he paused to check his bundle was wrapped tightly enough. On one side he'd improvised a pouch to hold his crown. As he touched its gold rim, he wondered if he was doing the right thing.

What if they make me undead? What if Brutan gets his hands on the crown again?

But he couldn't leave it here. It was part of him now.

Where the crown goes, I go.

Gulph crept along the path toward the lake. He was confident he could steal a boat without anyone seeing. *If I have to, I'll just turn myself invisible.* But what about when he'd paddled it to the crystal column that supported the ceiling? Climbing the column was one thing; reaching the crack through which he and his companions had fallen was quite another.

I'll be hanging upside down, like a spider. And if I lose my grip . . .

He shivered as he remembered his plummet into the cold water, how he'd nearly drowned as he fought his way to the surface. He realized now how lucky they'd been to be picked up so quickly by the couple in the boat. If they'd stayed in the water much longer, they might have encountered something far more dangerous.

The bakaliss!

He reached the shore. The silver water stretched before him, a smooth mirror reflecting the scintillating purple of the crystal ceiling. It looked as beautiful as it was perilous.

Several narrow-hulled boats were moored nearby. Gulph was halfway to the nearest one when a cloaked figure advanced out of the shadows. He backtracked, but the figure darted forward with uncanny speed and grabbed his elbow.

With a toss of its head, the figure threw back its hood, revealing a familiar scarred face and mane of red-gold hair.

"Mother!" he blurted.

"Don't call me that," said Kalia. "And what are you doing here? The lake is dangerous."

"I . . . I couldn't sleep. I thought a walk might help."

"You are lying." His mother's tone was matter-of-fact. "I am not surprised you want to leave Celestis. Your friends are in danger and you want to help them. I understand. You are brave—I saw that when you were faced with the undead ones. You will need that bravery if you are to defy the command of Lady Redina."

"How do you . . . ?"

"Hush. We have things to discuss, but not here. Come with me."

"But I . . ."

"Come."

Gulph followed her wordlessly as she led him along the shore to a small house made of yellow crystal. He felt confused and thrilled in equal measure. How did she know so much about him? Could he trust her? What did she want to talk about?

Shining through all these dark doubts was a single, brilliant thought:

She's my mother!

Kalia's home was small and cramped. Candles burned in alcoves set into the walls. The crystal magnified their light, so that the whole interior was filled with a cascade of flaming yellow. More alcoves contained jars and bottles. In the middle of the floor, a small black cauldron hung over the embers of a fire. It was half-full of a thick, green broth.

The home of a witch!

Kalia busied herself with the fire, adding more kindling and blowing on the embers until fresh flames burst forth. She seemed to have forgotten Gulph was there.

"Uh, what did you want to talk about?" he said at last.

"Be patient," the witch replied.

Gulph circled the little room, restraining the urge to touch everything. Kalia bustled to and fro, snatching jars from the walls and emptying their contents into the cauldron. To Gulph's surprise, most of the jars contained not liquid but sand of many colors.

In the flickering light—and despite the burn scars—Kalia's face looked very soft and very beautiful. Gulph thought about all the years they'd spent apart, and his heart ached.

If only I'd known you then. And if only you knew me now.

Soon the fire was ablaze. The heat was immense, and sweat broke out on Gulph's face. The sweet-smelling stuff in the cauldron started to bubble.

Kalia rummaged in a box and brought out a short crystal sword.

The blade was gray and dull. She dipped it into the cauldron and brought it out dripping.

"This quickens the blade." She thrust the sword into the fire. "And this binds the potion."

She held the sword in the flames for a moment, then handed it to Gulph. He took it hesitantly, expecting the hilt to be hot. Instead it was icy cold.

"Brave you may be," said Kalia, "but bravery alone will not defeat the undead. This blade will."

Gulph swung the sword experimentally. He fancied he could hear the blade hiss as it moved through the air. "Is this like the sword you used the other day?"

Kalia nodded. "Like yours, my blade is bewitched." She handed Gulph a belt from which hung a thick leather sheath. He put it on and slipped the sword inside.

"I can't believe you're not going to stop me leaving."

"Why would I do that?"

"But why would you help me?"

Kalia's hand closed on his wrist. "Because I want you to come back. You have a good heart—I can see it."

Before he knew what he was doing, Gulph had wrapped his arms around her and was hugging her tight, putting all the lost years into that embrace. When he let go, he realized that his cheeks were wet with tears.

Kalia laughed—a rich, tinkling sound.

"If I did have a son, I would wish him to be like you."

You do. And he is.

Gulph wiped his face with the sleeve of his tunic.

"I wish I knew why you cry so."

"And I wish—" he began, only to have Kalia cut him off briskly.

"No more words. There isn't time. What you wish is to go, and go you must. Now."

Before Gulph knew it, she'd bustled him out into the endless Celestian twilight.

"Go back to the shore. Take the first boat you find. Go with my blessing, boy. And make sure you return!"

Feeling a little dazed, Gulph trotted back toward the silver lake. All the way there, he kept his hand resting lightly on the hilt of the sword Kalia had given him.

His fingers fumbled as he untied the boat from its mooring. He clambered into its narrow hull and picked up the long pole that was lying there. Standing precariously, he held the pole over the side of the boat and let it slide down through his fingers. When he felt it hit the lake bed, he pushed backward, trying to imitate the smooth, rolling motion used by the man and woman who'd rescued them.

The boat slipped silently out onto the flat, silver water. Gaining confidence in his technique, Gulph worked his arms slowly and steadily, counting as he went, and hoped nobody was watching.

When he'd worked the pole one hundred times, he glanced back over his shoulder. The island had shrunk to a mere outcrop of crystal.

Looking ahead once more, he located the pillar of blue crystal he'd identified as offering the best escape route. It was thick at the base and narrowed to a slender waist before flaring wide again where it met the ceiling. The closer he came to the pillar, the more daunting was the prospect of climbing it.

I must be crazy, he thought.

He put both hands back on the pole, but just as he began to push down on it, a wave rolled out of the twilight and slapped the hull. The boat rocked sideways. By now the pole was slippery with water along most of its length, and Gulph lost his grip. He clawed desperately as it slithered through his fingers, and watched in despair as it toppled over the side and vanished underwater.

Crouching, he grabbed the side of the boat and peered into the water. The pole was nowhere to be seen. He searched the boat for some other means of propulsion—a paddle, perhaps—but in vain.

Gradually the rocking subsided. Gulph slumped in the back of the boat, staring at the crystal pillar. He'd made good progress across the lake, but he was still only halfway there. And now he was marooned.

His despair turned to fear as a new thought rose up to haunt him.

What caused the wave?

Forgetting the pole, he leaned once more over the edge of the boat. The old story whirled around his head.

The bakaliss killed the king . . . the bakaliss killed the king . . .

Would he see the bakaliss coming? Where did it live? Did it have a lair, some underwater cave? Or did it spend its time swimming just below the surface, waiting to drag its next victim into the deep?

The boat's hull was as slimy as the pole, and Gulph's hand slipped momentarily overboard and into the water. He jerked it back at once, but not before he'd glimpsed something.

A face? Was it a face, looking up at me?

He scolded himself. He'd seen nothing but his own reflection, and his overheated imagination had done the rest.

But it didn't look like me.

Tentatively, he dipped his fingers in the water again. The face appeared once more: the face of a boy, gazing up at him with intense, black eyes. His hair was a wild mane of red-gold that reached down to his shoulders.

Exactly like my mother's hair. And the same color as mine.

Gulph's heart was racing. The water lapped against his fingers. He stared deep into those coal-black eyes. He knew this boy. This boy was . . .

. . . my brother!

With a start Gulph realized he'd seen him before.

The battle. The giant bird. You were riding on the giant bird. It flew past when my father was coming for me.

Our father.

The face began to move. The eyebrows rose and fell; the mouth opened and closed. The semblance of life was startling. Gulph submerged his hand completely, reaching for his brother, wanting after all these lost years to make contact with someone who might know him, might remember him, might love him. . . .

The image splintered like a broken mirror.

Something bright red burst from the lake's shattered surface: a climbing, writhing wall of scales that reared up and over Gulph's head. It hung over him, dripping silver water, then smashed down onto the boat like a huge ruby hammer.

The impact catapulted Gulph into the air and turned the boat to splinters. As he flew he flung out his arms, controlling his tumble, but there was no avoiding the landing. He splashed down headfirst and the silver waters swallowed him.

He sank deep, grimacing as the water pressed into his ears. Thrashing, he pulled his way back toward the surface, but not before he'd glimpsed the red shape sliding past beneath him. Now it wasn't a hammer but a snake. It moved with sinuous grace, massive muscles flexing easily beneath its scaly skin. A forest of sharp orange quills sprouted from its back, waving in the current like lethal seaweed.

Gulph couldn't see its head. He didn't need to. He knew exactly what it was.

The bakaliss!

He broke the surface and began to tread water, looking frantically around in all directions.

Two breaths later a knot of red coils erupted from the depths, just a stone's throw away. The coils untangled, revealing long reptilian jaws lined with teeth that looked more like curved blades. Above the bakaliss's orange snout hung two enormous, colorless eyes. They had no pupils; they were pale and dull, like the eyes of a corpse.

The beast started gliding toward him, jaws agape. Waves grew around it. The silver water surged into its mouth, streaming out through a complex set of gills sitting just below its eyes. To Gulph those gills looked like slashes made by the claws of the world's biggest bear. Kicking his legs frantically to keep afloat, he fumbled for Kalia's sword. It had power over the undead. Could it help him against this monster?

But a splinter of wood from the smashed boat had wedged itself between the sword and its scabbard, jamming it in place. As he struggled to free the blade, his head dropped below the waves. He lunged upward, spitting out water with an anguished cry.

The bakaliss came on. Now Gulph could see every scale on its streamlined snout, every scratch on every tooth in its gaping mouth.

Its eyes were vast and bland and uncaring, empty holes into which he might fall . . .

Panic seized him. Water splashed once more into his mouth; once more he spat it out, marveling at how hot it was. Everything was hot. This wasn't a lake—it was a cauldron.

Mother's magic, he thought incoherently.

Gulph saw his hands turn translucent. For an instant they looked like crystal. Then they were invisible.

Not her magic! Mine!

The bakaliss was almost upon him. Was that confusion in its big, blank eyes? Impossible to tell.

Get away, get away, get away!

Gulph rolled onto his front, was about to thrash his way clear, changed his mind.

The more I thrash, the more I splash, he thought, suppressing hysterical laughter that was an eye blink short of madness.

Slowly, screaming silently inside, he paddled his way sideways, sliding out of the path of the oncoming bakaliss, careful not to raise a single ripple in the silver water. Out of the corner of his eye, he saw the monster first hesitate, then halt. It swung its massive neck back and forth like a scaly pendulum.

Gulph swam on, not breathing, panic burning him as the sun burns the desert.

From behind him came a gargling groan, then an unspeakable

sniffing that sounded more like grinding machinery than anything living. Warm wind sucked at the back of Gulph's head.

He immersed himself deeper into his own internal heat and kept paddling.

The lake's surface grew calmer. Gulph swam on, not daring to look back. Again he heard those dreadful, clattering sniffs. Another groan. A hissing noise, and a soft splash.

Now the water was mirror flat. Still he kept going, moving his arms and legs smoothly in a slow, steady rhythm that belied the terror still gripping his thoughts.

Don't look back, he kept telling himself. *Whatever you do, don't look back.*

In the end, of course, he did.

The bakaliss was gone.

Not trusting his eyes, Gulph continued to swim. Was the beast below him, waiting for the perfect moment to rise up and tear him to pieces? Was it behind him, tracking his every move, ready to bite him in half? Or was it ahead, poised to rear out of the water with its jaws split wide and swallow him whole?

His left hand touched something hard and cold. He bit back a scream, then saw it was a shelf of blue crystal.

The pillar!

He hauled himself out of the water and onto the tiny ledge at the base of the pillar, slithering like an eel and trying to make as little noise as possible. He was becoming visible again; the realization brought relief as he gradually began to accept the idea that he was safe.

Clinging to the pillar, he looked back across the lake. The crystal island on which the Celestians lived—and where his companions still slept—was a distant pebble. The cavern ceiling was an immense twilit sky dusted with sparkling points of light.

Of the bakaliss there was no sign at all. It had vanished, just as if it had never been there.

His heart slowing at last, Gulph turned his back on the silver Celestian lake and began to climb.

CHAPTER 15

Cedric? Are you all right?"

Elodie spurred Huntress—one of her favorite mares from the Vicerin stables—until they were trotting alongside Cedric's mount. He was slumped in the saddle. The rain, which had been falling all day, had plastered his dark hair to his head. Elodie didn't like his chalky complexion or the red rings under his eyes.

"I'm fine," Cedric replied. His voice wavered. Momentarily he let go of his reins to cradle the stump of his arm.

"I'll ride with you."

"You don't have to do that."

"I want to."

They rode side by side in silence for a while, heads bent beneath the rain. Elodie wished Samial was sitting behind her, but he was back at the castle, finding out what he could about Fessan.

The convoy stretched along the muddy road as far as Elodie could see, both in front and behind. It comprised one-quarter of the Vicerin army—both foot soldiers and cavalry—supported by a seemingly endless train of supply wagons.

The wagons were draped with thick furs. Beneath these, pouches of animal fat had been laced together to form insulating quilts. Squat chimneys jutted from their roofs, ready to carry away the smoke from the big braziers within. At the moment the braziers weren't lit.

When the wagons entered the Icy Wastes, they would be ablaze.

"They look like bears with wheels," Elodie said in an effort to raise Cedric's spirits.

"They look ridiculous," Cedric replied.

"At least they'll keep the soldiers warm."

"They still look ridiculous."

Elodie gave up.

The convoy crested a low hill. A village came into view. It was the fifth they'd passed since setting out from the castle. *"This will be a victory parade,"* Lord Vicerin had reminded Elodie as they'd passed through the gates, *"so be sure to hold your head high."*

As they entered the village, the standard-bearers raised the blue Vicerin flags. The village—Elodie didn't know its name—looked deserted. Burned buildings sagged in the rain; a dog slunk through the empty main street; fearful faces peered from behind broken doors.

This doesn't feel much like victory to me.

There was a stack of bodies beside one building. Elodie had seen such piles before, but the sight of it still took her breath away. So many dead, all of them awaiting burial. The war was spoken of with such casual ease in Castle Vicerin, yet here was the shocking reality.

Cedric was shaking.

"Are you all right?" Elodie asked again. "What is it?"

Sylva rode up, flanking her brother on the other side. She reached out a hand and steadied him, clearly afraid he would fall from his horse.

"I was here." Cedric's eyes were glassy.

"What?" said Elodie.

"Becktown. This is Becktown. Part of the Farrier estate. This is where I was . . . where I lost my . . ."

He teetered in his saddle. He looked as if he was going to be sick.

"This is all wrong," said Elodie. "How much longer before we reach Castle Darrand?"

"I don't know," said Sylva. "We're not exactly galloping along. And with all these stops to show off Father's power, we're moving even more slowly. A day. Maybe two."

Elodie calculated. The convoy's first destination—having meandered its way in supposedly glorious fashion through the outlying villages of Ritherlee—was supposed to be the castle of Lady Darrand. Once there, the plan was to make camp for a single night, arraying the Vicerin flags and weapons on the field before their enemy. A show of strength, Lord Vicerin had said.

A show of stupidity, more like.

After that—and assuming Lady Darrand didn't unleash her own army upon them—the convoy would break in two. Sergeant Stown would lead the insulated wagons south to the Icy Wastes, on a mission to defeat the Helkrags and find Elodie's brother.

As if that's going to happen, when Tarlan is far to the north in Isur.

A thought occurred to Elodie.

Why Stown? Why didn't they wait until Captain Leom could lead the convoy? He's the only one who knows Yalasti and the Icy Wastes.

Leom had been given chambers in the castle, where he was recovering from a fever brought on by his ordeal. The healers said he would be well in a few days. Surely the mission could have been delayed until then.

What doesn't Vicerin want Leom to see?

Lady Vicerin had stayed behind too, also complaining of sickness. That was less surprising. Elodie couldn't imagine her giving up even a few days of luxury for a forced march on a muddy road. While Stown led the convoy onward, Captain Gandrell would lead the remainder— which included Lord Vicerin, as well as Cedric, Sylva, and Elodie—to rejoin her at Castle Vicerin.

Up ahead, a large gray stallion broke formation and trotted back to join them. On its back rode Lord Vicerin.

"I trust that all is well?" He eyed Cedric with unguarded suspicion.

Cedric's face contorted as he straightened his back and sat upright in his saddle. Elodie clenched her fists. She wanted to shout at Lord Vicerin, tell him to leave Cedric alone. But if she gave him any cause to suspect her loyalties, she would be unmasked.

"I have been wondering," Lord Vicerin went on. He opened his arms, taking in the tremendous length of the army convoy. "Which unit is it that you plan to join?"

"I . . . I don't know, Father."

Elodie's heart went cold. Surely Lord Vicerin didn't expect his son to go all the way to the Icy Wastes? The lad could barely stay on his horse, let alone carry a weapon.

"Come, come," said Lord Vicerin. "There are so many to choose from."

Cedric stared dumbly at the line of marching men and horses. He looked lost and afraid. Elodie followed his gaze, for the first time fully appreciating the enormous scale of this operation.

How many soldiers can be left at the castle? Surely no more than a handful.

Then a thrilling realization came to her. Castle Vicerin was practically unguarded.

This is my chance. . . .

"Sylva?" she said, pitching her voice loud enough to override Lord Vicerin's blather. At the same time she slipped her feet out of her stirrups. "I don't . . . I don't feel very . . ."

With a theatrical groan, she allowed herself to slither from her saddle. The muddy ground rushed up toward her. She resisted the urge to stiffen her body against the coming blow.

This is going to hurt!

It wasn't as bad as she'd expected. She landed on her side in a puddle, the impact knocking all the breath from her lungs. Filthy water splashed over her, splattering her face and ruining her fine silk riding breeches.

"Elodie!" Sylva was off her horse in an instant. She knelt in the mud and pressed her hands to Elodie's face. "Are you all right? What's wrong?"

Elodie moaned, but didn't open her eyes. She kept her body limp.

More voices joined Sylva's. The commotion grew around her. Elodie kept her eyes shut.

"Give the girl room to breathe." That was Captain Gandrell, if she wasn't mistaken.

"Elodie . . ." said a thin, plaintive voice that could only belong to Cedric.

Wait . . . wait . . .

"Will none of you imbeciles help my daughter?" Lord Vicerin's reedy cry cut through the babble.

Fluttering her eyelashes, Elodie lifted her head out of the mud and made a feeble attempt to stand. Sylva's hands, strong and comforting, held her down.

"Wait for the dizziness to pass," she said.

Elodie stared at the circle of faces gazing down at her, their expressions ranging from concern to fear. She found Lord Vicerin's. The rain had washed most of the powder from his cheeks; the skin beneath was so pale it was practically white.

"I'm sorry, Father," she said. "It was seeing all those bodies. I just . . . I couldn't bear it."

Lord Vicerin produced a fan shaped like a butterfly and wafted it in Elodie's face. The flimsy thing only succeeded in spraying her with raindrops, but Elodie endured it without protest. As he fanned, he frowned up at the sky. The sun, making a brief appearance through the rain clouds, was beginning to sink toward the west.

"We must get you to shelter, my dear. Do you think you can ride?"

"I think so. It's just . . ." Elodie crumpled her face and pretended to cry. *With all this rain, nobody will spot that there aren't any tears.*

"I don't think I can go on. I can't face any more of this . . . this awfulness."

Peeking out through half-closed lids, she noted Lord Vicerin's brief show of frustration before he assembled his features into a mask of concern. Then, finally, he said the words she'd been waiting to hear.

"Then you must go back to the castle, my dear. An escort will accompany you, of course."

"Will you come with me, Father?"

"Alas, I cannot. I am sworn to accompany my men as far as Castle Darrand. The stand we will make there is vital to morale. You understand, of course."

"Of course." Elodie faked more sobs. "But surely you won't just surround me with soldiers? I need friendly faces too. And f-f-family."

Lord Vicerin's expression softened. "Of course, my dear. Sylva will go with you."

Sylva, still kneeling at Elodie's side, smiled warmly.

"And Cedric!" Elodie blurted.

"Cedric?"

"Of course," said Sylva. "Who better to protect us?"

Oh, Sylva! That's clever!

Lord Vicerin's eyes narrowed as he considered this.

"Very well," he said curtly. He turned to Cedric. "This is no easy ride, boy. Protect your sisters."

"I will do my duty, Father."

To Elodie's delight, for the first time since his return, Cedric was able to meet his father's eye.

The arrangements were swiftly made. Lord Vicerin personally selected twelve horsemen from one of the cavalry regiments, and assigned Captain Gandrell to lead them. As they made ready to depart, Elodie continued to feign wooziness, faltering as she climbed back into Huntress's saddle, and making a show of rubbing her head at regular intervals.

"Are you all right?" said Sylva.

"I'm feeling a lot better," Elodie replied. "Cedric—close your eyes."

"What?" He gave her a puzzled look.

"Close your eyes," she repeated gently. "Then you won't have to see the war. I'll ride beside you and guide your horse. That way it will look as if *you* are guiding *me*."

"I didn't think of that."

He smiled at her, seeming so surprised to be shown kindness that it was all she could do not to cry.

Trotting back along the muddy road, with Captain Gandrell leading, six soldiers ahead and six at the rear, they soon left the convoy behind. As they retraced their steps, the clouds thinned and the sun reappeared, bathing their faces in orange light.

"That feels good," said Elodie. She closed her eyes and drank in the warmth.

"You seem to have made a remarkable recovery," said Sylva. Seeing the knowing smile on her face, Elodie couldn't help but smile herself. "You did it for Cedric, didn't you? Thank you for protecting him."

Elodie turned her face back to the sun. What Sylva said was true. But there was so much more to her plan than that.

Sylva sighed. "I just wish we didn't have to spend another night on the road."

Elodie felt the same. It had taken the convoy two days to reach Becktown by way of winding village tracks. Even if they rode at a steady trot—and took the more direct South Dale road—they wouldn't reach Castle Vicerin before sundown the following day.

But who needs to trot?

Her smile widened into a grin. "Are your stirrups tight? And yours, Cedric?"

They both nodded, looking a little bemused.

"Then we won't be camping tonight! Hie, Huntress! Hie!"

Elodie spurred her horse first to a canter, then a smooth gallop. After a brief pause, Sylva and Cedric followed suit.

They left the rear guard standing and were soon speeding toward Captain Gandrell and the front-runners.

"Princess Elodie!" Gandrell called, but it was too late—they were already past, riding free and clear on the road to the castle.

The wind ruffled Elodie's short hair. For the first time, she wished she hadn't cut it off. How wonderful it would be to feel her red-gold locks streaming behind her like a pennant.

When I'm queen, I'll wear my hair long again. When I'm queen, and not before.

The soldiers soon caught up with them. Riding hard, Captain Gandrell drew alongside Elodie. His gaunt face turned toward hers. Was that the ghost of a smile on his thin lips?

"Are you determined to wear out the horses, Princess?"

"I'm determined to get home, Captain Gandrell."

"I see you are. Will you let me lead?"

"Just as long as you don't get in my way."

"Never, my lady."

And so they rode, sixteen horses galloping into the setting sun, pounding the mud to slush and slowing for neither the rise of a hill nor bends in the road. As the afternoon melted into evening, the rain returned, and Elodie rejoiced at the lash of the water on her face and the bite of the wind, because it reminded her that she was alive.

It was dark by the time they reached the castle. Huntress's black coat was flecked with foam, and she was breathing hard.

"Thank you," Elodie whispered, patting the horse's neck.

They slowed to a trot and passed through the gate, where Elodie spotted Samial. He was loitering in the light of a torch near the doorway that led from the stable yard into the castle, just as if he'd known they were coming.

Elodie reined Huntress to a halt, swung her leg over the saddle, and dismounted. She wanted to run over to Samial and let him know why they were back so soon, but she forced herself to be patient. Captain Gandrell mustn't suspect anything.

The captain leaped down from his own mount. "My men will take care of the horses. I will summon a guard to accompany you to your room."

"I'll probably be *in* my room before the guard gets here. All I want is my bed."

"Very well. Be sure to go straight there." Gandrell's mouth twitched in what was almost a smile. "Please."

If only Lord Vicerin was as easy to manipulate as you, Captain Gandrell.

"I'll go with her," said Sylva, preparing to dismount.

"No," said Elodie. "Don't worry. I'll be fine."

She walked briskly, but not too briskly, toward Samial. Now that she was here, every moment counted, because there was really only one reason she'd forced them to ride so hard.

Hold on, Fessan. I'm coming.

With most of the soldiers gone, this was her best chance of freeing him.

"We need a rescue plan," Elodie whispered as she and Samial

went through the doorway. "Is he still in the water cell?"

But Samial didn't seem to be listening. He was staring intently into the shadows at the end of the passageway.

"Samial, did you hear what I said? Is Fessan—"

"Elodie! Run!"

There was a sudden flurry of movement. The shadows unfolded, became the figure of a man, rushing at her. The man gripped her shoulder and spun her around. Something cold and thin touched her bare neck . . . then bit into it.

The pain was sudden and immense. It was as if a line of fire had been drawn across her throat and was now burning into it. Elodie tried to scream, but no sound came out.

Strangled! I'm being strangled!

She threw up her arms, trying to grab at the head of the man who was throttling her. Her fingers failed to grip his coarse, short hair.

Is this how Palenie felt, when Rotho strangled her to death in the Trident camp?

"Hold on, Elodie!"

Then the thing around her slackened. Pain still seared her neck, but suddenly she could breathe again.

"Witchcraft?" said the man who'd been trying to kill her. His voice was thick and gruff and full of surprise. "What is this?"

Drawing in agonized, rasping breaths, Elodie managed to turn in her attacker's grip. Samial was there, right behind her, his grimy fingers sunk deep into the would-be assassin's throat. The man's eyes bulged.

Then the noose tightened again, and Elodie felt herself slipping into a faint. Perhaps into death.

The knife!

She reached clumsily beneath her cloak. For a moment she thought it was gone. Then she had it: the ornate dagger Lord Vicerin had given her. Her fingers tightened on the hilt and she pulled it from its scabbard. She slashed blindly behind her, stabbing three times before she finally felt the blade sink into flesh. The man howled, his cry cut off by Samial's hands, and the pressure of the noose went away completely.

Clutching at her burning throat, Elodie finally managed to break free. She staggered back down the passageway, only to see Samial thrown against the wall. He slid down it, his eyelids flickering.

The man—a white-faced hulk dressed all in black—looked briefly puzzled as he tried to determine who had attacked him. Then he lunged for Elodie and tried to grapple the dagger from her hand.

As his large fingers closed around her wrist, she finally found the scream she'd been looking for.

The first to reach her was Cedric. He hurled himself at her

attacker. Even as he shouldered the man aside, Captain Gandrell and two of his soldiers fell upon him, dragged him out into the courtyard, and wrestled him to the ground.

Breathing hard, Cedric put his left hand—his only hand—gently on Elodie's shoulder.

"Are you all right?" he said.

Elodie tried to speak, but all she could manage was a wordless croak.

Sylva appeared behind Cedric, her normally rosy complexion turned to the color of chalk.

"Elodie!" She slipped her arm around her waist and hugged her tight. To Elodie's relief, Samial had picked himself up and stood close by, his eyes still wide with shock.

Then Captain Gandrell was there.

"He will be taken to the dungeon," he said, his face more skeletal than ever. "Do you know him, Princess? Is he one of that wretched Trident rabble?"

If not for the pain in her throat, Elodie would have informed him that Trident wasn't a rabble, and that the people he called wretched were her friends. Perhaps it was as well she couldn't speak. Instead she just shrugged.

"I don't think this had anything to do with Trident." Cedric had bent to the ground to pick something up. "Look at this."

Dangling from his fingers was a long strip of leather, thinner than rope, thicker than wire. Each end was capped with a curved handgrip that looked like ivory.

Elodie shuddered. She'd seen a weapon like this before. Rotho had used an identical leather strip to strangle Palenie.

"I know what this is," Cedric went on. "It's a garrote from Galadron. You can tell by the grips—they're carved from sea-wolf tusks."

The leather garrote swung hypnotically back and forth in Cedric's fingers. Elodie watched it sway, fascinated and repulsed by the thing that had almost killed her.

Galadron. The desert land where the sun never sleeps.

It was a phrase she remembered from her lessons. Galadron lay far to the west of Toronia, on the other side of the ocean. Its heart-land was said to be a scorching wasteland of white sand, a place of death and strange magic. Yet its coast was green and fertile, home to many large cities.

This man from Galadron had clearly also seen the empty castle as his opportunity to strike. But why were the Galadronians so intent on assassinating one of the heirs to the throne of Toronia?

Elodie could think of only one reason.

Invasion.

CHAPTER 16

I don't think I can do this much longer."

Tarlan kicked at the smooth surface of the stone platform in frustration, then dropped to his knees. He peered down into the water, willing Melchior to move.

But the wizard remained just as he had for the past few days: stiff and immobile. No breath lifted his chest. His spine was bent backward, his arms were thrust out, his fingers were clawed. His mouth was drawn down in what might have been pain or dread or both. He looked like a man undergoing the worst torture imaginable.

Sometimes, in the wastes of Yalasti, Tarlan had come across animals frozen in the ice. In what passed for the Yalasti summer, a sudden thaw might occasionally create a flash flood that cascaded down the mountain slopes, washing away any unwary creatures caught in its path.

Tarlan remembered a particular hunting trip he'd taken from Mirith's cave. He'd rounded a corner and there it was: a sinuous ice snake of frozen floodwaters, standing twice his height and extending far out of sight both up the mountain and down. Inside its glassy, blue-white confines was a black mountain bear, locked inside forever.

The bear had looked peaceful.

Melchior looked like he was dying.

"It's no good," said Tarlan, leaning down toward the water. "I've got to get him out."

"Wait more," croaked Theeta from behind him.

It took all Tarlan's willpower to stop himself from plunging his hands into the silver pool and dragging Melchior clear.

Oh, Mirith! What must I do?

His hand went to his throat, seeking the green jewel the dying frost witch had given him.

But the jewel wasn't there.

Neither was Mirith.

Mirith may be dead, but Melchior isn't. Not yet. Mirith told me to find him, and now he's told me to wait. Theeta's right. I just have to be patient.

But it was so hard.

He turned his attention back to the dull white stones embedded into the black walls of the crater. Melchior had promised that as his powers returned, the stones would begin to shine, just like the star constellations they represented.

They don't look any different to me.

Feeling glum, he took a strip of dried venison from his pouch and chewed it disconsolately. His supplies were getting low. He'd managed to keep warm at night by nestling with the thorrods, and had stopped his legs seizing up by walking endless circuits around the perimeter of the stone platform. But if he stayed here much longer, he was going to go mad.

Large wings obscured the light filtering down from the crater's mouth, high above, and suddenly Nasheen was there, landing silently beside her two thorrod companions. Concerned for his friends, Tarlan had sent her to check on the members of the pack who hadn't been able to make the journey across the sea to the Isle of Stars.

"Wolf moved," Nasheen said in her scratchy voice. "Tigron moved. Bear moved."

"They've moved? Moved where?"

The short feathers on Nasheen's brow flexed into something resembling a frown. This was quite a speech for a thorrod.

"Not sand. In trees."

Tarlan nodded in satisfaction. So they'd taken cover in the thin strip of woodland flanking the beach. That was smart. They'd be safe there.

He looked back at the pattern of white stones on the wall. Still no change. He sighed. Absently he scratched his hand. The gashes made by Brock when he'd first encountered the bear in his cage had scabbed over, but they were itching terribly. He thrust his hand down into the water, wanting nothing more than to cool the skin.

The itching turned to tingling. Realizing what he'd done, he snatched his hand out of the lake. He looked at the skin, suddenly afraid.

The gashes were gone. Where they'd been, there were no scars.

The water had healed him.

"I don't believe it! Theeta, did you . . . ?"

Turning, he saw his thorrod friend pecking at the bandages on her injured foot. The fabric had come loose during the flight from Isur, and now the angry scar on the stump of her missing talon was clearly visible.

Filled with sudden inspiration, Tarlan called her to the edge of the pool.

"Put your claws in the water," he said.

Theeta clacked her beak nervously. Had he ever known this gigantic bird to be nervous before? Tarlan didn't think so.

"It's all right. It's perfectly safe."

He touched his hand to the tip of her lethal beak.

Slowly, Theeta dipped her injured foot into the pool. She kept it there for a moment. Tarlan held his breath. Then she withdrew it.

The scar was gone. Theeta's stump was smooth with newly polished scales. The talon was still missing, but all signs of infection had vanished.

"Good foot," Theeta cawed.

"Yes!" Tarlan laughed. "Good foot!" He stared around at the blank white stones with renewed hope.

If the water does that to a hand—or a claw—what might it do to a whole body?

What might it do to a wizard?

"Come on!" he shouted at the walls. "Come on! Show me!"

A crash of thunder swallowed his words. The storm had grumbled throughout most of the previous day, so that Tarlan had begun to think that thunder and lightning were normal weather conditions for the Isle of Stars. But this morning he'd woken to find the sky quiet.

Now the storm had come back.

Lightning tore across the top of the crater. Its glare shattered the surface of the silver water, and for a moment Tarlan believed the storm was raging not in the sky but in the hidden depths of the pool.

"We're going to get wet again!" he shouted to the thorrods.

One of the white stones lit up.

Tarlan stared at it slack-jawed. Excitement fizzed through his veins. He thought he heard more thunder, but it was only the sudden pounding of his pulse in his ears.

Another streak of lightning ripped through the sky, through the water. A second stone flashed bright, then a third. Rain began to lash Tarlan's face, but he didn't care.

"Melchior!" he yelled, dancing on the spot. "Melchior!"

The silver water had turned choppy. Was the weather causing it, or something else? Glittering froth obscured his view of the submerged wizard. Had Melchior moved? He couldn't tell.

Thunder roared, then died, leaving a sudden silence in which Tarlan heard a new sound, very faint, very distant.

Somebody shouting.

More thunder. Skeins of lightning crisscrossed the sky. It was as if a giant had cast a net of light over the whole island. Again that eerie calm.

Another white stone winked into life, and another. A pause, then a frantic flurry of light as brilliance burst from one stone and leaped to the next, to the next, to the next. Dazzled and bewildered, Tarlan watched as a hundred stones started to burn, then a thousand, an intricate web of stars blazing from the night-black rock.

Again he heard shouting.

"They come," croaked Theeta.

Tarlan tore his gaze from the stones. "Who? Who comes?"

Theeta shrugged her massive wings. "See not."

Tarlan wanted to shake her. The thorrods were so smart, and yet had no imagination whatsoever.

But incredible ears.

"What do you hear?" He managed to get the question out before the thunder returned.

"Many come! Many cry!"

"Come from where?" asked Tarlan. Apart from the fishing village they'd glimpsed, the beach had been deserted.

"We go!" Theeta threw out her wings. Her black eyes were filled with urgency. Behind her, Kitheen and Nasheen were already in the air.

Torn by indecision, Tarlan hovered at the edge of the pool. Melchior had told him to stay and keep watch. But if Theeta was right—and hadn't he heard the shouts himself?—people were coming.

They mustn't find Melchior.

He raced across the platform and sprang onto Theeta's back.

No sooner had the three thorrods emerged from the crater than the wind picked them up and flung them out over the sea. Fighting to keep hold of the stiff gold feathers encircling Theeta's neck, Tarlan steered her in a rapid circuit of the island. All the way around he peered down through the driving rain.

The island was deserted.

"Where are they, Theeta?" he cried.

"Big wood!" shrieked Nasheen.

She swooped out to sea. Instinctively the other thorrods followed.

Lightning cut through the looming gray clouds, illuminating something enormous wallowing in the storm-tossed waves. Tarlan had never seen anything like it before, but he recognized it all the same.

It's a ship!

Mirith had told him about such things. Wooden constructions much bigger than mere dugout boats. Ships were so big they were like floating villages, self-contained vessels on which people might live for months as they traveled from one side of the ocean to another.

"They have masts," the frost witch had told him, "and sails to catch the wind."

"What are masts?" Tarlan had asked.

"They are like trees."

"And sails?"

"Like the wings of a thorrod."

The ship he saw now was every bit as big as he'd imagined, but the waves tossed it like a piece of driftwood. Tarlan drew in a sharp breath as it veered toward a ridge of toothlike rocks jutting from the water. Then, with a sudden surge, it rushed past them and into the shallows, heading straight for the Toronian shore.

It's going to crash, Tarlan thought. It was close enough now that he could see the bustle of activity on board. The sail furled like a conjurer's trick, the ropes that held it vanishing into the gaping mouths of a row of gargoyles on the ship's outer rail. Sailors in brightly colored robes raced efficiently across its deck, cranking handles and closing hatches.

Not crashing—landing!

"Theeta," he cried. "To the beach!"

Rain stung his face as Theeta swerved, leading the three thorrods around the ship, then dived toward the shore.

They touched down as the ship slid up the sand with a low, hissing sound that set Tarlan's teeth on edge. Just when Tarlan thought it would tip onto its side, two pairs of jointed legs unfolded, their flattened tips splaying on the sand to hold it steady. Now, instead of a ship, it looked like a huge insect.

A wooden walkway lowered from the front of the ship onto the beach. A group of men and women made their way down it. Their brightly colored cloaks were soaked through and tossed about by the wind, but Tarlan could see that they were embroidered with patterns—diamonds and circles, flowers and leaves.

"Not home," cawed Theeta softly.

"You're right," said Tarlan, sliding down her wet flank. The people now staring across the sand at him and the thorrods didn't look like they were from Toronia at all. Mirith had once told him about merchants who traveled from land to land, ships laden with goods for sale. *That must be why they're here*, he decided. *As long as they stay away from the Isle of Stars, that's all that matters.*

He strode to meet them.

"You won't find much trade here," Tarlan called. He held his arms wide, gesturing at the empty beach.

The men and women halted a few paces away from him.

"Trade?" said a broad-shouldered man with a neat beard and a bald head. He wore a long red cloak. "We don't come to trade, boy. We come to take."

Tarlan frowned. "Take what?"

"Toronia."

Tarlan stared at him, stunned. He shook his head. "You can't be serious."

A woman in a grass-green cloak gave him a strange smile. "Galadron can conquer anywhere. The reach of our empress is long."

Tarlan gave a snort of disbelief. *They're fools*, he thought. There couldn't be more than twenty of them on the beach; his pack could take them out in moments.

"Well, you won't get far," he said. "First you'll have to get past Lord Vicerin's forces in Ritherlee. Before you can take Isur you'll have to defeat an army called Trident. Oh, and did you know that Idilliam is overrun by an army of walking corpses, with the undead king Brutan in command? If I were you, I'd turn around now and go back to . . . where was it you said you were from?"

"Galadron," said the woman in green.

"Galadron." Tarlan tried out the strange syllables. "Where's that?"

"Across the seas." The woman crouched and scooped up a handful of sand. "But soon this land will be Galadron too."

The man in the red cloak scowled. "Enough, Lieutenant Dryssa," he snapped. "We don't have time to stand here listening to this filthy barbarian boy." He pointed to the thorrods waiting patiently farther up the beach. "He runs with the animals, for the empress's sake!"

The woman flushed. "I apologize, General Tyro."

Tarlan stared at Tyro with narrowed eyes. "You have no idea who I am."

"And you have no idea who we are!" The man threw back his cloak and drew a vicious, curved blade.

Immediately Brock charged out of the rocks at the edge of the beach. Greythorn and Filos sprinted out too, Greythorn's howl sounding over the noise of the storm. The wolf and tigron flanked Tarlan, Brock rearing up onto his hind legs. Tarlan was pleased to see General Tyro's eyes widen.

"Is this a threat, boy?" he said.

"It's a suggestion." Tarlan was struggling to keep his temper at bay. "Go home. There's nothing for you here."

General Tyro laughed. "Why would we leave," he said, "when we have barely begun to arrive?"

Tyro and the other Galadronians turned west to face the sea. Tarlan looked too. The storm clouds had shifted from the color of charcoal to a thick, dreamy purple. On the horizon was what looked like . . . *trees?*

Not trees, Tarlan realized, remembering the word Mirith had taught him. *Masts!*

He watched, his blood turning cold, as the clouds dispersed completely and the hazy line of masts resolved itself into a vast fleet of ships. They seemed to fill the sea, surging relentlessly toward shore. Tarlan cursed himself. Had he really thought these few wretched sailors were the only ones to have set out from Galadron? How could he have been so stupid?

"You tell us that Toronia is torn open by war," General Tyro went on. His blade flashed in the bursts of lightning. "Do you think we do not know this? Do you think we have no intelligence? No spies? Do you think we would come all this way unprepared?"

One of the Galadronian ships was very close now. Its hull was narrower than the rest, and it sat low in the water. Its sail was an immense red triangle piercing the flaming sky. Long oars worked the water, pulling the slender vessel effortlessly through the white-capped waves.

A tall man came to the rail—the ship's captain, Tarlan supposed. He wore copper-colored armor under his cloak. On his head was a red peaked helmet. Behind him, a line of soldiers, similarly garbed, stood to attention.

The captain raised his right fist. The Galadronians on the shore returned his salute.

"Welcome to Toronia, Admiral Merello!" Tyro bellowed. "I trust your voyage went well?"

"Better than yours, General. I avoided the worst of the storm. Shall I order the rest of the fleet to anchor offshore?"

General Tyro's answering laugh was entirely without humor.

"There will be no putting to anchor!" he shouted. "The fight to take back Toronia begins now! We will rest only when the first lights of the enemy have been extinguished!"

All eyes—Tarlan's included—followed Tyro's finger as it pointed south along the shore, to where a cluster of lamps flickered in the dim dawn haze.

The village!

Horror filled Tarlan.

"You can't attack them," he said desperately. "What did those people ever do to you?"

"They are barbarians," said Tyro. "They stand between us and Idilliam."

A little way up the beach, the first wave of ships had already made landfall. Unlike Merello's slender vessel, most of these had wide, square hulls. In front of their treelike masts was a squat turret. As the ships rode up the sand, ramps swung down from their bows. They looked like mobile castles, each with its own drawbridge.

Tarlan watched, appalled, as soldiers swarmed out of the ships. Their faces spanned all the shades between black and white, and the cloaks they wore over their coppery armor were all colors of the rainbow. At least half of them rode horses decked in golden armor. In the silky dawn light, the Galadronians were dazzling.

Tyro eyed Tarlan. "What weaponry do you think our troops will face? Fishing nets, perhaps? Or lobster traps?" He gave Tarlan a shove. "Now fly away with your forest friends, boy, before we kill you all."

Tarlan's rage boiled over.

"I am no boy!" he shouted, addressing not just Tyro but everyone in earshot. "I am Tarlan, son of King Brutan, born one of three! I have the right to stand here. You don't!"

Tyro's expression didn't change.

"You, a prince?" he sneered. "Not just filthy but crazy, too! So all this"—he swept his hand around in a circle—"belongs to you?"

"No," Tarlan replied. "But it certainly doesn't belong to you!"

He drew his sword. With blinding speed Tyro lashed out. The back of his hand struck Tarlan's chin. Bright stars exploded in Tarlan's vision and he reeled over backward, his head spinning. With a bellow of rage Brock swiped one of his massive paws at Tyro. The bearded man leaped back just in time to avoid the blow, although Brock's knifelike claws slashed his billowing cloak to ribbons.

"Theeta!" Tarlan yelled, scrambling to his feet. "To me!"

All three thorrods were already in the air. Filos and Greythorn were in motion too, driving into the enemy soldiers, howling and biting as they went. Tarlan grinned fiercely as the Galadronians scattered.

Three soldiers ran up to Brock, their short swords raised. Brock dropped to all fours and charged straight into them before they could strike a blow. Two of the men crumpled like rags, their bodies instantly limp; the third Brock crushed underfoot. Theeta landed hard beside Tarlan, dipping her head until her beak scraped the sand. Tarlan grabbed her neck ruff with his free hand and sprang up onto her back. Even as he jumped she was pushing off with her claws. Her huge, gold wings pounded the air, creating tiny tornadoes of sand as she powered her way up into the sky.

"Bad humans," Theeta observed.

They made straight for Brock, who was up on his hind legs again, battering at the circle of horsemen now surrounding him. Theeta dived into their ranks, slashing with her talons and scattering the enemy.

Gold feathers flashed nearby, bright in the dawn light, and Tarlan saw Nasheen and Kitheen following Theeta's lead. The two thorrods rose and fell, rose and fell, and with each new dive another line of Galadronians collapsed onto the sand.

But the invading ships were still arriving, a seemingly endless parade of vessels riding out of the ocean and onto the beach. Sails furled, ramps descended, and hundreds more horses poured out. Their riders wore the now-familiar blend of riotously colorful cloaks and brandished a dizzying array of swords and spears. And for all the ships that had beached here, at least as many had made straight for the village, plowing through the rows of houses that stood on stilts out in the water. Flames were beginning to rise from some of the buildings on the shore, and tiny shapes were scurrying to and fro like ants. Tarlan could hear distant screams.

This is hopeless, he thought. *We'll never defeat them by ourselves.*

They needed help.

Tarlan scanned the ground for his pack. Filos was making for Merello's ship. The ship's rail was lined with archers, each aiming a strange bow that looked like it was tilted onto its side. In just a breath or two, the young tigron would be in range.

"Filos!" he yelled, hoping she would hear him over the battle. "Come back!"

To his relief she swerved aside, just as a volley of short, red bolts flew from the weapons. They struck the beach an arm's length from her paws, raising puffs of black sand.

"To the woods!" he shouted, hoping the rest of his pack would hear.

Filos immediately broke away from the melee and began racing up the beach. After one final swipe of his massive claws—which felled four Galadronians in a single blow—Brock lumbered after her.

"Nasheen! Kitheen! See them to safety!"

As the thorrods shadowed Filos and Brock into the tree line, Tarlan looked around for Greythorn.

The wolf was circling Tyro, who was holding him off with his curved sword. Every time Greythorn snapped, Tyro swung his blade.

"Down!" Tarlan cried.

Theeta dropped like a rock, the air screeching through the stiff feathers at the ends of her wings. At the last moment, she pulled out of the dive and Tarlan swung his sword. Tyro looked up in surprise, taking a clumsy half step back. It was just enough to save him from decapitation. Instead of slicing through his neck, Tarlan's blade connected with his shoulder.

The thud of the impact sent shock waves all the way up Tarlan's arm. He couldn't tell if he'd struck flesh or armor. As Theeta wheeled around, Tyro's sword struck the side of Greythorn's head. The wolf flew sideways, blood pouring from the gash that had opened up below his left eye.

Stabbing his sword back into its scabbard, Tarlan wrenched Theeta around in a tight circle. Leaning precariously out from the thorrod's neck, he managed to slip his arm beneath Greythorn's body and heave the injured wolf onto Theeta's back. Screaming with the effort, Theeta lurched skyward, great beats of her wings compensating for the sudden extra weight. Tarlan held Greythorn against him, feeling the rapid drumming of the wolf's heart; his own heart was beating at least as fast, and his breath was coming in rapid spurts. His hands were slick with Greythorn's blood.

"To the Isle of Stars," Tarlan cried. "Faster than you've flown before!"

As they sped over the battlefield, a row of Galadronians raised their sideways bows. A scant breath later, a volley of bolts whistled past Tarlan's head. One struck Theeta's right wing, but passed straight between the feathers without so much as drawing blood.

Tyro's voice rang out over the battle. "Think you've escaped, boy? We'll come for you! Our assassins will hunt you down!"

"Not before we've defeated you!" Tarlan yelled back.

Theeta was flying faster than he'd ever known. Land gave way to sea, the Isle of Stars looming closer with every beat of the thorrod's wings. Squirming beside Tarlan, Greythorn let out a mournful howl. He was dismayed to see that the wolf's left eye had filmed over white. There was movement on the water below; two of the Galadronian ships had turned away from the village and were rowing in pursuit of Theeta.

"Faster!" Tarlan yelled.

"Fly fleet!" Theeta cawed. Incredibly, she sped up.

I hope you're ready with your magic, Melchior! If ever we needed a wizard's powers, it's now!

CHAPTER 17

The dungeons?" exclaimed Sylva. "But we were going to see if Mother's recovered from her fever. Anyway, you can't go to the dungeons, Elodie. They're not safe!"

"I've got to, because . . ." Elodie searched wildly for an excuse. "Because I need to talk to the man who attacked me! We have to know about the Galadronians and about why they want me dead."

"I think we can guess," said Cedric. "They want to make sure you can't take the throne. Anyway, Captain Gandrell will take care of all that." He glanced across the courtyard to where the captain was disappearing through the main castle entrance. "Come on. We'll see you safely to your room, and then—"

"Safe? Do you think any of us are safe with all these Galadronians prowling around?"

"There was only one of them," said Sylva doubtfully.

"If I'm to be queen, I have to know about everything that's going on in my kingdom. I'm going to the dungeon. Are you coming with me, or am I going alone?"

Tossing her head, she stalked off down the corridor.

Samial fell into step beside her. "Will they come?" he said.

"Of course they will."

And, of course, they did.

It didn't take them long to reach the dungeon. Here the naturally red stone of the castle walls was dank and covered with green moss. The ceiling was low and the only light came from torches burning in sconces on the walls.

As they entered the guardroom, the soldier on duty rose from his chair and challenged them; when he saw who his visitors were, he stood to attention.

"I didn't know you'd returned," he said. "Is your father with you? Does he know you're here?"

"Of course he does," said Elodie with a withering glare.

The guard let them pass.

She hurried to the cell in which the would-be assassin was being held . . . and marched straight past it.

"Where are you going?" called Sylva. "I thought you wanted to find out about Galadron."

Elodie stopped. *All right. Now to tell them the truth.*

"Will you help me do what I must?" she asked.

Sylva and Cedric exchanged glances. "Of course," they said in unison.

"Then help me now. Help me free Fessan."

"Fessan?" said Cedric, puzzled.

"Do you mean that man who was brought here with you?" said Sylva. "The fellow from Trident?"

"Yes. He's my friend—my very loyal friend. He's spent years fighting on behalf of me and my brothers. He's risked his life for us. I can't leave him here."

Sylva shook her head. "Loyalty is one thing, but . . ."

"Loyalty is everything, Sylva. Fessan believes in the prophecy. He knows it's real, and he'd do anything to see it come true. I have to save him."

Sylva nodded. "I understand. *We* understand. It's just . . . well, it's impossible."

"It's not impossible. Just dangerous."

Sylva looked around sharply. "Where's Cedric?"

Before Elodie could respond, Cedric's call floated down the corridor. "Elodie! Sylva! Come here, quickly!"

Sylva ran toward the sound of his voice. Elodie felt a cold hand curl into her own and saw Samial smiling at her grimly in the gloom.

"I'll help, Elodie," he said. "I'll always help."

She gave his ghostly hand a squeeze. "I know."

Cedric was waiting for them outside a large cell. Inside, staring out with pale, frightened faces, were dozens of children. Their clothes were filthy, little more than rags. Many were crying; all looked half-starved.

Sylva's hands flew to her mouth. "What's going on?" she asked. "Who are they?"

"Tarlan told me about this," said Elodie. Anger swelled inside her. "Vicerin has been kidnapping children from all the lands he's conquered. Sylva, I'm sorry, but your father is . . ."

"Is cruel," said Cedric flatly. "We know it, don't we, Sylva? We've always known it."

"We've got to get them out." Sylva sounded as if she was in a trance.

Elodie nodded, her thoughts whirling.

Fessan won't survive here much longer. But neither will these children . . .

"Go see if Fessan is still in the same cell," she said to Samial. "And if not, find him."

"I'll find him," Samial replied.

"Then go!"

As Samial scurried off, Sylva said, "Who were you talking to?"

"Never mind. You're right, Sylva. We've got to save the children. Sam—"

She broke off. Was it wise to reveal the existence of her ghostly friend?

She decided it was. "Samial! Wait!"

Samial trotted back and stood expectantly before her.

"Do you think you can steal the key to the children's cell from the guard?"

"Yes," Samial replied at once.

"Then do it now. And hurry!"

He darted away. Sylva and Cedric had been watching this exchange with slack jaws. To them, Elodie knew, it would look as if she were talking to thin air.

"Elodie," said Cedric slowly. "We heard rumors about Trident. About an army that was more than an army. You can . . . you can talk to . . ."

"Ghosts," finished Elodie quickly. "But there's no time for that now. We're going to free the children, and we're going to free Fessan. We're going to do it all tonight, before Vicerin returns. Then I'll tell you everything, I promise."

"Yes, but . . ."

"Never mind that! Can you create a diversion?"

"A diversion?" said Sylva. "I've got just the thing!"

Moments later Elodie was sprinting down one of the narrow corridors that connected the kitchens to the main castle. Her heart beat a rapid tattoo in her chest, urging her on.

No time! There's no time!

Rounding a corner, she collided with a maid carrying a steaming bowl on a tray. With a shriek, the maid dropped it and the bowl shattered, spilling what smelled like chicken broth over the stone floor.

"Begging your pardon, Your Highness, but I was taking that to Lady Vicerin," said the maid. "She's still poorly, you see."

"Sorry," Elodie called as she ran on.

A flight of stairs took her up to a suite of rooms on the first floor. These were the castle's guest quarters. Beneath her feet the floor changed from hard stone to polished wood. The painted faces of Vicerin ancestors stared down at her from the framed pictures on the paneled walls.

She stopped outside a door, considered knocking, then simply opened it. Inside sat the man she was looking for.

"Captain Leom," she said. "Will you help me?"

Leom didn't look well exactly, but he seemed a lot better than when Elodie had last seen him. He was clean-shaven, though gaunt, and his military uniform looked crisp and neat. But there were dark circles beneath his eyes, and a haunted look inside them.

"Help you?" he replied, rising slowly from the soft chair in which he'd been sprawled. "If I can, Princess Elodie. If I can."

Elodie spotted an untouched bowl of broth on a nearby table. It looked identical to the bowl the maid had dropped. "Are you well?" she said. "Are you eating?"

"As a matter of fact, I have not eaten anything for a whole day. I don't think all this rich Ritherlee food agrees with me. And do you know what? I feel much better for it."

"I'm glad." Elodie pulled out the thorrod feather from where she'd hidden it in the pocket of her dress. "Do you know what this is, Captain Leom?"

Leom's eyes widened. "A feather from a thorrod. A miraculous thing."

"Yes. And an important one. I found it here, in my own chamber. Do you know what that proves?"

The glint in Leom's eye told Elodie he was starting to guess. "Tell me," he said.

"My brother Tarlan flies with the thorrods."

"Go on."

"Vicerin lied to you. Tarlan was here, in Ritherlee—this feather proves it. Vicerin held him prisoner here in the castle. Tarlan escaped . . . but there are others still to be freed."

Leom's brow furrowed. "I thought there was something wrong here, but . . ." He pounded a fist into the palm of his hand. "Tarlan was here, you say?"

"Yes."

"So Lord Vicerin is a traitor to the crown."

"Yes. Captain Leom, will you help me?"

She held her breath as he rubbed his face. He lowered his hands and gave her a long, appraising look.

"What would you have me do, Your Highness?"

Outside, the gardens were on fire. The flower beds bloomed with flame; trees burned; mounds of hay and compost left by the gardeners blazed. Soldiers and servants stood in a ragged line, passing buckets of water in a human chain, trying in vain to douse the conflagration. There was smoke everywhere.

Well done, Sylva! Elodie thought with grim satisfaction. *Oh, well done, Cedric!*

"Is this the diversion you told me about?" said Leom as they raced past the confusion, then through the doorway that would lead them to the dungeon.

"Yes," Elodie replied. "It's quite a show."

Sylva and Cedric were waiting for them by the children's cell.

"Elodie, thank goodness," said Sylva. "I thought you were . . ."

Her voice broke off as Samial emerged from the shadows holding up a large ring of keys.

"Who's there?" whispered Sylva. Elodie knew the keys must seem to be floating through the air.

"Someone who knows magic, I suspect," Leom remarked, regarding Elodie with a quizzical eyebrow.

"It's Samial," Elodie said. "My friend."

She took the bunch of keys from him and picked her way through until she found one that matched the large black lock. The door swung open. At first the children didn't move. Several retreated, cowering to the back of the cell. Then Captain Leom dropped to his knees.

"It's all right, little ones," he said in a soft, deep voice. "You're safe now. I won't let anyone hurt you."

"Are y-you here to help us, m-mister?" stammered a small girl with dirty blond hair.

"Yes. I'm going to take you far away from here, to a place where Lord Vicerin will never find you."

"I'll give you gold if you'll take me, too," called the Galadronian assassin from his cell.

"Shut up!" snapped Elodie, rubbing her bruised and painful neck.

One by one the children crept out of the cell and clustered around Captain Leom. They gazed up at him adoringly, and Elodie knew her instinct to bring him here had been right.

"Hurry," she said. "Take them to safety, as you once took my brother."

"I will, Princess Elodie."

He began to make his way out of the dungeon, with the children in tow.

Elodie turned to Sylva and Cedric. "Go with him. The guard actually saluted Captain Leom when we came in, but I think he'll change his mind when he sees his prisoners on the loose."

"And if we can't convince him?" said Sylva.

"I have my sword," said Leom drily.

"What about you?" asked Sylva.

"I'm going to find Fessan."

"We'll come back for you, Elodie," said Cedric. "We won't leave you."

"No! Wait for me by the door to the garden. Be ready. When we come, we'll be coming at a run."

Without waiting for a reply, Elodie grabbed a fresh torch from a sconce on the wall, seized Samial's hand, and raced deeper into the dungeon.

The corridors gave way to rough tunnels. Elodie sensed they were descending deep underground, into the ancient catacombs over which Castle Vicerin had been built. Samial paused beside an open doorway.

"This is where they held him until today," he said.

Elodie peered inside and saw a tiny chamber with a low ceiling. Fixed to one wall was a set of manacles. There was a large puddle in the middle of the floor, and a drainage grille in the far corner.

"The water cell," Elodie breathed. She tried to imagine what it must have been like for Fessan, chained up to his neck in icy water.

It was a torture so typically Vicerin in its brutality. "Where is he now?"

"Not far. This way."

Hand in hand they ran farther through the maze of tunnels. At last Samial stopped. Before them was a low door made of hard, black wood. He took the keys from Elodie, sorted through them until he found the one he wanted, and plunged it into the lock.

Elodie held her breath as Samial opened the door, terrified of what she might see.

The cell was small and square, with solid earth walls and a muddy floor. It smelled like a sewer. There were no windows. When Elodie thrust the blazing torch inside, the man huddled in the corner cringed and threw his arm up over his face.

"Fessan!"

Handing the torch to Samial, she rushed into the cell. In the same instant, Fessan clambered to his feet and held up his fists. His knuckles were scabbed, and his hands shook. Elodie had never seen anyone less equipped to put up a fight.

"Fessan! It's me, Elodie!"

"I know who it is!" The words came out slurred. Fessan spat a gob of bloody saliva onto the damp floor. "Elodie the princess. Elodie the spoiled brat. Elodie the traitor!"

Elodie realized she was shaking all over. Tears spilled down her cheeks: tears of relief, that he was still alive; tears of shame, for the deceit she'd had no choice but to play on him; tears of pity, for the pain and anguish he'd suffered.

"I'm here," she said. She reached out to him, but he drew sharply back.

"Here? Yes, you're here. Come to gloat, have you?"

"No."

"How could you do it, Elodie? After all Trident did for you. After everything *I* did."

"I didn't want to." She forced her voice to remain steady. "It was the only way. The Vicerins would have wiped you out if I hadn't given them what they wanted. I thought they'd leave you behind with the others, but . . . If I'd known where you'd end up . . ."

"It's a nice story, Elodie."

"It's not a story. It's the truth."

"The truth? You wouldn't know the truth if it cut your throat."

Elodie's hand went to her neck, touching first the wound left by the assassin, then the gold chain from which her jewel was hanging.

"Please believe me," she implored. "I came to rescue you. You have to come with me. If we go now, I can save you."

Fessan bunched his fists tighter, then his hands dropped, revealing his face fully. Elodie gasped. His eyes were red and swollen; his cheeks were purple with bruises. Both his lips were bleeding.

"Why should I believe anything you say?"

Elodie was starting to despair. She turned to Samial, who was standing in the doorway to the cell, holding the torch aloft.

"We are running out of time, Elodie," he said anxiously.

I know!

Meanwhile, Fessan had spread his arms wide, exposing his thin chest. "Kill me," he said. "That's what you've come for, isn't it? If you haven't come to gloat, you must be here to stick a knife in me. Well, go on—get on with it. At least it will put an end to the torture."

Suddenly inspired, Elodie drew the dagger Vicerin had given her. Its jeweled hilt shone in the flickering torchlight. Then she turned it in her hand and presented it to Fessan, handle first.

"Elodie!" Samial shouted. "No!"

With trembling fingers, Fessan took it.

At once Elodie threw out her arms, mimicking his gesture.

"Put an end to it, then," she said. "If you really believe I'm a traitor, put an end to it now!"

The muscles in Fessan's arm twitched. For a moment Elodie was convinced he was going to do it. He would thrust the knife between her ribs and into her heart, ending her part in the long and terrible history of the kingdom of Toronia.

So be it, she thought. *I have done my best.*

Shaking now from head to foot, Fessan tightened his fingers on the dagger's hilt. His eyes were filled with tears. A vein throbbed at his temple.

Elodie closed her eyes.

She heard the blade clatter to the floor.

"You came," he sobbed. "Elodie . . . you came for me."

His arms closed around Elodie and drew her into a rough hug.

"I'm sorry," she sobbed. "I'm so sorry for everything. Can you forgive me?"

"Elodie, there is nothing to forgive."

They retraced their steps through the catacombs, Elodie doing her best to support Fessan while Samial led the way with the torch.

"Either the torch is enchanted," Fessan observed, "or we are in the company of one of your phantom friends."

They reached the guardroom. The guard lay sprawled on the floor beside his chair. Blood leaked from a puncture wound in his side.

As instructed, Sylva and Cedric were waiting at the garden doorway. When they saw Fessan's appearance, their faces dropped.

"You poor man," said Sylva.

"Did Captain Leom get away?" Elodie asked.

Cedric nodded, then ushered them all under the cover of a nearby gazebo. On the far side of the smoke-filled garden, a small group of servants was busy trying to put out a blazing outbuilding.

"There's a side gate," Cedric said. "Do you see it?"

He pointed through the smoke toward one of the sally ports set in the castle's thick outer wall. As children they'd used it in their games of hide-and-chase.

But this is no game.

"Can you make it that far?" Elodie asked Fessan.

"That far, and farther," Fessan replied.

"We told Captain Leom to wait outside as long as possible," said Sylva. "He will help you."

"What about you, Elodie?" said Fessan. "Will you not come?"

She closed her eyes. *I wish I could. But I can't, not yet.*

"No," she said sadly. "I have work to do here first."

"Then let me stay. Let me help."

"No. If you stay, they'll kill you."

She gave his hand a brief squeeze.

"Go now, Fessan. Go quickly, before one of us changes our mind. And . . . be safe."

"Is this really your wish, Princess Elodie?"

"Captain Fessan—it is my command."

"Then it is my duty to obey."

He nodded briskly, then slipped away, hugging the wall. When he reached the sally port, he glanced briefly back in her direction. Then he was gone.

"I've learned a lot today," said Sylva.

"What about?" Elodie's attention was still fixed on the darkness into which Fessan had vanished.

"My father." Sylva broke into racking sobs. Cedric wrapped his one good arm around her. Elodie joined the embrace, her heart going out to them both. The truth was hard.

They huddled together, while in the background the fires continued to burn. Elodie let the moment envelop her, and wished it would never stop. Then, reluctantly, she stepped away.

"Time to go," she said.

"We have to bring him down, don't we?" said Cedric. "Our father. That's why you stayed, isn't it, Elodie?"

"Yes," Elodie replied. *Oh, I'm glad you're here. Both of you.* "Sylva—do you want to do this? Can you?"

Sylva wiped her eyes.

"Just tell me what you want us to do, Elodie."

CHAPTER 18

Theeta reached the Isle of Stars well ahead of the two Galadronian ships. But she was tiring, and the ascent to the volcano's summit took longer than Tarlan had hoped. By the time the thorrod reached the lip of the crater, the first ship had already landed on the island's eastern shore.

"Wings burn," Theeta cawed.

"Keep going," said Tarlan. "We've got to get Melchior out!"

And we've got to do it before those Galadronians catch up with us.

Theeta descended swiftly to the silver lake inside the volcano. Even before she'd touched down, Tarlan was leaping from her back. He hit the stone platform hard, rolled, sprang to his feet, and ran to the water's edge. There was the wizard, lying just below the water's surface, with his limbs thrown out wide.

If ever we needed your magic, Melchior, it's now!

He was about to reach for him when a familiar voice sounded in his head.

Until all the constellations are lit, until all the numbers are counted, nothing must disturb me, or all is lost.

Tarlan couldn't tell if Melchior was somehow speaking to him, or if he was simply remembering the wizard's words.

He let out a growl of frustration. "I need him now," he muttered. "Those villagers need him now. But what if I wake him too soon?"

Torn, he went to retrieve Greythorn from where he lay on Theeta's back. He could help the wolf while he decided what to do.

Then he saw that the crater had changed.

The stars!

He turned in a circle, his eyes wide, the blood racing through his veins. When he'd left the crater, dozens of the white stones had still not been illuminated. Now not a single one remained unlit. They *blazed*, an impossibly complex network of light. It was as if the night sky had been carried down here.

So many!

His eyes flicked from one stone to the next, trying to follow the patterns they made. There was order here, a kind of language he could almost read. Understanding danced, tantalizingly close but always just out of reach. The more he looked, the more stones there were. If he carried on looking, their number would only increase, until the black rock of the crater wall was consumed and only the light remained. He began walking toward the edge of the platform, his arms outstretched, his feet marching of their own accord, his whole body driven by some greater power. . . .

"Tarlan, stop!"

Theeta's harsh voice broke the spell. Tarlan shook his head, found himself teetering on the edge of the platform, on the verge of falling into the water. He took a hasty step back. Something was thudding nearby. It was his heart, trying to climb its way out of his chest.

Greythorn!

Returning to where Theeta was waiting, Tarlan was alarmed to find the wolf unconscious.

"Greythorn, I'm sorry!"

He gingerly lifted the injured wolf from Theeta's back and carried him to the water's edge. Unlike his own, the wolf's heartbeat was so faint he could barely feel it.

"Don't die, Greythorn," he whispered. "Please, don't die."

Tightening his grip, he eased himself off the platform into the shallow water at the lake's edge. He bent his knees and lowered Greythorn's whole body into the lake.

As the water lapped around the wolf's muzzle, Tarlan hesitated.

I want to cure him, not drown him.

But Melchior hadn't drowned, had he?

Gritting his teeth, Tarlan plunged the wolf under the water. His gray fur fluttered in the silver liquid. His legs twitched. Bubbles streamed from his blood-spattered nostrils.

Tarlan held him under to a count of five, then lifted him out, grunting with the extra weight of his waterlogged fur. Then a large talon closed around Greythorn's body and lifted him clear.

"Thanks, Theeta."

As the thorrod lay Greythorn down, Tarlan clambered out and poured more water onto the wolf's face, wincing as it splashed into his wounded eye. Greythorn's chest heaved. The starlight from the glowing stones seemed to grow momentarily brighter. Tarlan placed his hand on the wolf's flank and was relieved to feel a strong, steady heartbeat. The fur on Greythorn's face rippled. Tarlan watched in amazement as the gash closed up, the skin sealing itself into a long, straggling scar.

The eye above the scar remained white and sightless.

Greythorn's other eye opened, rolled, then fixed on Tarlan. The wolf lifted his head and licked Tarlan's cheek.

"Wolf heal," Theeta cawed happily.

"Thank you," said Greythorn, his voice a soft, contented growl.

Tarlan threw his arms around the wolf's neck and hugged him.

"You're welcome!" he cried. "But your eye."

"I have another."

Greythorn struggled out of Tarlan's grip and shook his body

from head to tail. Water sprayed in a silver spiral, dousing Tarlan and Theeta.

Laughing, Tarlan stroked Greythorn behind his ears, then crossed the platform to where the wizard lay, still submerged in the magical lake.

Anxiously he scanned the network of shining stones. Were they really all lit? How would he ever know?

"Ships come," Theeta warned.

Tarlan wondered how long it would take the Galadronians to scale the side of the volcano. Once the enemy reached the crater's edge, they would be trapped down here like mice in a hole.

No choice, he thought grimly. *It's now or never. I've got to wake him up.*

"Your turn, Melchior," he said, and climbed down into the water.

The wizard looked just the same as ever, with his arms and legs thrown out and his face contorted into some unnamable expression. Tarlan slipped his hands beneath Melchior's back and heaved.

Melchior didn't move.

Tarlan tried again. Still nothing. The wizard might have been made of stone.

"Theeta! Come and help!"

The thorrod joined him and lowered her claw obediently into the water. But even with her huge talons and enormous strength, Melchior didn't budge.

"That's enough," said Tarlan, waving her away. "Let me think."

He looked again at the twinkling stars. *What have I missed?*

Plunging his arms back into the water, he laced them under Melchior's back and heaved. He felt the strain in his shoulders, in the tendons of his neck. The muscles of his thighs bulged with the effort.

"Theeta help?" the thorrod said.

Before Tarlan could respond, something struck him in the chest, knocking all the breath from his lungs and lifting him clear of the water. He flew through the air, arms flailing. The hard stone of the platform rushed up toward him . . . and then Theeta's wing was there, a welcome blanket of feathers that softened his landing.

Staggering to his feet, he took a hesitant step toward the lake again. All around him, the white stones burned like miniature suns. He took another step, and something pushed him back: a gigantic, invisible force.

The air crackled, and Tarlan's skin pimpled into gooseflesh. He saw that Greythorn's fur was standing on end, and Theeta's feathers were ruffling as if she were flying at high speed.

Tarlan tried to walk forward again. Again, the unseen hand pressed him back, this time with more force. The light from the stones strengthened. Something swelled inside the all-encompassing glow, and then a silver tree was rising up before him, its outline wavering and uncertain. Its shape shifted. Now it was no longer a tree but a tower of silver stone. It changed again, this time to a shimmering silver flame.

Tongues of white fire licked out from the stars, stabbing inward from every side of the crater toward the platform on which Tarlan, Theeta, and Greythorn were cowering. Tarlan threw his hand over his face, convinced this was death come to take them all.

Through his closed eyelids, he sensed the world turning red. Then, abruptly, the brightness faded. The crackling sensation subsided. All was still.

Tarlan lowered his arm.

Melchior was standing before him.

The wizard looked younger than Tarlan remembered, even though his face was still cracked with a thousand wrinkles. He seemed taller too—was that possible? His yellow robes flowed around him, moving with a constant, subtle liquidity, even though he himself was motionless. His staff was in one hand, and on his age-worn yet oddly youthful face there was a grin.

"Melchior," said Tarlan cautiously. "Is it . . . are you . . . ?"

The wizard's grin widened.

"Yes, my boy! And yes!"

With this cry, Melchior's whole body relaxed. His robes ceased their unsettling flowing movement. He took a step forward, flexed his legs in what might have been puzzlement, or perhaps wonder, and stamped his feet on the stone platform, one after the other.

"The world feels strong," he announced. "Or perhaps it is me. Who can say?"

"Are you back? I mean, did it work? Did it really work?"

Without speaking, Melchior spread his arms to indicate the dazzling constellations of shining stones that surrounded them. But were they quite as dazzling as they had been, Tarlan wondered?

Their work is done. They're already beginning to fade.

Melchior held up his staff. His fingers danced over the runes carved into its ancient surface. His lips moved rapidly. Tarlan heard no words, but something told him the wizard was counting.

A sparrow emerged from one end of the staff. Immediately it took flight, its wings humming in the silence. Every one of its tiny brown feathers looked as if it had been carved from oak. Theeta extended her neck over Tarlan's shoulder, watching with interest.

The little bird flew like an arrow to the opposite end of the staff, and vanished back into the wood that had spawned it. A moment later a second sparrow performed the same trick. Then three more birds appeared, and suddenly there was an entire flock of sparrows moving in an endless fluttering stream along the length of the staff.

Tarlan watched in delight with Theeta's huge beak resting lightly on his shoulder. Greythorn stood to attention at his feet, his one good eye fixed on the spectacle.

"Little wings," said Theeta.

Melchior's fingers fell still, and his lips stopped moving. The stream of birds flowed into the staff for the final time, leaving a lone sparrow, which darted suddenly toward Theeta. The little bird circled the head of its gigantic cousin three times, then returned to the staff and, with a single chirp, vanished inside.

Melchior, whose face had grown grave while he'd been performing this trick, relaxed.

"The magic is back," he said. With a slight frown, he plucked a single, minute feather from the end of his staff. He studied it for a moment, then rubbed it between his fingers, causing it to vanish.

"That was . . . amazing," said Tarlan. He could feel the wizard's smile reflected on his own face. Despite everything that had happened on the beach, he felt safe again.

Then he remembered the ships.

"I don't think we've got much time for tricks, though."

"No, indeed." Melchior's frown lingered. "There is a kingdom to be won. But before that, I must ask you a question, Tarlan, and you must be truthful with your answer."

Tarlan swallowed. He didn't like the sound of this. "All right."

"Did you wake me before my time?"

Tarlan briefly considered lying, then thought better of it. "I don't know. I don't think so. I had to . . . I had to leave you for a while. When I came back, the stones were all lit. I tried to lift you out of the water, but I couldn't. Then you . . . well, you came out of your own accord."

Melchior's frown deepened as he listened intently. When Tarlan had finished, he nodded slowly.

"All right. I understand. You did well, Tarlan. Very well."

Tarlan turned, breathing a sigh of relief. But Melchior's hand planted itself on his shoulder and turned him back.

"Now tell me, Tarlan, why did you have to leave me . . . and what made you come back?"

Tarlan shot a glance up at the crater's opening, a tiny circle of light hanging high above their heads. "There's so much to tell, Melchior, but I don't think there's time."

"Tell it quickly, then."

So Tarlan hastily explained about the invading fleet. "They say they're from Galadron."

Melchior's eyes widened. "Galadron," he repeated slowly. "Are you certain?"

Tarlan nodded.

"I traveled there once, long ago," Melchior said. He closed his eyes, as if remembering. "Before the Thousand Year War, Galadron was a good friend to Toronia. Then Toronia fell into conflict. Since then Galadron turned away from us. It wanted nothing to do with war."

"It does now," muttered Tarlan.

"Much must have changed." Abruptly, Melchior struck the stone with his staff. "You were right, Tarlan."

"Right? Right about what?"

"This is no time for tricks, nor is there any time to waste. Toronia is in no position to defend itself from invasion. We are all in far greater danger than we imagined."

Shouts rang down from high above. Tarlan felt the weight of Theeta's beak lift from his shoulder as the thorrod raised her head. He followed her gaze and saw tiny shapes moving at the crater's edge, silhouetted against the sky.

"Were you followed here?" said Melchior.

"That's why I wanted to hurry. Theeta—can you carry us all?"

"Theeta strong!" the thorrod said. "Fly now!"

Tarlan was about to help Melchior climb onto Theeta's back when the old man surprised him by springing up with an acrobat's easy grace. Turning his attention to Greythorn, he saw that the wolf was already settling himself into the thick feathers behind the wizard.

"That water is powerful stuff," Tarlan said as he joined his friends.

"Powerful?" Melchior's expression was severe. "My boy, you do not know the meaning of the word."

A shiver chased down Tarlan's spine. Then the wizard cracked a smile.

"But you will! Fly, you great bird! Fly!"

Despite the extra weight on her back, Theeta flew a fast, straight line up toward the open sky. The shining stones sped past, falling away beneath them like shooting stars. Although their light was indeed beginning to fade, they still blazed bright enough to leave lingering streaks in Tarlan's vision.

They are all lit, he told himself. *They are!*

And they were.

Except one.

It sat near the top of the scintillating bracelet of light through which they were ascending: a single, unlit stone. The instant he saw it, Tarlan's heart froze. He felt Melchior stiffen beside him, and knew the wizard had seen it too.

"What does it mean?" Tarlan cried over the rush of the air.

"Nothing."

"I woke you too soon. I knew it was wrong!"

"It's nothing," said Melchior again. Did the wizard sound troubled, or was that just Tarlan's imagination?

"You did nothing wrong, Tarlan. Pay it no mind. Remember the sparrow."

"Sparrows. There were lots of them."

"No. There was only one. *That* was the true magic."

Tarlan had no idea what the wizard was talking about. "You're sure the stone doesn't matter?"

"Tarlan, we have more pressing concerns."

With a deafening screech, Theeta burst out of the crater and into the clear air above. The morning sky was bright, and the storm had left the air crisp and clear. The comet hung directly overhead, a frozen spark thrown from some unseen celestial bonfire.

The volcano's slopes were swarming with Galadronian soldiers.

There are so many of them! Tarlan felt a stab of fear. *What can one wizard and one boy do?*

They were spotted immediately. Shouts rang out across the mountain and the air around them filled with whistling sidebow bolts. Several passed close to Tarlan's face.

"They mean to kill us," said Melchior conversationally. "We could climb out of range. We have a thorrod."

"I didn't wake you up to escape," said Tarlan. "I woke you up to fight!"

"How sad," said Melchior, "to wake to this. To find our old friends have turned enemy."

On the slopes below, the Galadronians were forming up into lines and reloading their sidebows.

"Melchior! We don't have time for—"

"They invade despite everything." Melchior's eyes drifted to the mainland, where the village was burning with flames as bright as the risen sun. "They think they can defy the prophecy."

"Can they?"

The wizard's eyes filled with infinite sadness.

"Nobody can say, Tarlan. Not even a wizard."

Melchior shuddered. Yet, at the same time, his body remained utterly still. Tarlan blinked, not quite sure what he'd just seen.

"Do you have your sword?" The wizard's voice was distant but immense. The morning sky darkened.

"Yes, but . . ."

"Have you ever put its blade into a man?"

"I've been in lots of fights, but . . ."

"Are you ready to kill?"

The question was terrifying in its nakedness. For a moment Tarlan didn't know how to reply. Then he saw Seethan dead at the hands of the elk-hunters, the cruel, powdered smile of Lord Vicerin as he gloated over the kidnapped children, and the mindless fury of Brutan's undead army.

"Yes," he said fiercely.

"Then that is what you will do. Bring us to them!"

"Yes, Melchior! Theeta—down!"

The thorrod instantly changed course, plunging toward the nearest slope and landing just short of the Galadronian front line. Melchior slipped smoothly off her back and onto the broken black rock of the volcano. Tarlan joined him, his sword drawn and his head thumping with anger.

Greythorn leaped nimbly down beside him and stood with his front paws splayed and his hackles raised, growling like thunder.

Theeta opened her lethal beak and screeched.

The soldiers at the head of the approaching army began to run toward them.

Melchior raised his staff, gripping it tight in his left hand and running his right over the carved runes. His silent lips moved. Tarlan steeled himself and held out his sword. What forces would the wizard unleash? Would there be fire? Given the way the sky was darkening, he half expected something like the previous night's storm.

Throw lightning at them, Melchior! Bury them in thunder!

There was no lightning. There was no thunder.

The soldiers on the front line continued to run, but somehow they didn't seem to be getting any closer. Tarlan squinted, trying to make sense of what he was seeing: perhaps two hundred armed soldiers bearing down on him and his diminished pack.

Not two hundred. Not that many. Only one hundred, perhaps.

The air was crackling around his head, just as it had inside the crater. The sky was the color of slate. The comet blazed, an all-seeing eye.

The soldiers came on. And yet . . . they didn't. Their legs moved, and their arms pumped, but they made no progress across the black rock.

Fifty. There are no more than fifty of them!

Beside Tarlan, the wizard had tightened his grip on the staff. His lips were a blur, now exposing teeth like ancient standing stones, now hiding them. The tendons in his wrinkled neck snapped taut. His tangled hair was a cloud of wild snow.

Now there were twenty men in the Galadronian army. Now ten. Tarlan took a hesitant step forward, forcing his way through the buzzing air. His skin tingled; his face felt hot and cold, both at the same time. What was he seeing? Where had the rest of the army gone?

They're all still there! It was so hard to see, so hard to comprehend. *They're . . . inside each other . . . behind each other . . .*

No, that wasn't quite right.

He took another step, peered closer.

Three men . . . folded around many. An entire army running without moving, crushed into the space of just three men . . .

Two men . . .

One man . . .

Melchior let out a ragged cry and Tarlan nearly jumped out of his skin. Gripping the staff with both hands, the wizard thrust it toward the stationary, oncoming soldier.

Soldiers?

"Quickly!" Melchior cried. "Before the numbers unfold."

Tarlan took another step toward the man . . . *men?* As he did so, his vision seemed to double, triple. He saw many faces hiding behind this single visage. It was like looking through a shattered window to spy on an immense crowd.

"NOW!" Melchior roared.

Tarlan drew back his sword, hesitated, then thrust it into the stomach of the frozen, running man, just below his copper-colored breastplate.

The blade entered smoothly, then jarred as it struck bone. Tarlan gritted his teeth against the sickening, grating sensation, plunged it home, twisted it once, twice, then yanked it free.

The man crumpled and began to fall. His eyes were already dead. Tarlan stumbled back, his guts climbing into his throat.

Behind him Melchior let out a long, sad sigh.

The crackling subsided. In the space of a single breath, the darkness fled the sky.

The man continued to fall. He also . . . *unfolded*. Now two men were falling, now three, now five.

Ten.

One hundred . . .

Tarlan continued to back away, breathless and unbelieving. The lifeless body of the man he'd killed lay sprawled before him. Beside it lay another. And another. Beyond them, spread across the volcano's jagged slopes, lay hundreds more. A sea of corpses.

All killed by a single stab of his blade.

Tarlan's fingers twitched open. His sword tumbled; when it struck the ground, it made a high ringing sound. His throat was dry. His eyes bulged.

Something brushed the back of his leg and he almost screamed. But it was only Greythorn.

"You bit the enemy," growled the wolf. "You bit deep."

"Big death," added Theeta, her voice unusually soft.

Tarlan nodded slowly, too shocked to speak.

Melchior joined him. The old man was leaning heavily on his staff and breathing hard.

"I didn't know how magic worked," said Tarlan at last. "I never thought . . ."

"Magic has many languages," Melchior replied. "The language I speak has few words. But it does have a great many numbers."

"We can defeat them all." The idea was both horrifying and exhilarating. But Tarlan supposed it was what they would have to do.

"Perhaps. How do you feel, Tarlan? Are you tired?"

Tarlan consulted his body. "No. Not really. It only took one stroke of my sword. I suppose . . . I suppose the rest was down to you."

Melchior nodded. He looked exhausted, his face haggard. "That is why I need to rest."

They sat for a while then, in the bright silence of the battlefield, while the sun soared into the waiting morning. Impatient as he felt, Tarlan endured the delay. Without Melchior's strength, what hope did he have of defeating the enemy?

Far away on the mainland, the village continued to burn. Meanwhile, the beach where the Galadronians had landed was emptying as the invading force headed inland.

I hope the rest of the pack is safe, he thought.

At last Melchior stood. Tarlan joined him on a crag of black rock, and together they looked east. The wind blew their hair back so that it mingled together: white and red-gold, woven into a single knot of moving color.

"Are you ready?" said Tarlan.

"Are you?"

"Yes."

Melchior raised his staff. "Then let us begin."

CHAPTER 19

Theeta flew in low over the beach where the Galadronian ships had landed. The squat vessels looked deserted but for a handful of lookouts posted high on the masts. Their faces turned to watch the giant thorrod and her passengers, but they made no move to attack.

Of the rest of the army there was no sign.

To Tarlan's relief, his pack was waiting for them on the sand. As Theeta landed, he beckoned to Nasheen. The white-breasted thorrod came forward; with a spry leap belying his great age, Melchior hopped down from Theeta's back and onto Nasheen's.

"Go to Filos and Brock," Tarlan said to Greythorn. "Run with them. Follow us into the village and help as you can. But be careful!"

"We will run," Greythorn replied, his one remaining eye bright. "But it is hard to be careful when you are busy biting."

Before Tarlan could respond, the wolf leaped down to join his companions on the beach. Filos and Brock, clearly overjoyed to see Greythorn healed of his wound, ran circles around him, yipping and growling their pleasure.

"Men gone," cawed Nasheen, nodding her head toward the notch in the cliffs through which they'd first arrived. "Big walk."

"All of them?" said Tarlan, looking east with some concern.

"They are an invasion force," put in Melchior. "What would they do but march inland?"

"Many stay." Nasheen indicated the burning village to the south. "Hot death."

"Yes," said Tarlan. "I know. And that's where we'll start!"

With a yell, he spurred Theeta into the air. Melchior followed on Nasheen, with the silent Kitheen bringing up the rear. Down on the ground, Filos and Greythorn sprinted after them, running almost as fast as the thorrods could fly; Brock followed at his own lumbering pace, his lips drawn back from his muzzle to reveal his enormous teeth.

The closer they drew to the village, the more Tarlan's apprehension grew. At least half the wooden buildings were on fire, with more igniting every moment. The long central street was filled with panicked villagers. Some of them had formed bucket chains to douse the flames; others were frantically trying to rescue their belongings from their doomed homes. More were simply running.

Down the many side alleys, Tarlan could see Galadronians systematically setting light to the remaining buildings. Each group of soldiers was clustered around a small cart. On the carts were metal barrels, from which jutted long spouts. The soldiers worked cranks and bellows, causing jets of flame to spurt from the ends of the spouts, igniting the thatched roofs of the buildings.

The fire's heat began to sear Tarlan's face.

"Stay back!" he shouted to the three animals on the ground. "Help the people who are trying to get out! Hold the enemy back! But don't go in there! You'll burn!"

His pack—tigron, wolf, and bear—didn't need telling twice. Tarlan could see Filos's blue fur beginning to singe, and he was relieved when Greythorn and Brock hustled her away from the wall of flame. The three animals prowled, keeping their distance but remaining alert, ready to help or hinder as events dictated.

Because it was wide, the main street was relatively clear of smoke and flame. Tarlan steered Theeta along it, keeping her level with the rooftops and looking for trouble.

It didn't take them long to find it.

A squad of Galadronians emerged from an alley with one of the fire machines. While three of them kept the villagers at bay with their swords, two armor-clad women pumped the bellows on the side of the cart. A third woman stood astride the metal barrel, her hands on a large lever, clearly waiting for the order to unleash the flames.

"Faster, Theeta!"

Tarlan held tight as the thorrod beat her wings against the hot, choking air, dipping below the eaves of a tavern and heading straight for the Galadronians.

"Hey!" Tarlan yelled. "Up here!"

The look of surprise on their faces was as gratifying as the panic with which they tried to swing the cart around. Tarlan wasn't worried. There was no time for them to take aim. Quick as the Galadronians were, Theeta was quicker.

As they flashed over the soldiers' heads, Tarlan felled the three swordsmen with a single sweep of his blade, Theeta's momentum lending a power to his blow that in no way compared to the magic of Melchior, but which felled more than one enemy all the same.

At the same time, Theeta lashed out with her talons, slicing apart both the bellows and the two women who were heaving at them. The woman on top of the barrel—now the only surviving member of the squad—yanked at the machine's lever.

This was clearly a mistake.

As Tarlan pulled Theeta up and away from the cart, the lever broke free from its pivot. The torn end struck sparks from the barrel and the entire machine exploded into flame. The Galadronians exploded with it.

Tarlan steered Theeta around in a wide circle, surveying the village. A group of Galadronians was gathered on the main fishing pier, torching the little boats moored there. He watched Kitheen dive and climb, dive and climb, a gold-winged engine of destruction, crushing two Galadronians in his beak every time he skimmed the pier's wooden deck.

He looked around for Nasheen, only to find the thorrod flying right at Theeta's side. "I have doubled the alleys!" the wizard called from her back. "Tripled some of them."

He pointed with his staff. Peering around Theeta's neck, Tarlan saw several of the Galadronian squads dragging their fire machines around impossibly tight corners, only to come up against unexpected dead ends.

"What did you do?" Tarlan rubbed his eyes, not sure what he was seeing. Was that one alley or two? Were there three streets meeting at that corner or five?

"I told you," said Melchior impatiently. "I counted the roads and made more. But it isn't enough."

"Can't you bring them all together, like you did before? Put them all in one place so I can use my sword?"

"They are too scattered. Besides, death is not the answer here."

Tarlan watched helplessly as the flames rose higher and higher. Most of the villagers had given up hope and were running, screaming, away from the fire. But the only direction left open to them was west, toward the sea. When they reached the water, they would be able to go no farther.

Burn or drown! Tarlan thought desperately. *Which would I choose?*

"What can we do?"

"You must stay, Tarlan. Do what you can. There are lives to be saved, even now."

"What about you?"

"I will try to count to seven. Hope that I reach it."

Melchior tugged at the ruff of feathers on Nasheen's neck, urging the thorrod over Tarlan's head and directing her out to sea. Tarlan watched, his stomach churning with both hope and despair.

Seven? What are you talking about, old man?

Directly below him, a jet of fire shot straight up from a collapsing building. Theeta veered sideways, narrowly avoiding being swallowed by the sudden eruption of flame. By the time she recovered, Nasheen was just a dot against the smoke-filled sky.

"Help! Help me!"

The cry was coming from a row of houses in the shadow of the falling building. Tarlan had no need to tell Theeta to head toward it.

Flames were steadily consuming each house in turn. Standing in the attic window of the last in the row was a little boy, no more than six years old. "Help!" he screamed again.

Theeta slowed, thumping her wings hard to maintain a steady hover in the billowing smoke. As Tarlan eased her closer, two more faces appeared behind that of the boy—a man and a woman. His parents, Tarlan supposed.

"You'll have to jump!" he shouted. "Hurry!"

Terror bloomed on the faces of the boy and the woman. The man's expression stiffened. He clamped his hands around the boy's shoulders and, without giving his son time to protest, threw him bodily out of the window.

The boy landed sprawling on Theeta's back. Tarlan grabbed his collar and planted him into the thickest part of the thorrod's golden ruff. Looking up, he saw the man and woman standing hand in hand on the window's wooden sill. Thick smoke gushed around them.

"Jump!" Tarlan yelled.

They jumped. At the same instant, Theeta edged a little closer to the building, which was now completely engulfed in flames. The man and woman landed awkwardly. Theeta lurched sideways from the impact and the man nearly slid off, but between them, Tarlan and the woman managed to drag him to safety. They clung on, coughing and choking, while Theeta powered her way into the clearer air over the sea.

"You saved us," the man croaked, his voice thick with smoke. He clutched at Tarlan's arm. "How can we ever thank you?"

"There's no need," said Tarlan gruffly. "But maybe you can help me."

"Anything!"

"Not all the army is here. Did you see where the rest went?"

The woman nodded. "They left just after the first attack. As soon as the fires took hold, the man in charge led them away. A big man in a red cloak."

Tyro.

"They went that way," said the man, pointing eastward.

Tarlan stiffened. In the east lay Isur—where Trident and Elodie were.

A thorrod can fly a lot faster than an army can march, he told himself. *I can reach her before they do.*

"What's that?" said the boy, pointing out to sea.

At first Tarlan couldn't make out what he was seeing. A long, gray shadow lay across the horizon. As he watched it, the shadow grew bigger, deeper. It seemed as if the ocean were trying to climb up into the sky. White foam appeared along the shadow's top edge, and Tarlan understood he was looking at a wave.

A gigantic one.

"Down, Theeta!"

They deposited the family on the wooden pier, where a crowd of fleeing villagers had gathered. By now the Galadronians had returned to their boats, which were making their way down the coast, presumably to their next target.

"Don't leave us here," wailed the mother as she climbed reluctantly down from Theeta's back.

"They've sunk our boats," said the man. "We've nowhere to run to."

"You won't need to run," said Tarlan. "But you may need to hold tight."

He left them staring upward with fearful expressions. As the two thorrods struck out for the open sea, Kitheen arrowed in at Theeta's side.

"Big water," said the great black-breasted bird, for once breaking his characteristic silence.

"You can say that again," Tarlan replied.

Nasheen was a speck of gold flying high above the immense wave's leading edge. She had to fly hard to keep pace with the rushing wall of water. Melchior was on her back—not sitting but standing, with his arms outstretched and the wind gusting through his froth of white hair. His yellow robe billowed out behind him.

"Melchior!" Tarlan yelled as Theeta and Kitheen fell into formation on either side of Nasheen. "What is this?"

"The wave of seventh waves!" the wizard shouted back.

"What?"

"Have you not heard of the seventh wave?"

"Melchior, I'd never even seen the sea until a few days ago."

"Next time you stand on a beach with your feet in the surf, count the waves. One, two, three . . . The seventh wave is always bigger than the rest. I have gathered all the seventh waves and multiplied them together. What better way to fight fire than with water?"

Only half understanding, Tarlan dragged his attention from the giant wave's foaming crest and gazed at the coastline, now very close.

"It'll put out the fire, all right. There'll be nothing left to burn. Melchior—this monster will smash that village to splinters."

"Wait," said Melchior with a mischievous smile. "Watch."

Tarlan's heart was in his mouth as the wave of waves bore down on the blazing village. The fire was truly out of control now, a seething mass of orange light looming over the last few remaining buildings on the waterfront. The villagers crowded the pier, cowering before the onrushing flames. Many had jumped into the water, where they clung to the wreckage of the fishing boats; a few were trying to swim out to sea.

If the fire doesn't kill them, this wave will.

He wouldn't have thought it possible, but the huge wave grew even bigger as it approached the harbor. Now it was twice the height of the fire, now three times. It was a cliff—no, a mountain—shining deadly blue in the fierce light of the morning sun.

"Melchior!" Tarlan cried.

The wizard stood immobile on Nasheen's back, his eyes closed, his lips moving.

Tarlan could hear the villagers screaming.

An instant before the wave struck the pier, it broke apart. What had been a solid wall of ocean water fragmented into a billion tiny droplets, each one scintillating in the sunlight like a tiny star. The droplets sprayed over the pier and into the flames, not the hammer blow Tarlan had expected but a gentle, endless rain.

The terror-stricken expressions on the villagers' faces turned to openmouthed wonder. They sank to their knees while behind them the fire hissed in fury. The water from the wave continued to rain down: a fine mist that smothered the flames and cooled the charred remains of the buildings. Tarlan moved his hands through the damp air, reveling in the departure of the baking heat.

The thorrods circled as steam rose from the ruins of the village. The survivors on the pier were helping each other to their feet, tending the injured, making their way slowly back into the ash-strewn streets. Many lifted their hands and waved their gratitude.

"It's going to take them a long time to put things back together," said Tarlan. He spotted the little boy, waving and grinning from ear to ear. He waved back.

"There is much work to be done," Melchior agreed. "But I sense you are anxious to be gone."

Tarlan nodded. "I have to defend the kingdom."

Melchior raised one drenched eyebrow. "Spoken like a king. So you are not just an angry young man?"

Tarlan flushed. "Oh, I'm angry, all right. All this is just the start. The Galadronians will burn every village between here and Idil-liam, if that's what it takes. They're heading into Isur right now. I've got to get back to Trident. If I can get ahead of the army, I can give Fessan the time he needs to rally defenses. And I can make sure Elodie's safe."

"Very well. I see you are determined. Nevertheless, these people are not yet saved. Many must still be trapped in the ruins, and the injured will number in the hundreds, if not more. And the dead must be buried. I will stay and help. Will the thorrod stay with me?"

"Of course," Tarlan replied. "Nasheen—can you carry Melchior a while longer?"

Nasheen regarded the leader of her pack with one beady eye. Steam swirled around her, turning her into a ghost bird. "Wizard strange," she cawed.

Tarlan guided Theeta close enough so he could reach out and touch the other thorrod's beak. "I know he is. But I need you to stay with him. And he'll need your help. Besides, I thought you liked him, don't you?"

"Wizard light. Wizard dark. Wizard friend."

Tarlan grinned. It was so hard to unwrap the many meanings compressed into the thorrods' words. But one thing was clear to him: Nasheen wasn't about to leave Melchior behind.

"That's settled, then. Theeta! Kitheen! Let's round up the others and make flight. There's no time to waste!" Tarlan turned to Melchior. "I'm glad you're all right again. Healed, I mean, or whatever it was . . ." His voice trailed off. He still had no real idea what had happened to Melchior inside the Isle of Stars. "I really didn't wake you too soon, did I? That star—the one that wasn't—"

"It is of no consequence, Tarlan. I am very glad you were there to help me. The prophecy holds. Remember that. Good is good, and the prophecy holds. Now, away with you!"

Grinning, Tarlan tapped his heels against Theeta's flanks and spurred the giant thorrod away toward the edge of the village. They emerged from the cloud of steam and his heart surged as he saw Greythorn, Filos, and Brock standing in a line, their ears pricked and alert for his return.

"Are you ready to run?" he cried. "We've got a long way to go!"

"Yes!" they cried in unison. "Lead us!"

So they set off, heading back toward the gap in the cliffs, the thorrods flapping steadily against a strengthening east wind, their flightless companions bounding eagerly along behind them. Tarlan didn't look back. He'd seen the sea, and although he thought it marvelous, he had other concerns now.

I'm coming, Elodie. And afterward . . . well, let's just see.

With the sun beating on their backs, Tarlan and his pack raced east.

CHAPTER 20

P arry left! And . . . thrust!"

Elodie stepped nimbly aside as Sylva struck halfheartedly at her with the sword. As Sylva stumbled, Elodie tapped her lightly on the back with the flat of her blade.

"It's no good," gasped Sylva. "I'll never learn."

"You will," called Cedric from the corner of the stable. He was sitting on a bale of hay, watching the practice duel. "You're getting better."

There was a wistful edge to his voice. *No wonder*, thought Elodie. *It'll be a long time before he's ready to raise a sword again.*

"You're a good teacher, Elodie." Sylva planted the tip of her sword on the hay-strewn ground and leaned on the hilt. Her face was bright red, and her hair had come loose. But her eyes were shining. "How did you learn all this?"

"A good friend taught me the basics," Elodie replied with a pang of sorrow. "Her name was Palenie. As for the rest—well, you learn fast in the heat of battle."

Sylva and Cedric were staring at her, both wearing an identical look of comic surprise.

"What? Did you think I spent all my time with Trident hiding away in a tent? Samial, tell them. . . ."

Samial—who was perched on another bale near Cedric—shrugged. He'd become such a part of Elodie's life that even now she sometimes forgot that nobody else could see or hear him.

"We believe you," said Sylva with a grin.

"I hear horses! They're back!" Cedric leaped awkwardly down from his hay bale and ran to the door. "Quick—hide the swords!"

Elodie plucked the sword from Sylva's grasp and handed both weapons to Samial. It was Samial who'd stolen them from the castle armory; now he tucked them out of sight behind a low bench in the corner of the barn.

Elodie joined Cedric at the door. A column of horsemen rode through the gate into the scorched garden, Lord Vicerin at its head.

"It's only been six days. I thought they'd be longer."

Elodie had wanted more time to train, to prepare for whatever might lie ahead. Still, it was satisfying to see the look of horror rising on Lord Vicerin's face as he surveyed what had once been a beautiful ornamental garden, and now looked like a battlefield.

"What has happened here?" he cried, his voice rising with fury.

Captain Gandrell steadied Vicerin's horse and spoke quietly to him. As Lord Vicerin listened, red flowers bloomed on his cheeks.

"Father does not seem best pleased about what's been going on in his absence," Cedric observed. He smiled grimly. "Let's see, there's the fire, Fessan's escape, the children . . . oh, and the assassin."

The captain continued to talk. The redness left Lord Vicerin's face, leaving it deathly pale.

"Where is she?" Lord Vicerin shouted, his voice thin and reedy. "Nothing is more important than the well-being of my daughter!"

Elodie snorted. *Of course it isn't. If I'm dead, your entire plan to control the throne collapses, doesn't it?*

She stepped out into the blackened garden.

"I'm here, Father," she called. "I'm all right. Sylva and Cedric are looking after me. They saved me."

Vicerin slithered clumsily off his horse. Having picked his way around piles of scorched vegetation, he gave her a perfunctory hug, then stood regarding her with a stern expression. Elodie endured first the physical contact, then the stare, without flinching.

"Where is the assassin now?" Lord Vicerin said coldly.

"We have him, my lord," Gandrell replied. "Would you like to—?"

"What we would like is to see his guts drawn from his belly and his body quartered to the farthest corners of Ritherlee! When we have seen this done, we shall take dinner! See to it, Gandrell!"

Ducking his head, the captain backed away and began to assemble an execution squad.

"You will not want to see this, my dear." Vicerin's tone remained icy. "You will take yourself to your chambers. Sylva, Cedric—you will see that she gets there safely. When this business is dealt with, we will review security arrangements so that nothing can touch you again."

Shaking from head to foot, Lord Vicerin turned on his heel and followed Captain Gandrell out of the garden.

"He'll double your guard," whispered Cedric as soon as his father was out of earshot. "That will make it hard to find your brother's jewel."

Not to mention getting away from here when I have it.

"We'll manage." Elodie rubbed her neck, which was now almost completely healed. She was glad they wouldn't have to watch the execution. It didn't matter that the Galadron assassin had tried to kill her; no man deserved to die in such a barbaric way.

"I suppose we'd better do as he says," Sylva sighed.

"Yes. But we haven't been to see your mother yet today."

Sylva's face fell. "We should visit her before we do anything else. I'm worried about her, Elodie. She doesn't seem to be getting any better."

◆ ◆ ◆

Lady Vicerin lay as still as the dead. Only her fingers moved, twitching minutely on top of the silk bedcovers. There was a dreadful greenish tinge in the sagging flesh beneath her eyes. Her breath was a thin, slow rasp in her throat. She seemed neither awake nor asleep, but trapped in some awful limbo between the two.

Elodie hovered near the window, allowing Sylva and Cedric to sit with their mother. The room was dim and she turned to open the drapes, hoping the sunlight would speed Lady Vicerin's recovery, or at least raise her spirits.

She'd no sooner drawn back one of the thick, velvet curtains than one of Lady Vicerin's maids bustled in and pulled it closed again. The room subsided once more into shadow.

"Forgive me, Your Highness, but Lady Vicerin don't like the light anymore," said the maid, bobbing her head.

"Oh? I just thought—"

"It's gloomy, I know. But the healer said."

Elodie looked around. "Where is she? The healer?"

The maid stared at her feet. "Went away."

"Went away? What do you mean? When's she coming back?"

Sylva and Cedric looked up from the bed.

"Begging your pardon, but I don't think she's coming back. I think she's been"—the maid glanced nervously at the door—"dismissed."

"Dismissed?" cried Cedric in astonishment. "Who would do that?"

The maid was wringing her hands and biting her lip. She looked as if she was about to cry.

"It's all right," said Elodie. "We just want what's best for your mistress. Please, tell us."

"It was him," the maid blurted. "Lord Vicerin. He said she wasn't doing her job, so he sent her away. He said there wasn't a healer in the kingdom could help her ladyship, and I tried to tell him about Frida, but he wouldn't listen, and now her ladyship's getting worse and worse, and nobody knows what to do!"

"I can't believe he did that," said Sylva. "There must be something we can—"

"Who's Frida?" Elodie interrupted.

The maid regarded her with wet eyes. "Frida of Hamblebury. They say she heals what can't be cured. They say she has certain . . . special ways. But Lord Vicerin, he won't even—"

"Where's Hamblebury?"

"Edge of the Darrand lands. Not a day's ride, I'd guess."

"Then what are we waiting for?"

"I still don't understand why Father would send the healer away," said Sylva as they descended the hill toward the village of Hamblebury.

Elodie said nothing. She'd lost count of the number of times Sylva had said this during the ride from Castle Vicerin. Cedric understood the depth of his father's evil; Sylva would work it out for herself, sooner or later.

As for Elodie, it seemed clear that Lord Vicerin simply didn't want his wife to get better.

But why?

The mist they'd been riding through was gradually thickening to fog. It bit into Elodie's skin with cold teeth. Their horses plodded patiently down the hill toward the village on a road that was now little more than a muddy track. The village itself was a scattering of ramshackle huts and barns strewn at random across the valley slopes. The buildings had a forgotten air about them, as if a giant had tossed them here and then simply walked away.

Shivering, Elodie pulled the hood closer around her head. Seated in the saddle behind her, Samial seemed unaffected by the cold.

I suppose there are some benefits to being a ghost.

The drab cloaks they'd chosen were a good disguise. Not only did they hide their finely embroidered Vicerin dresses, but they also afforded some protection against the mist, which in turn had given them excellent cover during their exit from the castle. Cedric had wanted to come with them, of course, but Elodie had insisted he stay behind.

"You have to cover for us," she'd explained. "If anyone asks, say we're sorting through all our childhood toys in the tower attic. Tell them it's the only place we'll feel safe until your father puts my new bodyguard in place. And whatever you do, tell them we don't want to be disturbed!"

Cedric had made no attempt to hide his displeasure, but he'd agreed all the same.

"Just be careful," he'd said as he waved them out of the castle gate.

Careful was exactly what Elodie intended to be. Hamblebury was part of the Darrand estate, which meant its inhabitants might well be hostile to any Vicerins venturing here. Hence the cloaks.

In any event, she needn't have worried. Although the village was busy with men and women going about their daily chores—chopping wood, winnowing grain, repairing roofs—its inhabitants seemed somehow sad and turned in on themselves.

Maybe it's the war. Or perhaps life in Hamblebury is just hard.

One of the villagers—a middle-aged woman with a spreading belly and tired eyes—did eventually look up at them. Elodie smiled at her and asked if she knew where Frida lived. The woman pointed toward a thatched cottage almost lost in the fog. Elodie thanked her and they rode on.

"What about the horses?" said Sylva as they dismounted. There was no hitching rail outside the cottage, just a stack of logs cut for firewood, and the horses wouldn't have to wander far to get lost.

"They'll be all right." Elodie nodded to Samial.

Sylva smiled. "Of course!" She might not be able to see the ghost, but by now she was becoming used to his presence.

Elodie knocked on the door. A boy of about five years old opened it. Upon seeing Elodie and Sylva, he called for his mother. A short, skinny woman appeared and studied them with shrewd gray eyes. Her hair was gray too, drawn into a tight bun, and her baggy black dress reached all the way to the ground.

"Strangers," she said. Her voice was surprisingly deep. "What brings you?"

"Are you Frida?" Elodie asked.

After a long pause the woman said, "Yes."

"My mother is sick," said Sylva. "Someone told us you might be able to help."

Another pause.

"I might. Come."

The door was low enough that they had to duck, but the cottage's interior was warm and welcoming, with a large hearth in which a fire blazed. Over the fire hung a cooking pot. Through another door Elodie saw a pantry stocked with what looked like jars of food and preserves. The boy was hiding in there, staring at them with wide eyes, his thumb corked in his mouth.

Elodie looked around, momentarily confused. She'd never been here before. *So why does it feel like home?*

"How does she ail?"

"What?" Elodie was still staring into the pantry. *Those aren't preserves. They're potions. And that isn't a pot. It's a cauldron.*

"How does she ail?" Frida repeated. "The sick mother."

"She's eaten hardly anything for days," said Sylva, who didn't appear to have noticed anything strange about the cottage. "Except for a few spoons of broth. Her skin is cold and pale, sort of greenish. And she won't . . . she won't wake up. . . ."

Frida gave Elodie a curious look, then shooed the boy out of the pantry. He ran from the cottage, still sucking his thumb. Frida rummaged among the shelves for a moment, then returned holding a small bottle of dark green liquid.

Potion, Elodie thought.

Her eyes roved over countless more bottles stacked on the pantry shelves. *That one cures backache*, she thought. *That one removes warts.*

She shook herself. How could she possibly know such things?

Frida placed the bottle into Elodie's hands.

"Use but a little," she said. "Too much, and she will sleep forever."

As she released the bottle, her fingertips brushed Elodie's skin. A jolt ran up Elodie's arm, and it was all she could do not to cry out. Frida's eyes widened, and she knew the gray-haired woman had felt it too.

"Witch blood!" said Frida. "Your mother?"

"Yes. My mother was a witch."

Sylva gasped beside her, but Elodie felt a rush of understanding. So that was why the cottage had felt so immediately homely. Her mother must have had potions too, and knowledge like Frida's, maybe even lived in a cottage like this. . . .

Questions were bubbling up inside her, but before she could ask them, the boy burst in.

"Men!" he wailed. "Men riding monsters!"

Fear filled Frida's gray eyes. "I knew he would come. Vicerin has left us alone until now. Now he is here!"

From outside came the sound of hoofbeats and long, wailing cries. Frida bustled the boy back into the pantry and opened a trap-door in the floor.

"Hide with us," she said urgently, lowering the boy into the cellar. "If Vicerin's soldiers see you, they will kill you."

"No," said Sylva. "They won't."

She threw off her cloak, revealing her dress with its blue Vicerin sash. Frida gasped.

"I am Sylva Mayanne Vicerin. And they will answer to my command!"

Before Elodie could stop her, Sylva had rushed out through the door. She hurried after her, the little boy's words echoing in her head.

Men riding monsters. What does that mean?

Outside, the mist swirled like torn silk. Hulking shapes moved through it: men on horseback, carrying swords.

But horses don't have antlers. And those weapons are too long to be swords.

"I thought it was my father's men," said Sylva, her eyes wide with confusion. "Who are they?"

A huge animal burst through the fog. It was twice the size of Elodie's horse. From the back of its domed head sprouted a pair of spreading antlers, much bigger than those on the stags' heads hanging on the walls of the castle. Its eyes were as black as the night sky.

On its back rode a man wearing armor made from bony plates, while over his head was thrown a scaly hood. The hood was lined with teeth. The face inside it was coarse of skin and dark with grime. He carried a bone spear from which hung a ragged white pennant.

Now she knew what they were: she'd seen drawings in her books of these wandering barbarians, hunting herds of elk on the frozen plains of Yalasti.

"They're Helkrags."

Beside the log pile, Samial was struggling with the two horses, both of which were rearing in terror. The Helkrag bore down on them, brandishing his spear. Huntress broke free from Samial's grip and kicked out with her back legs, causing half the logs to tumble outward in a wooden avalanche, right in front of the oncoming rider.

With an incoherent yell, he pulled his strange steed around and rode away into the mist.

Sylva retreated back into the doorway, only to meet Frida venturing out.

The witch's face was white with shock. "Helkrags! But they never leave the Icy Wastes!"

Elodie frowned. It didn't make sense. "Vicerin sent his army to Yalasti to wipe them out," she said. "What are they doing here?"

"Father's plan must have failed," said Sylva.

"No!" Elodie's mind was racing. The pieces fell into place. "This is what he planned all along. He never wanted to destroy the Helkrags. He wanted to recruit them!"

"But why would he do that?" Sylva wailed. "Why bring barbarians into Ritherlee?"

"Elodie!" said Samial, still fighting to keep control of the frightened horses. "We must go!"

The fog was hectic with bulky shadows and thick with distant screams. This was no mere skirmish; this was a full-scale battle. What chance would these villagers have against such a formidable foe?

Not much, Elodie thought grimly.

A sound like rising thunder signaled the approach of yet more riders. Three elks loomed from the mist, each carrying an armor-clad warrior. The one in the lead carried a white pennant at the end of his spear: the same man they'd first seen, now with reinforcements.

The nearest Helkrag—a huge brute whose hood was made not of scales but blue-and-white striped fur—spurred his antlered steed straight toward Elodie. He was wielding a heavy bone ax. Glad she'd come armed, Elodie drew out her sword and met his blow with its blade. The two weapons locked together. As the elk sped past, she ducked her head and twisted her body, wrenching the sword and tipping the rider off balance. He flew from the crude saddle and landed on his back in the mud. Completing her spin, Elodie drove her sword between two of the bony plates protecting his chest. It sank home with a satisfying crunch, and the Helkrag's body went limp.

"To your left!" shouted Samial.

Elodie whirled around to see the second rider swerving toward her. At the same time, the warrior with the white pennant was bearing down on Sylva and Frida.

Sidestepping, she let the elk run past, then spun to face it as its rider reined it into a turn. In the same instant, Samial pulled the lowermost logs out from beneath the stack of firewood that was still standing. The rest of the logs tumbled across the yard, smashing into the legs of the elk. Elodie heard snapping sounds that might have been splintering wood, or fracturing bones, or both.

With an unearthly bellow, the elk fell onto its side, its broken legs splayed horribly in the air. Unable to jump clear, the Helkrag was pinned beneath it. Both elk and rider lay helpless amid the scattered logs, writhing in pain, until Elodie stepped forward and cut their throats, one after the other. The entire encounter had taken little more than two breaths, and throughout it she'd felt nothing but icy calm.

By now the leader had reached the doorway. He brandished his ax in one hand, and his spear in the other. Sylva cringed back. Elodie had made her bring her sword, but in her panic Sylva seemed to have forgotten she was carrying it.

Elodie started to run, but she was too far away.

Then Frida threw out her hand. It was a curiously idle gesture; she looked as if she were tossing seed out for the chickens. Something glittered in the air.

When it met the Helkrag's face, it caught fire.

The flames were brief and bright. When they subsided, Elodie glimpsed the charred edges of the Helkrag's tooth-lined hood and the red mass of burned flesh where his face had once been. She clamped her hand to her mouth to stifle a scream.

The barbarian warrior slumped in his saddle, and the elk bore his body away into the mist.

"Elodie!" Samial called again. "We cannot stay here. There are too many of them!"

He was right. Shouts rang through the mist. Bone weapons

clashed against what Elodie guessed might be farming implements as, unseen in the fog, the battle raged throughout Hamblebury.

"We have what we came for," said Sylva shakily. "We have to go."

Elodie's hands remained clamped on her sword. What kind of queen would she become if she turned her back on those who needed her help?

I can't help. Not them, not here, not now.

But she could help Sylva's mother.

Shaking, she put her sword away.

"Samial," she said. "Bring the horses. We're leaving. Now." She eyed Frida and added, "Do you and your son want to live?"

Elodie remembered little of the desperate ride back to the castle. They hurried immediately to Lady Vicerin's quarters and found Cedric waiting outside the door. The minute she saw his face, Elodie knew something was terribly wrong.

"Oh, Sylva," he said, tears spilling over his cheeks. "I wish you'd been here."

"Here for what?" The shock in her eyes and the tremble in her voice made it clear that Sylva already knew.

Elodie followed them inside. Lady Vicerin lay in her bed, and Elodie's first impression was that she looked just the same as when they'd left.

Then she saw that the pale woman's chest was utterly still.

"She died not long after you set off," said Cedric, fighting to keep his voice steady.

"We were too late," Sylva sobbed. She rubbed her dead mother's hand, as if she were trying to urge life back into it.

Tears were pricking Elodie's eyes. She turned away. The drapes were open now that Lady Vicerin had gone and misty light poured through the window, bathing the bed with a cool, gray glow.

Frida tugged at her sleeve.

"May I?" said the witch. Her eyes were oddly alert.

"I think it's too late for potions."

"You speak the truth. But that is not my meaning."

Frida went to the bed and touched the back of her hand to Lady Vicerin's brow. Then she ran her fingertips down the dead woman's neck and pressed them against the top of her chest.

"Dead, yes," she said at last. "But not sick."

"Not . . . what do you mean?" said Sylva through her tears.

"This woman—your mother?"

"Yes."

"Then, I'm sorry to say, your mother was not sick. This is poison. Your mother was murdered."

Sylva and Cedric stared at Frida dumbfounded. Sylva's throat tightened, and her shocked eyes opened wide. Elodie felt helpless, wanting to offer her some kind of comfort, but knowing there was nothing she could say.

Elodie's eyes strayed to the empty bowl on the night table.

The broth! Captain Leom said he felt better when he stopped eating the broth!

Elodie felt cold all over.

Lord Vicerin. Every time, it comes back to you.

Everything was clear, painfully so. Vicerin had wanted Captain Leom out of the way before his men returned with the Helkrags.

But why kill Lady Vicerin?

Why would you want to poison your wife?

CHAPTER 21

Bracing himself, Gulph closed his fingers around the hilt of Slater's sword, which Ossilius had jammed into the door mechanism. He pulled, and for a moment he thought the sword wasn't going to move. Then, with an earsplitting screech, it came loose. Gulph flew backward, landing hard on the floor.

He lay there, panting, staring up at the low ceiling of the little storeroom. His whole body ached after the long climb up the crystal pillar and from scrambling over the many rockfalls during the even longer trek back through the tunnels. *It would be so easy just to lie here. Safe from the bakaliss. Safe from the undead.*

Safe from the prophecy.

But he wasn't safe. And neither were his friends.

He sat up, checked the crown was still safe in the bundle on his back, used the dim torchlight to find his way to the lever that operated the door, and pulled it.

As the huge bull-headed statue rumbled aside, he opened himself to the strange, scratchy feeling that came over him whenever he turned invisible. He looked down at his body as it melted away, unnerved by the control he was developing over his power.

Powers, Gulph thought, remembering how he'd been able to read the memories of Sidebottom John. *I have more than one talent now.*

A gust of wind extinguished the torch. Even as the flame winked out, sunlight exploded over him. Gulph screwed up his eyes; for days he'd experienced only the dim twilight of Celestis, and the torrent of light was overwhelming.

Gradually his eyes adjusted. He stepped cautiously outside. Accompanying the flood of light was a thunderous cacophony of noise: the crash of falling stonework, the roar of flames, the guttural cries of the undead.

Gulph looked up at the statue of the bull-headed man and realized with a start that he had no idea how to close it from the outside. Nor did he have time to work it out.

Rummaging through some nearby wreckage, he found a heap of blackened timbers—the remains of a burned wagon. Working fast, he propped them across the secret doorway, then stood back and appraised his work.

Not perfect. But it will have to do.

Gulph turned and took a hard look at what Idilliam had become.

Most of the buildings outside the city wall had been knocked flat. Rubble was strewn all around. Countless fires blazed amid the ruins, sending pillars of black smoke into the cloudless sky.

The undead were everywhere.

Crowds of them shambled through the ruins, tearing both at each other and at what was left of the outskirts of Idilliam. They all looked badly decayed, with flesh hanging from their bones. Many were little more than skeletons. The stench of rot was unbearable.

Gulph watched as one group of the undead grappled with another. A former soldier tore the arms from his opponent. The crippled corpse dropped to the ground and rolled sideways until its tattered shoulders made contact with the severed limbs. The arms reattached themselves, torn flesh knitting miraculously into broken bone, and the restored creature rose up in time to rip the head from the thing that had mutilated it.

Sickened, Gulph turned away, only to be faced by a gang of five corpses staggering in his direction. From the colorful hanging scraps of their clothing, he guessed they'd once been courtiers.

Fighting the urge to vomit, he drew Kalia's sword. To his relief, the blade had picked up his invisibility. He held it before him, reassured by its unseen weight, hoping desperately that its power remained intact.

But he didn't need to use it. The undead passed him by, leaving him free to make his way toward the distant city gates, which stood open. He ran most of the way, avoiding the undead as best he could, and breathing through his mouth in an effort to avoid the dreadful smell.

When he reached the open gateway, he stopped and stared.

On the great stone arch, impaled on long metal spikes, were two severed heads. The skin on their faces had turned a sickly green color and had clearly been pecked at by crows. But Gulph recognized them all the same.

One head belonged to Nynus.

The other was Magritt's.

For the second time in moments, Gulph felt all his strength drain away.

I can't stay here. I'd rather face the bakaliss than this.

He tried to tear his eyes from the decomposed faces of the former king and dowager queen. But he couldn't. So he closed them instead and conjured in his mind's eye the image of another face: that of his friend Pip, whom he'd come here to rescue.

The imaginary Pip smiled, and when Gulph opened his eyes again a great cloud of smoke had drifted over the arch to shroud the severed heads. Now that Nynus and Magritt were no longer staring down at him with their dead, accusatory gazes, he found the strength to move on.

Beyond the gate Gulph saw no evidence of the strange combat that he'd encountered outside. In fact, Idilliam appeared to be deserted. He picked his way carefully through the city, keeping to the edges of the roads to avoid the puddles of blood running down the central gutters.

Blood, but no corpses. Where are they all?

Peering in through the grimy windows of a tavern, he saw that the barroom was full of people. His heart lifted ... then he saw the torn flesh hanging slack from their faces and the raw bone jutting from the ends of their fingers.

He hurried on. All the buildings Gulph passed were filled with the undead. He saw nobody alive. As he made his way through the maze of streets, gradually approaching the great walls of Castle Tor, it dawned on him that Idilliam was no longer a city.

It's just one giant tomb.

Rounding another corner, Gulph found himself looking up at the towering stonework of the castle's western wall. With a start he realized he'd stood on this exact spot before, shortly after he and Nynus had escaped from the Vault of Heaven.

I climbed the wall. I wanted to get inside and rescue my friends. Then the guards came. ...

It seemed so long ago.

Now here he was again, in the same place, with the same hope. The glimpse he'd had of Sidebottom John's memories had shown his friends in chains. That meant they were probably in the castle, or perhaps the Vault of Heaven.

"Pip?" he breathed. "Where are you?"

The sun glanced off something shiny. It seemed to be hanging right in front of his eyes. The tip of Kalia's crystal sword! Gulph watched in dismay as the blade steadily became visible. In a moment he would be able to see the sword's hilt and his own hand wrapped around it. And then . . .

Gulph ducked into a nearby alley. Squeezing his way between two slumped, timber-framed buildings, he hid behind a mound of moldering crates and rotting vegetables. His heart was hammering.

Both his hands were now visible. He held his breath, concentrating, trying to conjure up those essential sensations—*sand, heat*—but to no avail. He let out his breath with a gasp. He'd never felt so exhausted.

Come on, Gulph! If they see me, you'll be just another corpse wandering about the ruins. . . .

Forcing himself to relax, he made ready to try again. But before he could collect his thoughts, the pile of rubbish to his right stood up.

Crying out, Gulph stumbled backward. What new monster was this?

The thing advanced. It seemed to be made of broken wood and compost: a hideous, lurching demon with misshapen arms and a head covered in fungus. Muck showered from it like poisoned rain.

Gulph held up the sword, aware now that most of his body was visible. The muck monster came on, shedding its outer covering to reveal what he should have guessed was underneath: the naked bones of one of the undead.

The tottering corpse made a sudden lunge. The fungus collapsed in an awful avalanche, revealing a grinning skull. A single toadstool jutted from one eye socket, its red-and-white spotted cap looking hideously jaunty.

Shouting again, Gulph swung Kalia's sword. The blade hissed through the air, crystal bit into bone, and the skeleton folded up like a child's puzzle. It hit the ground with a soft thump, no longer a monster, merely the remains of some poor soul who'd already passed on to a distant place.

A better place, I hope.

Gulph felt the rest of the invisibility leave him in a kind of gusting sigh. It was a relief. Using his power was like tightening all his muscles at the same time: tense and tiring.

But I'm going to have to do it again to find—

"Gulph? Is it you? Is it really you?"

The voice was frail and wondering. Lowering the sword, Gulph turned slowly around. Someone stood in the sunlight at the end of the alley: someone small, dressed in a grimy red jerkin and green britches.

It was Pip.

His throat too tight to speak, Gulph stumbled out of the alley and swept her up in his arms. He held her tight, and when her arms wrapped around him and hugged him back, he started to cry.

They stayed that way for a long time, until Gulph finally relaxed his hold and stepped away from his oldest friend. He looked her up and down, taking in her thin body, the filthy state of her clothes, the hollowness in her cheeks, and his joy turned to a fierce breed of sorrow.

"What have they done to you?"

"I'm alive." Pip's hand crept shyly to his cheek, then dropped again. There was an iron manacle around her wrist. "And so are you. That's all that matters."

"What about the others? The Tangletree Players?"

"They're all right."

"Are they really? Pip, what's this?" Gulph touched the manacle. She looked away. "He keeps us chained."

"Who? Who keeps you chained?" But he already knew.

"Brutan. We're *his* players now. He . . . I don't know how, but he sees to it that the . . . the dead ones don't touch us. We perform for him. It keeps us alive." Tears left clean trails in the grime on her cheeks.

"Well, you don't have to perform anymore. I'm here to rescue you, Pip. All of you."

She shook her head. "I don't see how . . ."

"I've learned a lot since I saw you last. Watch this."

Gulph took a step back. Forcing away his tiredness, he made

himself invisible. Doing so made his head throb. He held it for just a moment, then returned his body to the visible world.

Pip's face dropped. "Oh. Everything's changed, hasn't it, Gulph?"

The sadness in her eyes made Gulph want to cry again.

"Some of it's for the better, Pip. I promise."

"Do I know you, Gulph? Do I really know you?"

"It's me, Pip. It really is. I'll explain it to you, all of it, but it'll have to wait. We have to go to the others now. Will you take me?"

"Of course I will." But she didn't move, just stared unhappily at the ground.

"Pip? Are you all right?"

She lifted her head and whispered, "Come on, then."

Keeping to the narrow side streets, they circled around the castle until they reached the huge southern entrance. Like the main city gates, it stood wide open. A crowd of the undead milled around in the courtyard beyond, some walking in circles, many just standing still and staring at the ground.

Gulph held back, nervous about approaching. He'd spent many days here as Nynus's chief courtier. Castle Tor should have felt familiar; instead it seemed overwhelmingly strange.

"We'll be safe," said Pip. "You'll see. Can you do that . . . that trick again?"

Making himself invisible once more, Gulph followed her through the towering gates and into the courtyard. The walking corpses turned to watch Pip as she passed, the flames that served them as eyes brightening with greed. Skeletal hands reached for her, then drew back at the last moment, repelled by whatever unseen shield served her as protection. Gulph's hand twitched on the hilt of his sword. But they passed through the crowd unmolested.

Pip led him to a tower jutting from the inner curtain wall. She pulled open a door, kicking aside a swatch of black cloth that had blown against it. Gulph recognized the pattern: it was the standard of King Nynus, which had once flown on every mast over the castle.

Looking up, he saw a new flag fluttering in the breeze over the tower: the red pennant of Brutan, flying over Castle Tor once again.

Inside the castle, Gulph's sense of strangeness increased. He knew every twist and turn of its corridors; at the same time it felt like a foreign land. The fine tapestries that had once lined the ancient stone walls had been torn down. Every piece of wooden furniture they passed had been smashed. Pictures had been slashed or smeared with what looked like blood.

The devastation filled him with sadness. He adjusted the bundle on his back, sensing the weight of the gold crown inside.

The kingdom will know peace again. I'll make sure of it.

Like the rest of Idilliam, the castle was now inhabited by the undead. They thronged the junctions where the corridors crossed, and every time Gulph and Pip had to force their way through another crowd of corpses, Gulph gritted his teeth, convinced Pip would be attacked.

But although it was obvious the undead wanted to tear into her, Pip's immunity kept them at bay.

Will it be as easy coming out? Gulph wondered.

At last they reached the throne room. Gulph steeled himself. The first time he'd been here, he'd been wearing a ridiculous bakaliss costume and carrying a poisoned crown. Later, he'd served in the throne room under King Nynus, watching helplessly as he'd tortured children in a bid to find the triplets of the prophecy.

Pip must have sensed his hesitation. "What's wrong, Gulph? Do you want to go back?"

He shook himself. "I'm all right. I just heard an echo of something."

"Maybe we should turn around."

"What? Why?"

"It's just that . . . I don't think this is going to work."

"I'm not leaving you here. Not any of you."

Pip twisted her hands. Her face was a mask of agony. "Just go, Gulph. Please, this was a mistake. He's going to—"

A thick, broken voice boomed out from the throne room.

"Little one! I see you there in the shadows. Come to me. Come to me now!"

"It's too late for me," Pip moaned, "but you can still get away. Just go, Gulph!"

Shoulders slumped, she stepped into the throne room.

Go? Gulph thought. *That's the last thing I'm going to do!*

But he'd gone only three steps before he realized he could see his hands, floating in the air before him. He concentrated, trying to render them invisible again, but his head felt ready to burst. He looked down at his body in despair as, little by little, it formed itself out of thin air.

He stopped, torn between wanting to follow Pip and knowing that staying invisible gave him the only advantage he had: surprise.

All I need is a few moments of rest, then the power will come back.

But would it?

Heart thudding, Gulph peered through the giant doorway. The throne room looked much as he remembered it: a long chamber with a high ceiling. During Nynus's brief reign, he'd ordered the wooden shutters to be drawn over the windows, so sensitive was he to daylight. The shutters had remained in place, although many of the timbers were broken. The sun sliced through the gaps, thin swords of light cutting the dusty air.

At the far end of the room, standing on a wooden platform, was the throne. On it sat Brutan, Gulph's father and the undead king of Toronia.

Rotten flesh clung to his bones in malformed clumps. His once-fine robes had been reduced to shreds of dirty cloth. His face was little more than a vacant skull. In its eye sockets, red flames danced.

Skipping clumsily in a circle before the undead king were the Tangletree Players.

Noddy! Oh, there's Willum, and Simeon . . . Gulph's hand went to his mouth as he picked out each of his old friends in turn. He'd half expected to find them undead, mere shadows of their former selves.

Dorry! Gulph thought suddenly. *I can't see Dorry!*

As he watched, Noddy tripped over the wooden hobbyhorse he'd been riding. Metal clanked as he fell to the floor, and Gulph saw they were all wearing chains. No wonder their movements were clumsy.

No, he thought, *it's more than that. They're so tired they're about to collapse.*

A liquid bellow rose up from the end of the hall, accompanied by a repetitive thumping sound. The thumping came from Brutan's skeletal hand as he pounded it on the arm of the throne. The bellow, Gulph realized, was laughter.

"Up again!" thundered the undead king in his dreadful, broken voice. "Up again and fall! We like to see you fall!"

By now Pip had reached the spot where the players were going through their weary performance. As she helped Noddy to his feet, Brutan lurched up out of the throne. Despite his wasted appearance, he was still enormous.

"Little one!" he roared. "Come forward! What news?"

Gulph stared at Pip, confused. Did Brutan send the players out to spy on Idilliam? Was that why he'd kept them alive?

"You are the last, little one," Brutan went on. "Did you succeed where the others failed? Or does another one of you have to die?"

"Please," said Noddy. "We don't want to die."

"Oh, but you do it so well!"

Dorry? Do you mean Dorry?

An image formed in Gulph's mind: the undead king taking the little juggler and breaking him like a branch. Poor Dorry's face growing pale and slack, then flames rising in his dead eyes. . . .

"Well?!" bellowed the undead king, impatient for an answer. He rose from his throne and lumbered off the platform. He was huge and awkward, a dead man with the bulk of a bear and no more grace than a puppet.

The players stood in silence, their heads hanging. Only Pip looked at the oncoming king.

Brutan's hand shot out and grabbed Noddy around the throat. Noddy's shriek was cut off as fingers of bone dug into his flesh.

"You know something," growled Brutan, his burning eyes turned toward Pip. "Tell me what it is, or this one joins my army."

"Let him go!" cried Pip.

"I think not. What do you know?"

"Nothing!"

Noddy beat his fists weakly against Brutan's slime-covered arms.

"Pity," Brutan remarked. "This one is nearly done. Never mind, there are plenty more."

"All right!" Pip screamed. "I'll do it! Just let him go!"

Sobbing uncontrollably, she ran toward the doorway where Gulph was hiding. When she reached him, he opened his arms to catch her.

"Pip! What did he ask you to do? Why did he . . . ?"

To his surprise, Pip evaded his arms and seized him by the wrist. Kalia's crystal sword flew from his hand and hit the floor with a musical chime.

"I'm sorry," she wept.

Gulph was too shocked to protest. Strong despite her small size, Pip hauled him to the center of the throne room. One by one, the faces of the Tangletree Players turned toward him.

Slowly, Brutan released his grip on Noddy's throat. The fire in his eyes burned brighter.

Pip brought Gulph to a halt before what had once been his father. At the same time, the shadows behind the throne shifted, coalescing into the shapes of a dozen undead legionnaires. Rotten flesh hung beneath their bronze armor; in the narrow beams of sunlight, their bare skulls grinned.

"I'm sorry," Pip repeated. She began to cry. "King Brutan, please, don't kill them. Just let them live."

"Is this him?" grunted Brutan, cocking his grotesque head to one side. "Is this really him?"

Pip's hand left Gulph's wrist. Gulph reached for her, confused, wanting to comfort her, wanting to run. . . .

"Pip," he said. Pain pounded through his head. The whole throne room seemed to be spinning. "What's going on?"

She shook him off. She took a step toward Brutan.

"We made a deal!" she sobbed. "I've done what you asked. Now let the rest of them go!"

"What, Pip?" said Gulph. "What have you done?"

Pip gave him a final look, her face twisted with sorrow. Then she turned to Brutan.

"Here he is," she said. "I've found him, and I've brought him to you. Here he is, Brutan. Here is your son."

ACT THREE

CHAPTER 22

Elodie sat on the bench by her bedroom window. Outside, fog lingered over the castle, as if it had sunk to the bottom of a deep and featureless lake. Elodie guessed that noon was approaching, but she couldn't be sure; the sun was nowhere to be seen.

In her hands was the garrote.

Elodie turned it over, revolted by the slickness of the leather, fascinated by its intricate weave. She'd spotted it lying in the courtyard when they'd cantered back from Hamblebury, still believing they could save Lady Vicerin, and something had compelled her to pick it up. Now she couldn't put it down.

This thing nearly killed me.

Except that wasn't quite right.

That man nearly killed me.

The Galadronian assassin had been executed, yet still the thought of him filled her with dread. She ran her trembling fingers over the garrote, half expecting the evil thing to leap from her hands and wrap itself around her throat. To complete the task for which it had been made.

She started. Something had changed.

The leather had felt smooth at first; now it was coarse and gritty. The bench was changing too, its wooden surface shifting beneath her like a slowly rising wave, growing suddenly hot. Something like the sun baked the back of her neck, but when she turned to the window, she saw only the flat gray face of the fog.

A pale man-shape flitted across her vision. A soft thud made the air shake, although she would have sworn she'd heard nothing. A sigh followed, low and sad.

There was someone else in the bedroom.

The pace of Elodie's heartbeat doubled. She stood, fingers clenched on the garrote. She wasn't afraid, just . . .

On the edge. I'm on the edge of something. But I don't know what it is.

"Who's there?" she whispered, not wanting the guards she knew were outside the door to hear.

Nothing. No reply.

"Show yourself, ghost."

Still no response. The air was dry and hot. Her eyes stung, as if they were full of sand. Her mouth felt full of sand too.

Why would there be sand in my bedroom?

The man-shape reared up before her, suddenly *there*. She recognized him at once: it was the assassin who'd tried to kill her.

Whose hanged body had only just been taken down from the gallows.

Her hands flew up to stifle the scream. Her fingers opened and flung the garrote away. Instantly the ghostly figure vanished. A cold gust drove away the warmth she'd felt, and Elodie was once more alone.

She rubbed her eyes. They were clear.

With shaking fingers, she reached for where the garrote had landed on the bed.

If I touch it, will he appear again?

She drew back her hand.

What had just happened? Could she do more than just see ghosts? Could she make them appear before her? She felt as if her whole body was fizzing, her head throbbing as she tried to make sense of it all.

Frida knows magic, she thought. *Maybe she can help.*

Elodie wrapped her hand in a handkerchief and gingerly picked up the garrote. To her relief, touching it through the silk didn't summon the assassin's ghost again. She folded the handkerchief around the horrible thing and hid it in the pocket of her dress.

She went to the door. Pressing her ear to the wood, she listened to the murmured conversation of the two guards outside. The door itself was locked—she knew that without trying the handle.

"For your protection, my dear," Lord Vicerin had explained.

To keep me prisoner, you mean, was the thought she'd hidden behind her grateful smile.

She dropped to her knees and peeped through the keyhole. As she'd suspected, Samial was right there, perched at the top of the stairs. The guards, of course, had no idea they were in the company of a ghost.

Still thinking about Frida, Elodie rummaged in a drawer until she found the bottle of potion the witch had given her.

This came too late to help Lady Vicerin. Perhaps it can help me instead.

On a nearby table was a tray of small cakes that had been sent up to her after breakfast. Their gaudy colors looked ridiculous to her, so it was with satisfaction that she unstoppered Frida's potion bottle. She sniffed its contents: no smell. That was good.

She sprinkled a few drops of the potion over the cakes, hid the bottle once more, picked up the tray, and rapped her knuckles on the door. A key rattled in the lock and the door swung open.

"I have no appetite today," Elodie said, adopting the familiar role of the spoiled princess. "Send these back, or eat them yourselves—I don't care."

She was pleased to see the guard's eyes light up as he took the tray. The door closed, the key turned, and Elodie waited.

A few moments passed, then the door opened once more, this time revealing Samial's smiling face. He brandished the key triumphantly. Behind him the two guards lay snoring on the floor, surrounded by cake crumbs.

"Where's Frida?" said Elodie.

Samial led her through the castle's least-used corridors to Sylva's private chambers. There they found Frida holding Sylva's hand and talking quietly to her, while the witch's young son played with a set of wooden bricks in a corner of the room.

As soon as she saw Sylva's tearstained face, Elodie went to hug her.

"I keep telling myself it's a bad dream," Sylva sobbed. "But it isn't, is it?"

"Oh, Sylva."

"I hate my father for what he's done. And I hate hating him!"

"It's all right," Elodie soothed her. "You don't have to hate anyone." But the truth was that she couldn't imagine *not* hating Lord Vicerin.

"But how could he do it? She's dead, Elodie! My mother is dead—and he killed her!"

"We'll avenge her," Elodie said fiercely. "I promise."

Sniffling, Sylva pulled away and took Elodie's hands. "You shouldn't have come here. It's too dangerous now."

"We were careful not to be seen."

"'We'?" Sylva's red-rimmed eyes flicked around the room. "He's here, your . . . friend?"

"Yes. That's why I'm here—sort of. There's something . . . Sylva, I have to talk about . . . Oh, I don't know where to start."

Frida stepped forward.

"The beginning will do well, my child," said the witch.

They sat at the table in the corner of the room and Elodie related her strange experience with the garrote, which she placed on the table as grisly evidence.

Her words came out falteringly at first, but the more she spoke the easier it became. Soon everything was pouring out. Putting Samial's arrowhead beside the garrote, she told Sylva and Frida about how she'd met Samial in the Weeping Woods, on the fateful day when she'd first learned that she could see and hear ghosts. She talked about the ghost army: how they'd fought and how, after the Battle of the Bridge, she'd finally laid their spirits to rest.

"Keeping the arrowhead let me keep Samial," she explained, touching her fingers to the little metal triangle. Then she nudged the handkerchief in which she'd wrapped the garrote. "If I keep this, will the ghost of that awful assassin start following me around? If that's true, I want to be rid of it right now! There's . . . oh, there's just so much I don't understand."

"You have more choice than you realize," said Frida. "The ghosts do not command you, Elodie. You command the ghosts."

The witch's words sent a thrill down Elodie's spine. Yet still she felt daunted by everything that lay before her. "I just wish I knew which way to turn."

"You are one of three," said Frida, as if that explained everything. "There are no maps for your journey."

Elodie sighed. "That's the trouble. I feel as if . . . I know where I have to go, but I can't see how to get there. Too many obstacles are standing in my way."

"Then you have to go around them," said Sylva.

"Or knock them aside," added Samial.

"Knock them aside," Elodie echoed, for the benefit of the others in the room. She glanced at Sylva. "Lord Vicerin is one of those obstacles."

Sylva said nothing.

"It would take an army to knock *him* aside," Elodie mused.

She crossed to the window. Until now, her thoughts had been as foggy as the weather outside. But now something cut through them like a beam of light to reveal something solid: a plan. At last she knew what she must do.

"I need an army," she said, "so I'll raise one of my own. An army of ghosts."

Sylva stared at her. "Of ghosts?"

"Why not? I've commanded such an army before. This castle is built on the remains of a hundred fallen soldiers," she said, remembering the painting of the old Vicerin fort. "I can order them into battle again."

Sylva's eyes were wide. Beside her, Frida's face had creased into something resembling a smile.

"I believe you could," said Sylva slowly. "But how will you do it?"

Elodie's thoughts had already darted ahead to this. Her excitement was mounting. Now that she had a plan, everything seemed to be sliding into place, as if it was meant to be.

Maybe it is.

"That assassin's ghost didn't just appear," she said. "It came when I touched the garrote. If I can just gather the possessions of the dead, then . . . Frida, do you think it's possible? Will they come to me if I call? And if they come, will they fight?"

"You are one of three," Frida repeated. "You can touch the magic of the world."

Another shiver tingled down Elodie's spine.

"I think—" she began.

The door burst open and Cedric rushed in. Frida immediately left the table and gathered up her son, her face a mask of fear.

"Don't worry, you haven't been discovered," Cedric said to the witch. Then he turned to Elodie and Sylva. His face was red with exertion. "You have to come and see. They're in the courtyard garden, all of them!"

Elodie felt her stomach turning over. "Who's there?"

"Come and see!"

"I will stay here," the witch said, holding her son to her chest. "I would not be seen."

"You're safer with us," said Sylva. "We can protect you."

"I can protect myself."

Frida pulled open a deep pocket in her apron, revealing a collection of tiny bottles and what looked like twisted leaves.

Potions and powders, Elodie thought in wonder. *Enough to put a hundred guards to sleep. Or worse!*

"Hurry," said Cedric. "I don't know what's going on, but I don't like it!"

He led Elodie and Sylva from the chambers to a balcony overlooking the courtyard. Crouching behind the parapet, they peered out through the low stone pillars.

A dismal scene lay below them. The once-beautiful gardens that dominated the courtyard resembled a wasteland. The flowers in the beds were as black as the soil that held them; the arches that had once bloomed with roses were just charred stumps. The damp gray fog merely added to the sense of gloom, and once more Elodie had the unnerving sensation that the castle was drowning.

And we are drowning with it.

A wooden platform had been erected at one end of the courtyard. On it stood Lord Vicerin, resplendent in his ceremonial armor. Soldiers stood to attention on either side of him, their blue sashes brilliant despite the murky air.

A crowd of people were gathered in front of him. Most wore either military uniforms or elaborate costumes. Dozens of horses were lined up outside the stables, and as Elodie watched, more horses rode in through the gate carrying yet more visitors.

"The nobles of Ritherlee," Cedric whispered. "See—there's Lord Farrier. And the May-Henrys."

Scanning the crowd of lords and ladies, barons and dukes, Elodie spotted a face she recognized.

"There's Lady Darrand!"

The woman she'd met outside the council chamber stood tall and proud in her yellow robes. All around her, the visiting rulers of Ritherlee were deep in conversation. The murmur of their voices merged into a low rumble that filled the air as completely as the fog. Yet Lady Darrand was silent and wary. From the expression on her face, Elodie knew exactly what she was feeling.

You're afraid. And so am I.

"What are they all doing here?" said Sylva. "Why has Father summoned them?"

Lord Vicerin raised his arms. Gradually the hubbub subsided. One by one the nobles turned their heads toward their host. Vicerin swiveled his head, waiting for silence, then spoke.

"I am so glad you were all able to be here, and I welcome you with open arms, as friends. The differences that have grown up between us have damaged both this land and our relationships to the point of peril. Now it is time to set those differences aside and come together as one. Let us end this dreadful game we have all been guilty of playing, and build for ourselves a better world."

"Do not pretend we are your guests," cried a voice. Elodie wasn't surprised to see it belonged to Lady Darrand. "We come to Castle Vicerin because there is no other stronghold in Ritherlee that still stands. Your army has seen to that."

"And you are most welcome here." Lord Vicerin dipped his head and adopted a syrupy smile. "My castle—my *home*—will be your protection against the barbarian raiders who ravage our land."

"And I say thank you for it!" shouted a tall man in fine silk robes. "At least the Vicerin lands are still intact. Those Yalasti monsters have destroyed half my estate."

"And wasn't it Vicerin who destroyed the other half?" Lady Darrand snapped back.

Lord Vicerin stood patiently while the two nobles traded verbal blows. Elodie watched uncertainly, a knot of fear tightening in her stomach. She turned to Sylva and Cedric and hissed, "I don't understand. It was Vicerin who brought the Helkrags here in the first place."

"Father talks about games," Cedric replied, his hands gripping the balcony so tightly that his knuckles had turned white. "I fear he is playing one of his own."

"I don't like this," whispered Sylva. Her face was deathly pale. "I don't like this at all."

The argument spread through the courtyard, becoming a blur of voices from which Elodie could pick out only random phrases:

". . . pillaged our lands . . ."

". . . vicious brutes . . ."

". . . entire village slaughtered . . ."

And then, cutting through the tumult, Lady Darrand cried:

"Why do you keep us standing out here in the cold? We want to work, to plan the defense of Ritherlee against these Helkrags. I say, let the work begin!"

All eyes—including Elodie's—turned to the platform where Lord Vicerin was standing.

But the platform was empty. Lord Vicerin, along with his band of soldiers, was gone.

"Oh no," said Elodie.

There was sudden movement on the battlements overlooking the courtyard. Figures rose up from the shadows where they'd been crouching: hulking, fur-clad monsters wielding enormous bows primed with equally large arrows.

"Helkrags!" breathed Cedric.

More figures appeared on top of the adjacent wall, on the tops of the towers. Down in the courtyard, the nobles of Ritherlee looked silently upward, their heads turning in slow horror as they realized they were entirely surrounded.

On the battlements, several Helkrags broke free and began running along the lines of archers. They carried blazing torches, which they touched to each arrow they passed, igniting the fuel-soaked wads wrapped around the lethal tips. Some of the nobles started pushing through the crowd, seeking an exit.

Elodie saw with horror that every exit from the courtyard was blocked by armed Vicerin guards.

The light from the burning arrows lit up the fog, casting a baleful glow across the entire courtyard.

On a high balcony on a far tower, Lord Vicerin stepped back into the light. He looked first down at the crowd, then up at the Helkrags.

"Do not do this, Lord Vicerin!" cried Lady Darrand. She stood firm in a widening space left as the people around her tried in vain to flee. To Elodie's eyes, looking down on her, this warrior lady looked both small and invincible.

Vicerin regarded Lady Darrand with cold eyes.

"Kill them all," he said.

The first volley killed half the people standing in the courtyard.

The huge arrows impaled their bodies like spears; some arrows even passed all the way through and hit whoever was standing nearby. Even before the bodies hit the ground, they were starting to burn.

Elodie clamped her hand to her mouth. She wanted to look away, but couldn't. Beside her Sylva was screaming.

Some of those who'd survived the first attack were screaming too, running blindly in the hope of finding an exit from the courtyard, which was burning all over again. Others stood dumbstruck, frozen to the spot, their firelit faces blank with shock. Elodie looked helplessly up at the battlements, waiting for the second volley of arrows.

It didn't come. Instead a fresh wave of Helkrags erupted from inside the stables and proceeded to cut down the survivors. Their bone spears were merciless; their howls were like those of wolves. They worked steadily from one side of the courtyard to the other, a murderous wave that left nobody alive in its wake.

A few of the nobles had the presence of mind to draw their own weapons, but they were hopelessly outnumbered. Ritherlee screams merged with Yalasti howls. All too soon the screaming stopped. The howling continued for what seemed like an age; eventually it too died away.

"By the stars!" said Sylva hoarsely. "Oh, this is terrible. Elodie, what has he *done*?"

Cedric wrapped his arm around his sister and tried to comfort her. Elodie would have done the same had she not spotted a single person still standing in the middle of the courtyard.

Lady Darrand!

She walked with eerie calm across the courtyard.

It isn't a courtyard, thought Elodie wildly. *It's a killing field.*

Flames licked from the bottom of Lady Darrand's robes, once yellow, now charring rapidly black. They flew upward like flaming wings as smoke boiled around her. In her hand she held her sword.

"You will pay for this, Vicerin!" Lady Darrand shouted as she trod through the smoldering corpses of the fallen. She shrugged off her burning robes, revealing soot-stained armor. Her voice rang out, clear and strong. Across the courtyard, all else was silent.

Elodie rose to her feet, then realized that in doing so she was exposing herself.

Too late now, she thought bitterly. *It's too late for everything.*

As Lady Darrand continued her slow march toward the tower at the end of the courtyard, another sound pierced the fog: the unmistakable creak of a bow being drawn. In the corner of her eye, Elodie saw a single Helkrag perched on the edge of the battlements.

"Look out!" she shouted.

Lady Darrand's head whipped around.

The Helkrag loosed his arrow. It struck Lady Darrand in the vulnerable place where the plates of armor curved down around her neck. Her body folded and collapsed.

"No!" Elodie screamed.

She dragged her gaze up to the balcony where Lord Vicerin stood—and found him staring right back at her. Some instinct told her that it hadn't made any difference that she'd shouted out.

He knew we were here all along!

As their gazes locked, Vicerin puffed out his chest and proclaimed, "The noble houses are no more! Ritherlee now has a king." He summoned a pair of soldiers with a flick of his wrist, his eyes never leaving Elodie's. "Now—bring me my queen!"

CHAPTER 23

Y ou killed me!" growled Brutan.

He circled Gulph, moving with uncanny speed. Terrified, Gulph turned around and around, tracking his undead father's stumbling progress.

The Tangletree Players had retreated to huddle by the wall of the throne room, their faces pale and shocked. Pip was half-crouched and trembling, as if she wanted to act but didn't know what to do. She looked stricken.

It's all right, Gulph thought. *I know why you did it. You had no choice.*

"What will I do with you?" Brutan's voice was like churning gravel. A firestorm raged in the empty sockets of his eyes.

Don't take your eyes off him, thought Gulph, revulsion prickling his back. *Do that, Gulph, and you're lost. Oh, but he's so fast!*

"Will I kill you?" the undead king went on. "Or will I *turn* you?"

"I don't care what you do to me!" Gulph cared very much, but he wasn't going to let this monster see that. "Just let my friends go!"

"Friends?" Brutan continued his endless circling. With mounting horror Gulph realized he was steadily tightening his circuit. Closing in. "You mean the friends who betrayed you?"

Gulph risked a glance toward Pip. He wanted her to hear this. "Yes, I was betrayed," he said, "but not by Pip or anyone here. Magritt and Nynus were the ones who betrayed me. It was my hands that put the killing crown on your head, but they tricked me into doing it. I'm no murderer."

"You lie!" Brutan snarled.

"It's the truth, I swear it." Gulph was no longer talking to his undead father but to his oldest friend. "I only found out about the poison when it was too late."

Pip's hands flew to her mouth. "But . . . I thought . . ."

"You saw what you saw, Pip. I don't blame you for thinking it was me. In a way it *was* me."

"But it *wasn't*! You didn't . . . all this time I've been thinking . . . Oh, Gulph, what have I done?"

"What you had to do. It's all right, Pip. You didn't know. You were just trying to save everyone."

"ENOUGH OF THIS!"

The undead king lurched toward Gulph, clutching at his throat.

Instinctively Gulph bent his knees and sprang upward. Brutan's fingers whistled just a hairbreadth below his feet. Airborne, Gulph tumbled, tucking in his arms so as to spin more quickly, and flipped straight over the stooped body of the undead king. He landed lightly behind Brutan, but even as he straightened up, his onetime father was spinning to face him.

"Come to me, traitor boy!"

Brutan's arm lashed out, lightning fast. The bones of his fingers scraped Gulph's cheek. Crying out, Gulph scrambled backward, crablike, on his hands and feet. Brutan lumbered after him.

Heat and sand! Gulph had no idea why his invisibility seemed connected to those strange sensations. But if ever there was a time to summon them, it was now. *Desert trance!*

Nothing happened. He continued scrabbling across the floor. Brutan was gaining on him; if he tried to get to his feet, he would be caught. The Tangletree Players, watching in dumb amazement, fell back like a receding tide. And Brutan came on.

"Death? Or undeath? Which will it be?"

From the corner of his eye Gulph saw Brutan's undead legionnaires forming a barrier behind him. He was being herded. Hemmed in.

You cannot see me! he thought wildly. *I am the sun and the open sky and the deep, deep dune. I am the lost and ancient, the parched and the scoured, and YOU CANNOT SEE ME!*

Brutan stopped. The flesh of his face was almost gone, yet Gulph could still read his suddenly baffled expression. The undead king's bony fingers flexed.

"Where are you, trickster?"

Wouldn't you like to know?

Resisting the urge to simply bolt across the throne room, the now-invisible Gulph crawled slowly sideways on his hands and knees, taking great care not to make a single sound.

"Guards!" Brutan snarled. "Find him!"

The undead legionnaires lurched into action, swinging their swords randomly through the air where Gulph had disappeared: empty air, for Gulph had already managed to circle behind the cowering players. But what to do next?

Brutan had turned his attention to Pip. With a sudden lunge, he grabbed her shoulder and spun her small body to face his. He planted his free hand on top of her head, gripping it tight. Pip screamed.

"Show yourself!" roared the undead king. "Or I will tear off her head!"

"No!"

Shedding his invisibility with a reflexive shudder, Gulph sprinted toward Brutan. The undead king turned awkwardly, relaxing his hold on Pip just enough for her to slither away. At the sight of Gulph, Brutan opened his arms wide. Gulph was close enough to hear the tendons squeal like rusty door hinges.

Decayed lips peeled back from tombstone teeth in a hideous parody of a smile.

Gulph dropped to the floor, sliding beneath his undead father's hands, both of which brushed his flying hair. Brutan bellowed his frustration. Springing up, Gulph continued running, heading now toward the throne. Brutan lumbered after him and away from the astonished Tangletree Players.

To Gulph's relief the tiredness that had plagued him since his return to Idilliam was gone. He was filled with a kind of giddy energy; he felt as if he could run forever. Slowing a little, he allowed Brutan to gain. It was agonizing, hearing the creaking, ripping noises of the undead king's approach; even worse was the realization that the one sound a normal man would have made—that of labored breathing—was entirely absent.

The Great Throne loomed before him: a gnarled, black mountain that looked more like a vast and ancient tree than a seat for a king. Gulph ran straight toward it . . . then suddenly dodged, tucking his body and rolling sideways out of Brutan's path.

Unable to change course in time, Brutan crashed into the throne. Several of the twisted boughs broke off; one speared the undead king through the chest, and Gulph's heart missed a beat.

I've killed him again!

But Brutan staggered upright. Howling with fury, he pulled the branch from where it was lodged between his ribs. It juddered free with a dreadful scraping sound. He drew back his arm and hurled the dead wood at Gulph like a javelin. Gulph rolled again, and it missed him by a whisker.

Still howling, Brutan tore down the canopy of knotted timber that hung over the throne and flung it across the room. The canopy broke apart, becoming a storm of spearlike branches that scattered both the Tangletree Players and the undead legionnaires before it.

Recovering his balance, Brutan drew his sword.

Sword! Of course! You fool!

Gulph ran the length of the throne room to the place where he and Pip had entered. Halfway there, he turned invisible again.

Kalia's sword was lying exactly where he'd dropped it. He snatched it up and was relieved to see it melt into transparency the instant his fingers touched the hilt.

Back in the middle of the throne room, the undead legionnaires—there were six of them—had turned on the Tangletree Players. Willing himself to stay invisible, Gulph ran to the first and plunged his sword into its chest. The fire in its eyes winked out instantly, and what had been a lumbering, rotting monster transformed into a simple human corpse, which collapsed to the floor in a swift tangle of limbs. As it came to rest, Gulph fancied he could see relief wash over its lifeless face.

He managed to kill two more legionnaires before Brutan realized what was going on. The undead king stopped in his tracks, his eyes blazing.

"What are you doing?" he roared. For a moment Gulph thought Brutan was addressing him. But, incredibly, he was talking to the now-dead legionnaires. "Get up! Get up and kill them all!"

They'll never get up again, thought Gulph with satisfaction. Glancing sideways, he saw Pip's eyes widen with sudden hope.

The three remaining legionnaires, though clearly confused, had rallied. They charged as one to the spot where their comrades had fallen . . . and where the invisible Gulph was standing. Brutan, steadily advancing, continued to bellow his outrage.

Gulph met the first two legionnaires with the point of Kalia's sword. But with each stroke he felt the burst of energy he'd found fading. Trying to fight back the tiredness clawing at his limbs again, he swung at the third—a hideous, dried-out mummy of a creature—but slipped and fell sideways, and the blow failed to connect. As he recovered his balance, Pip gave a shout.

"Gulph! Look out!"

To Gulph's dismay he realized he could see Kalia's sword again; the blade shimmered ghostlike for a moment before condensing into solid crystal.

They can see me!

"Duck!" Pip yelled.

Without thinking, Gulph obeyed. The undead legionnaire's

sword whistled over his head. Gulph tried to tumble away, but his feet caught on one of the fallen bodies and instead of rolling he simply sprawled, dropping his sword.

Brutan's roars turned to thunderous laughter. The legionnaire loomed over Gulph, its sword raised and ready for the final killing blow. Gulph reached for his own weapon, but it was too far away.

He opened his mouth to scream.

The undead legionnaire burst into flames.

Gulph blinked, for a moment unable to comprehend what he was seeing. The legionnaire's mummified body was enveloped in orange fire. It stood, its limbs writhing, then it planted its blackening feet wide and raised its sword again.

"Kill it, Gulph! Kill it!"

And there was Pip, appearing from behind the burning legionnaire and brandishing the torch she'd used to set it on fire. She must have grabbed it from one of the wall sconces, Gulph supposed. If only it had worked.

But it did work, he realized, letting his sword lie where it was.

Sure enough, the legionnaire's movements were becoming gradually more erratic. Its mummified body cracked and shuddered as the flames swallowed it up. Then, finally, it collapsed.

Gulph rolled out of the way just before it hit the floor. Black cinders and burning embers exploded outward. He felt sudden heat on his ankle, then a foot kicked the flames away, and a small hand grabbed his wrist and pulled him clear.

"I thought I'd lost you," said Pip, helping him to his feet.

Before he could reply, bony fingers wrenched Gulph from Pip's grasp. They closed around his collar, squeezing his neck tight enough to make him cry out. His feet left the floor and he was turned, dangling, to find himself staring straight into Brutan's face.

"Never turn your back, boy!" he snarled.

Close up, the undead king looked like something from a nightmare. The skin of his face—what was left of it—had turned a putrid green. Beneath it, the white skull was pitted with tiny holes. Where the undead king's brain had once been, there now squirmed a mountain of maggots.

"You were a puzzle to me," Brutan went on. "But no more. I have decided what to do with you at last."

Gulph's clothes were tightening around his neck, choking him. The straps of his pack dug into his armpits; something wrapped inside it was digging painfully into his ribs—something hard and spiky.

The crown!

He struggled, but in vain. The undead king's grip was too strong, and Gulph's own strength had left him. He was exhausted beyond measure.

"Death is a world you will now know, boy," Brutan hissed, leaning close. The stench of his corrupted flesh was unspeakable. "My decision is made."

The undead king's hand tightened around Gulph's collar. A second set of fingers—just naked bones strung together by stringlike tendons—reached under his chin.

"First I will have your throat. Then . . ."

"Put him down!"

The blackness in Brutan's eyes flicked back to red, and Gulph had the overwhelming sensation that he had just blinked in surprise.

"Put him down right now!"

Brutan turned his head. Gulph looked past him to where the entire troupe of the Tangletree Players was standing. They'd made a rough semicircle around him and Brutan. Each of them held a blazing torch.

Gulph's heart swelled.

"Do you want to burn first," Pip asked Brutan, "or just die?"

Brutan's grip meant Gulph couldn't move his head to see her properly, but he noticed she was the only one not holding a torch. She was holding something, though . . .

"Enough of this game!" roared Brutan.

"We may be the Tangletree Players," Pip replied. Her voice trembled, and Gulph loved her for it. "But we don't play games!"

She hurled something through the air: a long, bright shape.

It spun, its keen edge making rainbows in the smoky air. Gulph twisted, instinctively reaching out for it, grateful yet again for the suppleness of his body.

His fingers closed on something hard and cold.

Crystal.

Gulph held up the sword and stared into his father's lifeless face.

"Do you know who gave me this sword?" he said. Brutan's jaws opened and closed, but no words came out. "My mother did. Kalia."

The undead king's eyes flickered in confusion. "Kalia is dead!" he hissed.

"No. She lives. You didn't kill her and you won't kill me!"

Drawing back his arm, he plunged the blade into the middle of Brutan's chest.

Nothing moved. Even the flames of the torches held by the Tangletree Players seemed frozen. Then Brutan's skeleton fingers unlatched themselves from Gulph's throat, and he dropped to the ground.

Gulph backed slowly away. His heart made thunder in his chest. Brutan swayed before him, one arm still outstretched, the other pawing feebly at the hilt of the crystal sword Gulph had buried in him.

After three steps, Gulph sank to his knees, fighting waves of dizziness, willing himself not to be sick. As if he were a grotesque reflection in some distorted mirror, Brutan dropped to his knees too. His ragged skull's mouth opened and closed, but no words came out. From somewhere behind his ribs came a shrill hissing sound. The fire in his eyes guttered.

Die, Gulph thought woozily. *Please, just . . . die.*

A small hand crept into his.

"You did it," said Pip. "Oh, Gulph, I knew you could. . . ."

Something flashed inside Brutan's eye sockets. Fresh flames, of a nameless color Gulph had never seen before. A tremor ran through Brutan's body. His hands closed around the sword's crystal hilt. The tendons in his arms screeched. The sword's blade screeched too as Brutan pulled it free. He raised it up, studied it with what might have been curiosity, or perhaps contempt.

Then he tossed it aside and rose to his feet. He rocked to and fro, clearly suffering from the wound Gulph had inflicted.

But the red fire in his eyes burned as brightly as ever.

Brutan, the undead king of Toronia, was still standing.

"It's time to go," said Gulph dully. "Now." But when he tried to move, his muscles refused to obey him.

It was Pip who dragged him out of the throne room, just as she'd dragged him in. The Tangletree Players followed in a tight group. Dazed as he was, Gulph recognized that they had formed a protective circle around him.

As they ran through the castle passage, enough of Gulph's strength returned for him to lead the way.

"Go left here!" he shouted when Pip hesitated at a junction in the corridor. "It's not far!"

From close behind them came the sound of shambling footsteps and a hideous, gargling voice.

"You will pay for what you have done!"

It was Brutan, moving slowly, but moving all the same.

"Hurry!" Gulph cried.

The instant they burst out into the castle courtyard, they found themselves facing nearly a dozen of the undead. Noddy cried out, but Pip ran on.

"They didn't attack us before!" she shouted. "Brutan put some kind of shield on me!"

"How do you know you've still got it?" Gulph called.

"I don't!"

Steeling himself, Gulph led the charge toward the shambling corpses. At first they advanced without wavering, and he thought they'd made a huge mistake. Then, as the Tangletree Players ran through their midst, the undead stumbled aside as if pushed by an invisible force.

"I wish I'd had you with me a few days ago," panted Gulph as they ran. No sooner had they passed through the gatehouse and out into the street beyond than Brutan appeared at the door.

"Take them!" he bellowed. "Bring them to me!"

Instantly the undead they'd just evaded turned and began to

chase them. One was close enough to claw at Madrigal, who was lagging behind at the back of the group.

"I think our luck just ran out!" Pip gasped, finding an extra turn of speed.

The undead pursued them first through Idilliam, then out across the battlefield outside the city wall. As they raced through the smoke and ruins, Gulph risked a glance back and was relieved to see the enemy trailing a long way behind.

You can say what you like about the Tangletree Players, he thought, *but we're fast on our feet!*

At last they reached the postern gate. To Gulph's relief the burned timbers he'd stacked across the doorway hadn't been disturbed. By now his lungs were laboring, and his breath was raw in his throat, but he'd mostly recovered his senses. In halting tones he explained to the others about the tunnels beneath the city and the lost realm of Celestis below.

"This is the only way down there," he said. "All we have to do is get inside and close the door behind us."

"And then we'll be safe?" said Noddy.

Gulph didn't answer.

They pulled aside the timbers and, one by one, entered the storeroom. Thankfully, none of the undead had found their way inside.

"There," he gasped, pointing to the mechanism that moved the statue. "That lever. If we pull it, the statue will slide back and close off the doorway. I think."

Simeon, ever the practical sort, spat on his hands, grabbed the lever, and heaved. Nothing happened. Frowning, he tried again. Still nothing.

"Noddy," he said. "Give us a shove."

Noddy joined him, then Madrigal, then Gulph, Pip, and all the others. The entire complement of the Tangletree Players set their collective weight against the lever on which their lives depended.

The lever refused to move.

Ordering the others back, Simeon peered at the mechanism to which the lever was attached. To Gulph it looked like a cage filled with toothed wheels. Simeon reached inside the cage and withdrew a handful of metal shards.

"Broken," he said. "Looks like someone jammed something into it."

Someone did, thought Gulph, remembering the sword Ossilius had used to wedge the mechanism closed.

What had saved them then had condemned them now. The door would remain open to the undead.

"What should we do?" said Pip.

"We've got no choice," Gulph replied. "It's Celestis or nothing. We have to go on."

"Brutan will track us here," Simeon warned. "He'll follow us down."

Gulph nodded wearily. The journey through the tunnels would be dark and dangerous; he knew that because he'd made it twice before. With Brutan on their heels it would be more perilous still. Yet that wasn't the worst of it.

The worst of it was that his father was still standing.

Even Mother's sword wasn't enough. He can't be defeated! Now I will never take the throne. Neither will my sister, my brother. Brutan will be king of Toronia forever.

CHAPTER 24

T rees move," said Theeta.

Tarlan looked over the vast expanse of the Isurian forest canopy. It was another ocean, this one made of glossy leaves and fine green needles. The only movement he perceived was the natural sway of the treetops in the wind.

But Theeta's eyes were much sharper than his own.

"What do you see, Theeta?"

"Trees move," the thorrod repeated unhelpfully.

Moments later, all became clear. In the distance, in the middle of a patch of young woodland, a long ribbon of trees was not just swaying—it was thrashing to and fro, as if some huge creature were beating its way through.

Not a creature. An army!

"We've found them!"

Tapping his heels against Theeta's flanks, Tarlan urged his thorrod steed lower. Kitheen, who'd been flying beside them all the way from the beach, followed silently as they descended.

"Filos! Greythorn! Brock! Are you there?"

Tarlan knew they were close. With every day that passed, the bond with his pack grew stronger. His knowledge of them was like a sixth sense, although not as powerful as his sense of sight or his hearing.

Not yet, anyway.

Sure enough Theeta's wings had barely skimmed the treetops before the three animals came into view. They raced through the thick undergrowth, bounding over deadfalls and plowing through stands of hawthorn and holly as if they weren't there. When they reached a small glade, they stopped and looked expectantly up.

Tarlan guided Theeta in to land beside them. Kitheen continued to circle overhead, keeping watch.

"We've nearly caught up with the Galadronians," said Tarlan. "You've done well, all of you."

"Men are slow in the forest," growled Greythorn.

"When can we fight them?" inquired Brock.

Tarlan grinned. "You'll get your chance. But we can't afford to take them on yet. Our first job is to join up with Trident again."

"The army is moving east," Filos observed. "Trident is east."

"I know. If we want to get to the Trident camp first, we'll have to circle around the Galadronians. We've got the speed, so we can afford to make a detour."

"Cold way," Theeta suggested.

It took Tarlan a moment to work this out.

"Yes, we'll go south," he agreed. "But not nearly as far as Yalasti, Theeta. Not even as far as the big river. Just far enough to make a loop around the army. Then we'll cut back north and be at the clearing before them."

"Fessan gone."

"Well, yes, I think he probably will be gone." Tarlan considered. "Fessan will have stayed long enough for the wounded to recover, but we know he wants to start recruiting again. I think Trident will have moved on by the time we get there, but they'll have left a trail." He grinned at the animals. "And I have the best team of trackers in Toronia."

"Then we fight?" asked Brock. He reared up on his hind legs, a mountain of tangled brown fur.

Tarlan gave the bear's massive foreleg a friendly slap and laughed. "There's no stopping you, is there, Brock? But you have to be patient. The Galadronian army is very big, and our pack is very small."

"Not as small as it was."

"Not now that we've got you, Brock, no."

The bear craned his neck and gazed deep into the forest. "Not Brock. *Them*."

There was a crashing sound behind Tarlan. He whirled in time to see several large creatures breaking through the trees and into the clearing: bears, at least ten of them, with more massing behind.

"Are you Tarlan?" demanded the bear in front, a squat black beast with a scar on his nose.

"Uh . . . yes." Tarlan found it difficult to speak with his jaw hanging open. He turned to Brock. "Where did they all come from?"

"From everywhere. When we were running to the sea, I met a bear. I told her my story. She told other bears, and they told more. Captive bears heard the story too, and rose up against their masters. When you freed me, Tarlan, you freed them. You freed them all."

Tarlan saw that some of the bears did indeed still carry the remnants of chains around their necks, or manacles on their paws. He promised himself that as soon as they found Trident, he would have Fessan's blacksmiths release them from these last shackles of slavery.

This is my true gift, he thought giddily. *It's not just talking to animals. It's setting them free.*

"You are welcome, all of you!" he cried, stepping toward the bears. "Will you really fight for me?"

"We will fight!" the black bear snarled.

"More come," croaked Theeta in Tarlan's ear. "You call."

Tarlan looked beyond the clearing, seeing only the darkness of the forest interior.

"More bears?" he said.

"More everything."

A thrill ran down Tarlan's spine. He closed his eyes and summoned his will. Heat washed through him, both strange and familiar. He touched the heat and, through it, touched the forest. Shapes were moving through the trees. *No, not shapes—minds!*

A wave of dizziness washed through him. He staggered; Theeta's wing caught him, held him upright.

"What's happening, Theeta?"

"Tarlan fly. Tarlan see."

Opening himself fully to the pulsing heat that was growing inside him, Tarlan clambered onto the thorrod's back and allowed her to carry him aloft. The forest was alive with movement. More bears were entering the clearing. A pride of red-furred forest cats was slinking along one of the half-hidden trails. Wild boars arrived from the slopes to the north, carving their way through low-lying brambles with great sweeps of their tusks. From the south came a volley of howls: packs of wolves, running to join the growing throng.

Joining the pack! Tarlan's temples throbbed. *My pack!*

"Join me!" he shouted. "Join me, all of you!"

His voice carried over the trees, but he knew that the real cry came from within. He felt it then: a vast, collective pulse. The force of all these individual animal lives, hunters and prey united, gathered as one below him. Gathered for him.

He spoke with something other than his voice.

Run with me! Fight for me!

With a sudden screeching, a flock of eagles burst from the tree-tops, each with a wingspan as broad as Tarlan was tall.

Fly with me!

By now the clearing was full. Tarlan could see Brock, Greythorn, and Filos moving among the newcomers, welcoming them.

Join me!

"There's no stopping us, Theeta!" Tarlan cried. "Fly, and let them follow!"

Theeta obeyed, turning south as they'd planned and beginning the loop that would take them ahead of the enemy. The eagles followed, a white-winged escort. On the ground below, what had begun as a random assemblage of mismatched creatures became a kind of organized stampede: bear and cat, fox and boar, horse and wolf, all running together, all following Tarlan's call.

Oh, Elodie, wait until you see what I've brought you!

By the time they reached the clearing where the Trident camp had been, the sun was beginning to set. The Galadronians were nowhere to be seen. Still, Tarlan suspected the enemy would be here by nightfall.

"Trident gone," observed Theeta as she landed.

"Yes," Tarlan replied. "Well, we expected that, didn't we?"

All the same, it was with some disappointment that he jumped down and surveyed the deserted clearing. He told himself not to worry, that Trident's absence was a good sign.

"They're off getting new recruits," he said, wandering out across the scuffed turf. "Let's see what clues we can find."

Filos and Greythorn emerged from the trees and into the low red light of the sunset. Beyond them Tarlan sensed the massive presence of the rest of his newly enlarged pack.

Stay back, he instructed them, sending the command not from his mouth but from his heart. Talking to the animals this way felt natural, as if he'd been doing it all his life.

"There was fighting," said Greythorn, casting his one good eye about the clearing.

Tarlan stumbled over an abandoned tent. To his dismay the fabric was ripped and stained with blood. Several swords lay half-trodden into the ground. The blade of one was broken clean in two.

What happened here?

Kitheen, who'd landed near the edge of the clearing, opened his black wings and cawed. Tarlan joined him and saw that the thorrod had found a line of freshly dug graves, marked with simple wooden stakes. Beside the graves lay the bodies of three dead men.

Carefully Tarlan turned over the nearest corpse. It wore the familiar green of the Trident army.

"They were attacked," growled Filos.

Tarlan nodded, appalled. "But by who?"

Something moved in the undergrowth to his right. Before Tarlan could react, a blur of gold shot past his head, and Theeta's talons thrust their way deep into the bushes. They emerged clutching a young boy dressed in the same green that adorned the corpse.

"Please!" screamed the boy. "Don't let it eat me!"

"She won't eat you. Theeta, put him down."

The thorrod deposited the boy gently before Tarlan. The youngster's face was grimy, and his tunic was torn, but his eyes were wide and full of life. A short sword was stuck into his belt. Its blade was scratched and its edge was notched.

"Please, Your Grace. I only hid 'cos I thought it was them. Please don't hurt me."

"Nobody's going to hurt you." It felt strange to be called "Your Grace." Tarlan wasn't sure he liked it. "Just tell me what happened."

"I thought you was them," the boy repeated. "Then I saw you was you."

"Who do you mean? What happened here?"

"It was them. The Vicerins. They ambushed us. We had no chance. I went up a tree and waited till it was over."

At the mention of the name Vicerin, Tarlan's whole body had turned cold. "When did this happen?"

"Not long after you left. You and the wizard. Where is he, Your Grace?"

"Never mind that. Where's Trident?"

"That's what I'm trying to say. There were too many of them. It's all over. Trident's finished!"

Distraught, Tarlan stared at Theeta. For the first time ever, he saw tears brimming at the corner of the thorrod's fathomless black eyes.

I never knew thorrods could cry. Oh, Melchior. I wish you were here with me now.

"Elodie," he said. "What about the princess? Where is she? Is she all right?"

"Oh, *she'll* be all right."

Something in the boy's tone made Tarlan's skin prickle. "What do you mean?"

"It was her that brought them here. I'm sorry, Your Grace, but your sister, it turns out she's a traitor."

Anger flashed through Tarlan. "That's not true! You're lying!"

"I wish I was. But I'm not. I saw it with my own eyes."

Tarlan's head felt ready to burst. "What did you see? Tell me!"

"The princess, she said how she was glad the Vicerins had come. She went riding off with them all high-and-mighty—begging your pardon, Your Grace, but she *did*—and there was poor Fessan all chained up. He'd have died fighting for her, so he would. And what did she do? Betrayed him. Betrayed us all!"

Tarlan wanted to shout at the boy to stop talking. There were too many words, and all of them were hurting him. With hunched and shaking shoulders, he turned his back and walked away.

He's telling the truth. It's there in his eyes.

Had Elodie really betrayed Trident? Tarlan couldn't imagine his sister doing such a thing.

But why would the boy lie?

I'm sorry, Fessan. You didn't want us to leave. If Melchior and I had stayed, would things have turned out differently?

Tarlan imagined Melchior vanquishing the Vicerin attackers with his magic . . . then remembered that until their journey to the Isle of Stars, the wizard had been just an old man who needed a stick to help him walk.

No. If we'd stayed, we'd be dead, or prisoners like Fessan.

He stopped pacing and returned to the boy.

"What's your name?" he demanded.

"Kassan, Your Grace. I . . . I'm sorry it all happened, really I am."

"So am I, Kassan. But there's nothing we can do about it now." He shoved his anxiety and confusion aside. *Enough thinking; time to act.* "What's done is done, and we have more important things to be worried about."

"We do?"

Tarlan eyed Kassan's sword. "Do you know how to use that?"

The boy puffed out his chest. "I surely do, Your Grace! I was the best student in the camp. Leastways, that's what Lieutenant Tagger said." His face fell. "He's dead now. I buried him, along with the others. There's still more to be done, though."

"Never mind that. I need every good swordsman I can find."

"Why? Is there going to be more fighting?"

"Yes, Kassan. Now tell me, do you know if there are any towns nearby?"

"Of course. There's Deep Poynt. It's the biggest town in all of Isur."

"Are you sure?"

The boy nodded. "I lived there before I joined Trident."

Tarlan shook his head, unsurprised. There was something inevitable about this whole encounter . . . about all the events of the past few days, in fact. He could almost feel all the many parts of the world moving around him, gradually settling into place like the pieces of some gigantic puzzle.

Crouching, he quickly told Kassan about the advancing Galadronian army.

"Where's Galladonika?" said the boy, frowning.

"Never mind. All you need to know is that the enemy is coming this way, and they'll attack anything lying in their path. From what you've told me, that means Deep Poynt."

Kassan's frown deepened. His hand hovered over the hilt of his sword.

"They're going to attack my home?"

"Yes! And you're going to help me defend it. As long as we stand, Kassan, you and me, Trident stands too!"

"You and me." Kassan looked doubtful. "We can't fight those Galladonikans on our own."

"We're not on our own."

Stepping away from the boy, he patted Theeta on the neck and strode out into the center of the clearing. The sun had vanished behind the trees, leaving the forest dark and brooding. Directly above Tarlan's head, the three prophecy stars shone in a purple velvet sky.

Spreading his arms wide, Tarlan called a single command: "Come!"

Even as his voice rang out across the clearing, he drew that word inside himself, where it grew hot and strong.

Come!

They came, the beasts of the forest and the birds of the air. The ground shook beneath hoof and paw, and the sky shrilled with the shriek of hawk and eagle. From one side came the bears, from another the wolves, from another amassed a crowd of boars and deer and low, slinking weasels. The ground to Tarlan's left began to shimmer as it covered itself with a carpet of snakes.

Through the center of the animal throng came the horses.

"So, Kassan," said Tarlan. "What do you think of our army?"

Kassan was openmouthed. His face was white, except for two spots of color on his cheeks, shining in the twilight.

"Will they eat us?" he quavered as a pair of giant grizzly bears loped past.

"Not us!"

Among the animals was a horse: a fine gray stallion with a thick black tail that Tarlan guessed must have escaped its owner.

Come!

He sent the command like an arrow. The horse reared, whinnied, then trotted up to him. It stamped the ground, snorting, and lowered its head, allowing Tarlan to stroke its nose.

"Can you ride?" Tarlan asked. The boy nodded. "Bareback?"

"My uncle taught me."

"Good. Every soldier needs a good horse. This one is called . . ." He spoke into the horse's ear: "Tell me your name."

The horse stamped once and whinnied.

Tarlan turned back to the boy. "Kassan, this is Windracer."

The boy was gaping. "You can talk to horses?"

"Yes."

"And he's . . . mine?"

"No, Kassan. Never think it. You and Windracer are equals. Look after him, and he will look after you. Now, can you lead us to Deep Poynt?"

The boy heaved himself onto the horse's back. He ruffled his fingers through Windracer's mane, then grinned at Tarlan.

"Follow me!" he cried, jabbing his heels into Windracer's flanks. They trotted north toward the edge of the clearing.

Follow! Tarlan sent the thought out to the gathered animals even as he raced back to where Theeta was waiting. *Follow, and soon we will fight!*

"Many come," Theeta remarked as she took them both into the sky.

"Yes, Theeta, just like you said."

They flew out over the treetops. Tarlan gazed down in awe, reassured to see Kassan riding confidently along a broken trail through the woods. Behind him ran Filos, Greythorn, and Brock, and behind *them*, widening like the head of an arrow behind its point, ran Tarlan's pack.

At last he let his thoughts return to Elodie.

What she'd done was unbelievable. Unforgivable. He wanted to confront her, to tell her how stupid she'd been. To shout it in her face.

Good riddance to her, he thought bitterly. *I didn't need a sister before. I don't need one now.*

But his brother . . .

"I'll save Gulph myself," he muttered. "And forget Elodie ever existed."

There was no use dwelling on it any further. Nor was there any point in wondering about the future. This was now, and that was all Tarlan cared about. The twilight air was cold, and the shadowy trees were filled with life. The darkness rumbled.

Battle lay ahead.

CHAPTER 25

In the courtyard, Lord Vicerin's loyal guards were dragging away the bodies of the murdered Ritherlee nobles. Others escorted the Helkrags to some deep part of the castle, perhaps to be rewarded for their performance, perhaps to be turned on and slaughtered themselves. Once the courtyard had been cleared, a large crowd was ushered out.

"He's sent men to get you," Cedric pleaded. "Elodie, they're coming!"

But Elodie needed to hear what the murderer had to say.

"Toronia is changing," Lord Vicerin said to the crowd. They listened intently, and Elodie wondered how long they had to live. "King Brutan has fallen. The fate of our glorious realm hangs in the balance. A new power is needed, if that balance is ever to be restored."

"What is he talking about?" sobbed Sylva.

"Please, Elodie," urged Cedric, tugging at her sleeve.

"Hush, both of you. I want to hear this."

She didn't want to hear it, of course, but she had no choice. Lord Vicerin might have gathered an audience, but his speech was addressed to one person alone.

Her.

"Here, today, this new power has arisen," Lord Vicerin went on. "Even as Castle Tor collapses into the darkness, so Castle Vicerin rises into the light. Even as the prophecy stars fail us, a new light illuminates our spirits. For I tell you that today a new king has come."

A tall man appeared behind Lord Vicerin: the chief chamberlain, resplendent in his blue-and-black robes. In his hands he carried a silver crown. He held it over his lord and master's head.

The watching people stood in utter silence.

The crown came down.

"Kneel before him," the chamberlain intoned. "Kneel before King Quentus of the House of Vicerin!"

One by one the members of the crowd dropped to their knees. Vicerin waved decorously, then his eyes fixed on Elodie's.

"Now that I am king of Ritherlee," he cried, "I will take my queen!"

Pressing her hands over her eyes, Elodie screamed . . .

. . . and awoke in her chambers, bathed in perspiration. The nightmare fell away. Outside the window, the fog was gone too, replaced by blue sky laced with delicate clouds. Somewhere, a lark was singing.

She climbed sleepily out of bed, clutching at the collar of her night robe. Her hand slipped down to the green jewel she wore at her neck. As always, she felt comforted by its presence.

Her eyes fell on the dress hanging in the doorway to the adjacent dressing room. The dress was gold, with a long, full skirt that split into dozens of shimmering ribbons. Each of these split again, and again, so that the bottom of the gown was a mass of delicate fronds designed to swirl and froth as the person wearing it walked along.

Not just any person, Elodie thought, recognizing at once the traditional Ritherlee design. *The bride.*

It was a wedding dress.

With dawning horror Elodie realized that everything she'd just dreamed really had happened the day before.

It wasn't a nightmare at all. I was remembering.

"Elodie? Are you all right?"

With a start she saw Samial standing in the corner of the room. His expression was grim.

"I watched you sleep," he said. "You had a bad dream, I think."

Elodie sat down on the end of the bed. She no longer felt sleepy. Now she felt sick.

"I wish it *had* been a dream," she replied. "How long have you been there, Samial? Were you watching me all night?"

Samial shook his head. "I spent most of the night trying to kill the new king."

"Vicerin is no king!" Elodie spat. Then she realized what Samial had just said. "What do you mean, you tried to kill him?"

"Just that. But I failed. I could not carry a weapon through the wall into his chamber, and when I tried to take a sword from one of the guards inside, they grew suspicious. I tried and tried—" He broke off, his expression miserable. "But I will not stop trying."

Elodie crossed the room to where he stood and hugged him. "Thank you, Samial. You're brave and true. But don't you see? You're all I have left."

"I want to help."

"I know. But, Samial, what if they found out about you, what if they took the arrowhead from me? I can't bear the thought of losing you, not now that I'm . . ."

She pulled away, biting back the words. Speaking them out loud might make everything worse. Might make everything . . .

. . . *real.*

"Not now that I'm trapped here forever," she finished.

The door opened and three maids bustled in. One carried a green sash, while the others held velvet-lined trays arrayed with green jewelry and flowers.

Green to match my necklace, Elodie thought. *Like it's some stupid trinket.*

A wave of revulsion swept over her. She ran to where the golden wedding dress was hanging, ripped it down, and hurled it across the room.

"Can't you see how wrong this is?" she screamed at the maids. "Can't you see that he murdered his own wife so he could marry me—his stepdaughter? If you want to help me, help me get out of here!"

They exchanged terrified glances, but before any of them could speak, a guard marched in.

"Is there a problem, Your Highness?" he said coldly.

Without thinking, Elodie made a grab for his sword. The guard reacted instantly, shoving her backward. She tripped over the trailing ribbons of the wedding dress and fell hard.

None of the maids moved.

The guard glared down at her.

And Elodie finally understood what the word "prisoner" really meant.

"I asked if you had a problem," the guard repeated.

"No." Elodie climbed shakily to her feet. She remembered something Fessan had once said to her.

A brave soldier knows when to raise his sword. A clever one knows when to lower it.

"Everything's fine," she went on. "I'm just nervous." She swallowed. It was like trying to choke down a stone. "It's a very big day."

"Well, if you're sure."

"You are dismissed," Elodie went on, trying to adopt the imperious air that had once come so naturally to her. The air of a queen.

But not the queen I imagined I would be.

The guard left. Elodie resigned herself to being dressed in the enormous wedding gown. As one maid fussed over her hair (and tutted over its shortness), another arranged her ribbons and jewels. Elodie endured it all.

They'll take me to the council chamber, she thought, frantically trying to imagine how she might escape. *They'll take me the long way around. They'll want to show off Ritherlee's new queen-to-be.*

She could think of half a dozen places where she might be able to give her escort the slip—her years as a child playing hide-and-chase with Sylva and Cedric meant she knew every corner of this castle.

But it will be crowded. They'll be lining the corridors, eager to see the bride.

No matter how hard she tried, she couldn't come up with a plan.

Castle Vicerin truly had become her prison.

At last she was ready. The maids stood back, admiring their handiwork.

"You look beautiful, Your Highness," said the first.

"That you do," said the second.

The third brought a mirror, but Elodie couldn't bear to look at her reflection. Instead she made her way into the small sitting room tucked behind the main bedroom. When one of the maids tried to follow her, Elodie waved her back.

"Please," she said, "I want to be by myself for a moment." The maids exchanged nervous glances. "It's all right. I just need a moment to . . . to compose myself."

As soon as she was alone, Elodie rummaged in the drawer of the little bureau beneath the window. Hidden at the back was a small bundle of cloth. She checked its contents: Samial's arrowhead and the thorrod feather.

I thought I could escape like you, Tarlan. She stroked her fingers over the feather. *Instead I'm trapped. And I'll never see you again.*

Elodie rewrapped the bundle and tucked it into the waistband of her undergarments, beneath the flowing folds of the wedding gown.

Once this was done, she returned to find the main door open. Four castle guards stood on the landing outside, dressed in their smart blue dress uniforms.

Elodie took a deep breath, let it out.

And now the nightmare really begins.

"All right," she said. "I'm ready."

As she'd known they would, the guards escorted her through the castle, taking a long, complicated route toward the council chamber. It seemed to Elodie that the whole of Ritherlee had indeed lined the corridors to watch. Their faces passed in a blur—in fact, the whole castle was blurred—and more than once she stumbled on the ribbons of her ornate gold dress.

"I am here. You're not alone." Samial's hand touched hers. "You've been strong before, Elodie. You can do it again."

"That's the trouble," she whispered. "I don't think I can."

Her foot tangled in the dress once more. This time she stopped herself from falling.

It will be all right! she told herself firmly, fighting back dizziness. *It has to be!*

But she didn't really believe it.

At last they reached the council chamber. The entire room was decked with flowers, artfully arranged in crisscrossing bands of color that, Elodie realized, represented all the noble families of Ritherlee. Before each display stood a small gathering of people in matching robes—representatives of those same families, she supposed.

He murdered your people! she thought, wishing she could say it aloud.

Then she saw the armed Vicerin guards stationed behind each of the groups, and decided that they probably already knew.

The giant banqueting table had been moved from the center of the room, and a wooden archway erected in its place. The archway was covered in flowers: white, blue, and green. Under other circumstances, it would have taken Elodie's breath away. Instead, her gaze only glanced off it, coming to rest on the blue-clad figure of the man she'd once called Father, and who now called himself king of Ritherlee.

As Elodie approached, Vicerin smiled, exposing his enormous teeth. The silver crown sat on his head, a delicate and strangely feminine accessory. Beside Vicerin stood the chamberlain, now wearing the gold robe of a marriage scribe.

Suddenly terrified, Elodie recoiled, only to feel the hand of one of the guards pressed into her back. She stumbled forward the last few steps and found herself beneath the archway, with Vicerin's fingers clamped around her wrist.

"Welcome, my dear," Vicerin crooned. "Are you ready for your big day?"

All at once Elodie's vision cleared. She stared straight into Vicerin's eager eyes.

"I would rather die than marry you!" she snapped.

Then she spat in his face.

Now it was Vicerin's turn to recoil. He drew back his hand and Elodie bared her cheek, waiting with a perverse kind of satisfaction for the slap. But it didn't come. Instead Vicerin dabbed the spittle from his face with a perfumed handkerchief and smiled.

"That may be so, my dear," he said. "But if you refuse, others will die."

Elodie's blood ran cold. "What do you mean?"

Vicerin snapped his fingers. More guards came forward, ushering between them a pair of figures Elodie knew all too well: Sylva and Cedric.

"It is so disappointing," Vicerin went on, "to discover that one's own children are traitors. So disappointing."

Elodie saw with horror that they were both in chains. Sylva's face was red and splotched with tears, while Cedric was sporting a black eye. Both looked as if they hadn't slept for days.

"I understand." Elodie glared at Vicerin. "Let's get on with it!"

Vicerin nodded to the chamberlain, who said in a penetrating voice:

"Welcome one, welcome all, to this marriage ceremony. Today we celebrate the joining of Quentus, of the House of Vicerin, to Elodie, also of the House of Vicerin . . ."

I'm not a Vicerin! I'm not!

As the chamberlain droned on, Elodie tried to close her ears against the words. She'd almost succeeded, when she heard Lord Vicerin speak her name in loud, ringing tones:

". . . Elodie, to be my true and only wife."

"Now it is your turn," said the chamberlain, turning to her. "Repeat these words: 'I take you, Quentus, to be my true and only husband.'"

For a moment she thought of simply turning and running out of the council chamber. The ribbons of her wedding gown would spray out behind her like a shower of gold.

Or like feathers. If I had feathers, I could fly far away from here, and never come back.

"Be brave," Samial murmured in her ear. "Be strong."

There was another stone in her throat. She swallowed it down. There were times when you had to lower your sword. This was one of them.

She straightened her back and stared at the far wall.

"I take you, Quentus," she said hoarsely, fighting back tears, "to be my true husband."

A sigh went through the crowd.

"And now you may exchange the rings of devotion," said the chamberlain.

"Give me your hand, my dear," said Vicerin, spreading Elodie's fingers wide and jamming a diamond-studded ring onto the third finger of her left hand. She recognized it immediately: it was the same ring that had once been worn by Lady Vicerin.

"I swear it's still warm," she murmured. "Couldn't wait to get it off her, could you?"

"Shut up, my dear," Vicerin growled through his tombstone smile.

"It's a shame I don't have a ring for you. Shall I just spit in your face again?"

Still smiling, Vicerin plucked a gaudy, gem-covered ring from his pocket and slipped it onto his own finger.

"No need. But thank you for the offer."

"You may now pass beneath the arch and enter the land of matrimony," the chamberlain said, closing the book from which he'd been reading.

Before Elodie could think, Vicerin had shoved her through the archway. Following her, he snatched up another silver crown—smaller and even more delicate than the one he wore himself—and placed it on Elodie's head. She closed her eyes . . . and again felt Samial's hand squeeze hers.

Don't leave me, Samial. Not here. Not now.

"Three cheers for the king and queen of Ritherlee!" someone cried from the back of the room. The room erupted with cheers; to Elodie it sounded like a badly tuned orchestra, and it was clear to her that most of the people applauding were doing so only because they feared what might happen if they refused.

I think I'm going to be sick.

Vicerin led her through the big double doors at the end of the council chamber and into the formal garden beyond. The sun shone down through a gap in a mass of gathering clouds, turning Elodie's dress into a dazzling gold beacon. The crowds gathered in the garden gasped when they saw her, and more applause broke out.

As Vicerin guided her through the throng, he waved and smiled.

"You must wave too, now that you are queen."

"I cannot be queen, because you are no king. I will be queen only when I and my brothers take the crown of Toronia as the prophecy foretold."

"And how will you do that, precisely?"

"I'll escape. You can't watch me every moment of every day."

"Mmm. And when you have escaped? What then?"

"I'll come back with my brothers and destroy you!"

"Ah yes, just like your precious Trident destroyed me?"

By now they'd reached the fountain in the middle of the garden. At Vicerin's command, it burst into life, sending water spraying high into the sunlit air. At a second signal, the water turned brilliant blue. Vicerin blue.

The crowd roared.

"Oh, my dear, I almost forgot." Vicerin beamed, reaching inside his ceremonial tunic. "I have a special wedding gift for you."

"I don't want it!"

"Really? But you accepted it readily enough the first time I presented you with it."

Elodie looked down. He was holding the jeweled dagger he'd given to her . . . and which she'd then given to Fessan.

"This was never really a dagger," Vicerin was saying. His voice sounded as if it were underwater. Elodie fought back the urge to scream. "It was a test. I was curious to see what you might do with such a thing. And now I know."

"Fessan," she mumbled through lips that had turned numb.

"Yes," Vicerin replied. "Fessan."

"What have you done with him?"

Vicerin's grin widened into a hideous leer.

"Now that, my dear, is the wedding present I *really* want to share with you."

He led her past the fountain to a wide expanse of lawn. By now the clouds had closed over the sun, and the day was turning rapidly cold. As Elodie stood shivering in her wedding dress, rain began to fall.

In the middle of the lawn was a wooden platform on which stood a sturdy wooden tower. Set into the sides of the tower was a system of ropes and pulleys, while at the top hung something shiny, mirror flat, and as sharp as a finely honed sword.

The blade of a guillotine.

"Bring him out!" cried Vicerin.

A squad of six guards climbed onto the platform, carrying between them a bedraggled figure Elodie recognized at once.

"No!" she cried. She surged forward, only to be held back by her own band of guards.

The guards forced their prisoner to kneel before the crowd. He was a sorry sight, with his torn green tunic and his head hanging low. The rain had already soaked his mud-splashed clothes and was dripping from his long hair.

One of the guards grabbed his head and pulled it back, and Elodie found herself staring straight into Fessan's anguished eyes.

"Please!" she sobbed, dropping to her knees before Vicerin. The ground around her was rapidly turning to mud, and it clung to the fine gold ribbons of her wedding gown.

She didn't care. All she cared about was saving Fessan's life.

"Spare him, please! I'll be your queen. I'll help you take Toronia, I promise. Please, just let him live!"

Vicerin glared down at her, his face a mask of contempt.

"This is a place of punishment," he said. "And this is *your* punishment, my dear. This is the price you pay for betraying me and freeing this prisoner from my cells."

"Then put me in the cell instead. Anything, please, I beg you. . . ."

"It is too late for that. The time has come. Without this man, Trident dies, along with any misguided ideas you might once have had about ruling this kingdom with your wretched brothers." He leaned close to Elodie, breathing hard. "This is where your so-called dreams end, Elodie. All of them!"

"You're a monster!"

Leaping to her feet, Elodie wrenched herself free of the guards and rushed to the platform on which Fessan was being held. She grabbed its rough timber edge and was about to haul herself up when Vicerin's hand yanked her back. She pulled free, started climbing again, then was hauled away so violently that she fell full-length in the mud.

The crowd gasped. Elodie clambered slowly to her feet. The gold dress had turned almost black. She wanted to cry. She wanted to shriek. She wanted to claw Vicerin's eyes from his smug, powdered face. She bunched her fist and drew it back, and Vicerin slapped her face.

"Leave her alone!"

Despite the blood in his mouth, despite the rain pouring down his face, Fessan's voice was strong and level. Hearing his prisoner speak, Vicerin looked around in surprise. Elodie took the opportunity to kick him in the shins, and felt a surge of satisfaction when he cried out in pain.

Her face stinging from the blow he'd struck her, she leaped for the platform once more, this time managing to climb all the way up before Vicerin's fingers clamped on her ankle. She kicked out, rejoicing as the heel of her foot smashed into Vicerin's nose, breaking it with a sickening crunch.

Vicerin reeled back, his hands pressed to his face. Elodie dodged around the hateful killing machine and threw her arms around Fessan's neck.

"I'm sorry," she sobbed. "I'm so, so, sorry."

"You will win in the end," Fessan answered. "You, Elodie, and your brothers. In the battle between good and evil, good will prevail. *You* will prevail."

Elodie was seized again: around the arms, around the legs, around the neck. Screaming, she was carried bodily off the platform and hurled into the mud.

"Let him go!" she yelled as she was pinned to the ground. "I am your queen! I command it!"

"Shut up!" howled Vicerin, still clutching his bleeding nose. "Hold her head! I want her to see something she'll never forget!"

Rough hands grabbed Elodie's head and held it rigid. She began to close her eyes, to shut out the dreadful scene unfolding before her, then realized that Fessan was still looking at her.

You will win, he mouthed.

I will watch it all, she resolved. *I owe it to you, Fessan. You won't die alone!*

The guards on the platform forced Fessan's head down into the curved wooden brace at the foot of the guillotine. A man stepped forward carrying a black hood in his hand. Elodie was horrified to see it was Stown.

"What's he doing here?" she shouted, trying to fight her way free again.

"Good service brings its rewards," snarled Vicerin, his voice muffled by his broken nose. "Sergeant Stown has been promoted."

Stown stared briefly at Elodie, showed his teeth in a thin smile, and slipped the black hood over his head. Through a slit in the material, Elodie saw his eyes glistening eagerly.

Stown swung a clamp over Fessan's neck, locking him into the apparatus. He picked up a large wooden bowl and was about to place it beneath Fessan's head when Vicerin cried out.

"No bowl! No bowl! Let his head roll!"

Stown shrugged and tossed the bowl aside. He wrapped his thick fingers into one of the ropes hanging from the wooden tower . . . and pulled.

No! Not yet. It's too soon. Please don't . . .

The blade fell, landing with a dreadful *thunk.*

As Lord Vicerin had commanded, Fessan's head rolled.

And Elodie saw it all.

"Take her to the White Tower!" Vicerin shouted as the rain flowed red with Fessan's blood. "Lock her away with my treacherous children! Let them all rot there together! This wretched girl has served her purpose. Now I never want to see her again!"

CHAPTER 26

I gave you shelter! I gave you aid in your time of need! And this is how you repay me?"

Lady Redina's face had turned white with rage. She paced back and forth in the shining crystal courtyard, glaring into the faces of each of the Tangletree Players in turn. Gulph stood as straight as his twisted back allowed, all too aware of how scruffy and bedraggled they all looked.

"We came to warn you straightaway," he said as sharply as he dared. *What else did you expect us to do? Stay up in Idilliam with the undead?*

"So I see! Could you not have had the decency to dry yourselves first? Or do you respect me so little?"

Gulph stared at the pool of silver water growing beneath his feet—beneath all their feet. When they'd emerged into the vast underground chamber that held Celestis, their only choice had been to drop into the lake, just as Gulph and the others had before. Luckily, Kalia had been keeping watch for them, and boats had arrived swiftly to pick them up.

Even more fortunate: the bakaliss had not found them first.

Facing the monster might have been better than this, thought Gulph glumly as Lady Redina unleashed another volley of furious curses.

"Not only do you have the audacity to return—against my strict instructions—but you tell me you have left open a doorway to the upper kingdom!"

"We tried to close it. Really, we did. But it was impossible. We thought the best thing to do was to come and warn you straight-away. Anyway, the tunnels under Idilliam are starting to collapse. The chances of an army coming through are—"

"*You* came through!"

Gulph lowered his head, abashed. "Yes, we did."

"Celestis has remained safe and hidden for a thousand years. Now we are exposed. Brutan will find us. His undead warriors will find us. And it is all your fault!"

"It isn't!" Pip stepped forward. "You don't know what you're talking about. Gulph saved us. And now he's trying to save you. If you were half as brave as he is—"

"SILENCE!"

Lady Redina's voice resounded off the emerald fountains, the ruby walls. Crystal flowers tinkled, echoing her outburst. Two armed soldiers stepped from a nearby doorway in the diamond wall of Lady Redina's splendid house, but she waved them back.

"I warned you!" she snapped. "I warned you that if you left Celestis, you could never be allowed to return! You ignored my warning. For that reason, I banish you! You will be taken from here without delay and cast out into the wastelands at the foot of the chasm. If I ever see your faces again, you will be killed instantly. Do you understand?"

Gulph was all too aware of the emotions of his friends: exhaustion, desperation, fear. He tried to imagine them facing up against the ranks of the undead who'd fallen into the chasm. He didn't think they'd last very long.

I've brought them all this way for nothing, he thought bitterly.

Kalia, who'd been standing to one side and listening to the entire exchange, stepped forward. She bowed deferentially.

"Sending them out into the chasm means certain death, Lady Redina," she said.

"I care not." Lady Redina turned away.

Kalia caught Gulph's eye, then went on. "Perhaps not, but do you not care about the defense of Celestis?"

Lady Redina stopped, turned back. "What is your point?"

"My point is simply this: Brutan is coming. We cannot escape that fact. Never mind casting blame—Celestis must prepare for invasion. And it must prepare now."

Lady Redina's face was paler than ever. "I am aware of this."

"Then let them stay, at least until the battle is over. They have proved themselves brave and resourceful—how else could they have evaded Brutan and survived the journey down here? Their knowledge of the undead king's ways makes them valuable. Let them fight for you. Let them prove their worth."

"They have no worth!"

Lady Redina stared long and hard at Kalia. Gulph held his breath.

"However . . . we will need every sword arm at our disposal." Lady Redina arched one eyebrow at Gulph. "If I give you weapons, will you use them well?"

"Your enemy is our enemy, Lady Redina," Gulph answered.

"Then, as a courtesy to Kalia, I will let you remain in Celestis . . . but only until this situation is resolved. As for what happens afterward . . . I make no promises."

Relieved, Gulph bowed low and nodded to his friends to do the same. "You are merciful, Lady Redina, and we thank you."

Lady Redina clapped her hands. Servants poured from the house and gathered around her. She barked orders to each in turn, instructing this one to summon the leaders of the Celestian defense teams, that one to rally the boat riders, another to call in all the observers and deploy them to the watchtowers.

Gulph listened, fascinated. Up to now, he'd seen Lady Redina as a rather remote figure, the kind of leader who sat aloof in her palace and allowed others to do all the hard work. Now he saw her sharp mind in action, as with a series of crisp instructions she set the defensive machinery of Celestis into motion.

She truly does rule Celestis. Don't ever forget it, Gulph.

"I will deal with the crystalsmiths," said Kalia when Lady Redina finally paused for breath. "I can instruct them on how to make the special blades we need to deal with the undead."

"We're going to need a lot of them," suggested Gulph.

"I know," Kalia agreed. "As for you, take your friends to my house. Stay there, and stay out of trouble." She lowered her voice. "You will be safe there, Gulph. I will see to it."

Gulph nodded. Despite everything, warmth stole through him. *She cares about me. Maybe she'll never believe I'm her son, but she does care about me.*

As they left the courtyard Gulph spotted a shriveled plant in a pot, its leaves black. It was the one he'd tipped his unwanted wine into.

Anxiety gnawed at him as he showed Pip and the others the winding path that led toward Kalia's house. If the poison had done that to a plant, what would it do to a human mind?

When they reached the lakeside, he stopped. "Kalia lives just beyond that rise," he said. "See—it's not far."

"But aren't you coming?" asked Pip.

"I'll catch up. There's just something I have to do first."

While Pip led the others on, Gulph made his way back toward the crystal house Redina had given them. When he was near, Gulph spotted the person he was looking for, seated on the end of a jetty jutting out over the silver water. Ossilius.

Gulph took a deep breath. By the time they'd parted, Ossilius had turned into a shadow of his former self. What state would he be in now?

The jetty, like everything else in Celestis, was made of crystal. Gulph could see the silver waters of the lake through its transparent planks. It felt like walking on air.

"Ossilius?" he said when he reached his friend. "Are you all right?"

Ossilius looked up. He was swinging his legs over the water like a child. Beside him was a plate of small purple sweets, which he was cramming into his mouth one after the other.

"Who are you?" he said dully.

Gulph's stomach turned over. "Don't you know me?"

"I never saw you before. Do you want one of my sweets?"

He offered the plate. Gulph shook his head, dismayed to see his friend—a captain of the King's Legion—in such a state.

An idea came to him.

"Captain Ossilius!" he announced, standing to attention. "Battle is imminent! I await your orders!"

Something flickered in Ossilius's eyes, and hope rose in Gulph's heart. Then Ossilius's shoulders drooped, and he mumbled, "It sounds dangerous." His eyes glazed over and he pressed another sweet between his lips.

There must be something you remember.

He brought out the crown from his pack. The gold shimmered in the constant purple twilight of Celestis, picking up the countless reflections of the surrounding crystal so that it seemed to glow with its own inner light.

"That's a pretty thing," Ossilius said. "Did you bring it for me?"

He made a grab for it; Gulph held the crown just out of reach.

"Do you know what this is?"

"I'd like to have it."

Gulph pressed on. "You must know what it is, Ossilius. You gave it to me yourself, when Nynus died. You said I was your king. You said you'd serve me. You said . . ."

"King? King of where? That's a very pretty thing."

Ossilius snatched at the crown. Gulph stumbled backward, horrified.

First Sidebottom John. Now Ossilius. I'm losing my friends, one by one.

Dread came over him.

Will the same thing happen to the others? To Noddy and Simeon?

To Pip?

Ossilius was on his feet now. He reached for the crown again and Gulph twisted aside, grabbing a crystal mooring post to keep himself from toppling into the silver water.

The water!

Without stopping to question—without thinking at all—Gulph rolled the crown out of reach and launched himself at Ossilius. He planted both hands on the captain's shoulders and shoved him off the jetty and into the water.

Ossilius went under immediately, too surprised even to cry out. He sank rapidly, bubbles rising from his mouth, and for a moment Gulph was terrified his friend was too drugged even to swim. Then he saw Ossilius's arms and legs begin to thrash. Gulph held his breath and hoped his friend was doing the same.

When Ossilius's head broke the surface, Gulph waited just long enough for him to open his mouth and take in a lungful of air. Then, reaching down from the jetty, he pressed his hands on top of the man's head and pushed him under again.

"Forgive me, my friend," he said, grunting with the effort. "The water healed us before—maybe it can save you now. . . ."

The second time Ossilius rose, Gulph saw that same brief flicker in his eyes. Was it recognition? Fury at being half drowned by someone he saw as a stranger?

Steeling himself, Gulph submerged him yet again.

This time when Ossilius surfaced, he was kicking and spluttering, reaching for the crystal planks of the jetty and throwing off Gulph's attempts to help him out of the lake.

"Let go of me, Gulph!" he cried. "I can do it myself!"

It took a moment for Gulph to register what he'd just heard. By the time he did, Ossilius had clawed his way up onto the jetty and was lying on his back with his chest heaving. He rolled onto his side, spat out a mouthful of water, then sat up and ran his hands through his sodden hair.

"Where am I? What's happening, Gulph?"

Gulph seized Ossilius's hand and gripped it tight. He could feel the grin spreading over his face, wide and warm. He couldn't remember the last time he'd smiled so broadly.

"It's good to have you back," Gulph said.

Making their way to Kalia's house, they had to jump to the side of the path to avoid a whole regiment of armed soldiers, dressed in glistening crystal chain mail, hurrying in the opposite direction. As the soldiers marched past, a messenger ran up and spoke to the officer at the front of the column.

". . . Undead seen in the upper tunnels," Gulph could just hear her say. "They are coming. . . ."

The words chilled his heart.

"At least they are taking the threat from Brutan seriously," said

Ossilius. He pointed to a line of boats forming on the lake to create some kind of waterborne defense.

"They need to," replied Gulph.

He watched as the soldiers disappeared along the path, unformed thoughts filling his head. *We have to take action too. Just like them. But what can we do?*

They reached Kalia's house and went inside. What Gulph saw made him grin. With the entire complement of the Tangletree Players crammed around the cauldron on its hearth, the cottage felt packed. The air smelled of fire and magic and fellowship.

Pip ran straight up to Gulph and pulled him into a hug. Then the others swarmed around him, throwing their arms about him and each other, and laughing. Noddy even danced a little jig.

"Is this how you treat your king?" Ossilius laughed, clearly enjoying the reunion.

The room fell silent.

"King?" said Madrigal, taking a nervous step backward.

"What do you mean?" said Noddy.

Gulph glanced at Ossilius, who nodded.

"You've all heard of the prophecy, haven't you?" Gulph said. His friends murmured that they had. Gulph took a deep breath. "Well, it's a long story—too long to tell now—but I'm not really who you think I am. I'm one of the triplets."

Silence fell again.

"Brutan's son?" said Noddy at last. "Is it true?"

"It is true," said Ossilius. "Gulph, show them."

Opening his pack, Gulph brought out the crown of Toronia. The Tangletree Players gaped first at the beaming band of gold, then at Gulph.

"By golly," Noddy breathed.

"W-what should we call you?" stammered Madrigal.

"I should have thought that's obvious," said Pip with a grin. "We call him Gulph."

He grinned back, his heart swelling.

"You can't tell anyone," he said, hiding the crown away again. "Especially Lady Redina. It's a secret. Nobody can know."

"We understand," said Pip solemnly. "Don't we?"

The others nodded their agreement.

Gulph squeezed her hand. "Thank you. Oh, I can't tell you how good it is to see you all again!"

"So, what do we do now?" said Noddy, clapping his hands together.

"We don't need to do anything," countered Madrigal. "We're safe."

"No, we're not," Gulph responded. "Brutan's already on his way."

There were cries of dismay all around, except from Pip. She stood with her hands on her narrow hips, studying Gulph. "You've got a plan. Haven't you, Gulph?"

Gulph considered this. The thoughts that had been drifting through his head during the walk from the jetty were beginning to gather together.

"Yes," he said. "I think I might."

"Do you want to go up against Brutan?" Ossilius asked warily.

"Better than that. I want to get rid of him, once and for all. We know the undead have been seen in the tunnels. The question is, how much time do we have before the actual invasion begins?"

"It is hard to say how the undead think," said Ossilius. "Even if a few of them have found their way down here, it does not mean they all will."

"Did Brutan know about Celestis?"

"Nobody knew about Celestis, Gulph."

"But he was the king."

Ossilius pondered this. "He knew the history of Toronia, better than most. If he has found his way inside . . . discovered the cracks that have opened up"—Ossilius's expression turned grim—"yes, I believe he will put the pieces of the puzzle together."

"Then we're agreed," said Gulph. "We have to do something. Right now."

He turned to Noddy, who had been listening to the conversation with his bright, attentive eyes. Noddy might have played the clown in the Tangletree Players, but in reality he knew more tricks than all of them.

"Noddy," Gulph said, "how would you like to make some fireworks?"

Outside Kalia's cottage, Gulph was saying good-bye to the Tangletree Players once more. *No sooner do I find you than I have to let you go.*

"Look after them, Pip," he whispered, hugging her tightly.

"Be careful, won't you?" She gave him a tearful smile.

"We must hurry, Gulph," called Ossilius from the end of the path. He pointed toward a low hill that looked as if it were made of pure emerald. A small army was massing there. "The Celestian forces are everywhere. If you want to leave without drawing attention to yourself, it has to be now."

"Good-bye, Pip," said Gulph. "Good-bye, everyone. I'll see you soon. I promise."

His heart heavy, Gulph turned from them and joined Ossilius, conscious of the extra weight in his pack. Once he'd explained his plan, Noddy had worked fast and hard. Now Gulph was carrying the fruits of his friend's labors.

Only these are the kinds of fruit that explode, he thought with a tingle of anticipation.

"Will you find John for me?" Gulph asked as they set off toward the causeway that would take them out of Celestis. "He should be with the others."

"Yes," Ossilius replied. "But not before I have seen you safely on your way."

"When you find him, dunk him in the lake, just like I did with you. You'll probably have to do it several times."

Ossilius nodded. "Do not worry about your friends, Gulph. They have me to protect them now."

"And my mother." Gulph hesitated, overwhelmed by the implications of what he was about to ask. "Will you do the same for her, too?"

"I fear she may put up a stronger fight than John," said Ossilius with a wry smile. "But yes, Gulph. I will see to it that Kalia is restored."

Restored! And then she'll remember me at last!

Gulph tried to imagine how it would feel to meet Kalia's eye and see not uncertainty but recognition. Understanding.

Love.

He thought it would feel very good.

Crossing the narrow finger of crystal that ran across the lake, Gulph and Ossilius had a good view of the Celestian shoreline, where hundreds of people were busy constructing crystal barricades and stockpiling glistening swords. Preparing for battle. To Gulph their activity looked both brave and hopeless. If Brutan succeeded in bringing his undead army down here, the Celestians wouldn't stand a chance.

There's only one person who can stop this invasion, he thought grimly. *And that's me.*

At last they reached the line of pillars marking the edge of the Celestian realm. Passing between them, they exited into the open space at the bottom of the chasm.

Gulph stared up into darkness. Behind him, within the crystal confines of Celestis, the eternal twilight lingered. In the world above, night had fallen.

They made their way to the chasm wall. Ossilius had his sword drawn, in case they were attacked by any undead fallen from Idilliam. But nothing moved in the darkness, and they reached their goal unmolested.

"Well," said Gulph. "Here we are. I suppose—"

Before he could say more, Ossilius had pulled him into a fierce hug. "Come back, Gulph. Be sure to come back. Fessan is still lost to me, and I fear he may never be found. I could not bear to lose another son."

Gulph felt as though his breath had been taken away. Did Ossilius realize what he'd just said? He'd been longing for Kalia to recognize him, yet it was this former captain of the King's Legion who had uttered the single word he never thought he'd hear from anyone.

Son. Is that really how he thinks of me?

His heart full, Gulph planted his hands on the cold rock of the chasm wall. High above was Idilliam. He had to get there before Brutan sent the rest of his undead army into the tunnels.

"Are you sure about this, Gulph?" said Ossilius. He was looking uneasily up into the blackness. "Nobody has ever climbed the chasm before."

"It's our only chance."

Gulph dug one toe into a crevice in the rock, put another onto a tiny ledge a little farther up. He pulled with his arms. He moved his feet again, one at a time, little movements, quick but careful. He'd made more difficult climbs in his life, but never one so high.

Don't think about it. Concentrate on where you are right now. One hand at a time. One foot. Little by little, Gulph. It's the only way.

In the blackness of the chasm, clinging like an insect to the sheer rock wall, Gulph began the climb of his life.

CHAPTER 27

The first thing Tarlan saw as they flew toward the fortress town of Deep Poynt was the flames.

We're too late!

His heart clenched as he guided Theeta over the burning buildings. The fierce orange glow of the fire lit up the night and sent waves of heat crashing against the thorrod's wings. Below, hundreds of people were fleeing, running out through the town's main gate and onto the hillside beyond.

Straight into the clutches of the Galadronians!

In desperation, he cast his eyes out across the landscape, seeking out the enemy.

"There they are, Theeta!" he cried, pointing at a line of soldiers lurking at the edge of the forest that surrounded the hill. "Why are they holding back?"

One glance back at Deep Poynt answered his question. The town was surrounded by earth embankments and thick, log-built walls. Sharpened wooden stakes jutted at angles from the embankments, looking for all the world like jagged teeth. Anyone trying to storm the defenses would be impaled on these stakes before they could reach the walls.

Having poured out through the high defensive wall surrounding their homes, the people of Deep Poynt were now taking shelter behind this barricade of stakes.

"Fireflies," croaked Theeta, swinging around to face the Galadronians again.

More soldiers had emerged from the trees, carrying the strange sidebows Tarlan had first seen on the beach. As he watched, they fired a tremendous volley of burning arrows into the heart of the town. No sooner had they done this than battalions of foot soldiers emerged from the trees. As they formed up into ranks, they beat their swords against their shields and yelled out battle cries. The shouting and clattering combined into a single, gigantic roar.

"Come on, Theeta!" Tarlan shouted over the noise. "There's no time to waste!"

If they were afraid, the Isurian townspeople didn't show it. But Tarlan could see how vulnerable they were. Although they were well armed with swords and conventional longbows, they were trapped between the town's outer wall and the ring of stakes, forced to cower behind their shields as the enemy arrows rained down.

As Theeta swooped in through the smoke, a group of townspeople emerged from the trees to the south. They'd somehow managed to outflank the Galadronians, catching the enemy off guard.

Tarlan's heart lifted as Isurian swords came down on the colorful armor of the invading soldiers. He clenched his fists tighter into Theeta's feathers, willing the people of Deep Poynt to succeed.

However, bravely as they fought, they were hopelessly outnumbered. The Galadronian archers fell back, allowing the assembled foot soldiers to advance and engage their attackers. The sound of clashing blades rose up to where Theeta was circling, high overhead, and the ground turned red with blood.

Suddenly Tarlan spotted a familiar figure striding through the melee, cutting down Isurians with great swings of his curved sword.

Tyro!

"The sooner we get rid of him, the quicker this will all be over," he muttered.

"Pack now," Theeta urged.

Tarlan nodded. "Yes. Let's go."

Tarlan guided Theeta away from the battle to a nearby stand of pine trees. The giant thorrod landed with difficulty on a densely wooded slope, where Kassan was waiting for them on his horse.

The boy looked pale and afraid. Windracer stamped the ground nervously.

"It's horrible," Kassan said the instant Theeta touched down. "My dad told me we were safe in Deep Poynt."

"I'm not sure anyone's safe against the weapons these Galadronians have brought."

"They'll smash the walls." Kassan was close to tears. "There's nothing we can do."

"They won't," Tarlan replied, holding tight as Theeta reared up, cawing agreement. "And there's plenty we can do."

His heart lifted as Filos, Greythorn, and Brock emerged from the trees. Moonlight flashed on their fur, then was briefly shadowed as Kitheen flew over their heads. The creatures on the ground halted beside Windracer and gazed expectantly up at Tarlan, while the thorrod hovered above.

"What are your orders, Tarlan?" growled Greythorn. His lips were curled back from his teeth, and his muscles were twitching beneath his gray pelt. Like his companions, he looked edgy.

"Is the pack ready?" Tarlan glanced into the shadowy forest. He could feel the presence of hundreds—no, thousands—of animals, all poised among the trees, awaiting their orders.

My orders.

"Yes, Tarlan," Greythorn answered. "We are ready."

"Good." Tarlan shouted up to the hovering thorrod. "Kitheen! Fly west as fast as you can. Find Nasheen and Melchior, and bring them back even faster. I have a feeling we're going to need a wizard before the night's out."

Kitheen continued to hold his place in the sky, driving his enormous wings relentlessly against the night air. The thorrod said nothing, as usual, but the furious gleam in his eye told Tarlan everything he needed to know.

"Don't worry," Tarlan told him. "You'll get your chance to fight. Now go! And fly like you've never flown before!"

Silently, Kitheen turned away and accelerated toward the distant ocean. By the time Tarlan had taken three breaths, he'd dwindled to a tiny dot and vanished from sight.

"Thorrod fast," Theeta remarked.

"Like the wind." Tarlan had never seen such a turn of speed from any of the thorrods. However well he thought he knew these giants of the sky, still they managed to surprise him. He turned back to Greythorn, Filos, and Brock. "Now it's your turn."

Brock rose onto his hind legs. "We fight now?"

"Soon. I need the three of you to rally the pack, and then wait. Make sure they're ready and that they understand the difference between the Galadronians and the people of Deep Poynt. Tell them that the enemy wear clothes of bright colors and have metal armor and weapons that curve like"—he glanced up at the sky—"the crescent moon. But they have to wait until the moment is right. That's very important. Don't let them advance on the Galadronians."

"How can we fight these enemies if we don't go to them?" Filos asked.

"You're not going to them."

"We're not?"

"No! I'm going to bring them to you!"

The three animals had emerged from the forest appearing nervous. Now they stood tall, stiff-necked. They looked ready for anything.

If I'm strong, they're strong too, Tarlan thought, his chest swelling with pride.

"Kassan!" he cried as Theeta lifted him once more into the air. "Be ready!" As they climbed skyward, the boy's face fell away, a pale oval glowing bright in the moonlight.

Returning to the battlefield, Tarlan saw that more of the Isurians had emerged from their defenses to engage the enemy. He wasn't surprised. Their town was already burning; what choice did they have but to fight?

He watched tensely as four Isurian men charged down the hill, waving their swords and screaming. Two were cut down instantly by arrows; their comrades ran on without even slowing. Each man felled several Galadronians before they themselves fell.

Tarlan was impressed by their bravery. Though the Galadronians had more sophisticated weapons and greater numbers, those defending the town battled ferociously.

Of course they do, he thought grimly. *They're fighting for their lives.*

It didn't take him long to spot Tyro again: the big man's bright red cloak was unmistakable. His face was splashed with blood; his beard was soaked in it. He was crimson from head to toe.

Tarlan drew his sword and drove Theeta into an accelerating dive.

"Tyro!" he yelled, the wind whipping the words from his mouth. "I'm coming for you!"

Tyro looked up. He seemed more pleased than surprised. Whirling his sword, he made rapid hand signals to a rank of nearby archers. Their sidebows lifted in unison. At once Theeta began weaving from side to side.

Tyro's arm came down. A volley of arrows buzzed through the air, barely missing them. Trusting the thorrod to carve a true course through the deadly rain, Tarlan shouted again.

"You won't win, Tyro!"

"Bring them down," bellowed the bearded man. "Kill the barbarian! He must not leave alive!"

More arrows flew. Theeta dodged them all, swinging left and right. When they were almost upon Tyro, she extended her legs and opened her claws.

"No!" warned Tarlan. "Remember the plan!"

Cawing her frustration, Theeta retracted her claws and swooped over Tyro's head. The wind she made almost knocked the big man over. Tarlan heard him curse in a guttural language he didn't recognize. Then they were past, climbing hard into the night.

"Around!" Tarlan urged. "Go around, Theeta. Head straight for the woods!"

In no time at all they'd left the battle behind again. Glancing back, Tarlan saw Tyro waving his sword in triumph.

"Retreating so soon?" the Galadronian commander shouted after them. He made more hand signals; at once a whole battalion of his army—Tarlan guessed it was perhaps one hundred soldiers— separated from the rest and ran in pursuit of the low-flying thorrod.

Just as Tarlan had hoped.

Theeta flew low, staying in sight of the pursuing enemy at all times, drawing them on. At first Tarlan worried that the dense forest would hold them back; to his relief he saw that the leading wave of soldiers carried lightweight machines with whirling blades. These contraptions sliced easily through the thick undergrowth, creating a wide path along which the rest of the battalion could follow.

So that's how they got here so quickly from the coast.

Tarlan closed his eyes, sent out his thoughts. He could sense his pack waiting. It was vast: a mighty army armed with tooth and fang, waiting in the shadows for the order to attack.

Not yet, he told them as Theeta's wings clipped the topmost leaves from the trees. *Not yet.*

Battle cries rose up from the Galadronian soldiers. Theeta had slowed a little, allowing them to close the gap almost to nothing. Arrows began whistling past Tarlan's head.

Not yet . . .

There was movement in the trees ahead: a huge, shifting surge, like some gigantic hidden beast taking a breath. Tarlan didn't exactly see it, didn't exactly hear it. But he felt it, like a pulse of heat in his belly.

"NOW!" he roared.

The instant he shouted, Theeta began to climb.

"Hold thorrod," she cawed.

It sometimes took a while for Tarlan to interpret the deceptively simple language of the thorrods. This time he understood at once. Thrusting his fingers into the ruff of feathers at her neck, he gripped tighter than he'd ever gripped before.

"I'm holding, Theeta!" he yelled.

Theeta flipped all the way over onto her back, reversing her direction, and plunged down toward the Galadronians. For an instant Tarlan was hanging upside down, his hands buried deep in her feathers, his legs flailing. Then, as Theeta completed her roll, he was secure on her back once more, his legs gripping her heaving flanks, his black cloak streaming out behind him, the wind blasting his face.

"Now!" he screamed. "To battle!"

The forest erupted.

First to advance was a line of giant bears, lumbering through the undergrowth on all fours, bellowing like thunder. As they met the Galadronian front line, the soldiers gaped in stupid surprise. Before they could react, the bears reared up, batting aside first the tree-cutting machines, then the men who'd been carrying them.

Immediately behind the bears, running fast, came a huge pack of gray timber wolves. Greythorn was leading them. When they reached the bears, Greythorn let out a single, piercing howl; the bears dropped low, allowing the wolves to climb their hunched backs and leap at the throats of the second wave of Galadronians.

You think you've got an army, Tyro? Tarlan thought deliriously. *Now* this *is an army!*

By now Theeta had reached the lowest point of her dive. The tree canopy was too dense for her to descend all the way to the ground, so she flattened her wings against the air, reducing her speed to nothing in the time it took Tarlan to take a single breath.

"Stay close!" Tarlan shouted in her ear.

He threw himself off her back, grabbing at the nearest tree and dropping in a barely controlled fall through its branches to the ground. Landing hard, he drew his sword and ran into battle.

The Galadronians had begun to fight back. Their shock at being ambushed had turned to fierce resolve. Moonlight flashed off a fearsome array of curved swords. Tarlan saw a leaping stag pierced by a dozen arrows. The majestic creature crashed dead to the ground, its huge antlers smashing apart against the trunk of a tree.

A pair of eagles emerged from the darkness. They flew at the faces of the sidebow archers who'd brought down the stag, raking the enemy with their talons.

"Die, you mangy cat!"

Tarlan turned to see a tall Galadronian woman raising her sword over the fallen stag. Something was trapped beneath it, struggling to free itself: a lithe creature with blue-and-white striped fur.

"Filos!"

Tarlan hurdled a fallen tree and sank his blade into the Galadronian's side, fortuitously finding the gap where the plates of her armor met. She fell back, dead.

"I can't get free!" Filos cried.

"Brock!" Tarlan shouted. The bear was hugging one of the Galadronian soldiers to him and roaring in fury. When he released his gargantuan paws, the man collapsed like an empty sack. Brock bounded over and set his weight against the dead stag while Tarlan helped Filos out from beneath it. To his relief the tigron was unhurt.

"Thank you." Filos licked his face, then hurled herself at the nearest Galadronian.

Tarlan followed her, surprised to see how few of the enemy were still standing. There were bodies everywhere, and the ground was thick with blood. Apart from the dead stag, he couldn't see a single member of his pack with more than a superficial wound.

The ground shook beneath his feet, and Kassan rode up. There was blood on the boy's sword.

"It worked!" Kassan shouted. "Your plan worked, Tarlan. They're dead, all of them!"

Tarlan watched as three wild boars ran their tusks through the last few Galadronians; then the forest was still. He was suddenly aware of the breath rasping in his throat, the sharp tang of blood in the air, the steam rising from the panting bodies of a thousand animals.

"This is only the start," he said grimly. "All of you—follow me!"

They emerged into the open, close to the outer defenses of Deep Poynt. Tarlan's heart sank immediately. The Galadronians who hadn't pursued them into the forest had penetrated beyond the outer ring of stakes—many of which now lay useless and half-buried in the ground—and were fighting hand to hand with the town's defenders. The gates were still wide open, and the town was ablaze.

"We need Melchior," Tarlan muttered.

"Who's Melchior?" asked Kassan.

"Someone who can help us beat them. But he has a long way to come."

"Then we'll just have to hold out until he gets here."

Tarlan liked Kassan's straightforwardness. Up to now, he'd regarded humans as frustratingly complex: all hidden meanings and politics. It was refreshing to find someone who said things how they were.

"You're right," he said, ruffling the boy's hair. "Tell me, who's the leader of Deep Poynt?"

Kassan pointed to a spot where the fighting was thickest. "We call him The Hammer."

Tarlan saw a mountain of a man draped with loose leather armor. His hair was a thick red thatch. His eyes blazed vivid green. He was wielding not a sword but an enormous iron hammer, twice the size of any blacksmith's tool Tarlan had seen.

"He's the Defender of Deep Poynt," Kassan added. "He looks even bigger up close."

Tarlan thought for a moment, then called Filos, Greythorn, and Brock to him. They were more than his companions now, he realized. They were his lieutenants.

"Take the pack. Lead them around the town. Stay low. Don't be seen. As soon as you're ready, attack the Galadronians on their north flank. The hill is steeper there—they won't be expecting it."

As the three animals began to carry out his orders, Tarlan summoned Theeta down from where she'd been circling.

He pointed at The Hammer. "Take me to him."

As they flew in over the outskirts of Deep Poynt, Tarlan wasn't surprised to see Tyro plowing through the lines of defenders, working his way steadily toward the gates of the fortress.

Does nothing slow that man down?

"You call that rabble of animals an army?" Tyro shouted up as the thorrod's shadow passed over him.

"They're better than an army," Tarlan answered. "They are my pack."

He pulled Theeta around so that she was hovering directly above Tyro's head.

"You're dead!" Tyro shouted up. "All of you, dead already! As soon as we take this fortress, the rest of Isur will bow before us. Galadron has come, boy. Nothing can stand in our way!"

"I can!"

His defiance was answered by a volley of arrows. Theeta veered away, carrying Tarlan on toward the town. Her chest heaving, she landed on the fortress wall, close to where The Hammer was beating back a fresh Galadronian onslaught.

Having felled the last of the enemies around him, the gigantic warrior bent his head toward an Isurian soldier who'd been tugging at his leather tunic. Swiveling on his heels, the Defender of Deep Poynt stared at Tarlan. Moonlight twinkled deep in his striking green eyes.

"Are you a miracle?" His voice boomed out over the battlefield. As he spoke, a lone Galadronian rushed up behind him. Without looking, The Hammer casually swept his enormous iron weapon out behind him, meeting the skull of his attacker. He continued speaking as if nothing had happened. "You do not look miraculous, yet you ride a thorrod. You bring an army of animals."

"Never mind what I am," Tarlan replied. "You need my help, and you need it now."

"Oh, but I do mind what you are. You have a look about you, boy. Your hair is red, though not as red as mine. Red with gold, some might say. The color of prophecy, they are telling me."

The Hammer raised one shaggy red eyebrow. His broad mouth twitched with what might have been humor.

"We don't have time for this," said Tarlan. "You have to retreat into the town—or what's left of it. Get inside and close the gates. We'll hold them off until help arrives."

The half smile became a grimace. "Retreat? The Hammer has never retreated, boy!"

Suddenly Tarlan was tired of debate. He was tired of shouting down to these squabbling humans, trying to make them see what to him was so clear.

"Well, you're going to retreat now," he told him.

He was aware that other Isurians were looking up at him. Some looked confused; some looked awestruck; a few looked nervously at The Hammer, clearly wondering how their leader would react to being spoken to like this.

The Hammer's mouth opened. The Hammer's mouth closed.

"Tell me why I should do this, boy," said the man-mountain.

Tarlan hesitated. The words he knew he had to speak felt wrong. Yet they also felt *right*.

"Because your future king commands you!" he roared.

A long gasp rippled through the crowd. The iron hammer slipped through the meaty fingers of its owner and hit the ground with a colossal thud.

On Theeta's back, Tarlan waited.

"Do as he says," said The Hammer slowly. He looked dazed, as if he couldn't quite comprehend what was coming out of his mouth. "Behind the walls. Close the gates. Everyone. Now!"

The retreat began immediately. Even before Theeta had taken to the air again, the rearmost ranks of the Isurian defenders had fallen back inside the town perimeter and were urging their companions to join them.

Leaving them to it, Tarlan guided his thorrod steed back over the battlefield just in time to see Brock, Filos, and Greythorn leading the gigantic pack of animals up the nearby slope to meet the Galadronians' northern flank. But his excitement turned quickly to dismay as a line of swordsmen cut down the leading ranks of foxes and wolves. At the same time, sidebow arrows flew high and far, biting into the animals bringing up the rear.

We're too exposed!

"Drive them into the woods!" Tarlan yelled.

Hearing his battle cry, the bears surged forward with renewed energy, Brock in front. Filos led in a wave of big forest cats that penetrated deep into the Galadronian ranks, and then wheeled around to push the enemy down the slope they'd just climbed. The fighting was intense, but gradually the animals began to force the invaders away from the town and toward the trees.

"Hold your ground! Hold your ground, curse you all!"

It was Tyro, shouldering his way toward the front line, stabbing his sword at the attacking animals and using its flat edge to slap his own soldiers into action.

"Down, Theeta!" Tarlan yelled.

With a terrible shriek, Theeta tipped into a dive.

Tyro looked up. The instant he saw them bearing down on him, he pulled a short throwing knife from his belt, from which at least ten identical blades were hanging. He drew back his arm and threw it upward; thin blades protruding from the knife's hilt made it spin in the air like an arrow. It was aimed straight at Tarlan.

Acting purely on instinct, Tarlan lifted his sword. The knife struck it with such force that his arm was wrenched back. A bolt of pain shot from his fingers to his shoulder and, horrified, he watched his sword fall from his hand and disappear into the battle below.

Tyro's face was split into a grin. He was already aiming another knife. "Now I have you, barbarian!"

"Go!" Tarlan yelled.

The instant Tyro let the knife fly, Theeta twisted sideways. The air beside Tarlan's head screamed as the knife flew past. It missed him, just barely, but his throbbing fingers struggled to find a grip as the thorrod bucked and turned. With a sickening lurch he fell.

He landed sprawling on the battlefield, just curling his arms over his head in time to cushion the blow. The wind blew from his lungs. Tarlan lay still for a moment, fighting for breath and trying to shake the ringing in his ears.

When he did, he could hear Theeta's cries of panic.

Then a voice: "I have come to finish you, barbarian!"

Tarlan rolled over. Tyro was looming over him and lunged, thrusting his curved sword with blinding speed. Tarlan rolled again and the blade stabbed the muddy ground beside him. Scrabbling on his elbows, Tarlan tried to squirm away.

"Not so fast." With a grin, Tyro pulled back his boot and kicked Tarlan hard in the ribs. Pain exploded through Tarlan's chest. He tried to move, but his limp body refused to obey him. All he could do was watch as Tyro raised his sword above his head.

"All things come to an end, barbarian," Tyro growled. "Even prophecies. It's time for you to die."

CHAPTER 28

Gulph clung like a spider to the sheer cliff face. His arms were bunched tight to his chest, his fingers gripping a tiny ledge no wider than his thumbnail. His toes were crammed into a pair of crevices so small that even a mouse wouldn't have considered using them as holes. His legs were racked with painful cramps. His whole body shook.

Above him the chasm was a smooth vertical wall. He'd climbed through the night, yet he still couldn't see the top. He couldn't see any more handholds, either. There was nothing to hold on to. There was nowhere to go.

Let go. Just let go and fall. You've done your best. It's over.

But he couldn't do that. Life was a precious thing, and he wasn't ready to let go of it.

Besides, he had a job to do.

Ignoring the pain in his fingertips, in his toes, in the spasming muscles of his arms and legs, Gulph forced himself to breathe deeply. Doing so calmed the rising panic. But it didn't solve his problem.

He studied the wall above him, willing the solution to appear. In the light of the setting moon, the rock looked like polished silver. Nothing.

He looked to his right and saw more of the same featureless rock. Nothing there, either.

Tendrils of mist wafted past him, ghostlike. The drop—the endless drop—hung beneath him like the mouth of a waiting beast. He could feel it, a tremendous presence made all the more terrifying for its emptiness.

I won't look down. I won't!

Feeling only despair, Gulph looked to his left. Another expanse of smooth, unblemished stone.

So this really is it. I can't . . .

He looked harder. There was a thin crack running vertically up the rock face. It was a long way away—he would have to stretch his arms to three times their length to reach it.

Impossible.

It was so tantalizing: a route up the cliff within sight but out of reach. To get to the crack, he would have to cross an impossible span of unyielding stone.

"Or jump," he said aloud.

It was his only choice.

Slowly he straightened his arms, lowering his body a short distance back down the cliff. Now, instead of having bent arms and straight legs, the opposite was true. His compressed thighs protested; his stretched shoulders howled.

Only one chance at this, Gulph. Make it count.

He looked again at the crack. It was hard to gauge the distance properly in the failing light of the moon.

Don't think. Just jump.

Gulph jumped.

The leap was pure agony: a twisting, sideways kick that seemed to send every part of his body flying in a wholly unnatural direction. The instant he jumped, he unlatched his fingers and toes from their holds; he felt a sharp stab of pain as one of his fingernails tore off. He threw out his arms, blindly seeking the crack that he would surely never reach . . . and felt his battered fingers slip neatly into it.

He grabbed at the rock, cramming his hands deep into the crack, seeking fresh handholds and finding them. His feet scrabbled for a moment; then they too found purchase. Gulph tensed his entire body, freezing himself in place, trying to assess whether or not he'd found safety, or just another trap.

The rocky edges of the cracks held firm.

Sweat broke out all over his skin. His breath spurted from his mouth in sharp, steaming gasps. His heart hammered.

I made it!

He looked up. The crack extended up the chasm wall as far as he could see.

But it wasn't *all* he could see.

Above him the sky was glowing pink with the first light of dawn. Cutting across it was a sharp, horizontal line of rock.

The top of the chasm!

Gulph began climbing again.

Some time later—he had no idea how long—Gulph pulled himself up over the lip of the chasm and flopped down, his chest heaving. He was weary beyond measure. To his relief a nearby pile of rubble hid him from the view of anyone looking out from Idilliam. Beyond his hiding place the deserted battlefield stretched all the way to the distant city wall. Above, the sky had turned from pink to pale violet. Unable to move, he simply lay there, aching all over.

Slowly the pain began to ebb from his arms and legs, his hands and feet. His finger still throbbed where the nail had been ripped away; he tore a corner of cloth from his shirt and used it to bind the wound.

He also tried to imagine what it would be like climbing back down again . . . then quickly steered his mind away from the subject. The very idea was unthinkable.

You'll have to do it sooner or later. Sooner, probably—if you stay here too long, you're bound to be caught.

He clambered slowly to his feet.

One thing at a time, Gulph. Right now you have a job to do.

Coaxing his body back to life, he adjusted the pack of fireworks on his back and hurried across the wasteland surrounding the outer wall of Idilliam. The place seemed deserted, but he summoned the energy to make himself invisible anyway. He had no desire to attract the attention of the undead.

He ran beneath the city gate, shuddering as he passed under the decaying heads of Nynus and Magritt, still impaled on their spikes. As soon as he was inside the city, he began to see the undead: not exactly hordes of them, but enough walking corpses wandering the streets to make him anxious.

They can't see me, he told himself. *I'm safe.*

But he didn't feel safe at all.

He made for the nearest building—a half-collapsed wooden structure—and hid behind its shattered walls.

Inside one of the surviving rooms, a group of undead warriors was sorting through a pile of swords and spears.

They're gathering their weapons! thought Gulph grimly. *Getting ready to invade Celestis!*

Opening his pack, he took out the first of the fireworks Noddy had made from the powders they'd found in Kalia's storeroom. Gulph jammed the tightly bound tube into a gap between two planks, struck a spark from his tinderbox, and lit the fuse.

He'd just reached the safety of the opposite side of the street when the firework exploded in a mushroom of orange sparks and flames. There was a chattering series of loud cracks, like popping grain on a stove top. Three breaths later, the entire building was ablaze.

Through the window, Gulph saw the undead dropping the weapons and reaching blindly for the exits, but already the wooden building was an inferno. He watched with cold excitement as their decayed bodies turned white-hot and burned away to ashes.

Just like the legionnaire in the throne room. Thank you, Pip, for giving me the idea. It might take me all day and all night to burn down Idilliam, but I think it's going to work!

The flames crossed quickly to neighboring buildings. With a surge of excitement Gulph decided this might not take as long as he'd feared. He hurried to the next crossroads and used another firework to ignite a large warehouse filled with the undead. By setting fires on street junctions, he reasoned, he would make the fire spread faster and farther.

He reached an open square dominated by a towering structure that was all too familiar. It looked like a gigantic, malformed bird's nest balanced on enormous stilts.

The Vault of Heaven!

Gulph shivered, remembering the dreadful days he'd spent trapped inside that awful prison. He supposed it was empty now, since all the prisoners had been taken out by Nynus to help destroy the bridge.

Oh, but I can't resist this!

He planted one of Noddy's largest rockets into the ground, aimed it at the underbelly of the Vault, and lit the fuse. The rocket flew, burying itself with a tremendous explosion in the woven structure of the prison.

The Vault of Heaven began to burn.

Gulph ran on toward Castle Tor. All the streets behind him were burning now, first one building erupting into flames, then its neighbor, and so on, until Gulph realized with a jolt that the flames had already cut him off from the main gate.

Don't think about it. There must be a hundred ways out of this city.

By the time he reached the castle, his invisibility was beginning to flicker on and off. He fought to control it, but he was so tired that his efforts met with little success. He just hoped he'd caused enough panic among the undead that they wouldn't notice him.

He tossed a firework into a hay cart that was drawn up near the castle wall, then raced on toward the main gate tower. Flames pursued him, and as he passed beneath the portcullis he saw that the spiked wooden gate was already on fire. The flames had circled behind him, reaching the castle faster than he'd anticipated.

It's out of control, he thought with satisfaction and no small measure of fear.

The courtyard inside the gate tower was empty. On its far side rose the wall of the inner keep. Smoke was pouring from the windows. Screams came from within.

Gulph was halfway to the main door when a figure appeared on a balcony overlooking the courtyard. It was a massive, monstrous thing, half man, half skeleton. Velvet robes hung in tatters from its slumped shoulders. In its eye sockets burned flames even brighter than the fire that was consuming Castle Tor.

Brutan!

Summoning all his will, Gulph concentrated on the strange sensations with which he could summon—and sustain—his invisibility.

Sand! Heat! Desert magic!

To his relief Brutan's burning gaze passed over him, unseeing. Then, to his surprise, the undead king clambered awkwardly over the balcony's parapet, dropped the short distance to an external staircase, and began to descend.

The reason for Brutan's hasty departure became clear as a jet of flame burst over the balcony, which crumbled and fell with a deafening crash into the courtyard. The undead king was consumed by a billowing cloud of dust and smoke, and for a moment Gulph's heart rose.

It crushed him! He's dead!

But his hopes were dashed when Brutan staggered clear of the debris. Shaking himself, the undead king ran across the courtyard to Gulph's left, stumbling awkwardly toward another set of stone stairs. He kept his skeleton hands clamped to his chest, covering the wound Gulph had inflicted with Kalia's crystal sword.

So it did hurt him, Gulph thought. *But where's he going?*

There was another crash behind him as the gatehouse collapsed into a burning heap of shattered stones and broken timber. A wave of heat rushed over Gulph, forcing him toward the keep. With mounting horror, he watched as the flames began systematically to destroy the wooden outhouses lining the courtyard walls.

Brutan's looking for a way out, he realized. *He knows he's trapped. And now I'm trapped in here with him! If only I'd gone back to the chasm sooner!*

But he knew he couldn't have done that.

Not until he knew Brutan was dead.

Gathering all the strength that had carried him here from the depths of the chasm, knowing this might be his only chance to finish things once and for all, Gulph chased after the thing that had once been his father.

The stairs climbed steeply, curving up and around the outside of the castle's main watchtower. Gulph kept his distance and remained invisible. The last thing he wanted to do was run blindly into a trap.

As Gulph ascended, he found himself looking down over the whole of Idilliam. To the east the sun was rising, turning the sky to pale gold. Its rays spread across the city, skimming the tops of the trees that grew in Isur, on the opposite side of the chasm. The beauty of the faraway forest canopy made Gulph's heart ache.

This could be my kingdom, he thought, panting as he forced his aching limbs to climb. *Once Brutan is gone . . .*

A different kind of canopy hung over Idilliam. Instead of

treetops, here were glowing red fountains of fire. Gulph marveled at the destruction he'd brought to the city, and wondered if it would ever stop.

As he climbed higher and higher, the watchtower narrowed. Gulph slowed, glancing down. The tower was affixed to the outer corner of the castle keep, which in turn overlooked the chasm surrounding Idilliam. If he slipped on these stairs, he wouldn't just fall to the ground.

He'd fall into the chasm.

One more turn of the stairs would bring him to the top of the watchtower. Brutan was somewhere up ahead, out of sight.

There was a roar of flames behind him.

He stopped in his tracks.

The steps he had just come up were on fire. Flames spurted and he raised his arms to protect his face. Heat scorched his invisible skin. Panic bubbled inside him.

Brutan ahead, the fire behind. I'm trapped, and it's all my fault . . .

He scrabbled on upward, away from the rising fire.

I was a fool to think it was all going to work out, he thought bitterly. *Me, rule Toronia as a king, with my siblings at my side? Why did I ever believe it?*

When he could run no more, Gulph sank to his knees. Above, the fire cast a lurid glow over the darkening sky. The prophecy stars looked down, patient and cold.

It's failed. Because of me, the prophecy is over.

Smoke was billowing out over the chasm. Somewhere, far below, Ossilius was waiting for him to return. Pip too—poor, gentle Pip. And farther away, somewhere in Toronia, were the brother and sister he'd never met.

Now I never will.

He couldn't change any of it. Yet there was still something he could do.

I can make sure Brutan really is gone. I can do that at least. Before the end . . .

He wiped his eyes. "Come on, Gulph," he told himself. "One last trick."

Gulph stood. He rummaged inside his pack. His hand met something hard: the crown of Toronia. He ignored it. The crown was useless to him now. Instead he let his fingers explore the pack's interior until he found what he'd known was there: a tightly wrapped tube filled with explosive powder.

A firework.

The last firework.

Fresh flames licked around the corner of the stairs, just below him. Gulph ignored them and proceeded up the final twist of the tower.

The staircase ended at the edge of a wide observation platform fixed to the top of the tower. Wind gusted, threatening to throw Gulph off the stairs and into the chasm. Resisting the compulsion to look down, he crouched low and ascended the final few steps to the highest point in Idilliam.

Brutan was standing in the middle of the platform with his back to Gulph. His shoulders were hunched. His hands were clasped to his chest. The remains of his robes whipped in the gale blowing across the top of the tower.

Trapped! Gulph thought with a curious mix of satisfaction and despair. *Just like me.*

Holding the firework behind his back, he took three hesitant steps toward the undead king. Behind him the fire ate up the steps he'd been climbing barely a moment before. Flames began to lick up around the edges of the platform.

His whole body began to tremble. He wondered if he was still invisible, then realized with horror that he couldn't be.

Because his father was speaking to him.

"I can see you," the undead king growled, the exposed bones of his jaws opening in a hideous grin. "Even when I could not see you, I knew you were following me. I could smell your blood."

The wind gusted. Fighting to keep his balance, Gulph sank to his knees. His fingers and toes were numb. The climb first up the chasm wall, and then up the steps of the burning tower, had robbed him of all strength.

"Begging for your life, boy?" roared Brutan approvingly. He seemed unaffected by the hot and howling gale. "It won't do you any good!"

Sand! thought Gulph desperately. *Heat!*

But there was only the heat of the fire.

Brutan took a lurching step toward him.

"So what do you plan to do, boy?" he roared. "It is a long way down. But I believe I can survive the fall. Can you say the same?"

Trembling, Gulph tottered to his feet. With his free hand, he fumbled his tinderbox out of his pack. The wind pounded him. From somewhere, he found the strength to resist it.

"I may fall," he said, speaking slowly and clearly. "But you won't. I'm going to see to that."

From deep inside Brutan's ruined chest there came a sound like breaking wood. With sick revulsion Gulph realized the undead king was laughing.

"And how, precisely, do you plan to stop me?"

"With this!"

In one smooth movement Gulph brought the firework around from behind his back and snapped open the tinderbox. The flames in Brutan's eye sockets flared with sudden surprise.

Gulph scraped the flint across the metal lid of the tinderbox, praying that the wind wouldn't blow out whatever spark he was able to create. Light flashed, and instantly the fuse of the firework was burning. The fuse, Gulph saw, was very short.

He stood, drew back his arm.

"This is for the prophecy!" he yelled. "This is for Toronia! This is for Kalia, my mother! This is for the siblings I'll never meet. But most of all, this is for me!"

And Gulph hurled the burning, spitting firework straight at the face of the undead king. But Brutan moved faster than Gulph could have imagined, ducking low and turning his ravaged body to the side. Gulph watched with rapidly unfolding despair as the firework flew harmlessly over Brutan's shoulder.

As it exploded, bright fire of all colors—red and green and gold—blossomed behind the undead king, a halo of dazzling sparks and fizzing embers. A tremendous bang resounded across the platform, and black smoke blasted Gulph's face, stinging his eyes.

The wind sucked the smoke away, leaving the air clear, though still laced with the lingering smell of flash powder.

Brutan was still standing. His tattered robes were smoldering, but he was otherwise unharmed.

Flames boiled around the edges of the platform. The fire was everywhere. Gulph could feel his hair and skin beginning to singe. He looked wildly around. There was nowhere to go.

Brutan's eyes were filled with glowing red malevolence. His fingers snapped shut like bony bear traps. The platform shook as he advanced on Gulph, his arms outstretched.

"Enough games! Now I will fall!" roared the undead king. "And I will take you with me, to serve among the ranks of the undead!"

Gulph backed away until his feet had reached the edge of the platform. The flames licked at his back. Brutan lunged for him, his fingertips slashing the air right in front of Gulph's face. He ducked, ran sideways around the perimeter of the burning platform, stumbled, and fell to his knees.

Just one touch! That's all it will take. He'll grab me—and then he'll jump. By the time we hit the ground, I'll be just like him.

Gulph stood. He could see nothing beyond the wall of flames surrounding the platform. He was trapped in a crucible of fire. Idilliam had ceased to exist. Toronia had ceased to exist. There was just him and the monster that had once been his father.

He knew at last what he must do. He felt strangely calm.

"Come to me, boy!" roared the undead king. "Come to me forever!"

"No," Gulph told him. "I lost you a long time ago, Father. And now you've lost me."

Bending his knees, Gulph sprang backward, performing a perfect backflip through the flames.

So this is how it ends, he thought, and fell into the chasm below.

CHAPTER 29

The sky was brightening. A halo of pink and violet, framed by trees. Tiny clouds, racing like snowflakes. A flock of birds flying so high they were little more than specks of dust.

Tarlan saw it all in extraordinary detail, knowing that it would be the last thing he ever saw.

Tyro loomed over him, blotting out his view. The bearded man's sword hung high in the air, ready to descend.

Then he froze. His mouth slowly lolled open, blood first trickling from his mouth, then gushing. His body began to jitter.

Tyro collapsed to the ground beside Tarlan. A long, slow sigh blew from his mouth. His eyes rolled up until they showed only the whites. His chest heaved once, then was still.

A large, shaggy creature stood where Tyro had been. The

bear's huge claws were dripping with Tyro's blood. "Brock!" gasped Tarlan, struggling to his feet.

"You saved me," Brock said. "Now I save you."

Tarlan staggered toward the bear and flung his arms around his thick neck.

With a flurry of golden feathers, Theeta landed beside them. Her eyes were bright and gently she laid her huge beak on Tarlan's shoulder. "Alive," she cawed softly. "Tarlan alive."

Tarlan stroked her beak. "I am, Theeta. And we still have a battle to fight!"

He glanced around for his sword. It was nowhere to be seen, but glinting beside Tyro's body was his curved blade. Tarlan picked it up and swung himself onto Theeta's back. With one powerful beat of her wings, they were rising above the battlefield once more.

Theeta accelerated toward the defensive ring of wooden spikes, where Filos and two forest cats were under sustained attack.

Trapped against the spikes, the creatures were flailing desperately at an advancing line of swordsmen. Smoke from the burning town surrounded them. Filos fell awkwardly on her back, blood oozing from a wound in her neck. Behind the foot soldiers, a smaller gang was readying one of the flame machines Tarlan had seen them use in the fishing village.

"Faster, Theeta!"

Theeta made straight for the wheeled machine, stretching her talons out at the last moment and ripping its crew from their posts. The cart tipped over, spilling fuel from its barrel and crushing one of the operators beneath it. But the swordsmen had butchered one of the forest cats and were now turning on the fallen Filos and her remaining companion.

"Theeta—turn!"

But Tarlan could see they were too late.

A horse galloped out of the smoke. On it rode a shrieking boy: Kassan. He plunged his sword into a foot soldier, then pulled his steed around and whistled.

Galadronian heads turned.

Two dozen wild horses burst into view. They rode down the enemy, hooves trampling their bodies into the ground. The horses reared, whinnying in triumph. Kassan gave Tarlan a ferocious smile, then led the horses back into the fray.

Filos rose unsteadily to her feet. Her companion nuzzled her with obvious concern.

"Are you all right?" Tarlan cried.

"Sore," Filos replied. "But I will live. And there are many more enemies to fight."

The tigron was right. With something close to despair, Tarlan took in a quick sweep of the battlefield. Bodies lay strewn everywhere. The colored robes of fallen Galadronians fluttered in the morning breeze, but it seemed to him that many more of the dead belonged to his pack.

They're killing us! Little by little, we're dying here.

Things were hardly better near the town. Although most of the Isurians had managed to get inside the fortress walls, they still hadn't closed the gates. Flying nearer, Tarlan saw why: The gates hung broken from their enormous hinges. They would never shut again.

The Hammer had positioned himself near the entrance. A small band of ferocious-looking men surrounded him. Together they formed the last line of defense against the invaders. Tarlan's heart swelled as he saw Greythorn and a contingent of wolves fighting at The Hammer's side.

But we can't hold out much longer, he thought desperately. *They're too many . . .*

"Thorrods come!" Theeta's screech pierced the air, echoing across the battlefield. Down on the ground, the animals in Tarlan's dwindling pack looked up. The Galadronians looked up. Even The Hammer stopped, checking his great iron bludgeon in midswing and raising his head from the carnage.

Two dark specks hung in the sky, far to the west. As Tarlan watched, they grew bigger . . . and bigger.

"Kitheen! Nasheen!" he yelled, raising both hands above his head in triumph. "Melchior!"

The two returning thorrods drew nearer, growing huge. The light from the rising sun met them head-on, turning the gold feathers on their wingtips to moving lines of fire. Both had their beaks open; both were shrieking out a high-pitched call in what Tarlan thought of as thorrod deep-speech, a language so strange and ancient that no human could ever hope to decipher it.

Whatever it meant, the sound of it turned his blood to ice and his bones to powder.

He could only imagine what it was doing to the Galadronians.

Melchior was standing upright on Nasheen's back, ignoring gravity, heedless of the lurching of his airborne steed beneath him. His white hair shone. His staff was raised. His eyes flashed.

"Tarlan!" Melchior cried as soon as he was close enough to be heard. "How many legs do they have?"

Tarlan blinked. He'd been waiting for fire to spurt from the wizard's staff, or magical lightning to fill the sky. He scolded himself; he'd already learned that Melchior didn't work like that.

"What do you mean?" he shouted back.

"Your animals. Your pack. How many legs?"

Tarlan stared down at Filos and the cats. "Four?" he yelled back uncertainly. What was the wizard planning?

"Four!" Melchior bellowed. "My thought exactly! Rally your pack, Tarlan. Bring them in. Bring all of them in. Make them run! Make them run now!"

Setting his confusion aside, Tarlan raised his voice and called to the animals. At the same time, he sent his thoughts flying out over the battleground like a desert storm.

"Come to me!" he roared. "Come to me!"

And . . .

Come to me, all of you! To me! To me! Come here! Come now!

Tarlan's pack came. Gray wolves crested the slopes. Horses turned in their tracks and galloped toward the town. Snakes writhed. Bears blundered in, mountains of muscle and fur. Eagles flocked. The animals *swarmed.*

The Galadronians turned to face the oncoming tide. Behind them the spiked defenses of Deep Poynt prevented their retreat. Yet Tarlan's pack looked pitifully small against their enormous numbers.

Like a wave about to smash itself to pieces on rocks.

Tarlan remembered the fishing village.

Like a wave!

Light flickered along the length of Melchior's staff. It sank into the runes, winked out. The wizard's lips moved. Nasheen's wings flapped slower and slower . . . then stopped altogether. The still air surrounding the motionless thorrod boomed softly.

"What comes?" wondered Theeta.

"Magic," Tarlan replied.

The first wave of animals was dominated by the bears. Brock led them, running fast and true. He bore down on one of the

Galadronian soldiers, drew back one massive paw, and struck out, his claws whistling through the air.

His claws!

Tarlan blinked, not trusting what his eyes were telling him. Brock had too many claws.

No, it's more than that.

Brock's blow knocked the soldier down. The three soldiers standing beside him fell too. Brock spun around, bellowed, swiped again. His limbs were a blur, but even from this distance point, Tarlan could see there were too many of them.

Brock has four paws on each arm! He has eight legs! A whole forest of claws!

The sight was so odd, so unnatural, that Tarlan couldn't believe what he was seeing. Yet it was happening.

The rest of the bears thundered in behind Brock. Each of them was just one animal, but it was also four. Wherever there was an exposed Galadronian neck, four sets of jaws bit down. Wherever the enemy was massed together, four sets of claws scythed through their flesh. The bears were more than they had been. And more than their adversaries could contend with.

It's like on the Isle of Stars, Tarlan thought, remembering how Melchior's magic had condensed hundreds of Galadronians into a single body. This was the same thing, only backward: instead of reducing the presence of the enemy, Melchior had somehow multi-plied the power of Tarlan's pack.

Wolves followed the bears, snapping with their many muzzles. With each bite, four wounds opened up. It was the same with Filos and her cats.

Here came the horses, each one galloping not only on four legs but also on sixteen. They ran hard, moving faster than any creature Tarlan had ever seen on the ground. The herd hit the Galadronian flank like a battering ram, instantly killing those soldiers unlucky enough to be standing at the edge and knocking the others aside like dolls.

Tarlan glanced at the wizard, still standing on the back of the hovering Nasheen. Melchior had begun to stoop, bending his back like that of a very old man. He was no longer holding his staff up in the air, but leaning on it instead. He looked tired and haggard.

It's no wonder. All that power has to come from somewhere.

A great cry rose up from behind him. Tarlan turned to see the Isurians running out from behind the Deep Poynt defenses, led by The Hammer. Shouting in triumph, they fell upon the invading army, only to find their enemy scattering before them.

In fact, Tarlan noted, very few of the Galadronians remained standing. Melchior's intervention had turned the tide so radically that, with a single assault, Tarlan's pack had brought the battle to an end. Those soldiers still alive had no stomach left for the fight; instead they raced for the shelter of the forest. The animals chased them, running no longer on their multiplied legs but quite normally on all fours. Already the magic had left them. Tarlan suspected that even a wizard as powerful as Melchior couldn't sustain such a spell for long.

Indeed, Melchior had now sunk to his knees on Nasheen's back. The thorrods' wings were moving again, guiding her in a rapid descent toward the edge of the town. Kitheen circled her protectively, his tail feathers twitching with concern.

Urging Theeta in pursuit of the fleeing army, Tarlan shouted down to his pack.

"Come back! Let them run! The battle is over! We've won!"

The animals obeyed instantly, turning on their heels and heading back toward Deep Poynt. Theeta landed beside her thorrod companions. The three giant birds nuzzled each other with obvious affection, cawing softly. Even the taciturn Kitheen seemed moved by the events of the morning.

"You did well," said Tarlan as Filos, Greythorn, and Brock ran up. All three animals were covered in blood, but as far as he could see only the tigron was injured. Kassan rode up behind them, his face streaked with mud. "You too, Kassan. All of you—you're better than any generals a commander ever had."

They were too exhausted to respond, but the looks on their

faces—a complex mix of pride in their achievements and adoration of their leader—brought a lump to Tarlan's throat.

He went over to Melchior, who was climbing down stiffly from Nasheen's back. When the wizard's feet touched the ground, he stumbled. Tarlan reached for him, but Melchior waved him away.

"No, no, my boy, I'm not nearly as crumbly as I look. It was a hard number to find, that's all. I'm recovering already, see?"

To prove his claim, he balanced his staff vertically on the tip of his finger, then threw it up in the air and caught it deftly.

"Victory is ours!" The ground shook as The Hammer stomped over to them. "Your soldiers are strange, lad, I'll say that! But they fight like—" He laughed as he realized what he was about to say. "Like animals!"

His good humor was infectious, and Tarlan found it hard not to laugh along with this giant of a man.

Still chuckling, The Hammer slapped Tarlan on the back. It was like being hit by a cart. Then the big warrior's face became serious.

"You have saved Deep Poynt, boy. I owe you a great debt."

"You don't owe me anything."

"I disagree. If there is ever anything I can do for you—anything at all—you have only to ask."

Tarlan grinned. "I'll remember that."

The Hammer gave a curt nod. "In the meantime, my men and

their weapons are yours to command. The battle is won. But the war is not over."

"War? What war?"

The Hammer turned Tarlan around and pointed east with one meaty finger.

"The Galadronians have clearly struck farther inland. See? Idilliam itself is burning."

Tarlan gaped. Sure enough, a colossal plume of smoke towered above the trees. It was much bigger and blacker than the smoke rising from the buildings burning in Deep Poynt.

"There are n-n-no m-m-more Galadronians," he stammered. "We defeated them all."

"Then what is happening in Idilliam?"

Tarlan stared at the smoke. His whole body turned suddenly cold.

Gulph!

"Theeta!" he cried, racing over to the thorrods. "Can you fly?"

"Thorrod tired," Theeta replied, her dark eyes drooping.

"I know, my friend, I know. But I need you. My brother needs you. Can you fly? *Will* you?"

"Fly slow."

"No. Not slow. Fast. Faster than you've ever flown before!"

Theeta regarded the smoke rising from distant Idilliam.

"Brother die," she cawed softly.

"I hope not. Oh, Theeta, I hope not!"

As soon as Tarlan had climbed onto Theeta's back, Melchior's hand closed on his ankle.

"You must not go, Tarlan," said the wizard. "Whatever fate has befallen Idilliam, you cannot help."

"I can try!" Tarlan kicked Melchior's hand away. "Now fly, Theeta! Fly!"

Flapping her wings with slow, labored strokes, Theeta heaved herself into the sky. As they rose, Tarlan threw one final glance down at the battlefield.

He saw dead bodies strewn everywhere, both animals and men. The ground was dark with the blood of the slain. He saw Filos, Greythorn, and Brock moving among the animals of the forest, passing out the news that their work was done . . . for now. He saw Kassan rounding up the horses. He saw The Hammer organizing the townsfolk into groups to tend to the wounded, bury the dead, repair the defenses, put out the fires. Only Melchior was still, staring up at him.

As Theeta flew on, Deep Poynt shrank to a smoke-shrouded speck in the trees. Then the forest swallowed it completely, and it was gone, as if the battle had never happened, and the place and all the people in it had never existed.

Meanwhile, Idilliam was growing larger and larger, and the scale of the fire that had consumed the city became evident. What Tarlan had first assumed was a single cloud of smoke was in fact a thousand separate plumes, each one rising from balls of orange flame blazing from one side of the city to the other.

What happened here? Who set Idilliam alight?

But there was another question that caused him even more concern.

Where's my brother?

The closer they drew, the more nervous Theeta became. The air was hot, thick with smoke and burning embers. Tarlan's eyes stung, and every breath seared his lungs.

"Fire bad," Theeta observed.

"I know. But we have to keep going!"

A low pass over the city walls revealed streets choked with fumes and littered with the wreckage of collapsed buildings. Apart from the flames, there was no movement, no sign of the undead army that had once occupied this place.

They've all burned. Everything's burned.

"Gulph!" he shouted. "Gulph! Where are you?"

Theeta aimed herself toward the huge stone edifice of Castle Tor. The air was a little clearer here, even though orange flames had completely consumed the castle keep and most of its subsidiary towers.

Nobody could survive this. Tarlan felt drained of all emotion save for a huge, welling anger. *I'm too late.*

"What was the point?" he yelled as Theeta circled the blackened castle turrets. It had all been for nothing: Gulph was dead and Elodie had turned traitor. His quest to regain Melchior's magic on the Isle of Stars had been in vain. Toronia was lost. He was lost. The prophecy meant nothing.

I don't care about Toronia! I don't care about prophecies! I just care about my friends.

But so many of his friends were gone too. Seethan, the wise, old thorrod who'd been butchered and burned by the Helkrags. All the loyal creatures who'd fought for him in the battle at Deep Poynt, and who now lay dead.

And Mirith. Of them all, it was Mirith he missed most.

It's over. I wish it had never begun.

"Not man," Theeta cawed.

"What did you say?" Tarlan pawed tears furiously from his eyes.

"High tower. Not man."

They were far above the castle now, on a level with its topmost tower. This slender stone needle was surrounded by orange fire. Flames darted up the spiral staircase that wound around its exterior.

A figure was moving on the top of the tower.

"Fly closer, Theeta!"

Theeta obeyed. The figure resolved itself into the shape of a man . . . or something that used to be a man.

Brutan!

Tarlan had seen this monster once before, when he'd flown over the chaos of the Battle of the Bridge. That fateful moment when he'd seen his father for the first time. His brother, too.

Now Gulph was surely dead.

But I can avenge him!

Anger filled Tarlan's body. His head throbbed with it. His fingers clutched tight onto Theeta's ruff of feathers; his heels clamped hard against her heaving flanks.

"Fast, Theeta! As fast as you can!"

Thorrods were silent in flight, Tarlan knew that. Yet even as they swooped toward him, Brutan turned. Close up, he was more of a monster than Tarlan could have conceived—a mutilated mountain of a man whose face was no more than a skull draped with rags of flesh, whose arms were slabs of raw meat hanging from gore-streaked bone. Brutan's chest gaped with some kind of open stab wound, from which green pus oozed.

And the empty eyes of the undead king blazed with fire. With anger.

"You have no right to be angry!" Tarlan screamed. The wind whipped hot sparks against his face. He paid them no heed. "The anger is mine. Do you hear me? The anger is mine!"

The chest of the undead king swelled. Pus flew from the wound in a syrupy spray.

"Who are you to defy me?" Brutan roared, raising his arms

over his head as if he planned to drag the speeding thorrod out of the sky.

"I am your son, come to take you out of this world forever!" Tarlan roared back. "I am Tarlan, one of three! And this is for my brother!"

Theeta tucked in her wings, increasing her speed yet more. Smoke streamed past them. The tower loomed. Brutan brandished his sword.

Theeta's hooked beak slammed into the center of Brutan's chest. Her momentum carried him forward, and for an instant Tarlan was looking straight into the flaming eyes of the undead king.

The eyes of what had once been his father.

"This is the end of it!" Tarlan yelled. "The end of it all. The end of *you*!"

Brutan's arms flew out sideways. Theeta tossed her head, almost casually, flinging him over the edge of the platform as if he were no more than a scrap of meat. Brutan tumbled once, twice, falling out and away from the tower in a great, curving arc.

Falling into the fire.

Theeta tracked Brutan as he fell. Tarlan watched as the flames tore at his ravaged body. First to burn were the remains of his clothes; then what was left of his flesh ignited. Smoke gushed from his mouth. His bones caught fire. Deep inside his chest, something glowed white-hot, brighter than the midday sun.

And then, with a vast and soundless concussion, Brutan's body blew apart. Where the undead king had been, now there was only a bright, expanding cloud of sparks and ash.

Brutan was gone.

With a tremendous, shuddering crack, the base of the tower exploded. The tower dropped away, the stonework fragmenting as it fell into a growing cloud of gray dust that billowed out across the burning city. Theeta rode the wave of pressure that accompanied the tower's collapse and soared out over the chasm, away from Idilliam and all that had happened there.

Away . . .

In a single breath Tarlan's anger was gone. Everything was gone. He felt hollowed out. Yet he also felt strangely renewed. Once, his life had been simple. Now even though his heart was filled with grief, he knew it could be simple again.

"It's over." He fell limp across Theeta's back. "All of it. Everything that happened was all for nothing. And now it's time to leave it all behind."

"Crown lost."

"Yes, Theeta. Lost to me, at least. If Elodie wants the crown, she's welcome to it. As for me . . . I've finished with Toronia."

"Find thorrods."

Smiling, Tarlan patted her neck.

"Yes. Let's find them. The others, too. All that matters is that we're together."

"Fly fast."

"No, we don't have to go fast. Just far. Fly far, Theeta. Far away from here."

"Fly where?"

Tarlan smiled. Thorrods almost never asked questions. When they did, you could be sure you'd reached a moment of great importance.

A turning point.

"It doesn't matter where, Theeta. Just as long as it's away."

Behind them the morning sun shone through the smoke as Idilliam continued to burn. Ahead the sun's rays illuminated the forest where Tarlan's pack was waiting. They would meet up, and then they would set off together on a new journey that had nothing to do with prophecies and crowns, but which was wholly their own.

The battle was over. It was time to go.

Away from Toronia. Away from everything.

EPILOGUE

Clouds hid the night. There was no moon; there were no stars. The comet that had dominated the darkness in previous days was gone. Even the three prophecy stars—those bright points of fate about which lives had turned—were invisible.

Elodie stood at the window of the cell at the top of the White Tower, truly a prisoner at last. She gazed through the metal bars and into the blackness beyond.

It's like staring into an abyss.

That made her think of Idilliam, the Battle of the Bridge, and of her fall into the chasm surrounding the city.

Of how her brother had saved her.

Oh, Tarlan, where are you now?

Had he found his way back to Isur after his journey to the Isle of Stars? Had his mission to restore Melchior's powers succeeded? She had no way of knowing. But a dreadful suspicion clawed at her heart.

If he finds anyone from Trident, they'll tell him I'm a traitor. They don't know I was trying to save them. They'll say I turned against them—against him . . .

As for Gulph . . . who knew what had become of him?

She touched the empty place at her throat where her green jewel had once hung. Having it snatched away by Lord Vicerin, at the very moment she'd been bundled into her cell, had been the final blow to fall on the most painful day of her life.

With a deep sigh Elodie turned from the window. She could feel the night at her back. It was like a living presence.

"Are you ready?" she said.

Sylva and Cedric looked up at her from where they were kneeling on the floor. The room was dimly lit by candles, and the flickering light played across their faces.

"You'll have to be quick," said Sylva. "The guards are sure to be back soon."

"I'm just waiting for Samial," Elodie replied. "As soon as he gets here . . ."

As if he'd heard her words, Samial appeared at the window. "I have brought you what you asked for."

He perched on the ledge outside the cell window and handed

her a small canvas bag through the bars. Elodie took it, then peered outside.

"I gave your note to Frida," he said. "She gathered everything you asked for."

"You did well."

Joining Cedric and Sylva, Elodie laid the bag's contents on the stone floor. A moment later Samial was at her side, having melted through the wall as if the solid stonework was no more than a thought.

"So many dead," said Cedric, sorting through the little pile of objects with his one remaining hand.

Elodie picked up the items one by one. A gold necklace. A coin. A charred scrap of silk. A silver charm. Each item had belonged to one of the heads of Ritherlee's noble families. Each item had been in their possession when they'd been murdered by Lord Vicerin. A fine soot covered them all.

"He set fire to all the bodies," Samial explained. "Even the ones that were already burned."

"He wants to destroy all memory of them," said Elodie. "Well, he won't succeed."

She picked up the last of the items: a silver signet ring with a decorative seal. The last time she'd seen this ring, it had been on the finger of a woman she'd grown to admire. A woman she'd once thought might actually be the one to stand against Lord Vicerin.

Lady Darrand.

"All right." She placed the ring back in the pile. "I'm ready."

"Do you really think this will work?" asked Sylva.

"It must. It's our only chance to escape. Our only chance to bring him down."

"Our father," said Cedric quietly.

"Yes. Your father."

My husband, she thought with a shudder.

Cedric looked at her. "Then what are we waiting for?"

Elodie closed her eyes.

At first she saw nothing, felt nothing. She tried to focus her mind, but her thoughts kept slipping away.

Concentrate, Elodie!

But how? How was she supposed to know what to do?

She took a slow, deep breath, felt the air flooding into her lungs, then emptying itself out.

She did it again, and this time something moved in the darkness behind her eyes. Tiny lights flashed in the corners of her awareness, like sparks, like fireflies, like . . .

Like grains of sand dancing in the desert wind.

The sand whirled, thickened, took form. She wasn't just seeing the shapes it made; she was *feeling* them. They filled her up, rasping against her, the emptied-out husks of people turned hot and dry and lifeless by the scouring of sand and sun.

No. They are not without life. They are beyond *life.*

A pressure was growing inside her. The wind howled.

Heat! she thought in exultation. *And sand! This is it! This is where my power comes from. I don't understand it. But I know it. And I can use it!*

The wind became a storm. The storm wanted to escape the confines of her body. She was its prison, and she had the power to make it free.

Escape! Freedom! If I give it to you, can you give it to me?

The shapes inside her were spinning. A tornado. The heat was too much to bear. Fighting to hold herself steady in the darkness, she opened her mouth, expecting the storm to erupt from her.

But what came out were words.

"Come now!" she cried. "Come now, all of you! I am here! Be here with me! Come now!"

Elodie opened her eyes to flickering candlelight. She'd expected the room to be turned upside down, ravaged by the storm she'd unleashed.

But the storm had been inside her all the time.

"Did it work?" said Sylva, anxiously looking at her. "Are they here?"

Elodie looked past her sister toward the window, not quite trusting her eyes. Were those figures she saw, or just wisps of smoke? For a moment they swirled, a line of drifting pillars that were somehow both dark and light at the same time. Then, one by one, they began to solidify into the shapes of people.

The nobles of Ritherlee. You're here. Oh, you're really here.

Of course they were.

She had summoned them.

The more she stared at the ghosts, the more real they became. Here was an old man standing proud and tall, there a stout young woman who looked both tired and ferocious. Their bodies were hazy, so that Elodie could see the stone walls of the cell through them, but with every breath she took they became more solid.

More real.

"Elodie?" said Sylva in a quavering voice. She'd turned around to face the window, and now her eyes had grown wide with shock. "I can see them!"

Elodie gaped at her. "You can? Really?"

"So can I," said Cedric in a small, wondering voice. "You must be getting stronger, Elodie."

By now the line of ghosts had become almost completely solid. One of the women stepped forward. She wore a yellow robe over shining armor. Her face was pale and determined. Elodie recognized her at once.

"Lady Darrand," she said, rising to her feet.

The ghost regarded her, then put her hand to her hip. Slowly, with infinite care, she drew her phantom sword. Then she dropped to one knee and bowed her head.

Behind her, the rest of the Ritherlee nobles did the same.

The ghost of Lady Darrand tilted her head up until her eyes met Elodie's. Outside the window, the night's black shroud seemed to flutter, as if something unseen had suddenly changed.

All the hairs on the back of Elodie's neck stood on end.

"We come to answer your call, Your Highness," said Lady Darrand. "What is your command?"

Turn the page to read an excerpt from

♦ BOOK THREE ♦

A KINGDOM RISES

The triplets face their greatest challenge yet.
Can they take the throne?
Will they survive?

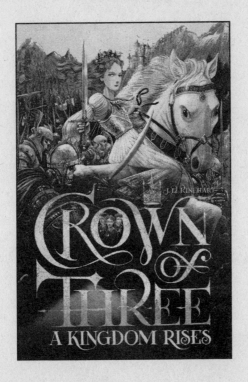

Tarlan slumped facedown on Theeta's back. His breath rasped in his smoke-scorched throat. His face was wet with tears.

Away, he thought. *It's time to go far, far away.*

He pulled himself to the downy hollow that lay between Theeta's warm neck and her huge, beating wings. After resting there for a moment, he stuck his head out into the open air and peered down.

Far below, the city of Idilliam burned. As Tarlan watched, the spindly tower rising from the ruins of Castle Tor crumbled and vanished into the smoke. Only moments earlier, he and Theeta had been swooping over the top of that very tower in an effort to save Gulph.

But we failed! My brother fell—and I never even got a chance to meet him!

Yet he hadn't fallen alone. As they'd flown past, Theeta

had shoved the undead monster King Brutan into the flames too. Brutan the tyrant, father to Tarlan, Gulph, and their sister, Elodie, was now just ash on the wind.

"We got justice, Theeta," Tarlan said through his tears. "Brutan killed Gulph, but he paid." He swallowed hard. "It isn't enough, though. It will never be enough."

Theeta remained silent.

"What was it all for?" Tarlan sat up, wiping angrily at his wet face. "The battle at Deep Poynt? All for nothing!"

"Star story," croaked Theeta. "Life light."

The thorrod's strange way of speaking frequently left Tarlan puzzled. Not this time.

"I don't care about the prophecy! I don't care about my so-called destiny. So what if some old legend says that Gulph, Elodie, and I are supposed to rule Toronia? Oh yes, our father's dead, like the prophecy said, but things are worse than ever. Gulph's dead! Elodie's turned traitor! As for me . . ."

He broke off.

I won't cry again! I won't!

"I'm done with humans. Just give me clean air, and a stream to drink from. That's all I had in Yalasti. I should have stayed there."

"Fly far," said Theeta.

"That's right, Theeta. Far away." Tarlan took in a deep breath, let it out slowly. "But there's one thing I have to do first."

Tugging gently at the ruff of golden feathers around Theeta's neck, Tarlan steered the thorrod away from the burning wreckage of Idilliam and back toward the green forest realm of Isur. Before long, they were circling over Deep Poynt.

As Theeta approached the slopes surrounding the fortified hilltop town, Tarlan's heart lurched. Where it wasn't scorched by fire, the battlefield was torn to mud. Tarlan saw that littering the ground, lying in pools of their own blood, were the bodies of bears and horses, tigrons and wolves. His loyal friends, who'd fought beside him. Who'd fought *for* him. All dead. He stifled a moan.

I had no right to lead them into battle, he berated himself. *What did it matter to those poor creatures who rules this land? Toronians, Galadronians... what's the difference?*

Turning his attention to the town itself, Tarlan watched as a group of men erected scaffolding around a jagged hole in the circular defensive wall. Once, this had been the gateway to Deep Poynt. Now the townsfolk were laboring to repair the considerable damage caused by the Galadronian war machines.

Directing the work was the Defender of Deep Poynt, a giant of a man with a bright thatch of red hair, known as The Hammer. Beside him stood a wizened old man in a grubby yellow robe. As Theeta's shadow passed over them, both men looked up.

Theeta opened her beak and screeched. The men repairing

the town defenses clapped their hands to their ears. Even the animals lying wounded or wandering among the dead raised their heads to see what the commotion was.

Among them were two more thorrods.

"Nasheen!" Tarlan shouted. "Kitheen!"

The enormous birds lifted their wings and screeched back their greetings. A little of the weight lifted from Tarlan's heart.

My friends! My pack!

Theeta landed beside the thorrods and touched her beak to theirs, each in turn. As she was doing this, a blur of blue and white sprinted over the grass and leaped onto her back. Tarlan wrapped his arms round the young tigron's neck and allowed her to cover his face with hot, slobbering licks.

Filos purred. "I'm glad to see you, Tarlan!"

"Enough, Filos! You'll drown me!"

Filos tugged him to the ground, where Greythorn and Brock were waiting. Tarlan embraced the wolf and the bear in turn, taking care to be gentle with Greythorn's wounds.

"How's your sight?" Tarlan said, stroking the matted fur around the wolf's left eye. The eye itself was filmed over white.

"One eye does me well enough," Greythorn replied.

"Brock killed many enemies!" thundered the bear. He flexed two sets of massive claws in front of Tarlan's face. "Brock will fight whenever Tarlan commands!"

Tarlan pushed Brock's paws firmly away. "I won't be asking you to fight again, Brock. I won't be asking anything of you at all."

The big bear's brow contracted into shaggy confusion. "Brock does not understand."

Filos nuzzled his hand. "Tarlan? What's wrong?"

Tarlan ruffled the fur behind the tigron's pointed ears. "Nothing. Everything's going to be all right."

They were all looking at him expectantly: Filos and Greythorn, Brock and the thorrods. Behind them, a much larger group of animals and birds had begun to gather, the survivors of the animal army Tarlan had led against the invading Galadronians. His pack.

"Tarlan!"

A bony hand planted itself on Tarlan's shoulder and spun him round. Tarlan found himself face-to-face with the old man in the yellow robe.

"Melchior," he grunted. "I'm not staying."

The wizard frowned, multiplying the wrinkles on his age-worn face. He rubbed a bony hand through his matted white beard. "What do you mean, Tarlan?"

"Leave me alone!"

The frown became a look of concern. "What happened in Idilliam? Did you find Gulph?"

Tarlan pulled away. "I was too late! He died! Are you satisfied now?"

A ripple of growls moved through the watching crowd of animals. Melchior's eyes grew wide.

"Dead?" said the wizard, leaning heavily on his wooden staff. "Do you mean . . . ?"

"What do you think I mean? Gulph is dead. So your precious prophecy is dead too."

"What happened?"

Tarlan glared at him. "What does it matter?"

"Tell me."

"He fell into the fire. Is that enough for you? The whole city was burning and Gulph fell into it."

"But did you *see* him die?"

Tarlan shook his head. "I didn't need to. Nobody could have survived those flames. Nobody! Gulph is gone! And soon . . ."

Tarlan bit back the words. Turning his back on Melchior, he knelt before his pack.

"I'm sorry," he said, bringing his anger back under control. "I should never have asked you to fight for such a worthless cause. You're better off without me, all of you."

Both Greythorn and Filos stared at him in shock. Brock the bear shifted uncomfortably from one paw to the other. Nasheen and Kitheen lowered their heads. When Tarlan looked toward Theeta, she fixed him with her most piercing glare.

"You're free," he went on, the words choking in his throat. "All of you, free to go your own way. You don't have to follow me anymore."

Silence descended. Dampness from the grass soaked into Tarlan's worn leggings. He waited for them to reply. At the same time, he hoped they would say nothing.

"When you found me," said Greythorn at last, "I was a prisoner in Vicerin's castle. You released me." The gray wolf fixed Tarlan with his one good eye. "You freed me long ago, Tarlan. If I follow you now, it is because I choose to."

"You saved my life," said Filos. "Where you go, I go."

"You opened Brock's cage," rumbled the bear, looking lost.

From behind them—seemingly from across the entire battlefield—a discontented growl began to rise. The collective unhappiness of Tarlan's pack.

Exchanging an inscrutable thorrod glance, Nasheen and Kitheen stepped forward together. To Tarlan's surprise, it was the black-breasted Kitheen, normally so reluctant to speak, who voiced their thoughts.

"Stay, boy," cawed the giant bird. His eyes were dark and ferocious.

I can't, thought Tarlan, scrambling to his feet. *One moment longer and I won't be able to go through with this.*

He turned to Theeta, only to discover she'd flown silently to an empty spot on a nearby slope. From that distance she stared at him, her expression unreadable, her wings wide and poised for further flight.

"I'm sorry," he said to the others. "Good-bye."

His heart breaking, he turned his back on them and walked toward where Theeta was waiting. No sooner had he begun to move than Melchior was blocking his path.

"Tarlan, you're wrong." The wizard's voice was soft but strong. "The prophecy is not over. If you leave now—"

"I *am* leaving!" Tarlan tried to push past the wizard, but Melchior's hand seized his wrist. "Let me go! Didn't you hear me? Gulph's dead! Elodie's gone back to the Vicerins! It's over!"

"But don't you see? Gulph might still be alive. You and Gulph and Elodie are destined to rule Toronia. The prophecy says so, and the prophecy is powerful. More powerful than the fire you saw, more powerful than any of us can comprehend. Even an old wizard like me."

"Yes! Listen to the wizard!" boomed a new voice.

Over Melchior's shoulder, Tarlan saw The Hammer striding up. Behind the big man came a straggle of Deep Poynt townsfolk. Tarlan groaned. So much for leaving without a fuss.

"The prophecy brings hope," The Hammer continued. "Without hope, we are nothing."

"Then we're nothing," cried another voice from the crowd. "The boy's right. It's all been in vain."

More shouts rose up.

"What about the prophecy?"

"Forget the boy! We've a town to rebuild!"

"Listen to The Hammer!"

The voices blurred into meaningless chatter. Tarlan wrenched free from Melchior and ran to Theeta. He pressed his forehead against the huge, hooked beak of his closest friend.

"Tarlan go," Theeta croaked softly. "Theeta go."

You think you understand, Tarlan thought. *But you don't.*

"I'm sorry, Theeta. But I have to leave you, too. I'm . . . I'm not safe to be around."

"Theeta go," the thorrod repeated.

"No. Stay with the others. Look after them. They're going to need you."

Theeta swiveled her massive head to stare down the slope to where the other thorrods stood. The rest of Tarlan's pack pressed close against the flanks of the giant birds, looking confused and anxious. The people of Deep Poynt, including The Hammer, had fallen silent and were watching Tarlan with open curiosity. And why not? Had he not so long ago told them he was their king?

Melchior, the wizard who seemed always to know what to do, stood motionless, his wrinkled face drawn down into a mask of sadness.

Tarlan looked deep into Theeta's eyes.

You found me. He didn't trust himself to speak. If he opened his mouth, all that would come out would be the splintering sound of his own breaking heart. *You saved me when I was a baby, lost in the snow. You brought me to Mirith, the frost witch who was like a mother to me, when my own true mother was lost.*

But you, Theeta . . . it was you who really brought me into the world.

He cupped his hand against the lethally sharp tip of Theeta's beak. The tiniest movement from the thorrod would have driven a hole through the middle of his palm. It was the ultimate display of trust.

"Good-bye, Theeta."

His feet dragging through the mud, Tarlan walked away.

For the first fifty paces, he had to pick through the ruts and scars of the battle-torn earth. Eventually the descending slope turned to rough pasture, and the going became easier. Ahead rose the waiting wall of the Isurian forest. All the way to the trees, Tarlan plodded with his head down, each footstep a dull echo of his thudding pulse. There were no thoughts in his head, just a thick roaring sound. He wasn't stepping out into the world, he was sinking into it, as a boy might sink into quicksand. The world would draw him down until it closed over his head. After that, all would be dark.

A faint rustling sound penetrated his daze. Blinking, he looked first around, then up. A shadow flitted over his head. Warm air wafted his face. Sunlight flashed, dazzling him.

Shielding his eyes, Tarlan watched in wonder as Theeta dropped from the sky to land an arm's length in front of him. Her golden feathers were ablaze. The sun reflected in the depths of her piercing black eyes.

"Tarlan go," the thorrod croaked. "Theeta go. We go."

"But—"

"No speak. We go."

The golden light filled Tarlan's head, driving away his powers of speech. No words, no thought. No people, no pack. Just him and Theeta.

Tarlan climbed onto her back. The thorrod kicked the ground with her huge talons. Her broad gold wings pumped the air once, twice, a hundred times. The world fell away. The high air was pure, like a cold mountain stream. Tarlan breathed it in and felt clean.

"Thorrod fly," said Theeta. "Fly far. Never stop."

It wasn't in the nature of thorrods to ask questions, but Theeta's slow circling told Tarlan she was waiting for instructions. He looked down at the forest, now a sun-dusted patchwork of green, then back over his shoulder toward the south, where his icy homeland of Yalasti lay.

Tarlan turned his attention north. He had no idea what lay in that direction. He'd never been there.

"That way, Theeta." The feel of his voice was amazing in his throat, as if he'd never spoken words before. "North, until the sun goes down. Then we'll stop to rest. After that, we'll go on."

"Never stop," said Theeta, powering ahead through the crisp, bright sky.

"That's right, my friend. We'll never stop."

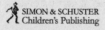